Tex, the Witch Boy

by

Stuart R. West

Tex, the Witch Boy

COPYRIGHT © 2022 by Stuart R. West

Cover Art by *TWJ Design*

The Wild Rose Press, Inc.
PO Box 708
Adams Basin, NY 14410-0708
Visit us at www.thewildrosepress.com

Publishing History
First Edition, 2022
Trade Paperback ISBN 978-1-5092-4297-9
Digital ISBN 978-1-5092-4298-6

Published in the United States of America

On the street, the car stopped, grew louder, and reversed toward the barking dog. Quickly, I jumped over the fence, braved myself, and ran like hell through the front yard toward the street. Before I reached the pavement, the oncoming taillights grew larger at an alarming rate. I dashed across the street. Fishtailing in reverse, the car swam toward me. The tail end of the auto barely missed me, the ensuing rush flapping the back of my shirt up. I tore into the yard. Car brakes slammed on. Gears shifted as the car lurched forward slowly and then stopped. I felt eyes peering into my back as I continued my survival run. The driver once again raced down the block and turned onto the next street, attempting to cut me off.

This time I went up the street through the back yards. I couldn't keep this up much longer, not with my aching leg.

About four houses from the top of the street, I peeked around the corner of a large bush. The silver car slowly rumbled by. It crawled another two hundred feet or so before the headlights shut off, the motor idling, the car at a standstill. If I could make it another two houses up the street, it would put about four or five houses between us.

Praise for Tex, the Witch Boy

"A funny and intriguing story about a boy who discovers he's a witch. This kept me laughing right through to the end. We need more YA authors like Stuart West for all those reluctant teen readers. Teachers? This belongs in your library."

~ Suzanne de Montigny, author

"Right from the start, Stuart West's novel grabbed my attention and never let go. I loved experiencing the world through the eyes of Richard "Tex" McKenna, along with the entire cast of fabulous characters. The story transported me right back to high school, this time experiencing it from Tex's (often hilarious) point of view. West managed to tug at so many emotions—from bittersweet family matters to a gut-wrenching bully scene. Both the suspense and mystery kept me turning the pages, but the thing I loved most was the healthy dose of humor that embeds the overall book. It kept me reading long past my bedtime. Can't wait for the next one!"

~ Tamara Lowe, author

Dedication

I'd like to dedicate this book to the two muses in my life:
my wife, Cydney, and my daughter, Sarah.
They've inspired me and supported me through times of self-doubt.
Couldn't have done it without them.

Prologue

I didn't choose to be a witch, no way.

Ever since I discovered my witchy destiny last fall, my life's been pretty screwed up. I mean, it had been before, but not to this extent. First of all, I'm a guy. I should be a warlock or wizard, something cool like that. I'm even allergic to cats. How lame is that for a witch? But had I not been a witch, several people I care about wouldn't have survived last fall. Even though not all of them made it out alive.

I'll never forget last fall, much as I'd like to.

I hate autumn. When the leaves tumble, so does the temperature, ending the possibilities and hope that the lazy, hot summers in Clearwell promise. Gone are the days of sleeping in, swimming, hanging out, and laughing with friends. If you're lucky enough to have them.

Those days get replaced with tyranny, captivity, bullying, cliques, ignorance, and just about the entire gamut of ugly humanity encapsulated within the halls of good ol' Clearwell High School. And if the Fates or gods, or whatever it is you believe in, choose to torture me in such a situation, they're equally cruel about the surrounding environment. The cold, brittle weather outside complements the sterile gray inhumanity within the classrooms, with a new winter storm looming practically every week. If I survive high school, I'm taking a cue from the birds and going where the warmth is. I'll gladly be a Florida witch.

So, Clearwell, Kansas. I've heard all the Kansas jokes, including the tired ones about Dorothy and Toto. The few foreign exchange students I've met believed there were still cowboys roaming the plains of Kansas. Actually, Clearwell's a suburb of Kansas City—about thirty minutes from downtown—and the only shoot-'em-ups we experience are between warring urban gangs.

Yes, the weather sucks in the fall and winter here, but the neighborhood Dad and I live in isn't too bad. The houses are old enough to look different from one another, unlike the suburbs further south, which my friend Olivia calls "stupid yuppieville." Fortunately, they're far enough apart I don't have to go to sleep listening to whatever Mr. Cavanaugh next door does late at night.

The neighborhood's overseen by what I used to call "The Tree Watchers." Giant trees—maples, oaks, everything—are littered throughout the yards. As a kid, I saw them as vigilant protectors, watching over me as I slept, keeping me safe from what lurked in the dark, barely outside of the swaying tree limbs' reach. Even though it sucks when it's time to rake up their shed skins each year, it used to comfort me, knowing they stood as a final barrier against the scarier things in the world. I sure could have used them last fall.

The house Dad and I live in rests in the middle of Oak Street, a nice, average neighborhood. It's mostly quiet because of all the old people living there. It's been this way for as long as I can remember. But last year, the old folks started dying off. I remember looking out my upstairs bedroom window late one winter night and seeing flashing lights next door at Mrs. Hathaway's house. I watched, terrified, yet fascinated, as they took Mrs. Hathaway out on a stretcher. A mask and tubing grew out of her face, giving her the appearance of a cyborg going back to the factory for maintenance. The next morning, Dad told me Mrs. Hathaway had 'passed away.' I became very familiar with the term "passed away" during the next couple of years.

So, there came an eventual "greening" of the neighborhood. A changing of the guard brought in younger people. Though there were no other teenagers, I quit feeling like I was living in an old folks' home. Mr. Cavanaugh moved in next door, taking over the left-behind shell Mrs. Hathaway inhabited. There wasn't much known about Mr. Cavanaugh, other than he was single and sat on his porch most nice evenings, *watching*. I never understood what he was watching, but that's what he did. Dad didn't say too much about him. He only grumbled that he thought Mr. Cavanaugh was in sales, and I should "keep my distance."

One rainy day, shortly after Mr. Cavanaugh moved in, I had a weird encounter with him. Outside, killing time, I tried to catch raindrops in my mouth from the tree branches. (You have to make your own fun in Clearwell.) Completing this pointless exercise in random boredom, I ran up to my room, throwing myself across my bed. The doorbell rang, and I heard Dad answer it. Curious, I listened from the stairwell leading down to the front door. Mr. Cavanaugh complained I'd been making faces at his cat, Benny, trying to scare it. Mr. C. rambled on, demanding retribution for my wanton acts of feline terrorism. Having lived a life full of blame for things I didn't do, I wasn't surprised, but thought, "Wow, *this* is stupid." I can think of lots of endeavors more worthwhile than making faces at a cat. And honestly, would a cat even care?

Dad shut the door with a slam, uttering "Jeezus" not quite under his breath. I came down the stairs, yawning and stretching my arms (intimating, "Who me? I wasn't eavesdropping!"), and asked who'd been at the door.

"Ah, just the neighbor, son," he said. "Go back to your homework, and I'll get dinner ready soon." I loved my dad, and if we weren't such a non-touching, non-feeling family, I would've hugged him right there. Adults usually didn't stand up for me.

My dad's in a wheelchair. He wasn't always. I barely remember his walking, but I do. My youngest memories are when he'd come home from his banking job, toss a couple of bank datebooks at me because he knew I liked to draw my own comic books in them, and swing me up on his shoulders. He was six feet four inches tall, so my mom always freaked out he'd bang my head on the ceiling. "Here we go, Tex," Dad would yell.

I don't remember it, but the story goes one day my perfectly healthy dad walked into the backyard to get some logs for the fireplace, and he went down. Simple as that, no drama, no fuss, just *phut!* He collapsed and was confined to a wheelchair for the rest of his life. The doctors studied, poked, prodded, brought in specialists, and finally, one specialist diagnosed him with MS. (I used to think this stood for "mystery sickness" since apparently, no one knew anything about it.) The specialist called this "not an extreme example of multiple sclerosis." I'd hate to see the *extreme* cases. But Dad could actually walk a few steps and even drive a little if an emergency should call for it.

This explains why I, Richard "Tex" McKenna, a sophomore at Clearwell High School, have my driver's permit at age fifteen. Due to Dad's "circumstances" (as the doctors and drivers bureau called them), I got a permit and a total crap-heap of a car, so I could take Dad to work and drive to school. Best of all, it saved me from the hell known as the school bus.

My mother's death last year also played into my ability to drive early. Small favors. But I don't like talking about that.

Anyway, let me take you back to that fateful fall.

Chapter One

I'd only known Olivia since the start of our sophomore year, but already she was one of the few people I could honestly call a friend. One week after school started, a short girl wearing a beat-up jean jacket, a Clash T-shirt, and a streak of orange adorning the long black hair hanging over one of her eyes, burst into speech class. She carried a folded-up piece of paper and a sense of excitement about her. After Miss Swanson studied the paper, she announced, "Class, this is Olivia Furman. She's a new student here, so please make her feel welcome. Olivia, go sit over by Richard." Since I was short on friends and "school cred", empty seats usually surrounded me.

Once Miss Swanson assigned the latest group project (which I always hated, since I felt like the overweight kid, always chosen last in gym class), Olivia turned to me and said, "Okay, what's the deal with that Hastings tyrant?" Arville Hastings was the notoriously scary, hard-ass vice-principal of our beloved school. Right then, I knew I wanted Olivia in my corner.

"What happened?" I asked.

"I just came from that jerk's office." Her one visible eye lit up. "He spent forty-five minutes telling me I needed to stay away from the stoners, the slackers, and the freaks, and if I wanted to make it, I should dress more appropriately and get to know people like the cheerleaders and the football team and..." Olivia listed off every notation with her bejeweled fingers. Out of breath with indignation, it took her a minute to notice my chuckling. Suddenly, she burst into a loud guffaw, attracting the irate attention of Miss Swanson.

"Is there something funny about our group project, Richard?" Miss Swanson asked.

"No, sorry. We're just trying to come up with a topic for our group speech." I leaned in closer to Olivia and whispered, "Welcome to sophomore year of 'Tyrant High.' I'm Tex, by the way."

"I thought your name was Richard."

"Well, I suppose technically, it is. But Richard's such a stupid name, and I've learned the nickname for Richard is something far worse."

Olivia stared at me until she realized what I meant and bellowed out another donkey laugh. With lightning speed, Miss Swanson stood over our huddled heads, arms akimbo, attempting to intimidate us into silence.

"Do you have a topic for your group speech, yet?" Miss Swanson barely kept her anger simmering under the surface of her matronly manner.

"Yes," blurted Olivia, "teenage anarchy!" And with that, we both did our worst at stifling a rush of joyous laughter. I also realized a friendship had been forged from the fires of speech class. Literally saved by the classroom bell, Olivia was spared another visit to her new friend, Arville Hastings. The Fates smiled upon us that day.

****

Mid-October, I drove Olivia home from school through the leaf-strewn streets, her house five blocks from mine. An uncharacteristic quiet weighed heavily over us. Earlier, we'd been stunned by the shocking news delivered over the school's barely intelligible intercom system.

The muffled mumblings of Arville Hastings had interrupted the ritual of watching the clock count down and crackled, "Attention, students. It's with great sorrow…that I…report the sad passing away of football running back and student Matt Rimmer late last night."

If Hastings was capable of being dumbfounded over anything, this was it. Not just any student had been killed. *A football player*.

"Tomorrow's first class will be devoted to talking with your teachers about how this makes you feel…and for those who need it, our counselors will be available all day."

Great. The burned-out counselors will be available from eight to three; then it's time to turn off that grief, fellow students, and head home.

"Man. I still can't believe it, right?" said Olivia. The orange strand of hair swayed in front of her eye with every bump and jab my old Chevy delivered along the brick-laid street. Olivia called my car the "Battle Bucket" in honor of it being a quick getaway from the constant threat of high school bullies. "I mean, Matt Rimmer wasn't even one of the worst of the jerks. Too bad it wasn't Bellman or Malinowski."

"Hmmmm…" That's all I managed to sputter out. Even though in total agreement with her, I didn't want to get karma pissed off at me any more than it already was by wishing death upon someone else. Olivia, on the other hand, never feared tempting karma by speaking her mind, although she baited the anger of bullies quite a bit by doing so. She's a dangerous person to be friends with, but well worth the trouble. "Yeah, Rimmer was one of the more…benign, I guess, of the football players." Rimmer managed to hurl a few insults my way in the past, but at least, he kept the violence out of our 'relationship.'

"Benign," hooted Olivia. "Where in hell do you come up with these words, Tex?"

"I don't know." But I *did* know. "Benign" was a word I had become agonizingly familiar with last year. "Did you hear how he died?"

"Someone said they found his body in Mission Park early this morning, and he'd been beaten up and strangled," Olivia said. I found this hard to believe. Rimmer was a pretty big and healthy guy. Who could jump a football player? And didn't they usually run in packs like wild wolves?

"Where'd you hear that?" Sometimes Olivia's flights of fantasy took her to the most extreme places. And I didn't think she had too many friends besides me, Ian, and Josh. She was one of those girls *every* other girl hated, so she found acceptance with me and the rest of my freak show, as they called us.

"Ah, I dunno, just overheard it, I guess. Man, I really, *really* don't want to have to deal with this first hour tomorrow. All the drama, the handwringing…everything!" I pulled onto Olivia's street, Maple Avenue (the people in Clearwell loved naming everything after either trees or Native-American stuff), while Olivia zoned out for a minute. "Why would anyone kill Matt Rimmer?"

I shrugged. "Beats me, O. Besides, we don't know for a fact he was strangled. What you heard might've been just gossip."

"*Crap*. My mom's home!"

I met Mrs. Furman once, and honestly, I didn't find her nearly as bad as Olivia made her out to be. You could tell she used to be one of those women considered pretty years ago, but time—and whatever *real* drama had transpired in her life—chiseled out some hard knocks on her face. She seemed quiet, friendly enough, tired, and…well, *sad*. I think Olivia would've hated any parent she had to deal with because the notion of *rebellion* seemed pretty important and romantic to her. Her dad left when she was a lot younger, and she never talked about him.

"Okay, here's where *you* get off, young lady," I said in a mock-serious voice. I jumped out and rushed around to open her door from outside since it wouldn't open from inside. Just another astonishingly crappy thing about my really crappy car.

"Why, what a gentleman." Olivia fluttered her one visible set of eyelashes. She gave me a hug, and I nearly jumped out of my skin. Olivia'd never hugged me before.

"Hey, relax, Tex." She laughed. "It's just a hug." She smiled widely, exposing perfect white teeth.

"Sorry, I'm just not used to hugs."

"Well, get used to them." She leaned in for another hug. This time, I embraced her fully and somewhat awkwardly.

"So remember, stay away from the stoners, the slackers, and the freaks…" she said, finally breaking our embrace.

I finished our departing ritual. "And always be the best little anarchist you can." I waved, got in the car, my thoughts all about Olivia. My smile soon faded, though, as a sudden shiver zip-lined through my body. I could feel something dark and unsettling coming down on us here in Podunk, Kansas, USA, God's world.

****

Ruder than a mean cheerleader, dusk shoved daylight away. I pulled into our driveway, scraping the bottom of the Battle Bucket's muffler along the way.

Too early to pick up Dad, my homework already finished in study hall, I felt antsy.

With nothing better to do, I thought I'd try and find out how exactly Matt Rimmer did die. My old computer (inherited from Mom) fired up, and the screen-saver photo of Mom greeted me with a knowing smile. A few clicks later, I found the local newsfeed story regarding Matt's death.

Details were minimal, probably the norm for an unsolved murder. Matt's body had been found in Mission Park by an early morning jogger. The only available information about his death stated he'd been "assaulted." With no elaboration on the type of assault, that could mean practically anything. After he'd been late coming home from football practice, Matt's parents had reported him missing. The story quoted Coach Jensen as saying, "Matt was a good and upbeat kid. It's a great loss to everyone who knew him."

Curiosity got the better of me, and I flipped over to social media to see if my suspicions on my peers' behavior would be proven correct. Sure enough, some enterprising student had already set up a memorial page for Matt, with literally dozens of testimonials morbidly crying from the screen, claiming the tragedy as their own. Many tributes started with "I didn't know Matt well, but…" and went on to provide their side of the story. I imagine some of these poor fellow school travelers didn't know him at all. At the first sighting of a cheerleader remarking about Matt's beautiful green eyes, I could take no more and shut the computer down.

I harbored no ill-will toward Matt. Sometimes I sort of got the feeling he went along with the name-calling half-heartedly because he thought of it as expected of him. I also felt bad for his family. I know what tragic loss feels like. What I can't stomach are opportunistic vultures who try to up their lot in high school life by jumping on the bandwagon of a popular student's tragedy. I know this sounds more than cynical, but hey, I'm a teenager, and that's my worldview. But…the murder of someone I knew well enough to be called a "fag" by? Wow. *Murder*. It's really bizarre when it lands in your own backyard.

****

I heard a forlorn, rhythmic ringing coming from outside. Through my bedroom window, I saw a plain white van driving slowly, a bell clanging on top. Something seemed off. The ice cream man hadn't been seen or heard around here since the beginning of summer. For the first three agonizing weeks of June, the gaudily illustrated ice cream truck persistently cruised the streets of our neighborhood, blaring out the mind-piercing tune of Scott Joplin's "The Entertainer." It got to the point every time I tried to go to sleep, the infernal song played on a loop in my mind.

After three weeks, I heard nothing. One of two things might've happened. Either the ice cream vendor gave up, realizing there weren't too many age-appropriate customers in the hood; or one of the neighbors (Mr. Cavanaugh, cough) had complained about the song. Either way, the truck vanished in June. And now, here it was again.

Yet this was a different ice cream truck. Gone were the colorful paintings of cartoon Bomb Pops dancing jauntily on a summer's day, now replaced by plain, dingy white van paneling. If it weren't for the tell-tale sign of a bell on top, ringing methodically as slowly as the van traveled, you'd have no idea the van was slinging ice cream. And why would the ice cream man make a less than triumphant return in the middle of October? This time of year, I'd rather have hot cocoa than a popsicle.

This murder business had me on edge, and at the back of my mind, I saw harbingers of doom instead of sugary-cold sweetness and frivolity. Time to shake off the chills. I reached for my favorite knit cap in its usual slumbering spot on my desk and found nothing.

Panic surged that I'd lost it somewhere. Mom had given it to me. She knew my personality better than anyone. A circle and a diagonal line blocked out the smiley face symbol emblazoned on the center of the green cap. When Mom had handed it to me, we just looked at each other and shared a laugh. No words were exchanged. They didn't need to be.

I didn't find it in my dresser, so I pulled a few boxes from the top shelf of my closet. A tiny swag bag fell. Picking it up, I untied the green ribbon holding it closed. The white handkerchief opened, exposing what looked like bay leaves and other herbs. I found it weird Mom had hidden some homemade potpourri in my closet. I didn't think my closet stank *that* much. What scent it used to carry had long fled, so I tossed the folded cloth and its contents across the room smack into the wastebasket. *Three points*! Maybe I should go out for basketball? *Not*.

****

Just off of Elm Parkway, I pulled the Battle Bucket into the bank's parking lot and shut off the engine. I guess the Bucket had different ideas as it stubbornly coughed and spat even after I took the keys out. I opened the bank door and did the usual desultory waves to my dad's few remaining coworkers, who were lucky enough to have survived the lousy economy so far. I noticed at least one look that fairly screamed, *Get a haircut*!

"Hey, Dad." I lurked in the open doorway, hoping not to get the stench of rampant capitalism on me.

"Hi, son." Dad had already wheeled himself halfway across the room from his desk. A proud man, he never wanted anyone to see him being pushed in his chair. I respected this, even though it obviously wore him out. Once we were outside, our unspoken routine allowed me to assist him into the car.

"How was your day?" I asked. "Did you devastate many families by turning down their loans?"

"Yes and no." Dad sighed, with a faint glimmer of a smile. "Hey, I heard about your schoolmate. Such a terrible thing! Was he a friend of yours?"

"Dad, he was a football player."

"Right." Dad always worried about my friends, as he didn't approve of my small coterie of what he called ragamuffins. On the other hand, he resigned himself to the fact I'd never be one of the Popular Kids.

"Bill said the Rimmer kid was beaten and then choked. They don't know if he died from the beating or strangling yet." Bill Pearson, the omniscient security guard on duty at my dad's bank, still had many connections to the local cops and acted as my dad's one-stop gossip shop.

"Yeah, I'd heard that. Just crazy."

"I want you to be careful, Tex." Briefly, he dropped his granite façade of stolid "Pack Leader." Fear and worry crossed his aging face. After everything we'd been through, it scared me a little to see him lose his composure. "Just…be careful."

For the next several minutes, the only sound came from the Bucket's start and stop sputter. Through the falling darkness, Dad gazed out the window. Leaves swirled about in a sudden gust of wind, spinning like a baby tornado.

"Son," Dad said, breaking our silence, "we need to talk about your mother." *Much* more uncomfortable than the silence, my least favorite topic. Over the past couple of months, Dad, in his awkward fashion (it runs in the family), had been trying to bring up the subject of Mom. Whenever he does, I nearly break out in a sweat. Waves of anxiety pour over me to the point I physically can't talk about it.

"Not now, Dad. Sorry…" I strained my eyes at the now slightly blurry intersection ahead. "I don't want to."

"Well, I'm sorry, too, that you don't want to talk about your mother, but we need to." Dad stared me down. *Hard*. "I told her I would," he added quietly. He snapped his head back to stare out the window. I could tell he wished he could take back that last sentence.

****

That night, we went through the motions of dinner,

pushing frozen peas around our plates as if playing solitaire soccer. More small talk routinely rolled out of our mouths about our so-called lives, each of us carefully avoiding hotspots. Only too happy to go to bed for once, I raced up the stairs as Dad rolled into his downstairs bedroom.

Closing my eyes, the freshly remembered dulcet tones of "The Entertainer" ravaged my brain. I wondered what the Fates—or whatever sarcastic smartass who sets up the pieces in the game of Life—had in store for me. A lot of weirdness rained down upon me today, and I wondered if some strange cosmic puppeteer had yanked away my umbrella to punish me or if things were connected. Matt Rimmer's murder, Dad's cryptic mention of Mom's wanting him to talk to me, annoying ice-cream men making a return from the graveyard of cold confections, bags of potpourri, missing caps, back-talking cars…anything and everything raced through my head like a bad fever-dream.

There was a scritch-scritch-scratching at my window, and by the moonlight, I saw the lonely gnarled hand of the giant oak Tree Watcher. Waving goodbye. No longer a child, on my own now, the oak let me know he wouldn't be able to keep me safe from what lies in the darkness any longer.

Chapter Two

Upon entering sociology class, I spotted Ian, grinning ear to ear, a positively manic twinkle in his eyes. Crazy weird as Ian is the angriest person I know.

"Dude," Ian said, practically salivating, "you ready for this?" More antsy than usual, his black-painted fingernails scratched at the desktop as he scooted up and down in his chair.

"Not really. I just want to get through the day. Like every other day."

A crowd of one, I valued Ian Stapleton, the only holdover friend I had from grade school. We met in the fourth grade and immediately bonded over our many surprisingly similar interests: horror movies, comic books, Guitar Hero, Alternative Rock, and surviving school bullies. Last year, Ian self-diagnosed himself as manic-depressive—which I believe—but he refused to tell his parents or do anything about it. I think he considered it a cool type of suffering; the kind old movies used to project upon James Dean and that sort. Ian thrived on being different. He shined a great big spotlight on himself, wearing a big metaphorical "Kick Me" sign on his back, practically begging to be bullied. The typical "emo" kid, he wore the dark clothes, moped about with a down-turned head, and used gallons of product on his shaggy, black-dyed haircut. He hadn't always been like this. In grade school, he looked like any other kid. But in our freshman year, he decided to go for a "makeover," wanting to be the Great Misunderstood Emo Kid. And we all know how well that goes over with the jocks and bullies.

At first, the change kinda threw me. I couldn't figure out why he did it. But after our first year in High School Hell, it made more sense to me. It was Ian's—possibly misplaced—sense of preserving his individuality. After failing to fit into *any* of the school cliques—and we both tried drama, band, etc.—rejection gets old after a while. So he figured *the hell with it. I'm not going to change to belong to any stupid group. I'll just be myself.* Of course, if he logically thought this through, he'd realize he did change for the very reason he didn't want to change by reforming himself. But I thought maybe I'd wait a few years to clue him in on this.

The really weird thing, though, among myself, Olivia, and Josh, Ian has the most normal—some would say best—home-life. His parents are happily married. He has one older and one younger brother, who both stay out of trouble, get good grades, and are just "livin' the dream." There might be some unspoken envy in our little group of misfits, at times wishing we were in Ian's black emo tennis shoes. Yet inexplicably, he's always angry, if not at the injustices in school, then at how his family treats him.

I once saw Ian totally go off in his bedroom, after his mom told him to wash the dishes. He threw a chair across the cluttered room, destroying one of his Star Wars action figures, while making a sort of growling sound. Shortly after this, he bounded downstairs, washed the dishes, and we commenced playing Guitar

Hero.

****

A quiet hush suffocated the classroom, occasionally broken by a sob from one of the cloned Clearwell Indians cheerleaders in the front row until Mr. Jensen entered the room. I refused to call him "Coach," because he was no coach of mine. But as my homeroom and sociology teacher, and as far as coach/teacher hybrids go, he really wasn't too bad. He sat down behind his too-small desk, his knees visible over the desktop.

"Does anyone want to start?" he asked, looking around the room solemnly. Aside from Ian's sliding up and down in his chair, the students didn't budge. "All right, then. You all know we've lost a much-loved student...to tragic circumstances." Tired-looking, he shook his blustery red face slowly. "Matt Rimmer was a good student, a good football player...and a good kid whom I was glad to know."

At this, Miss Nameless and Vapidly Pretty Cheerleader totally broke down, crying and moaning as if she were possessed by a soap opera diva. "Susie, would you like to go talk to Mr. Sherwood?" Clearly out of his element, Mr. Jensen couldn't solve this with a few well-thought-out football plays. A couple of other girls leaped up, draped their arms around the hysterical Susie, and escorted her out of the room.

"Sudden death is..." started Mr. Jensen. He took his glasses off, wiping them and staring at the floor. A strategic ploy, I thought, to keep the students from realizing how helpless he felt. I couldn't help but empathize with him.

I wanted to look over at Ian, but I could see out of

the corner of my eye his wide smirk. Yeah, maybe it is time for him to look into a little medication.

The intercom buzzed. Mr. Jensen looked thankful for the disruption. Answering it, his back turned toward us, his head hung low, muttering "yes" a few times. His rounded, large shoulders, straining against a gray sweater, made him look like a giant tombstone. He turned around and locked a now-composed gaze on me. *Uh-oh*, I thought in a flash of panic, *what's wrong with Dad now?*

"Tex, you're wanted in Mr. Hastings' office." The only teacher who called me "Tex," Mr. Jensen hung up the intercom.

Worried, I stood, a little thankful to exit the post-death-watch vigil scenario playing out in the room. But experience had taught me a visit to Hastings was never a good thing. Down the empty hallways, I stumbled, occasionally hearing an anguished howl or sob from one of the classrooms I passed. The beaten, gray lockers stood as silent as military guards as I felt like a prisoner strolling his last mile to the death chair. *Dead Man Walking!*

What could Hastings possibly want with me?

****

This would be my second visit with Arville Hastings since I started my incarceration at Clearwell High School. The first go-round happened last year, the inevitable capper to the hilarious hi-jinx that introduced many important players in the unfolding drama called My Life.

Late last April, during my final hour, gym class (which is a very special ring of hell unto its own), we were lined up on the gym floor. Like good dutiful little

20

soldiers, we counted off our assigned numbers so Mr. Sowers, the gym teacher and basketball coach, could take attendance before deciding what sort of punishment to dole out.

The routine began. "One?" "Present!" "Two?" "Present!" "Three?" "Absent!" "Four?" "Present!" On it went, until we got to number sixteen, and silence filled the gym. A small, quiet kid with huge eyes and a mop-top haircut had the unfortunate luck to be number sixteen. I didn't know Josh Berillo well then, had no idea what came over him, but he had forgotten his number. The punishment for forgetting one's designated gym number is the entire class does twenty-five push-ups. Mr. Sowers licked his lips sadistically. In his exaggerated good ol' boy fashion, he said, "Oh, by golly, fellas, it looks like number sixteen forgot his number! Drop and give me twenty-five." He blew his whistle, groans went through the line, and down we went. Strike number one for poor little Josh Berillo.

That day's sensitivity training class revolved around dodge ball, a particularly heinous form of torture, since we, the freshmen, had to go up against the older students from Mr. Jensen's sophomore class. Josh, apparently, hadn't learned the secret to successful dodge ball playing—stick your hands in the air, let an over-passing ball graze your fingertips, then with a disappointed look on your face, bellow, "I'm out, coach!" I watched from the sidelines as Josh became one of the last freshmen standing. I pitied Josh as the sophomores and juniors pummeled him with an onslaught of terror, showering a torrent of red rubber balls down upon his small body. Not only did he take a physical beating, he clearly drew attention to himself, with taunting names hurled about.

"Take that, Mole!" *Mole* had become Josh's unfortunate nickname amongst the brutes and savages. I suppose he did resemble a mole, at least superficially. Josh always wore shirts too big for him, and they were usually fashion-challenged turtlenecks. With his small, mop-topped head barely rising above the collars, his large, wandering and scared eyes peering out, he became an instant, weaker target for the stronger animals in the menagerie. Strike number two for Josh.

After the fun ended came shower time. The perfect end to a perfect day. Josh and I belonged to the secret club of Those Who Would Prefer To Not Take Communal Showers. We all had our reasons. I was self-conscious about my body. My pubic hair hadn't come in—hell, my voice hadn't even changed yet—and I thought, it's last hour, why can't I just shower when I get home? I did everything possible to avoid the showers.

However, the sadists in charge deemed showers mandatory. If you couldn't cleverly avoid them, you were forced to strip down, go by the "towel givers" and hit the communal stalls. The towel givers were always upperclassmen—handpicked by Jensen and Sowers, usually football and basketball players—who reveled in handing out insults and smacking us with towels. I guess their form of extra credit or whatever.

On that fateful day, a particularly evil couple of thugs comprised the towel givers. Bob Bellman, star football player and psychopath extraordinaire, was without a doubt the scariest person I'd ever met. Standing at over six feet tall, a blond buzz cut perched atop his completely black unibrow, making his cold gray eyes even scarier. Whenever he smiled, exposing his smoke-stained teeth, you knew trouble was headed your way. Notoriously whispered about by frightened students, Bellman had attained legendary school boogeyman status. His sadistic ways were well known, and only the most naïve, foolish, death-wish-seeking kids would stand up to him. One story had him nearly beating a freshman to death with his football helmet until three fellow footballers pulled him off. I didn't know anything about Bellman's personal life, and I really didn't want to. Up until this point, I had successfully stayed out of his way and under his radar, and that suited me just fine.

Bellman's faithful sidekick, the equally terrifying Johnny Malinowski, lorded it over us as the other towel giver that day. While Bellman had wide-open crazy eyes, forecasting his insane intentions to cause unwarranted pain and agony, Malinowski's eyes were narrow slits. One could never predict his mindset. At times quiet, Malinowski could turn on a dime, flying into an inexplicable rage of bullying brutality.

I had had several encounters with this particular sociopath. From the first week of my freshman year, Malinowski had shoved me into a locker, tried to trip me several times (which I always saw coming, so just stepped over his outstretched foot—thus pissing him off more), punched me in the back, and called me various names, including the extremely charming "faggot."

When it came time for Josh to walk the gauntlet between everyone's favorite sociopaths, he held his hands cupped over his junk. *Uh-oh*, I thought, *there's strike three*.

"Hey, Johnny, look at this one!" Bellman exposed

his rotting teeth in a hideously greenish grin. "This fag ain't got no junk!" He took a towel, rolled it up, and let it fly on Josh's back. *Whap!* Josh stood stoically quiet, but his round eyes fairly screamed in terror.

"What a pussy," said Malinowski, equally eloquently. "Let's see if he's got anything in the shower." *Whap! Whup!* The bullies corralled Josh toward the large shower stall with their rolled-up towels, two drunken cowboys rounding up their herd. The majority of the boys quickly fled the locker room to avoid the drama, some with pained grimaces on their faces, others in sweaty panic. I'd been dithering around, still in my jockstrap, trying to figure out how to get out of a shower.

So far, I've always lived to see another day by adhering to what I call my Golden Rule. This simply is Survival 101. I learned it a long time ago in grade school. Keep a low profile, fly under the radar, don't call attention to yourself, don't get involved in the target practice of bullies, and maybe—just, *maybe*—you'll live to see graduation. Josh apparently had been poorly educated, as no one taught him about dodgeball or the Golden Rule.

I pitied Josh, as I knew it could've just as easily been me in the showers because the Fates are a fickle bunch of bitches. But in the name of self-preservation, I knew I had to get the hell out of there.

I pulled my jeans on over my jockstrap, foregoing underwear. From the shower stall, Josh's scream echoed through the mostly emptied locker room. *Where in the hell are the coaches?* Probably holed up in the attached office area, doing God knows what. Disregarding my self-preservation, I raced to the stall.

Bellman had Josh pinned to the floor, one beefy leg on his back. He twisted the hot water knob, the steam gaining and rising. Josh screamed again—in his defense, I don't think he ever cried or pleaded with them—and Malinowski embellished the torture with his whipping towel. Then Bellman cranked the hot water valve all the way.

Screw the Golden Rule! I ran to the coaches' shuttered office window. I pounded on the windows, yelling for help. Mr. Jensen, wearing headphones, pulled the door open quickly.

"They're *killing* him!"

Jensen threw the headphones into a corner. He raced down the locker room corridor ahead of me, toward the billowing steam and ever-rising screams.

"What in *God's* name are you *doing*, Bellman?" Mr. Jensen's voice shot through the stall like a bullet. For a big man, he moved fast. He shoved Bellman into the wall with a resounding thud. Bellman, obviously stunned, pulled back his arm, ready to land one on Mr. Jensen, until what little reigning sanity he had left must've finally, thankfully, taken over. He dropped his arm to his side, fist still curled. I ran in, turned off the hot water. I grimaced at Josh's red back.

"Are you okay?" I later thought, what a stupid question. Of course, he wasn't okay. Malinowski stood in the corner, grinning, waving his towel back and forth, a mad dog's wagging tail.

"Tex, see if you can get him to the nurse," ordered Mr. Jensen. "I hope to God she's still here. If she's not, call an ambulance." Josh managed to get himself up on his feet. I put his arm around me, hobbled him into the locker room where he managed to pull his jeans on, and we walked once again by the Stall of Doom.

"Tex…" sneered Bellman. He spat on the ground, glowering at me as I walked by.

"Shut your *mouth*," screamed Mr. Jensen. But it was too late. Now—like Josh—Bellman's radar had pinpointed me.

****

In her office, the nurse seemed even crankier than usual. She examined Josh's back, declaring first-degree burns (I would've gone second-degree, but, hey, I'm no cranky nurse) when the door rattled open.

Mrs. Carbody poked her pelican-like nose in and sniffed. "Mr. Hastings would like to see you boys now." One of the front office paper-pushers, Mrs. Carbody prided herself on busting kids who faked letters of sickness from their parents. If you could get one by Mrs. Carbody, you had a nice future in forgery.

"Josh will have to stay for a bit," said Nurse Cranky. "The other one's all yours." With a regal flourish of her hand, she dismissed me. I followed Mrs. Carbody down the now-empty hallway to the main office, where I took a seat by the front desk. Mrs. Carbody alternately peered at me over her glasses and shuffled papers. Her phone rang. She nodded several times before saying, "Right away, Mr. Hastings."

Hasting's door opened. The ugly, grinning Bellman, followed by the slithery Malinowski, and finally, Mr. Jensen, exited. Bellman spotted me. As soon as I registered in his psychotic brain, he raced toward me. But not fast enough. Mr. Jensen grabbed Bellman's collar and redirected him toward the hallway door. "Go Home! *Now!*" After Jensen shoved them out the door, he came toward me, shaking his head back and forth. "I'm sorry… I'm sorry about your friend." Clearly upset, maybe even a little ashamed, he shuffled out the door.

"Mr. Hastings will see you now," said Mrs. Carbody. *Yay*, I thought.

I knocked on the daunting wooden door, wondering if it was specially installed per Arville Hastings' wishes. Everyone knew about his notorious one-team task force in intimidation. The world's biggest Clearwell Indians supporter, he'd go to great lengths to protect his sports boys. If you didn't play football, you didn't make it into Hastings' football-focused tunnel vision. Rumor has it he's even instrumental in recruiting promising players out of grade schools.

"Come in," bellowed a Southern-tinged, husky voice. A big man already, Hastings' favored cowboy boots made him even bigger. His hawk-like nose jutted out from his square head, ever ready to sniff out troublemakers. Frankenstein's Monster from Texas. *Yippie-ki-Arghhhh!*

He stacked papers on his desk, ignoring me as I entered. *Welcome to Intimidation Central.*

"Why did you and the other boy…Josh…start a fight with the other fellas?" Finally, he looked up at me.

I couldn't believe it, yet I shouldn't have been surprised. "We didn't! And I'd hardly call it a 'fight.'"

"That's not what the other fellas just told me. Why would they make something like that up?" Hastings still hadn't offered me a seat, so there I stood, swinging in the wind, so to speak.

"They were burning him in the shower! I just ran to get Jensen's help. What did Mr. Jensen say about it?"

He glared at me, unemotionally. *Blink!* I willed him. *Blink! Do something*!

"All right," he said. "Well. Someone's not telling the truth here." And I bet I knew who he thought that was. "Detention next week for you and the Berillo boy. Dismissed."

My first meeting with Arville Hastings came to a close as he looked down at his papers again. I thought about arguing with him but realized it'd be a wasted effort and may buy some extra detention time. So I left, slamming the door much too loudly.

****

So, in a haze, my mind filled with the worst possible outcome, I stumbled toward my second visit with Arville Hastings, with no idea why. I had several minor encounters with the local bully-pen since last year, but by no means could they be considered 'fights' even by Hastings' limited definition. Deciding to bypass the scrutiny of Mrs. Carbody, I headed straight toward the imposing door. It pulled open before I could put my hand on the golden doorknob. Paul Jacobson, an amiable enough stoner, looked at me and said "Duudddde," which was code-speak for *what a crock of crap you're in for*.

Flanking Hastings on both sides stood two bald men, arms folded, a set of genie bookends. One I recognized as our figurehead of a principal, Bob Smithson. A quiet man, Smithson appeared to be afraid of the students over whom he presided. The only time anyone ever spotted him was when, once a month, he stood on the front steps of the school, greeting students whose names he never learned. Likewise, I'm sure most of the students wondered who in the hell he was.

"I understand you didn't get along with Matt Rimmer," said Hastings. I could see his desktop manner hadn't improved since last year.

"Where'd you hear that?" I asked. "I didn't even know him."

"Someone said there've been names exchanged between the two of you in the past," Hastings drawled. Principal Smithson shifted uncomfortably, itchy to escape and hide behind the doors of his mysterious office. "Care to explain that?"

What I cared to do was sit down because I felt the wind knocked out of me. "Well, he called me a few names in the past, but I pretty much kept my mouth shut and didn't talk to him. As I said, I didn't even know him. We didn't exactly run in the same social circles or have sleepovers or whatever." I gazed longingly at the chair in front of me, wondering if anyone had ever been invited to luxuriate in its brown plush comfort.

"Settle down, son," said the other bald bookend. "We're just gathering information and are questioning as many students as possible." Meaning the students on Hastings' "special list," containing the names of "school troublemakers," I'm sure. "I'm Detective Ryan Cowlings by the way, of the Clearwell Police Department."

"Okay." I nodded, wondering why Cowlings let Hastings run his investigation. I directed my full attention to Cowlings. "Look, I barely knew Matt, and I sure didn't wish him dead. Even if I did, look at me. I'm one hundred ten pounds soaking wet. Do you really think I could jump a football player?" As soon as I said this, I wished I would have phrased that a little less…incriminatingly. Hastings sat up, looking as though he'd just extracted a confession. "Why aren't you questioning the local psychopaths who're capable of hurting people, like Bob Bellman or John Malinowski?"

Cowlings shot a look to Hastings. The hard-ass vice-principal narrowed his eyes and gave a shake of his square head, signifying this was a dead-end according to his expert profiling techniques. "Those boys were Matt's friends…and teammates," snapped Hastings. "I hardly think they'd do something like that."

"But since Matt called me names, I'm your primary suspect?" I shot back. "Too much CSI for you," I muttered under my breath.

"Hold on, hold on," said Cowlings. "No one's said anything about suspecting you of any wrong-doing. Richard, isn't it? We just want to see if you've heard anything. When was the last time you saw Matt Rimmer?"

"I really don't know. Maybe a week ago? In the hallway? I usually tried to avoid him and the rest of the Clearwell Indians. And, no, I haven't heard anything."

"Okay," said Cowlings, proffering his hand toward me. "Here's my card. If you think of anything unusual, or if you hear anything, please give me a call."

Principal Smithson audibly sighed and leaned against the window, obviously glad to have another interrogation finished. The golf course beckoned.

I didn't say anything. I didn't *want* to say anything. The unbelievable absurdity was too much to grasp, and I didn't know whether to laugh or to break down and cry. Either one could incriminate me. Hello, paranoia, old friend! One last glimpse of Hastings glaring at me under a furrowed brow was all the fuel I needed to propel me the hell out of there. Without a word, I left quickly, while feeling their stares burrowing into my back, trying to get a peek into my guilty soul.

****

While Ian, Josh, and I met for lunch down in the boiler room with Red, I still felt anxious. Ants in the pants anxious.

Red—one of the two school janitors (the other being Carl, an old cantankerous dinosaur of a man)—was cool enough to give the three of us a safe haven at lunchtime. I believe Red relished the company, as it gave him a chance to hold court and regale us with fascinating (fake, I wondered sometimes) stories of his sexual conquests, and how he had been the basketball star of Clearwell High School ten years ago until he blew his knee out.

We first met Red late last year under unusual circumstances. Ian and I were walking around one school night, bored, looking for something to do. Ian came up with the not-so-great idea to egg our school in a grand showing of anti-school anarchy. So, armed with eggs, we set out on our nocturnal mission.

Very few lights lit up the building as we propelled our poultry bombs onto the school walls, concentrating on the street side (for a fast getaway) where the gym sat next to the janitor's lair. *Whack! Splat!*

I hurled my last egg onto the janitor's serrated, pull-down metal garage door. It flew open with an awful grinding sound. A tall, lanky redheaded man in coveralls spotted me and gave chase. Incredibly, even with my one-hundred-foot head start, he caught up with me in no time. He grabbed me by the scruff of my neck and shook me thoroughly, dragging me back to the garage.

"*Hey!* Hey! Why the hell'd you *do* that?" He stared at the egg decoration and shoved me down onto a metal folding chair. After a long bout of fuming silence, he finally let his anger go and handed a bucket of water and rag to me. I shook in fear, hoping this wouldn't turn into a huge "contact the parents" sort of ordeal. Anger also gnawed at me as Ian got away and left me to take the blame and hold the bucket, even though it had been his brilliant idea.

"Clean it up," he ordered. He stood over me, watching while I mopped up the mess, like some giant red-haired prison orderly in a jumpsuit. "Why'd you do it? Why'd you egg the school?"

"I don't know." Which was the truth. But I didn't think he'd buy "youthful shenanigans."

"Do you go to some rival school or something?"

"No. No...I go here." Not one of my more eloquent times.

"*What*? Why would you do that to your own school? Do you egg the house you live in?"

"No." For a second, I thought how ridiculous it'd be to egg your own home. "I guess I just don't like it here much...that's all."

Silently, the big red giant rubbed his chin. "Come down to the boiler room at lunch tomorrow," he finally said. "And bring your partner in crime with you. Don't worry. I'm not going to report this to your parents, or Hastings, or the cops." He pushed me out into the cold, night air and shut the serrated garage door. "People call me Red," he shouted as an afterthought.

It took a few weeks to get Ian to visit Red. Terrified Red would hand us over to the authorities for our act of random terrorism, Ian fought my invite. But when I told Ian that Red wanted to teach us self-defense, he finally relented.

Red had guessed the reason I hated school was bullying, so he offered to show us some boxing and karate moves. Of course, once he realized Ian and I had neither coordination nor muscle, he changed tack. "Come get me when you're in trouble," he sighed, giving up the good fight. "If I can't teach you, then I can at least try and help you." Eventually, Josh joined us in our safe lunch place, and soon bullying became a generally ignored topic. The subject matter covered became all about sex, Red's glory days in basketball, cars, or how to fix things. It flowered into an education being acquired below the school in the boiler room, miles apart from what happened in the upstairs classrooms; and perhaps better, too.

****

Red enthralled the three of us with a wild tale about some girl he picked up in a bar the other night, when a loud, obscene litany of curses grew louder and closer. The banging, slapping sound of feet on the metal stairs and the spider-webbed, adorned black stockings told me who came visiting. Hurricane Olivia on a rampage.

Goddamned fascist sexual pig bitches is a more sanitized version of what Olivia yelled.

"O', what's going on?" I asked. "Why're you down here?"

The three of us sat dumbfounded—Olivia never ventured to the boiler room. She thought it just a little *too* geeky even for us and gave us grief for lunching with one of the janitors. In all honesty, she was probably right about this, but we needed a guaranteed safe lunch place. For thirty glorious minutes per day, we didn't fear bullies.

"Those *bastards!* Those *pigs* think just because I'm a girl, I'm not capable of killing someone! They didn't even bother talking to me! *Bitches!*"

"Olivia, you're the only one I can think of who's mad because you're not a murder suspect." Thank God for Olivia's bringing *something* funny to this solemn day.

Olivia looked positively pissed at our amusement, and it stoked her internal fires higher. "*Oh, yeah! Real* funny, dorks! *Goddamn it!* I'm just as dangerous as any of you geeks, and I can prove it! I know they talked to you, Tex, and to Ian, and probably even Josh, and they never considered me because they're nothing but a stupid boys' club of *fascist, sexist pigs!*" She paused long enough to take a look around and grimaced. "And it's…really, really *gross* down here!"

I couldn't deny the boiler room ruled in grotesquerie. Red had papered the brick walls with old pin-ups, leaving all sorts of female anatomy exposed. Crushed beer cans filled nooks and shelves. Fast food wrappers adorned the floor. Exactly what a high school boy's bedroom would look like if not for the domineering designer tastes of parents.

Red tossed back his floppy mane of hair and said, "Well, hello there," For a moment, I thought he looked like the golden, boyish basketball star he bragged about in his prime, even though his advances were wildly inappropriate in more ways than one. "They call me

Red."

Definitely *not* the way to Olivia's heart. Her visible anger built as she huffed and puffed, for once at a loss for words. I braved myself for the terror we brought upon ourselves.

"And *more* sexist creeps," she screamed. "Well, Red, I'd tell you to go get a room with your paper girlfriends, but you probably *live* here, and you're a *creep,* and this crappy-ass school is nothing but a boys' club, and I can murder someone, too, and I've had it with *all of you.*" She stormed up the stairs, still ranting, and I honestly have no idea how she managed the stairwell in her rage.

"Um, we'd better go see if she'll be okay," I said. Ian and Josh sheepishly agreed.

"Man, I hope one of you guys is hitting that." Red grinned, master of the sensitive.

We looked at each other and chuckled nervously, neither manning up nor denying Red's inquiry. And for a moment there, I noticed something odd that hadn't struck me before. Did I resent Red's crass come-on to Olivia, even just a little?

Chapter Three

"Look, O', I'm really sorry for laughing at you." She sat steaming silently in the Bucket as I drove her home. "I guess I just kinda needed it. Believe me, I would've gladly traded you places instead of being grilled by Hastings."

"We laugh at *others*." Oliva's gaze remained locked on the windshield. "Not at each other." The Bucket ground loudly over a fallen tree branch that looked like a giant leper's lost gnarled finger. "Whoa."

"Hang in there, Battle Bucket." I patted the dashboard. "You can do it, girl."

Olivia's angry veneer nearly vanished, but I realized too late I'd just supplied her with more ammo. "And here we go again. Why does the Battle Bucket have to be a female? And *why* do men always *insist* their cars are women? It's like women are only good to be driven and told what to do and where to go, like a car, with no minds of their own, and only you big, strong men can tame the wild beast!" She finally turned toward me. "I never thought you'd be one of the sexist pigs, too, Tex!"

I knew that if I looked back at Olivia, I'd burst out laughing. A *deadly* move. So I bit my lip, concentrating on the road, hoping not to start round two. Finally, she let out a whooping roar of laughter, the flag of peace at full mast again.

"I promise not to refer to the Battle Bucket as a female again. I'll call him Ben." We shared laughter, cathartic after all the gloom of the day. "I'm seriously sorry though, O'."

"It just sucks, that's all." Olivia settled in comfortably and kicked her feet up on the Bucket's dashboard. "That whole place sucks. Most of it's a boys' club full of sexist pigs, bullies, and perverts, young and old. And they're so stupid...they talked to you and Ian as possible murder suspects."

I had to agree with everything she said. The tyranny of bullies at Clearwell High didn't just stop at the students' level. It carried on from gym teachers to regular teachers, all the way to his booted highness himself, Arville Hastings. I once read the behavior of school bullies could be explained as youthful immaturity. But how does that explain adult bullies? And what about the ninety percent of Clearwell High who aren't bullies? I guess "youthful immaturity" is reserved for the chosen sociopathic few. My grandmother used to tell me school days are the best days of your life. She lied.

"Well, at least they didn't talk to Josh," I said. "At least, not yet. Hey, maybe they'll talk to you tomorrow." I imagine the only reason they didn't suspect Josh was he was too small and therefore, not a perceived threat. I sometimes wonder if crime ever got solved in Clearwell.

"Whatever..." Olivia slashed her hand down, end of subject. I couldn't be happier we were letting this dialogue die. "Just remember, we've got to stick together. We're all we've got."

"You're right." I pulled onto Olivia's street. In

front of us, the dirty, white ice cream van slowly chugged down the street, its bell dinging at intervals. "Hey, Olivia…you ever seen this van before?"

"Ugh…no." Her lip turned upward in disgust. "What? Is it some pervert selling Bomb Pops out of the back of his van?"

"I don't know. I first saw him on my street last night and thought it was weird because of how the van looked and the fact it's October." The van's bell maintained a slow, solemn pattern, totally devoid of any "good humor" whatsoever. The tinted back windows proved impossible to see through. A film of dirt and dust obscured the license plate. I sped up to within three feet of the van.

"Tex, *what* are you doing? You gonna shake down the ice cream man for a cone?"

The bell stopped crying. The van sped up, quickly vanishing down the street, orange and yellow leaves stirred up by its departure.

"Huh…weird." A tingle of fear ran down my back. My knuckles on the steering wheel grew whiter than usual. "I guess it's quitting time for the ice cream man."

"Hey," said Olivia, already forgetting the runaway ice-cream van. "Don't forget tomorrow after school, I got a stupid detention to go to. I'll walk home, so you don't have to wait."

"No, that's cool. I'll wait for you. I want you to be safe."

"*Ha*! You boys need me to keep *you* safe. But thanks for the ride. Meet me in front of Miss Swanson's class about an hour after school lets out."

"What'd you do this time, anyway?"

"All I did was call Swanson an uptight beeyotch.

Can you believe that *crap*?" I shook my head and chuckled, while Olivia remained stunned at the unfairness of the Universe. "Well, she *is* an up-tight beeyotch."

Regardless of Miss Swanson's beeyotchy status, Olivia was right about her ability. She *could* take care of herself and had rescued the three of us from close scrapes before. But I still couldn't help but be afraid for her. For all four of us. Something dark was stirring underneath the boiling surface of the stewpot that was Clearwell, Kansas, and some mad chef was ready to serve it up to us.

****

As I pulled into my driveway, I noticed the cats. At least eight cats milled about the front door and along the dying hedges by the bay window. I spotted a calico, a black cat with white paws, several yellow and white striped cats, and Benny, Mr. Cavanaugh's cat. Great. Something died and attracted a cat convention to our front yard. I walked toward the front stoop, cautiously avoiding contact as one stray cat hair would set my eyes itching and watering. The cats turned their attention to me and rubbed against my jeans, purring their internal motors.

"Scat," I said in a hushed whisper so as not to excite them further. "Get away."

"Richard?" said a voice from behind me. Mr. Cavanaugh. His tone reminded me somewhat of a cat's purring self-satisfaction. "Ah…there you are, Benny. And it looks like you have some friends, too." He grinned oddly, waiting for some sort of corroboration.

"Hey, Mr. Cavanaugh." I didn't want to rile him regarding a cat controversy of my devilish doing. "I don't know why the cats are all here. Maybe a dead bird…or something." The cats encircled me like I was an open can of tuna.

"Maybe they just *like* you." His smile appeared to be on autopilot, stretched and frozen into place. This man makes a living in sales? "How was school today, Richard?" Now, this was something new. As long as Mr. Cavanaugh lived next door, he never once inquired into my academic achievements. "I understand the police talked to you today." So, *this* is what he wants. "About the death of the…Rimmer boy, is it?"

"Well, they questioned a lot of people. It really wasn't much of anything."

"Ah…did they tell you anything about the…murder?" The way he drew out the word "murder" sounded like some stuffy old British constable in a forties B-movie. "How it…happened?" This intrusive questioning, delivered through his Cheshire Cat-like grin, was way unsettling. And how in the world could Cavanaugh know this? Does news travel that far and fast in Clearwell? As far as I knew, creepy Cavanaugh never appeared to leave his porch.

"I really don't know anything, Mr. Cavanaugh." Here I was again in a ridiculous situation. A wild group of cats wanted to crown me their king with feline pomp and circumstance, while their court jester interrogated me, seemingly oblivious to the cats on parade at my feet.

"Well, tell your father hello for me." He turned his grin into a disgruntled frown, ending our conversation. "Come along, Benny." The cat ignored his owner, only having eyes for my pant legs. Mr. Cavanaugh bent to pick him up. "Naughty little kitty…" he continued chanting as he walked back to his front porch.

"Okay, cats, I'm done here." I brushed them aside as well as I could without harming them. I sneezed once, ran up the two steps, unlocked the door, and squeezed through as narrow an opening as possible. I looked out the door window and saw them sitting on the stoop, staring up at me. I'm much disliked by everyone at school, but suddenly I'm irresistible catnip to every neighborhood cat? What's happening?

****

Upstairs, I immediately felt uncontrollably anxious. I walked past my mom's old study where she used to do her real estate work. I hadn't been in there since she died. We kept the door shut. Whether closed to preserve memories within, or to keep them from painfully flooding out, I didn't know, but shut it remained and had been since her death.

I put my hand on the doorknob and felt a large static shock course through my body. It seemed like a beckoning sign. The seal had been broken, and now felt safe for me to remember.

I pushed the door open and looked around. After a year, it surprised me to see the place practically devoid of dust and smelling quite fresh. There sat her old desk that must've been passed down through many generations, still covered with the last house listings she'd been working on. On the mantle above her desk rested her collection of rubber duckies. A strange collection for someone her age, but I remember Mom as always being different from the local PTA moms. She always stubbornly—defiantly—did things her way, let the Greek chorus of gossiping housewives be damned.

I pulled open the bottom drawer of her desk, and in

it sat a long cardboard box. I opened the folded flaps; inside were dozens of long thin candles of varying colors. Most were white, but some were colored—blue, gray, yellow, green—and some were striped. I never remembered having seen my mother burn any of these candles anywhere in the house. *Was Mom an Avon lady on the side?*

When I opened the closet door, a loud squeak indicated the only sign of neglect in the room. An odd wooden box, about eight by eight inches, sat on the top shelf. I grabbed it and opened it. Lying in the center was my folded green knit cap, the one Mom gave me. Surrounding it were various odd knick-knacks and remembrances of my childhood, including baby teeth (*gross*), pictures I'd drawn, and once again, more bay leaves, herbs, and a handful of cloves. The box had been hand-made, the amateurish carpentry betraying these origins. The bottom appeared to be a thin piece of plywood. What a weird "memory box." And why would Mom snag my cap from me to put in there?

I looked back at the shelf. The white Styrofoam head adorned by the long red-haired wig Mom had bought seemed to stare down at me, giving silent, tacit approval for my trespassing. I collapsed against the wall beside the door, sliding to the floor. A sudden outburst of violent sobbing brought on a wave of memories, as I held my head between my knees…

****

Two years ago, it was a day like any other, a comforting thought. One of the last ones I remember having. My mom handed me my sack lunch as I left for another happily bland day in my last year at grade school. She stopped me and gave me a long, lasting kiss on top of my uncombed hair.

"After I take your dad to work today, I have an appointment. I may not be here when you get home from school, so try and make your dad dinner just in case, okay, honey?" Her red hair brushed up against my face. In the privacy of our home, I welcomed my mom's coddling, but never in public, natch. What happens at home, stays at home.

"Right, Mom." I raced out the door, actually excited about new possibilities at school. "Love you, Mom!"

"Love you, too." I looked back from the corner bus stop and saw her in the doorway, suddenly tired-looking. Possibly crying. I got on the bus and at first, thought nothing of it. But as the day grew long, my new "friend" Paranoia pawed at me, nudging my imagination into the worst scenarios possible.

Why would Mom miss dinner because of an appointment? She'd never missed a meal with us in her life. And why had she been crying? That day, the hours crawled by slower than usual. By the time the counselor's office summoned me, I nearly wet myself out of fear.

"Richard," said the school counselor, "your father's here in a taxi to pick you up. Your mother's in the hospital."

****

The cab driver dropped us in front of Clearwell County Hospital. I didn't remember much about the trip other than my dad attempting to tell me what was happening.

"Tex, your mother has breast cancer." Lines on his forehead rippled. His grimace appeared wracked with

43

physical pain.

"How bad is it?" I knew about cancer—it can kill anyone at anytime. But to my younger mind, cancer hadn't yet achieved Boogeyman status.

"We don't know yet." He wrapped his arm around me. "We were hoping the bump they found was going to be benign...um, not harmful overall...but it turned out to be...malignant...harmful. They're going to have to operate. And it's a pretty serious operation."

"Why didn't you *tell* me?" I had nothing else to say. So many emotions ran through me. Betrayal for not being told the truth, incredible anger at the unjust Fates, sadness for more trauma to my family, and fear for my mom's health and life. "Why didn't you tell me? *Why*? *Why* didn't you *tell* me?" I cried in a continuous chant. The cab driver, obviously tired of listening to it, turned on his radio.

"Shhhh, son." Dad held me tighter than he ever had. Or has, to this day. "We didn't want to worry you." Then Dad started crying, too.

****

Dazed, I pushed Dad in his chair through the cold, sterile hallways of the hospital. My vision had blurred from non-stop crying in the taxi. Torn between wanting to shout at the people staring at us, "*What are you looking at?*" and being pissed off at the people ignoring us, I wanted it both ways. But most of all, I wanted life back as it was this time yesterday.

We arrived at Mom's room on the fourth floor. Upright in bed, even without makeup on, she appeared as beautiful and healthy as ever. Surely the doctors had made a mistake.

"Tex..." Her eyes implored me to come to her.

44

"How was school today?"

"Why didn't you tell me?" The tears started again as I hugged her. Talking about school seemed rather pointless. "How are you? Why didn't you tell me? What's going to happen? Why didn't you *tell* me?"

"Tex, when I said goodbye to you this morning, the lump in my breast still could have been just a benign cyst." That word—*benign*—again. "There was no sense telling you until we knew what we were dealing with." She smiled wanly.

"What's going to *happen*?" I wanted the bottom line, tired of the baby pampering. "What are we going to *do*?"

It's funny how life can change so suddenly sometimes. A real laugh riot.

"We have two choices," explained my mom, the only dry-eyed person in the room. "I can either have a radical mastectomy—have a breast removed—or they can take the lumps out and treat me with chemotherapy and radiation for the next six months." No pampering going on now.

"It's your choice, Elizabeth," said Dad. "Whatever you decide, you know Tex and I'll be here for you." His voice broke. I couldn't stand the sight of Dad like this, and it triggered more of my own crying. The endless back and forth crying jags went on for the next several hours until they kicked us out of the room. Just business as usual for the hospital staff.

****

Mom decided to go through with the chemo and radiation treatments and thus began Our Cancer Year. She knew it wasn't a perfect science. She knew of the side effects, and that it might not be successful. But damn, she fought hard.

After the initial operation, the doctor released her into our care. Although bedridden for several days, not once do I remember her losing faith or wallowing in self-pity as I surely would've done. She constantly smiled, joked, talked to me about school (which I tried to get out of for a couple of days, as I thought I wouldn't be able to concentrate anyway).

By the second day, she got up, no moss on her, and prepared our lunches for the upcoming day. I helped her with her stretching exercises and took walks with her, becoming somewhat her personal coach. Her optimism proved contagious and gave me hope we'd survive this.

Then the treatments started. She'd drive herself to the hospital and be back home several hours later. But when I jumped off the bus every day, ran into the house, hoping to hear some miraculous end to cancer, more often than not, I found her napping, one arm slung over her eyes, the other holding onto a big bowl.

About the time her hair began to fall out, I noticed some of the fight had left her. When awake, she seemed like a sad former shadow of herself. She walked around in her bathrobe, resting in strategically placed chairs throughout the house. She'd smile, ask about school, then lie down for "some shuteye," she'd call it. I don't know how she did it, but every day she still managed to take Dad to work and pick him up again.

"Tex…" she said one day, sitting in one of the kitchen chairs. "I think it's a good idea if we get your driver's permit early." Her eyes looked half-glazed.

"Um…okay, Mom, but I'm only thirteen." The thought of operating large machinery out in the big, bad world when I could barely find my way around on my bike, terrified me.

"Yes, honey, but we have extenuating circumstances." My mom never held back with her large, wonderful vocabulary, definitely a trait I picked up from her and carry with me to this day. "I'm sure the driver's bureau will work with us on this."

Of course, Mom was right. Apparently, such things were relatively commonplace (but not in *my* family!), and seeing as how I had two currently debilitated parents, the bureau rewarded me with a driver's permit at the ripe ol' age of thirteen. The provisions allowed me to drive to school and back, take my dad to work and back home, and take my mom to her medical appointments. "No joy-rides or fun driving!" croaked the froggy-voiced bureau puppet from behind his desk. I wanted to ask, "Mr. Puppet, just what in *hell* makes you think there's *anything* fun about driving?" But I kept my mouth sensibly shut.

Dad volunteered as my driving coach, and we definitely had some hair-raising adventures. Every weekend, we'd journey out, my dad gripping onto the "Oh *Hell*, Handle" above the passenger window with white-knuckled intensity. Not until late in the game did I notice he kept his eyes shut half the time. He made me nervous, his fear obvious by the way he'd scrunch down in the seat or raise one knee in a defensive position (not an easy task for him to do). By the end of each lesson (*in terror*, Dad probably thought), I felt a little more accomplished, while Dad let out a sigh of relief, sweat beading on his forehead. To this day, I'm still not sure if Dad's comfortable with my mad driving skills, but I've not once been ticketed or been in a wreck.

Soon, Mom had lost all of her hair and her eyebrows had fallen out. Proud as ever, she wouldn't let this stop her from going out in public. She donned a colorful bandanna and put makeup on again. One day, after I brought Dad home from work, we found Mom sitting at the kitchen table, staring at a white Styrofoam head covered with a red-haired wig. It looked as if she was in the middle of an intense stare-down contest and on the losing side.

"Well, guys, what do you think?" She grinned and held the atrocity up. "What do you make of my new wardrobe addition?"

"Put it on and let's see how beautiful you look," Dad said. So artificially red, the wig could've made a stop sign jealous, at least ten steps removed from Mom's natural strawberry-blonde coloring. Long and curved at the ends, the fake hair resembled a 60s Go-Go dancer's mane gone wild. Dad and I exchanged quick, nervous glances.

"This is what the hospital set me up with. Don't worry, dear, they said the insurance would cover it." Finally, she let out a loud, whooping laugh, the happiest I'd heard her in months. "Okay, I think it's going back." Later, I found out she never sent it back. Don't know why. Maybe she kept it as a war trophy.

Dad looked instantly relieved as we all ridiculed the bald-faced runaway head of hair from hell. Mom proudly decided to work with what she had and garnered a very stylish collection of bandannas to wear for all occasions. She also gained neighborhood notoriety for being so brazen as to not hide her cancer or hair loss.

Around these interesting days of Our Cancer Year,

I took it upon myself to learn to cook, my time to take care of my parents. Okay, maybe calling it "cooking" seemed like a stretch. Totally over-reliant on the microwave, I started by burning TV dinners, and this supplied much-needed mirth over those several long months. Sitting down at the dinner table, I could see Dad's face, torn between amusement and dread, at what new monstrosity I would serve up. Mom beamed at me and never failed to tell me how proud of me she was as she forced herself to choke down burnt mystery meat.

At the end of those early meals, Dad would lean back, look to the ceiling, and sigh. "Well...*that* was interesting."

We'd burst out laughing, generally ending with Mom's coughing, and we'd just as suddenly stop.

Soon, I'd graduated to burning hamburgers on the stovetop and developing skills for powdered mashed potatoes. Dad joined me in my cooking endeavors, wanting to help (but I suspect driven by dread of my next culinary offering). We were "giving back" to Mom—as awful as those early meals were—and she watched proudly. Weirdly enough, in those scary, sad, unsettling times, we, as a family, seemed to grow. We found small pleasures in the mundane details of everyday living we used to take for granted.

Between school, driving, cooking, and taking care of my parents, I had never been busier. The year flew by as well. One spring day, I came home to find Mom crying at the kitchen table, where she conducted all the important details of her life.

"Mom? What's wrong?"

"Tex...the cancer is in remission." I had a crash course in cancer education over the past year. This was good news. "I'm going to be all right."

She rushed forward, threw her arms around me, and we did a crazy circular dance for minutes, knocking everything over in our way. From all the whooping and screaming, our neighbors probably thought we were being massacred by a serial killer.

"I've got to call your father!" Her eyes bugged out, filled with crazy hope. "No, *wait*! Let's drive down to his work and tell him there!" She hopped up and down like the girls do at school, squealing like they're on fire. "You drive! *No*! I'll drive!"

Off we went, my mother driving, speeding through the neighborhood. As I grabbed onto the "Oh *Hell*, Handle," I found sudden empathy for what my dad must've experienced. Mom bolted for the bank door before I even got out of the car. By the time I entered the bank, Mom and Dad were hugging. He knocked off work early and suggested the three of us go out to eat and celebrate.

"No offense, boys," said Mom, grinning, "but…thank *God*!"

****

Three months later, while preparing dinner, the phone rang.

"Son…there's been an accident." Dad's voice sounded tinny and far away as if from an old-fashioned radio, followed by an uncomfortably long radio silence. "It's your mother. Terrible…accident."

Mom had picked up her real estate business again. While driving back from an appointment along I-35 during that wintry late afternoon, a semi-truck slid on a patch of ice, jackknifing in front of her. Her car ran head-on into the overturned truck, killing her instantly.

****

Earlier, I had explained the "Golden Rule" regarding bullying. This holds true in life as well, especially when you're dealing with those tricky, arbitrary bitches known collectively as the Fates. When dealing with the Fates, you should always try and run under the radar and not draw attention to yourself. If they don't know you exist, they can't screw up your life. Once you're on their radar, they know you're there, and they become bound and determined to toy with your life, ensuring that a life full of happiness is snatched right out from under you.

The Fates noticed how Mom cheated Death and decreed, *No, we can't have that.* So in their constant game of selfish one-upmanship, they took notice of my family's happiness and decided it should be short-lived. I envision them sitting in their courts, bored with the usual wars, plagues, pandemics, and famines, thinking how much fun it would be to bring a smaller tragedy to fruition for their own petty amusement. With a few small moves of the McKenna family chess game pieces, the unfair Fates smiled and said, *Let's change it up.*

Good move, the kiss-ass lackeys replied as their all-knowing, unjust tyrannical leader smiled from his golden throne. And we, the poor, helpless, pitiful game-pieces have no other choice but to suck it up and see if there's any game left in it for us. Because it's clearly out of our hands. There's no such thing as creating and following one's own destiny. Just…fate decided by cruel gods.

At that time in my frozen, emotionally stunted life, all I could think was *game over*.

****

That night, as I picked Dad up, we drove home, business as usual. I told him how Hastings and a cop grilled me about Matt Rimmer. He clenched his eyes shut, obviously pissed off.

"You want me to talk to this Hastings?" he asked.

"No, Dad. That'll just make things worse. It'll blow over."

We drove along through the early falling dusk in silence. I thought about everything I found in Mom's office and the memories it brought cascading back like an inexhaustible waterfall. I had questions. And if I couldn't control my life—if the Fates were cruel arbiters of our lives—at least I might be able to control the talk I knew I had to have with Dad tonight.

"Dad, I want to talk about Mom. I'm ready to talk about her tonight."

Chapter Four

In the kitchen, dinner preparations were being wrapped up. Since Mom died, we'd graduated to more advanced meals. Tonight's menu offered chicken breasts stuffed with crabmeat. It's too bad Mom couldn't see how far we'd progressed.

"Son, have you heard anything else about the Rimmer boy's death?" Dad pounded out the chicken breasts with a plastic-wrapped can of pumpkin pie filling.

"No, not really. Just a lot of wild rumors and the usual gossip. Nothing specific." I chopped the crabmeat into small bits as we avoided all things "Mom," an unspoken understanding between us the eminent chat would happen after dinner. Right now, "family time" reigned.

"Bill Pearson said the boy was beaten brutally with a pipe and then strangled." Dad shook his head in disbelief. "Who would do such a thing?"

Even though I could think of at least two likely candidates for such savagery at school, I decided I wouldn't worry my dad unnecessarily with this information. "Beats me."

"Did he have a lot of enemies?"

"No, he was well-liked. But I barely knew him." I sensed the best course to give Dad some peace of mind was distancing myself from the sitch.

"Just watch yourself." Dad stopped flattening the chicken to catch my eye. "Be careful."

Dinner was good, although neither one of us had much of an appetite. We pushed the food around on our plates, talked about the weather and other waste-of-time topics, dreading the inevitable. After we ate, silence hung heavily in the small kitchen, the clock ticking away anxiously on the wall above us.

I washed the dishes, and Dad dried them. We sat back down at the dinner table, where we always had our talks. The same table where I found Mom crying, a different lifetime ago.

"Dad…" There was no turning back now. "What exactly was Mom involved in?"

He looked sharply at me. "What do you know?" We danced nervously around each other, both of us afraid to take the lead.

"Today, I found some weird stuff in her office. I found a ton of strange candles, a homemade box with some of my stuff in it—"

"Son…" he interrupted. "Son, your mother was a practicing witch."

There. He'd said it. I sat dumbfounded, not knowing how to respond. It didn't come as a total surprise, as the clues were all there. But it did seem unworldly having heard it out loud, hanging in the tick-tocking kitchen like a thrown dagger.

"Okay," I finally said. "*What* does *that* mean?"

"She comes from a long line of witches. Her mother was one, and her grandmother was one. Apparently, it's hereditary. I understand your mother was…very talented and powerful."

"Grandma was a witch…" I thought about the frail

little, facial-haired lady I used to kiss on holidays. Imagining her stirring a cauldron brought a smile to my face.

To my amazement, Dad smiled, too. "Yes, that's what I was told." He folded and unfolded his hands, his "bank-side" manner.

"So, the candles I found? Did she use these for…spells?" Not only did this topic seem surreal, but it astounded me at how matter-of-factly I coped with this bombshell information.

"Yes, she did. But I need you to understand something. Your mother was very careful to practice only white magic. And she was careful to not use it for selfish purposes. Otherwise, she once told me, things could go bad *very* fast."

"What kind of spells? What 'white magic' did she do?" The air seemed almost hazy—the kind of atmosphere you experience as a kid on Christmas morning with the magical glow of Santa's trail still lingering in the air.

"I saw her do a lot of good things over the years." Dad shut his eyes as if in pained concentration. "Do you remember when your cousin Billy nearly died? When he had pneumonia so bad, the doctors didn't think he'd live another day?"

"Yes…" I didn't really remember, being three at the time. But I'd heard enough about it when we gathered at my cousins' house for Thanksgiving dinner.

"She saved his life with one of her spells. Either that or he miraculously recovered on his own, but…" He spread his hands as if that explained it all. "She was also the one who called the police anonymously five years ago about the missing Barton boy. She'd found out where he was with a...with scrying—you know, divination of a sort—your mom called it."

I *did* remember the Barton kid going missing. He'd fallen into a storm drain, and thanks to a call to the police, they found him safe, scared, and hungry.

"She did many things," Dad continued. "Most of what she did wasn't on the scale of saving lives, but she did little things to help people out as often as possible. She knew I was...uncomfortable...and even a little skeptical about all this...witchcraft...so she kept it from me as much as she could. But I did become a believer. I just didn't understand most of it, so your mom decided what I didn't know wouldn't hurt me." Dad's voice cracked ever-so-slightly before quickly recovering. "I didn't know this about your mom for the longest time. Years after we were married, she told me about it. Like we're doing now...it happened at this very table."

"But...we went to church every Sunday. How could Mom have been a witch...if she was religious?" Every Sunday, the three of us would trudge down to the Hall Avenue Baptist Church and get an hour-load of Godliness shoved at us. Then, life resumed as usual. Dad and I stopped going to church once Mom died, her funeral the last time either one of us set foot in a church.

"No...no, no!" He laughed and shook his head. "Look, Tex, I don't understand witchcraft at all, nor the extent of what your mother was practicing, but I guess it's possible to believe in and worship God, while still being a witch. In fact, I think she incorporated God into her practice." This was getting nuttier by the minute. Everything I thought I knew about my mother was apparently only half-true. And my limited understanding of witchcraft (from movies, mostly) hardly seemed like gospel either.

"Oh boy." I hung my head, my hair grazing the table. "So, Mom was a witch who helped people by using 'good witchcraft' and..." I stopped, trying to mentally order all the questions I had. "If this were true, why didn't she cure your MS? Why didn't she protect herself from dying?" This last question unleashed some surprising rage at my parents—for lying to me, for getting sick, for dying. Especially if it could have been prevented. I pounded the table with my fist, rattling the fruit bowl at the center.

"I don't know for sure, Tex. But I suspect your mother had a lot to do with my MS not being as severe as it could've been. She was extremely cautious about using her powers for selfish reasons, as I told you, but I do think she put a protection spell on me after I was first diagnosed. I *know* she put a protection spell on you."

"Was the spell...a small handkerchief filled with herbs and stuff?" Too bad I'd thrown it out, but by now I was so pissed off I didn't care about being "unprotected."

"Yep, that much I do know," said Dad, happily able to supply something concrete. "As for her own protection and health, well...we both know she was a pretty selfless person. And, I guess she was afraid of invoking...black magic."

"Dad, I don't get *any* of this. This changes *everything*!"

"Hey, nothing's changed. Your mother's still the same person we always knew and loved. If anything's changed...it's just the fact she protected you more than you knew. She wanted me to tell you about this when she was first diagnosed with cancer...in case she died."

"*Why*? What good does it do to know this *now*? Maybe I'm better off not even knowing about this...craziness!" Crazy didn't begin to describe it. It almost felt like my mom's memory had been sullied.

"Well..." Dad sighed, shutting his eyes again. "There *is* something important you need to know, Tex. I said being a witch is hereditary...that makes *you* the next witch in line." He scratched at the table, rubbing out an invisible smear. "You're a witch, too."

I stared at him in disbelief. Then I laughed, long and loud. What else do you do when you're told you're a witch? My life was confusing, hectic, and scary enough without this bird-dropping of mind-blowing crap being unloaded onto my shoulder. Bullied high school murder suspect by morning, witch by night. That's me. Yay.

"This is...*unbelievable*." I ranted to the dead-bug-filled light fixture above me, in my best teenage dramatic diva performance. "*Now* what am I supposed to do, Dad?"

"I know this is hard to take..." He rolled his wheelchair across to my side of the table. He laid one hand on my shoulder.

"'Hard to take...'"

"Here..." He unfolded a piece of paper from his shirt pocket. "Your mom wanted you to contact this person. She'll be able to help you and answer more questions than I can."

I looked at the name and address on the paper. Mickey Goldfarb.

"Dad," I said, regaining myself somewhat,

"okay…but, why do you want me to go see your bookie?"

He stared at me blankly before we shared a much-needed, tension-breaking laugh.

"Just go see her. I've never met her, but your mom talked about her on occasion. They…worked together, and I guess she helped your mom learn some things."

Worked together. On what? Boiling cauldrons? Ancient curses? "Fine, I'll go see her," I said resignedly. "Whatever. But I can't after school tomorrow because Olivia's got a detention, and I have to wait to give her a ride home."

"Oh?" Dad lifted his eyebrows. I believe he saw this as an escape route from the current uncomfortable topic of witchery. "Your girlfriend?" He grinned, hoping one uncomfortable topic would supersede the other.

"No, Dad, she's *not* my girlfriend." We'd been through this many times, and I know Dad wishes she were my girlfriend. Sometimes I suspected Dad thought I might be gay. Bad enough his son is a witch and all that…

"Okay, but don't wait too long to see Mickey. I think she'll be able to, if nothing else, make sense of this…mess…" Dad's voice trailed off quietly as if he were sorry I'd been dragged into this. "Goodnight, son…"

I watched him roll away from the table and felt a sudden sense of compassion for him. While I cried like a little kid about my small(ish) problems, here lived a man whose wife and health were plucked cruelly and prematurely from him. He never whined or dramatically thrust his hands toward the uncaring gods screaming,

Why me? At least that I ever saw or heard. He coped with quiet dignity.

"Dad?" I walked up behind him and placed my hand on his shoulder. He covered mine with his stronger hand.

"Yes, son?" He looked up at me.

"I really miss her...I miss Mom." Here came the tears again. The eighth wonder of the world today, my inexhaustible supply of tears just wouldn't stop. Step right up and see the incredible tear-flowing Tex, the witch boy!

"I know, son. I miss her, too." Silence ruled, proximity to one another comfort enough.

"But you know..." Dad hesitated as if he didn't want to finish. "Just because your mother's passed away...doesn't mean you can't still contact her."

I thought about this while Dad went off to bed.

****

The next day, Ian and I listened to Red talk about fixing his old Impala (stored above us in the school garage, which doubled as half-maintenance area and half auto-mechanics class), and how he'd take us "cruising for chicks" when he finished the job. Neither Ian nor I particularly cared anything about cars, but the appeal of "cruising for chicks"—particularly those outside the realm of Clearwell High School—did hold a mysterious allure of pleasures beyond our limited lifestyle and knowledge.

Josh ran down the stairs, dropped his skateboard onto the cement floor, and wheeled it over in a casual show of mini-wheeled expertise. He kick-flipped it up into his hands, practically completely covered beneath his oversized, brown turtleneck.

"Hey." He jerked his chin at us.

"Hey" became our standard greeting after Olivia put a ban on our using the fist bump. She'd said, *Leave that fist-bump to the Neanderthals*.

Red only had three folding chairs in the boiler room, and Josh usually lost out as he had farther to travel from class. He sat down on the floor next to us.

"What's up, Josh?" asked Red, flipping his curly hair out of his eyes.

"Not much..." Josh unwrapped his peanut butter and jelly sandwich, the only thing he appeared to eat.

I considered Josh to be a world-class skateboarder. Josh's skating prowess even impressed Red, golden boy supreme of the basketball courts. If everyone has a special talent—Ian's would be video games, Olivia's tart and sharp tongue. I suppose mine is, I don't know, *witchery*. Josh definitely ruled as King of the Skate Park. No one could turn a board inside out like him. A mini-legend at the Summit Skate Park, he presided royally with his never-ending repertoire of Ollies, kick-flips, shoves, and pushes. If the bullies who maliciously called him "Mole" could see him in his natural habitat, I had no doubt he wouldn't be cursed with his undeserved anonymity.

The summer when I got to know Josh after the shower incident was a fun one. He taught me, Olivia, and Ian to skateboard, at least to the best of our limited, two-left-feet abilities. Ian picked it up better than Olivia and I had, but even he cast a pale shadow of the skateboarding accomplishments of Josh. But the learning process provided our otherwise dull summer with hours and days of entertainment. As our circle of friendship grew stronger, our bumps and bruises grew larger and bluer.

I even saw Josh outrun Bellman and Malinowski on his skateboard once. If Josh wasn't at the skate park, then he could be found skating around the sidewalks at school. One day while getting into the Bucket, I spotted Josh racing and flipping off the front sidewalks when Bellman and Malinowski crossed his path. Of course, ugly words and threats spewed from their mouths while Bellman stabbed his hotdog of a finger at Josh. As I prepared to dash the Bucket up there to give Josh a getaway ride, he calmly held his own. While he didn't say anything to the bullies, he grinned and circled around them as a cat would casually tease a barking dog. Suddenly they gave chase, and Josh high-tailed it, fast as a bottle rocket, leaving the chain-smoking football bullies doubled-over and breathing hard on the sidewalk. Bellman, after all, had already developed a beer-gut at the age of sixteen.

The next day, I asked Josh about the incident. He just smiled, a Rock God Skate Boarder, and he knew it. Too bad no one else took the time to discover this about him.

During that last, fun summer, Ian and I were invited to Josh's house for dinner, an eye-opening experience. We sat down at the table alongside Josh's parents and his two older twin brothers, Bernie and Bobby, home from college for the summer. Practically indistinguishable, Bernie and Bobby were two large, muscular behemoths of boys. Giants compared to Josh, they amiably punched and teased one another. The Berillos appeared not too financially stable (later verified by my dad), accounting for Josh's ill-fitting wardrobe. I just wish they had better tastes than all the colors of the earth turtlenecks.

At dinner, Josh's dad—a permanently scowling and seemingly verbally challenged man—murmured a prayer then yelled, "Let's eat!" The twins noisily chased after meatballs with forks and fat fingers, while their dad struggled to suck up a tremendously long piece of pasta. He craned his head around the table impatiently, as if he couldn't believe his misfortune to be punished by the world's most stubborn pasta. Then he shook his head from side to side, like a dog with his favorite squeak-toy, spraying sauce over the table. He stopped and stared at everyone in turn, expectantly. Expecting what, I couldn't be sure, but it felt extremely uncomfortable. Finally, the twins belly-laughed like hyenas, and Josh and his father joined them.

Josh's mother attempted to hide her smile and said sheepishly, "Honestly, Bob," but soon joined them in their giddiness. Ian and I exchanged stunned glances of disbelief but also relief because we understood it was okay—and expected—to laugh. I experienced something long forgotten—the enjoyment of a family sharing something. Sure, it might have been considered sorta' civil savagery, but while watching Josh's family hooting and flipping sauce at one another, I immediately felt at ease. Also, a melancholic sense of what I'd lost hit me hard. After that, I went to Josh's house for dinner at every opportunity.

After dinner, the twins pulled me aside and quietly thanked me—in a manner much different from their tableside behavior—for helping Josh at school. I told them I hadn't done anything. Refusing to believe this, they went on about how Josh said I'd practically saved his life. They also promised a form of protection if we were ever bullied again. Even though it was comforting to know we had backup if necessary, I thought it rather futile. When school started up again, they'd be back at college. This time I thanked them, pointless as it may've been, but it reassured me that not every large lunk-head reeked of evil.

****

I finished my tuna sandwich and tossed the wrapper at Red's wire trashcan.

"Oooooh, *missed*," yelled Red. "From where you were, Tex, that should've been an easy two-pointer."

We all took turns trying to hit the basket with the rest of our trash. "Damn, boys, am I gonna have to teach you a thing or two out on the courts?" asked Red.

The prospect of extra-curricular sports didn't sound too appealing, so I quickly changed the subject. "I guess Olivia's one and only trip down here did her in, huh?"

"Yeah," said Ian, grinning. "She calls it the 'Dork Dungeon of Depravity' and swore she'd never set foot here again."

"She was a pretty hot little thing," said Red. "I'm telling you, one of you guys better bust a move soon…before it's too late." He creased his brow, visually daring us to accept his challenge.

Once again, "redirection" proved to be my most efficient weapon. "Hey, have any of you seen a dirty white ice cream van around here lately? One with nothing but an old bell on top?"

"Somebody's got the munchies," said Ian, laughing harder than merited. "Do you need a push-up, maybe with little itty-bitty sprinkles on top?"

"Actually," said Red, "I think I *have* seen it…"

Lost in thought, he stroked his hair with his long, thin fingers. "I think it's been cruising around here after school. But it was weird 'cause I never saw it stop once…and it didn't ring the bell much."

"That's the one." I didn't let them know how suddenly fearful this made me. "Huh…weird…" I said casually, to blow off any more talk of mysterious ice cream men. But part of me thought…could this ice cream guy be Matt Rimmer's killer?

I also debated if I should share what I knew about my mom—and myself—with my friends. On one hand, I understand the feeling of betrayal when loved ones keep something important—something you have a right to know, something you've *earned* the right to know— from you. On the other hand, it sounds way too crazy to even believe. Then again, I knew my friends would act as my support group, and maybe—just like that summer of skating, bruises and camaraderie—we could learn together. And yet, something told me, I didn't have enough information to share with them yet. And something even deeper, from a dark place, told me if they knew, they'd possibly find themselves in the path of danger.

****

Mostly surrounded by freshmen waiting for a working parent to pick them up, I hung out in the cafeteria and finished my homework. The school policy stated that at three forty-five, students had to vacate the premises and wait outside or be invited into a supervised classroom. So when the cafeteria clock turned three forty-five, I gathered my books and backpack, realizing I had another fifteen minutes before Olivia would be released from the pointless exercise known as detention.

I'd only had a couple detentions myself, one for "loitering" in the halls after school, a paradox because you'd think the faculty would appreciate students desiring to stay longer in their Halls of Education. For over an hour, I wrote my name continuously on notebook paper until my hand cramped, and time stood at a standstill. I wondered who created this sadistic form of torture when the time could have been better spent furthering my education by doing—oh, I don't know—homework, or something.

Olivia and Ian were unintentionally vying to see who could rack up the most detentions. One detention provided all I needed to know to opt out of their competition. Ian's seemingly random acts of aggression always brought about his detentions, while Olivia channeled her talents into "fighting the man" and railing against what she saw as acts of injustice. I'm not sure how calling Miss Swanson an "uptight beeyotch" fit into her one-woman crusade (true as it may be) against unfairness, but it gave Olivia the lead in the contest.

I went to the maintenance garage to see if Red could be found working on his car, or whatever he did all day to earn his paycheck, but it was vacant. Then I poked my head down the stairs to look for him in the boiler room. Still no sign of him.

I sighed, resigning myself to the fact I'd have to risk another detention by loitering outside Miss Swanson's classroom, waiting for Olivia to finish the written manifesto of her name. Those capital "O's" would probably be hell on her hand.

Miss Swanson plastered her door window with a

handwritten sign reading "Swanson–Speech," so I couldn't wave at Olivia to light a fire under her. Feeling the burden of my backpack, I slid down alongside the slick, gray lockers, landing with a plop onto the checkered linoleum floor.

As soon as the door swung open, I hopped up, ready to get the hell out of there. Instead, I stared into the frightening visage of Bob Bellman. A lop-sided grin stretched across his face once he remembered he hated me.

"Hey, pussy," he spat. "Narc." He said this as quietly as if in a library, but then I realized how stupid that comparison sounded. Bellman's never been in a library, probably didn't even know what one is.

"Well, which is it?" I asked, wishing my inner censor had kicked in before my words came out. "Am I a feline? Or a narcotics officer?" Too late.

Bellman's smile grew wider while he tried to grasp if I'd ridiculed him or not. "You're dead is what you are." He came at me, invading my personal space. His noxious, nicotine-tinged breath rolled off him, potent in its pungency. His unibrow formed a horizontal exclamation point above his crazy-eyed statement. Two inches separated my distance from the face of evil.

"Tex…I remember how you tried to get me expelled. You're *so* dead." He shoved me backward as I fell with a metallic clang against a locker. With one arm braced against my chest, he pinned me against the wall.

"Look, I did *not* try to get you expelled…I didn't do *anything* to you." His other arm stretched above my head, hand flat against the locker, like he wanted to offer me the kiss of death. I squirmed, attempting to slip off my backpack, hoping it would be a valid weapon to knock him back if necessary.

"What kind of pussy name is 'Tex'?" He pushed the words through his grime-covered teeth as if it pained him. "There's only two things from Texas with horns, and that's steers and queers."

Idiotically, I obliged him. "You didn't even get the movie quote right." My stupid mouth and brain weren't communicating with one another. "What you said doesn't even make sense."

"Make sense of *this*!" He blind-sided me with a fist to the side of the head. Half-stunned, I dropped, my vision giving way to sharp slivers of light. By the time I could see clearly again, he'd wrapped the straps of my backpack around my neck and pulled it tight. As he pulled the nylon straps tighter, my breath cut off.

"Let's see you do some smart-ass talking now!" He dragged me down the long hallway by the constricting straps, chuckling. My fingers attempted to loosen the straps around my neck. I flailed wildly for anything to stop our progress. With nothing to grab but dust from the slick floor, my vision fled again. I heard myself choking as if from far away, a horrible gasping sound.

My God, he's going to kill me!

I panicked, scrabbling as hard as I could. He dragged me toward the stairwell where some of the more barbaric forms of torture take place. The bullies preferred this venue because between classes they sat empty, and sound didn't travel down the hallways. One of my last fully coherent thoughts had been the story of how Bellman and Malinowski had set John Scranton's hair on fire last year in this very same stairwell.

About to surrender to unconsciousness, I heard a door open from a distance. A voice trumpeted, "*Hey*!" I barely made out the pitter-patter of running feet before it grew louder. Suddenly, like a banshee, Olivia yelled, "Take your paws off him, you damn, stinking *ape*!" I deliriously remembered we had watched *The Planet of the Apes* recently.

Bellman let out an agonized, inhuman scream. The straps around my neck loosened. Bellman writhed, twisted, and tossed one of his bloated hands toward his back.

"What did you *do* to me, you *slut*?"

Able to get up on my hands and knees, I gasped for breath. I looked up just in time to see Olivia grab the fire extinguisher from the sunken-in shelf on the wall. She flipped it upside down, a punked-out firefighter, and released a long, white foamy blast onto Bellman, giving him the appearance of a bakery explosion victim. As a loving, parting gesture, Olivia picked up the extinguisher and brought it down upon Bellman's snow-white head. The audible thud sounded sickening as Bellman went down, still raging and cursing us.

Olivia grabbed my shoulder, gave it a quick pinch, and said, "Come on, Tex, we gotta go!" I got up, shook my head to wake from the nightmare. We ran to the safety of the stairwell, my earlier, imminent port of departure. As an afterthought, Olivia spied the fire alarm and pulled it. Maybe not necessary, but typically Olivia.

We bounded down the stairwell, the persistent ring of the fire alarm chasing us. But even over the calamitous ringing, I could hear Bellman bellowing in animal-like rage, "Kill you! I'll *kill* you*! Pussyfaggotbitchslut!* I'm gonna *kill you*!"

Olivia threw open the door to the field where the

marching band practiced. We had to hightail it to the nearest street, go around the fence, and carefully take the long way back to the school parking lot. Olivia quickly surveyed the now-empty field like a well-trained spy and said, "Let's go!" I think part of her enjoyed this, nearly giddy because she thought our team "won one." But I knew there'd be "overtime." I just hoped it wouldn't be "sudden death."

****

Miraculously, our covert effort to return to the school parking lot, unseen by faculty and Bellman alike, proved successful. We crawled into the Battle Bucket and slowly and quietly—as quietly as the Bucket stubbornly agreed to—drove away without uttering a word. I practically held my breath until we were two blocks away, fearful the slightest audible syllable would bring the rats running.

"Are you all right?" Olivia asked, breaking the silence. She looked concerned. And flushed with excitement. "I tried to text you that Bellman was in detention, too, but Swanson busted me. I almost got another detention! So…are you okay?"

"I don't know." My hands trembled on the steering wheel, my voice unsteady. "I think so. That sick bastard…he tried to *kill* me."

"Well, I got him pretty good for you."

"I saw your whole kung fu ninja extinguisher act." I mustered a weak smile. "But, what did you do to make him let me go?"

"When I saw him dragging you down the hall, I grabbed the largest pin off my purse—the Sex Pistols—pulled out the needle and *jammed* it into his back!" Olivia's eyes lit up with passion and fire. "See? Here it is." She proudly held up her victory weapon. Dried blood stained the needle.

One step away from traumatic crying, I chose laughter instead. "Olivia...you're a warrior." I was truly in awe of her. Not only did she single-handedly take down the largest, scariest bully known to Clearwell High (and I bet a first for him), she also retained her weapon.

"You're damn right I am!" She flexed a muscle.

"You know we're in for one helluva storm of trouble, right?" I hated to sour her well-deserved mood, but I wanted her to be aware of the inevitable consequences.

"I already showed you I can handle Bellman."

"I know you can, O'. I mean, you're damn quick on your feet with a virtual arsenal at your fingertips—the pin, the fire extinguisher, the alarm. But, *really*...was the alarm necessary?"

"Yep!" We burst out laughing, releasing the pent-up emotions brought on by sudden danger.

"God, you're so brave." I felt a little ashamed. Inadequate and weak. "All I could do was come up with some snappy comebacks...and they weren't even that good." In my eyes, I let Olivia down, worried she wouldn't respect me. I had no idea I suffered from the prototypical fragile male ego.

"Tex...no." She abruptly turned serious. "You're the brave one. *You* are." At that moment, she did something she rarely did. She pulled the hair back from her covered eye, tucking it behind her ear. "Pull over, Tex." She gripped the steering wheel and tugged it toward a parking lot we were passing.

"Okay." I pulled into the lot.

71

"Look at me, Tex. *Look* at me. You're the brave one. Out of all of us, you're the bravest. I don't know how you put up with everything…with your mom dying…your dad in a wheelchair…the bullying…but you do. And you keep going. That's why we look up to you. You keep us together."

"Thanks, O'." I've never thought of myself as brave before. I run from every potential fight. Smart, maybe, but brave? I never realized my friends thought of me this way. "Thanks for trying to make me feel better."

"It's *true*, idiot! Have you ever known me to lie to make *anyone* feel better? *Duh!*"

I snorted, and Olivia howled with glee. The unrestrained natural abilities of Hurricane Olivia worked their miraculous talents on me once again.

"Okay, whatever," I said. "But we need to talk about our plan. And we need a plan."

"Check." She nodded half-seriously.

"Regarding the faculty and the um…fun with fire equipment…" Olivia tried, but couldn't hide her anarchic smile. "We deny everything. We saw nothing. We did nothing. If any teacher, or Hastings, asks you— and you *will* probably get your day in the hot seat—tell them you left detention five minutes earlier than you did and met me in the parking lot. Miss Swanson probably won't remember a difference of five minutes."

"Got it." Totally enjoying the whole cloak-and-dagger thing, she had no clue of the danger she'd put herself into. She'd now become a blip on the radar— Bellman's hateful, vengeance-fueled radar. And the thought of what Bellman might do to her made my skin crawl.

"They'll probably ask if Bellman left before you did. Tell 'em you really don't know. You just wanted to get the hell out of there and go do your homework like a good, little student."

"Okay." She snorted, homework a relatively alien concept to her. "But what about Bellman? Surely he'll rat us out."

"I doubt it. Do you *really* think he wants the school to find out he was beaten up by a girl?"

"*Hoo-yah!*" Olivia roared, once again channeling her inner warrior. "Okay, but what's to stop him from pointing you out?"

"He won't do that."

"Why not? He *sucks*!"

"Because…he'll want to get revenge on me Bellman-style. Having me suspended or expelled won't be enough for him." As I methodically worked this out, I wondered if divining the future could be part of my newly-discovered witch powers.

****

Once we reached Olivia's driveway, I realized I only had a little while to pick Dad up from work. Time does fly when you're having fun. We sat in the driveway for a few more minutes synching up our stories.

"It's okay to tell Ian and Josh about what happened, I guess, but nobody else," I said.

"Like I want to talk to anybody else at that dump." Olivia glared at me like she couldn't believe I'd even question her discretion.

"And, O', be careful. Text me whenever you can."

"Always." She reached across the seat and hugged me. I walked around, let her out the passenger door, and saw her safely inside.

It dawned on me life had recently grown more complicated, and real danger was in my future. But even after my near-brush with death, my recently revealed heritage, and a murderer running loose, Olivia loomed largest in my mind. She's magnificent, funny, smart, courageous, a great friend, and yes, hot. What this meant to me, and what I planned to do about it, scared me, possibly more than the events of the past weeks.

Chapter Five

Dad and I shared some awkward dinner conversation, both of us ignoring the previous night's bombshell event. I suppose he felt what needed to be said had been said, and didn't see any need to go backpacking again through the rugged wilderness of discomfort. I couldn't have been more thankful, as I mentally waved at the large elephant in the kitchen.

I kept quiet about the Bellman event, so as not to upset Dad. I needed to man up and adhere to the strict code of confidentiality I swore to Olivia. Should it come out, I'd address it then. But I felt confident my plan would work, and he'd never need to know the truth.

After dinner, I excused myself and told Dad I'm going to visit Mickey Goldfarb.

"Okay, son," he said. "Be careful. And if there's anything you need to ask me about your mother, don't be afraid to do so." He looked relieved after saying it.

"Thanks, Dad. Don't know when I'll be home, but I've got my key." I bolted toward the door.

"Hold on a sec… Technically, you're not supposed to be driving this time of night, unless for school or my work."

"I'd say this was homework, wouldn't you?" He nodded and said goodnight. I stepped outside and nearly tripped on a trio of cats on the stoop, staring expectantly at me. Their tails swooshed madly from side to side.

"Oh, great. The cat brigade's out in full force again." I glimpsed over to Mr. Cavanaugh's front porch, and like magic, he appeared. As I made my way to the Bucket, he sprang from his wicker chair, watching me carefully over his wooden railing.

"Richard?" he called out softly. Well, at least soft enough for me to pretend I hadn't heard him. I hopped in the Bucket and sped off. No time for nosies.

****

Mickey Goldfarb lived twenty minutes away, just a few blocks from where Josh lived. Nestled in the poorer part of Clearwell, her little blue two-story house appeared well kept. Given the time of year, her full and green manicured yard looked astonishingly vital. The most beautiful garden I'd ever seen surrounded the screened-in front porch. A full visual onslaught of exploding colors and flowers brimmed with life. I imagined their gaping, reaching flower buds crying out, *Feed me, Mickey*! Late October, we'd already had our first killing frost, so here lay proof Mickey Goldfarb had achieved miraculous gardener extraordinaire status.

I walked up the little broken sidewalk in the center of the yard to her porch door. The only sign of yard misbehavior was the tall green grass strands stretching through the sidewalk cracks, yearning for sunlight and rain.

I knocked, never having really understood proper screen door etiquette. Does one bypass the preliminary door and go straight to the front door? Like a stubborn woodpecker, I pounded at the screen. I finally relented, pulled open the porch door, and proceeded to the oddly-colored yellow front door.

Another five minutes passed, I finally saw a tuft of blue hair through the small window atop the door.

"Who is it?" rang out a craggy voice. *This is starting out soooo great.*

"Um, hi, Mrs. Goldfarb. I'm Tex." I suddenly felt very stupid and wanted out of there. "Tex McKenna... My dad said I should talk to you...I guess." I spoke too loudly, over-enunciating, because, hey, old people have a hard time hearing, right?

The door opened a crack, pulled taut by a chain. "You're Elizabeth's boy?" I snatched a peek at a brown eye peering over glasses, riding low on her nose. "Well...what do you want?" I kinda' thought my dad would've taken care of the preliminary meeting courtesies. Otherwise, it looked like I was in for yet another interrogation.

"I don't know, ma'am. My dad said I should see you and ask you about...well, certain powers...that my mom and I... Can we talk about this inside?" Embarrassed about the whole witch thing, really, I preferred not to have the entire neighborhood hear about it.

The door banged close. More rattling ensued with one chain than I thought possible. "*Goddammit.*" I sincerely hoped she had aimed her curse at the pesky chain rather than me. Finally, the door swung open. There stood Mickey Goldfarb, all five feet two inches of her, her curly, blue hair contributing at least four inches of her height. I always wondered how blue hair happens. Is it natural? Or do certain old ladies buy blue hair dye, believing this to be the hip new fad?

"Well, come in." She frowned, none too happy to

be interrupted. Whatever she'd been doing. Placing love spells on the retired guy next door, no doubt. Her glasses balanced at the very tip of her long, slender nose. How did she keep them afloat? She wore a long, blue robe. Pink fuzzy slippers peeked out underneath, the kind one would find on an infant. Hardly my idea of what a witch should look like.

"Get the hell outta' the way, Sampson!" She kicked at a fat, black cat. Ah! She *is* a witch! The cat dutifully obeyed her, and I could've sworn, almost nodded in her direction. Four more cats crawled out from seemingly nowhere to stare at me, tails whisking back and forth rapidly. Okay, crazy cat lady, we better make this short as my allergies are going to get the better of me soon.

"So you're Elizabeth's boy," she reiterated, scrutinizing me from head to toe. After her initial inspection, she concluded, "You need a haircut."

"Yeah, I get that a lot." I sighed. The cats brushed against my legs, purring for approval.

"You've grown some since Elizabeth's funeral." I didn't remember seeing her—or meeting her—at my mom's funeral. But that didn't mean anything. I'd gone through the entire proceedings as if in a dream-state, barely acknowledging anyone else.

"Yes, ma'am." How else does one respond to your growth notice?

"Oh, cut the 'ma'am' crap, kid." She guffawed. "That's for little old ladies!" *Huh.* "Call me Mickey." Even standing just inside her door, the cat hair began to take its toll on my watering eyes. "Your name's 'Tex'?"

"Yes, ma...Mickey."

"What kind of name is Tex, anyway?" She eyed me with suspicion.

"What kind of name is Mickey?" Okay, internal self-censor, you really need some fine-tuning. She stared at me, somewhat taken by surprise at my teenage insolence. Finally, she chuckled, her mirth ending abruptly in a coughing fit.

"Okay, okay," she said between spasms. "You've got your mom's attitude, kid, and I like it." She reached into her robe pocket and pulled out a package of cigarettes. "My doctor says I should quit." She jabbed one into her mouth. "So I try and smoke outside as much as possible. Let's go."

"Um…okay." I didn't understand her logic, but any chance to get away from the cat hair, I jumped at. Besides, I didn't want to risk getting her pissed off at me. She shoved me in front of her, making a sort of "shoo-shoo" sound. I could tell she was more used to dealing with cats than people.

"Get back, Sampson." She aimed her pink-covered foot again in the black cat's direction. "Make way, Delilah," she directed toward a calico cat. She pulled the door shut behind us and ushered me to a floral-patterned swing on the porch. "Sit, sit." She pushed me down onto the damp plastic seat covering.

"It came from my dad, actually."

"What did? The attitude?" She looked puzzled, and I couldn't blame her. Overwhelmed, my mind raced in too many directions at once.

"No…my name, Tex. When I was younger, my dad loved old western movies. He tried to get me into them, but I never really liked 'em. But he loved to play cowboys with me, and pretty soon he was calling me 'Tex' more than my real name. It was always, 'Which way did they go, Tex?' or 'What coach did you ride in on, Tex?' So, it just stuck over time. And my attitude *did* come from my mom, I guess, and I can see that I'm talking way too much." I ran out of gas and slumped back onto the swing.

"Heh." Mickey snorted, alternately laughing and coughing. "I never much had no use for them westerns, but I wouldn't kick that Clint Eastwood outta' bed."

Okay, gross, I thought as I watched Mickey gaze dreamingly through her screened porch, momentarily lost in a lustful scenario.

She fired up her cigarette. "You want one, kid?"

"Um…no thanks. I…uh…gave it up last year." Real cool, Tex, trying to impress a little old blue-haired lady by lying about smoking. What's next? Taking her "cruising" in the Bucket?

"Whatever, kid." She exhaled a huge cloud of smoke. "So, what do you know about your mother?"

"Well…turns out I don't know as much as I thought I did." Having said this out loud brought home the painful truth of the statement. "I just found out yesterday she was…I guess, a practicing witch."

"Kid, she wasn't just a practicing witch. She was one of the best, most goddamn talented witches I'd seen in a long time. She pulled off some spells I thought were just myths in *The Book of Witchcraft*. Years ago, she came to me to learn. But let me tell you something, sonny-boy, she ended up teaching me quite a few things!" She blew a perfect smoke ring into the air, punctuating it with her index finger.

"Were you her…coven leader?" I didn't know anything about witchcraft, really. Just what I'd seen in horror films.

She burst out laughing. "Why put a title on

everything? There's not really a 'coven' as you call it in Clearwell. Some of us are witches, some of us are Wiccans, some of us just practice the craft and some, like your mother, are born into it with strong supernatural leanings. Elizabeth said you had the gift, and I can tell just by being around you, kid." Her short stubby legs kicked back and forth, like a little kid on a playground swing, unable to reach the porch floor.

"What do you mean? How can you tell?"

"I can see your aura, kid." She studied the perimeter of my head like a police detective would a chalked murder victim outline. "And it's a mighty strong one. That's one of my special abilities."

"Well, what do I *do* with this…witchcraft?"

"It's gonna take some time, kid." She stubbed out her cigarette in an overflowing bucket beside the swing. "That's enough for tonight…I've got to watch my stories." She rocked back and forth a couple of times to build up momentum and popped out of the swing like a geriatric gymnast.

"That's it?" I asked.

"Look, kid, what do you want from me?" She turned back toward me, faster than I thought possible. "You want some *Karate Kid* crap? Fine…go wax my car." She held out what I took to be an imaginary sponge.

"I just thought…I could learn more about my mother." I sank lower into the cushion, deeper into my funk. "And more about my so-called powers."

She sat back down and in that moment, appeared twenty years younger. "I told you, this is gonna take time. I'll tell you about your mom, and I'll teach you things and show you how to use your powers properly and responsibly. But, whatever you do, do *not* try anything on your own until you fully understand what you're dealing with." This was not the same cranky little old lady I'd been dealing with five minutes ago. I could see why Mom sought her out.

"But, Mickey…" I started and then stopped. I didn't want to whine, nor involve anyone else in my problems.

"But, what?" She pursed her lips, challenging me with her glare. The piston-like pumping of her short legs fired up again.

"I'm in trouble…I need help. I need to be able to protect my friends…" I trailed off, the overwhelming last call of the locusts drowning me out.

"Okay, okay. *Now* we're getting somewhere." She wore a self-satisfied smile across her face. "I could tell you were in some form of worry when you first showed up. Your beautiful aura was a little ragged around the edges, like you lately took a beatin' or something."

"I think my friends and I could be in danger. There're these crazy kids at school who want to kill us." I couldn't believe I shared this with a blue-haired witch I just met.

Once Mickey saw—or felt, maybe, in her case—the sheer terror that had locked me down, her smile melted away into a concerned frown. "Why, you're *serious*, aren't you, kid?"

I just nodded, a stupid bobblehead.

"All right." She folded her yellowed fingers into her lap and stared sternly at me. "Everything I said still holds true. I *will* help you, but it will take time, knowledge, and practice. We'll just step up the urgency."

I continued nodding, silently, afraid if I let loose more verbal diarrhea, she'd change her mind about helping me.

"But you just remember what I told you, kid!" She poked me in the chest with her smoke-ring popping finger. "Do *not* do anything on your own until you're ready." Her eyes narrowed into slits, far above her gravity-defying glasses. "If you think you're in trouble now, you should see the crap-load you'll get in if you screwed up with the craft! There's some dark and damned dangerous things out there, kid, that you don't go messin' with."

"Yes, ma'am."

"I mean it! You understand me, kid?" I'd seen many faces of Mickey Goldfarb tonight, but her scary 'you kids get outta' my yard or else' face seemed the worst. "And don't call me *ma'am*!"

"Yes, Mickey," I said, trying to slink even further down into the comforting protection of purple and brown-covered patio furniture. Apparently, it was "National Scary Confrontation Week," and everyone forgot to tell me.

Mickey must've sensed my intimidation and put her friendly grandma visage back on. "Tex…does your life feel like it's out of your hands sometimes? Do you ever feel like you've got no control over whichever way your life turns? Like there's something else controlling you, and you ain't got no say in the matter even though it's your own goddamned life?"

"Yes." Leave it to a little blue-haired old lady to perfectly sum up the awful and angsty teenage experience in very few words.

"Hee, looks like I struck a nerve." She slapped the

back of my head. Damn, if the old lady didn't pack some muscle. That one's going to bruise.

"Here's lesson number one in witchcraft, kid. Witchcraft ain't about the cauldrons and alla' that crap. Sure, they may be tools of the trade in some form or other, but witchcraft is about dealing with your relationship with nature, more than anything else. It's about finding the perfect balance between outside forces—what I call nature, but there's lotsa' other names for it—and your life. You need to bring them together into a nice symbiotic relationship. You understand me, kid?" Pokity-poke went the finger. Noddity-nod went my head.

"If you learn the ropes right, you're gonna find your life becoming less…hectic…and making more sense. The spells and potions and fun stuff come as a sort of bonus, but you've got to understand what I'm tellin' you first."

"I could really, *really* use something like that in my life."

"Okay, that's your first lesson," said Mickey. "Consider that one on the house. The next lesson won't be." She began her bounding allez-oop exercise to get out of the swing again. Up she went.

"Um…I don't have any money." It disappointed me to find out she had intentions of charging me for her knowledge. What happened to the pride in being a mentor and all that junk?

"It don't have to be nothin' big, kid. Look at it as bringing me an offering for my witch smarts…just bring me a pack of smokes."

"Mickey…I'm not *old* enough to buy cigarettes."

"Humph." She rubbed her small chin. "I guess that

must've been hell on you when you used to smoke, huh?" Mickey went through her routine of laughing then hacking. "You're so fulla' crap, kid. Okay, I guess you can't bring me any whiskey either, huh?"

"No." This was going to be a real roller-coaster ride with her.

"All right, then." She sighed resignedly. "Bring me some of the extra crispy... I love me some fried chicken." She had the same lustful gleam in her eyes as when she had conjured up Clint Eastwood earlier.

"Okay." For the first time that night, I laughed. "*That* I can do."

She opened the front door, shooing her cats out of the way. "Oh, and, kid, let's meet in another couple of nights. And you've heard of using the telephone, right?"

"Um, yeah..." Even though phoning people seemed like an outdated form of communication, I thought it best not to let Mickey know this.

"Well, use the damn thing!" She slammed the door in my face. "I'm in the phone book," she bellowed from within the house.

And that ended my first meeting with a witch. At least that I *knew* about.

****

No shocker, the next day of school proved intense. I arrived minutes before my first class started, no need to be in the war-zone longer than necessary. I pulled into the parking lot, turned off the Bucket, and flipped my phone out.

—*R U all right?*— I texted Olivia.

Seconds later, she replied:

—*YUP. In class. No sign of Bellman.*—

—Good. Check in a lot.—

I ran through the parking lot, muttered "Good morning" to principal What's-His-Face standing on the steps, and bolted to sociology. My eyes never strayed from looking straight ahead. If I passed Bellman, I never knew it.

I threw open the door, and saw by the clock, I had a few more minutes. I motioned for Ian to come out into the hallway. Ian took his feet off the chair in front of him and shuffled out.

"What's up?" he asked. "You look freaked out."

I quickly filled him in on what happened after school yesterday. Best to forewarn our allies, I thought, and I knew Olivia would tell Josh since he shared her first hour.

Ian giggled uncontrollably. "Damn, I wish I could've seen it. Olivia's bad-ass!"

"Yeah, she *really* is. Be cool, be cool." Ian's laughter drew unwanted attention. "Just be on the lookout. I don't know if Bellman's gonna go after you or not. He might not even know we hang, but I can guarantee O' and I are on his hit list." Having said it aloud brought home the urgency and sheer terror again.

"Okay…" Ian finally settled down. "Here comes Jensen. Let's get in before we get another detention."

My phone beeped.

—Uh-oh— read the text from Olivia. *—I'm being summoned.—*

The lords and masters of Clearwell High were working fast today. The long hour of sociology crawled by at a snail's pace.

****

The bell rang, and I ran toward Olivia's class.

Didn't spot her anywhere. I hoped she didn't lose her cool and mouth off.

—*How did it go?*— I texted her.

Blindly making my way toward algebra class, I stared at the phone, practically willing it to respond.

—*Awesome!*— she finally texted back. —*Wait till U hear about it!*—

—*Cool. Come have lunch downstairs 2day?*—

—*Ugh!*— she wrote. —*OK. Gotta go.*—

It was a long haul until lunch, and I half expected the intercom to summon me for another round of interrogation with Hastings. While sweating it out, the hours dragged by. I thought no news seemed even scarier than bad news. It meant Bellman would indeed take matters into his own ham hock hands. Suspension or even expulsion sounded like better options.

****

"Bellman's such a punk-ass," said Red, alternately amused and horrified. "You shoulda' come got me, Tex."

"You weren't around, Red. Even if you were, I really didn't have time to do anything. From the moment that bastard saw me, he started choking me."

"Let's see him pick on somebody his own size for a change." Red shook out his floppy head of hair. "Sorry I wasn't here. There was a leak in the girl's toilet upstairs. Duty calls."

"It's cool. It all happened so fast. I just gotta lay low for a while and hope it blows over." False optimism, my old fickle friend.

"I'm so sick of him," said Josh quietly, fear filling his eyes. I'm sure it brought back memories from his shower incident. "Can't you tell Hastings—or even,

Jensen—what happened, Tex? Maybe we can get him suspended?"

"Not without me and O' both facing suspension. Besides, Hastings always protects his pet football players."

Olivia's black flats flapped down the stairs into view. Ranting again, but this time out of empowerment, not rage. "Oh, yeah," she called out, half-mockingly. "Here comes O', don't *jack* with me!"

Red, smiling, leaped up from his rusty folding chair and offered it to Olivia. "Well, if it ain't the junior flyweight champion of Clearwell High. Have a seat…you earned it."

Olivia surveyed the peeling, brown chair and the garbage surrounding it. "Uck…I'll stand." Okay, now she acted like the daintiest Welter Weight champion of Clearwell High. Red laughed, plopped back down, and rested his lanky legs on top of a cleaning solvent drum.

"Okay," I said, "what happened? I'm dying here."

"*Omigod,* you won't believe it!" Her visible eye widened with excitement. "Before class even started, Hastings called me in." Olivia looked vindicated now that someone thought her capable of performing acts of vandalism or mischief. "Hastings wanted to know if I saw or heard anything about Bellman when I left detention."

"What'd you tell him?" asked Ian, nearly as excited as Olivia.

She covered her eyes with her black-finger-nailed hands and then repeated the gesture over her ears and mouth. "I see nothing, hear nothing, speak *nothing*. Just like we talked about, Tex, I said I left detention, and there was nothing going on in the hallway. Told

Commandant Hastings that I *think* I left before Bellman, but couldn't be sure. Hastings stared me down, trying to break me, and finally said 'Miss Swanson is pretty positive you left just a few minutes *after* Bob did.'" Olivia enjoyed her spotlight of notoriety. She even offered a hilarious, yet not very accurate impression of Hastings, embellishing him with a German accent.

"Uh-oh." Why in the world would Miss Swanson be so alert as to notice when her detention students left? She needed to get a life.

"I matched old Hastings' stare and lied like a champion," Olivia continued. "I said 'Well, hell, I really don't know, but I didn't see *anything*.' I finally asked Hastings what had happened, anyway. He didn't want to tell me at first, but finally—*finally!*—told me. Get *this*! Bellman told Hastings that three—or *however* many—guys from South High jumped him, stabbed him, and beat him up with a fire extinguisher!" Olivia laughed uproariously. She took pride in Bellman's blaming her actions on three rival school *male* students. "It was pretty much as you said it would be, Tex…although I never thought Bellman would come up with a story like *that!*"

"Ha!" Red shook his head. "Bellman got his ass whipped by a *girl* and had to blame it on three guys they'll never find."

Olivia whipped her head toward Red. "Yeah…that's right! A *girl!* Don't screw with *me*, you sexist *pig!*" We all laughed, this time Olivia joining us. With her mood so victorious, even Red's little dig at 'the inferior sex' didn't derail her.

"Well, Bellman found a story that'll keep him out

of trouble." I did my best to rein in the celebratory party as I found it premature, and just wanted to keep everyone on their toes. "And if it's further investigated, it'll go nowhere. So…that puts us in a holding pattern. Bellman's not the kind of guy who'll forgive and forget. He's not wired that way. Let's not forget he's *crazy*."

Josh nodded vigorously, his chin covered by his turtleneck.

"Do any of you have him in any of your classes?" I asked, looking solemnly at them in turn. No, was the consensus. We were lucky to be all sophomores, while Bellman ruled in terror as a junior (maybe several times over). "Have any of you seen him today?"

"I saw him before lunch," crowed Olivia. "His eyes were still red from the bath I gave him!"

"O', you didn't say anything to him, did you?" I dreaded the answer. It's impossible for Olivia to withstand rubbing salt in the wound.

"I didn't *say* anything. Just laughed at him! And walked right by him doing it, too!"

"Olivia…*please* don't antagonize him. Don't make it worse than it already is." And I knew telling Olivia *not* to do something was as good as sending her a gilt-edged invitation to a party. Usually, I love her for it, but not in this case.

"Okay, okay," she said, smirking like a kid caught with her hand in the cookie jar, who planned on going back for seconds nonetheless. "It's just *too* easy."

I sighed. "Well…anyway. The longer we can stay out of his path maybe some of his anger will burn off. Right now, it's Thursday, and I'm just trying to make it through the week." This didn't sound like much of a challenge, but it felt like going for the Gold Medal in Survivalism. "He's not in my seventh-hour gym class, but he *is* in the upper-class gym class at the same time. I could have an encounter with him in the locker room." It'd been on my mind all day. Like one of Dad's westerns, an imminent showdown would be held at High Noon. The villagers would shut their doors and windows, leaving me alone to fend off the notorious Bob Bellman.

"I'm glad I'm not in gym anymore," said Josh. "Sorry, Tex." After last year's shower escapade, Josh found a family doctor who wrote a letter recommending he take "remedial gym" for medical reasons. I always envied this loophole as the easy-peasy gym kids never did anything more physically challenging than walking. Yet, because of some misplaced sense of pride, I never asked Dad to find me a willing doctor. Now, I deeply regretted that decision.

"It's cool, Josh. I totally get it."

"What's with those jackasses?" asked Ian. "Is gym the only class they ever take?" As students, two years of gym were required and then our tour-of-duty in Torture 101 could be put behind us. After my second and current year, I vowed to never set foot in a gym again.

"Ian, we're not dealing with brain surgeons here," Olivia said. "Gym is all they know and probably the only decent grades they get." We all nodded and silently agreed with her.

"Tex, my garage is right across from the locker room," said Red. "I'll be sure I'm upstairs—in the garage—during your seventh hour today. If you need me, I'll come runnin'." This actually gave me a small sense of comfort. Red glanced at Olivia to be sure she noted his grand gesture of selfless protection.

"Thanks, Red," I said. "I appreciate it. If you hear me screaming, run in with your fists a-blazin'." And, I knew first hand, that's what Red did best. Running.

****

While sweat-inducing and futile, gym class proved surprisingly quiet for the most part. Thankful that the juniors and seniors played football outside, I gladly ran my endless and pointless laps inside the relative safety of the gym. Bellman was nowhere to be seen. Now I just had to get dressed and out of there as fast as possible.

While running my umpteenth lap around the "world's smallest indoor track" as Mr. Sowers called it, my blood ran cold as the upperclassmen came into the gym from outdoors. There stood Bellman, big and ugly, mouth wide open, glowering at me. He slowed his gait, his gaze burning into me, as he entered the locker room.

Mr. Sowers ended our torture at the fifty-minute mark and blew his whistle. "Golly, gee, fellas," he drawled, "that was pathetic. Put me out of my misery, and go hit the showers." He enjoyed belittling our lack of physical prowess every chance he got.

Maybe Bellman had already showered and left before me. Reluctantly, I entered the locker room, honed my tunnel vision technique, and hustled toward my locker. My shower would have to wait until I got home, no sense in putting myself at risk in the stalls. I threw my jeans on and tied one shoe while sitting on the bench. If I had to leave suddenly at least I'd be half-dressed.

Thick, hairy legs planted themselves in front of me.

I looked up. Bellman stood naked, his junk inches from my face. From head to toe, hair and muscle covered him, capped off by a burgeoning beer belly. He leaned down and whispered in my ear, "You're dead." His calm unsettled me more than his usual out-of-control shrieking.

"I'll get you," he continued. "And your little slut, too." It took all the control I had to not ask him if he tried out for the role of the Wicked Witch in the school production of *Wizard of Oz*.

Inches above my head, he smashed his fist into the locker. I said nothing, frozen with fear. Breath plumed from his nostrils, his mouth. The rank odor of nicotine wafted down. He hit the locker again with a loud rattling bang. He pulled his hand back and clenched it in front of my face, forming a threatening fist. His knuckles grew white, one of them bleeding. Predatorily, he licked the blood off with a grin.

"What's going on here, fellas?" asked Mr. Sowers, poking his head into the locker alley. "Bellman, go get dressed. McKenna, hit the showers…you smell!"

"Yes, Coach," Bellman said. His unblinking eyes never left me as he barely acknowledged Sowers' existence. He strutted off, staring at me like a vulture surrounding an already dead carcass.

"Okay, Coach." For once, I was glad to call Sowers "coach" for his intervention probably saved me.

No shower for me today, though, thank you very much.

I waited for Sowers to go back to his office, threw on my other tennis shoe, grabbed my shirt, and ran into the gym. In case Bellman waited for me in the hallway outside the locker room, I didn't mind at all taking the long route to the parking lot. I opened the door onto the football field. While running for my life, I finished dressing, pulling my shirt on. Recently, I'd perfected the art of multi-tasking.

Chapter Six

On our way home, I told Olivia about my hair-raising encounter with Bellman. Of all the reactions I expected from her, disgust won the day as she wrinkled up her nose at my description of Bellman's standing buck-naked in front of me.

"*Gross*. So he was just standing there? With his big, ugly junk just hanging in your face? *Gross!*"

"Yeah, that's about the size of it," I said, hoping it didn't sound like some lousy pun. Olivia still didn't take this seriously and it concerned me. After her successful takedown yesterday, she felt recklessly invulnerable. "O', he means business…and it's nasty, life-threatening business."

"His junk in your face? That kind of nasty business?" Maybe I scarred her for life with my description. "I always thought he was a closeted gay guy."

"Yeah, well, the last thing I'm concerned with right now is Bob Bellman's sexual orientation." I sighed. "Actually, he's probably 'omni-sexual.' Sex with men, women…animals." If you can't beat 'em, join 'em, I thought, trying to find the levity Olivia sought comfort in.

"Okay, really, *really* gross!" While Olivia's laughter rang out with abandon, mine felt forced.

"Just stay out of his path. Do *not* confront him,

provoke him, and for God's sake, don't laugh at him."

"Yes, Father," she said. But I knew she wouldn't hide or run away from anyone.

"I *mean* it, Olivia. He threatened my life and *yours*, too. He's all about the 'cray-cray.' I *believed* him when he threatened to kill us." The Bucket backfired at that instant as if in agreement. Olivia released a small, surprised yelp before turning it into another laughing jag.

"Oh, he won't hurt me," she said. "He's afraid of me now. Seriously, Tex, we're not dealing with a murderer here or anything. He's just a kid. A hairy, gross, scary bully kid…but that's all he is."

I could see Olivia truly wanted to believe in the good inherent nature of mankind, but here her rose-colored optimism did no good.

"But, he's *not*. He's not just a kid. Hell, I don't think he ever had a childhood. He's absolutely crazy and capable of anything. You saw that first-hand yesterday. If you hadn't come to my rescue, I really think he was going to kill me."

Olivia sat silently, lost in thought. "Okay," she said quietly. "Okay, I'll stay out of his way." I looked over at her and sadness overwhelmed me. I'd popped her balloon full of sunshine and bunnies. Disheartening, to say the least, when you discover the world is a horrible and unjust place, full of darkness and little hope, something I'd painfully discovered myself several years back.

****

I dropped Olivia off and headed straight for Chicken Heaven. Mickey and I had agreed to meet tomorrow night, but the urgency of my school situation set me on edge. I needed to move our meeting to now. I hoped to get some sort of "protection spell" as my friends and I definitely needed it. There was no way we could hold out much longer.

I bypassed the screen door this time and knocked on Mickey's front door.

After a few minutes of silence, I heard her tell one of the cats to move. She yelled, "Who is it?"

I sighed, thinking I'd better get used to this ritual. "It's Tex, Mickey! I brought chicken." I held up the red and white bucket offering to the window but remembered she couldn't look out because of her height.

The long rattling of the chain commenced as she screamed, "*Goddammit!*" At least, Mickey's behavior seemed consistent, something I could count on.

The door swung open. Dressed in the same robe and slippers, I wondered if she had a multitude of blue robes or just lived in the one. She held her head back to peer at me through the ends of her glasses. She didn't appear happy.

"I know I'm a day early, Mickey, but something came up, and I was hoping we could meet this afternoon." She fumed at me in silence. Once again, I held up the sacrificial bucket of chicken, hoping it would lick any wounds. "Chicken?"

"Well, dammit, come on in then. Still haven't learned to use a phone, I guess. Kids, today."

"Sorry, Mickey. I also thought since tomorrow was Halloween, you might be busy."

Her mouth fell open, and she fell back a step, looking as if I had just drop-kicked one of her cats. Hands on her knees, she guffawed loudly before giving into a racked, coughing fit.

"Oh, kid, you kill me. Halloween! You think just because I practice witchcraft that Halloween is my Christmas or something?" She sat down on a nearby beat-up ottoman, still chortling hysterically.

"Well, kind of." I shrugged, feeling totally stupid but not knowing why.

"All Hallow's *Eve*." she cried. "Boil, boil, *toilet* trouble! Let me go get my cauldron!" Okay, so the only person who can teach me about witchcraft is now making fun of my lack of witchcraft knowledge.

"Kid, Halloween is strictly amateur hour for us witches. It's like New Year's Eve for alcoholics! Ain't nothin' special about a day created to sell candy. Good God! Halloween…" She shook her head in disbelief.

"Okay." I sighed. "If we're done having a good laugh at my expense, here's some chicken." I held out the bucket, hoping the power of it would prevail and make me quit feeling like a jackass. Jackpot. She greedily snatched it from my hands and looked inside.

"Extra crispy?" She gazed at me skeptically.

"Nope," I said, hoping to get this one right, "nothing but the original recipe."

She smiled broadly. "Good boy. Come into the kitchen." Like a herd dog, she prodded me ahead of her into the small, dark kitchen. She flipped on a power-saving light that stubbornly lit up the orange-painted walls and green cabinets. I noticed five or six pet bowls on the floor next to the refrigerator, covered with photos of small children. *Were they her grandchildren, or did she lure them in with candy and cook them in her oven?*

It surprised me how clean the linoleum floor and

countertops were, as I earlier got the impression being the world's greatest housekeeper didn't interest Mickey. In front of the open kitchen window sat a small round table adorned with a bowl of plastic fruit. Only two chairs sidled up to the table—not many more would have fit comfortably—and a floral patterned placemat lay at the window-facing side. Mickey loves her floral patterns. The table itself appeared in immaculate condition even though it looked old, possibly older than Mickey.

Mickey flapped at me to sit down in one of the chairs. She pulled open a drawer, intently studying the contents before deciding what she wanted. She said "Ah!" and whipped out a placemat and flung it down in front of me along with a handful of napkins. A Santa Fe motif adorned the mat with two coyotes howling next to an abstract cactus. "This is the best placemat I have for a boy." It somewhat amused and touched me with the thought she put into it. Maybe she had a placemat for every occasion and visitor.

"Okey-dokey, let's eat." She grabbed a chicken leg and nibbled at it, with small but determined bites. Like an ear of corn, she worked it around in a circular fashion.

"Hey, Mickey, can I ask you a favor?" Mickey's cats had begun to circle the wagons and nestled against my legs. One particularly bold brown and white cat kept trying to jump into my lap. I nudged him away with my foot.

"What, you mean more than I'm already doing for you?" She stopped eating and held the bone in front of her like a miniature baseball bat.

"Yeah, I guess. I'm allergic to cat hair, so could

we…I don't know…put the cats away or something?" She continued to stare quietly. "Maybe just for a little while?"

And, we're back to her rowdy shrieking and coughing. "Oh, kid, you just *kill* me!" I sure hope she had thoroughly chewed her chicken, as I couldn't remember my Heimlich maneuver technique very well.

"Um, I'm glad I kill you…"

"Okay, okay," she said, her chuckling winding down. I totally slayed it today. If I ever decide to do stand-up comedy, I'm going to plant Mickey in the front row at all my gigs. "Tex, you're some kinda' witch! Whoever heard of a witch who's allergic to cats?"

Mickey stood and raised her hands above her head. "Sampson, Delilah, Romeo, Juliet," she yelled, "upstairs, just for a little bit." The cats stopped cold in their tracks. They whipped their heads from around my legs to look at her, as if saying, *you can't be serious.* Deciding seriousness ruled, the cats sprinted for the kitchen door, and I heard them stampede up the stairwell.

"So, I see you're a Bruce Springsteen fan," I said, trying to find some common ground with her. I assumed she named the four aforementioned cats after the lyrics from the Springsteen song, "Fire."

"What are you talking about, kid? Wait…is that the kid on that soap opera?" Mickey considered everyone a kid. I decided it best to drop it.

"Is that better, Tex?" she asked after the last cat vanished upstairs.

"Yes. For a little while at least." The cats may've vacated the kitchen, but their hair lingered behind them.

"How'd you do that? With the cats?"

"Why, they're my familiars, of course. That's why it's coconuts for you to be allergic to cat hair! Every witch benefits from their familiars."

"What is a 'familiar,' exactly?" I knew I risked her ridicule again, but I realized learning from Mickey was like a fishing expedition. I needed to keep the bait flowing freely.

"A 'familiar' can be a pet. Sometimes even a person. But that's rare. Usually they're animals," she explained, holding court with her chicken bone as her gavel. "Some witches believe familiars are spirits. My cats are mine. I believe the animal world is closer to communicating with the spirit world than we are, so I use my cats to help with messages and even spells, sometimes." She looked at her chicken leg, decided it'd served its purpose, and laid it neatly at the edge of her placemat.

"Mom didn't have any cats. She couldn't have any because of my allergies." Mickey rummaged through the bucket for a thigh. Not at all hungry, I fidgeted around with my chicken breast.

"Kid, just because you didn't have any pets, don't mean your mother didn't have any familiars. They could have been neighbor pets, or birds, or anything she may've consulted with a few times in the yard."

I thought of my feline visitors at home. "Mickey, I've been…ah…quite popular with cats all of a sudden."

"What do you mean?"

"Lately, there've been lots of cats coming to my house and bothering me." Mickey dropped the thigh onto the placemat with a *thump*. I braced myself for another round of crazed laughter.

"Kid, I don't know if this is a good thing or not," she said thoughtfully. She rubbed her chin and looked toward the ceiling, one eye shut. "Some spirit has a message for you. The familiars are either trying to communicate it with you...or warn you."

"Were these my mom's familiars?" Both excited and nervous, I welcomed Mom finally entering into the conversation. "Is my mom trying to contact me? Does she have something she wants to tell me?"

"Too early to tell, kid. And we're gettin' way too ahead of the game for you to go messin' around with the spirit world and familiars." She picked up the thigh and began to meticulously chew at it again. "We'll get to that in good time. I may have to come over and see these kitties for myself. As for your mother, well, these may or may not have been her familiars. Just leave 'em alone for now."

"*Gah*! Every time we start to get somewhere, or talk about my mom, you shut me down! This is...*frustrating*." I knew I shouldn't lose my patience with Mickey, but this irritatingly endless and pointless dance routine just put me more on edge. "What *can* you tell me about Mom?"

"Okay, kid, didn't anyone ever tell you about patience and all that?" She wagged her finger at me. "I ain't rushin' this for a reason as I told you the other night. To learn—and learn right—you got to take your time. I'm not yankin' your chain. This is a safety issue." She leaned in toward me. "Your mom would agree with me, and don't you forget that, kid."

"Fine. Sorry. Could you please tell me a little bit about my mom to start? About her...witchcraft?"

"All right… Let me finish my food first." She nibbled noisily while staring at me. I finished my piece of chicken as well as I could.

I stood up holding the chicken carcass and asked, "Where's your trash, Mickey?"

"Hold on, hold on…" She bounded up, opened a drawer, got a plastic bag, snatched the bone from my hand, and put it with hers inside, sealing it with an efficient zip. "You never know when you might need these."

"For spells?"

"*Hee*! Don't be dumb." She laughed and slapped the back of my head. "For the *cats*. *For spells*, land's sake! You've got a lot to learn, kid."

We retreated into the living room where she prodded me toward a long white sofa. I sat down with a *flump* as the soft, deep cushions threatened to swallow me. In front of the sofa a rickety dinner tray, decorated with yet another floral pattern, threatened to topple. Sitting next to me, Mickey looked like a tiny, wrinkled child awash in a sea of white upholstery.

I glanced about the room where literally hundreds of porcelain eyes ogled me. Tiny figurines of small children in sleepwear, most accompanied by lambs or cats decorated every nook, corner, and cranny of the room. Many were praying, a lot of them with their back flaps open, exposing their butt cracks. I fought the urge to get up and turn them facing the wall. The clutter—especially of these demonically angelic porcelain faces—felt suffocating.

"Ah, you're appreciatin' my collection, I see," she said proudly.

"Yeah…" *Or something.*

"Tex, as I told you last night, your mother came to me one day and wanted to learn how to use her powers. There are two different types of witchcraft...white magic and black magic. Your mom was always very careful to keep on the side of white magic, and it's a thin line separating the two."

Mickey snuggled into the sofa. I worried she might sink too far into the impossibly plush sofa and suffocate.

"I taught her some simple spells," she continued, "and before long we were practicin' together, and she was showing me things I'd never dreamed possible. But she made it clear she only wanted to use her powers for good, and she didn't want to use them for her own self-gain. She was a smart woman, your mother was, and she understood that once you start using spells for your own purposes, you were gettin' closer to crossin' over into that black magic." She shook her head in a pained manner. "Once you start doin' this, you're getting closer to making deals with dark powers you don't want no kin with."

"Mickey, are there practitioners of black magic here? I mean in Clearwell?"

She paused for a minute. "Oh, kiddo, you'd be surprised. There's a huge group of witches in Clearwell, both white and black." She suddenly seemed a bit less confident, more worried.

"In Clearwell, Kansas?" I asked stunned. "Why in this Godforsaken place of all places?" I couldn't believe it. I figured my mom was just an anomalous one-off because I didn't understand why anyone would want to live here, let alone an entire group of witches.

"Oh my, yes! There are a lot of witches on both

coasts, Florida, and some of the Northern states, but I'd have to guess we have the most witches located here in Kansas. Let me show you something…" She began her routine of swinging her short legs back and forth for momentum and popped off the sofa as nimbly as a woman half her age. At the bookshelf, she snagged an Etch-A-Sketch and brought it back to the sofa.

"My great-nephew left this here. I ain't had time to mail it back to him yet." Okay, so she *did* have great-nephews and didn't just eat kids.

She started turning the round white knobs, faster than I would've thought her age allowed, reminding me of Ian on his video game module. She turned her drawing toward me. "You know what this is?" It was a five-pointed star encased within a circle.

"Sure, it's a pentagram." I've seen enough horror films to recognize this. *Score one for me on witchcraft knowledge!*

"That's right, Tex." She beamed at me proudly. *A first!* "And it's probably the most important tool of the trade in witchcraft. Now…what would happen if you laid a giant pentagram over the United States of America?"

I thought for a minute before the light bulb clicked. "Kansas is the center of the pentagram. And the areas you said have high witch populations represent the points."

"Gold star for the kid. Many witches think the center of the pentagram represents the main area of mystic power, so they migrate here, hoping to ramp up their powers. For some, like your mother, it works great…but you've got to have some powers to begin with."

I guess that explains why Mom moved from Denver, her birthplace, to Kansas. I never could think of any other reason.

"I had no idea that Kansas of all places was such a hot-spot for witches." I knew we still had the Klan running about some areas—and sure, there would always be the occasional one-off satanic death-metal high school incident—but this seemed unreal.

"You better believe it, kid. Now, the pentagram is used in spells and usually you draw it on the floor or some parchment paper. Talented witches like your mother can get away with drawing it in the air, other times they can draw it on the surface of an object. Many witches see it as a way to control the elements with each corner representing God or man and fire, water, earth, and wind. This is how your mom liked to look at it."

"Yeah, Dad said she was sort of a Christian witch." And it *still* didn't make any sense to me.

"That's right. And I've never seen anyone pull it off like her before. She believed that the upper-point of the pentagram pointed toward God, and that he was ultimately responsible for the good things she could do." She folded her hands, deep in thought. Thankfully, she sat up on the edge of the sofa so I didn't have to worry about the sofa eating her alive. "She never did give enough credit to herself, your mom."

"I always thought witchcraft was the worship of Satan. Do you really believe my mom was a God-worshipping witch?" I suppose I wanted to believe this, even though it went against my current beliefs of the universe; the agnostic in me wanted to worship reason and nothing else. Except for maintaining a healthy fear of the Fates.

"Kid, didn't you know your mother better than that? Haven't you been listening to a thing I've told you? Witchcraft is open to interpretation. That's part of the beauty of it."

"I guess. I'm just learning about a side of my mom that two days ago I never knew existed. I'm trying to make sense of it all."

"Let me tell you a story," she said. "When I was a kid, about your age, I reckon, I was going to a Catholic school. I started questioning the stories in the *Bible*. One day I asked the ol' nun who was teaching class, I says, 'I'm having a hard time believin' all these stories about arks and parting of the seas and Adam and Eve. How can I believe in something that don't make no sense? How come none of these miracles are happenin' today?' Well, most of the class looked at me like I was the Devil himself come to roust them all to Hell, but the ol' nun, she just looks at me and says, 'Sometimes you're not supposed to take the *Bible* literally. Sometimes, it's best to interpret the teachings as fables, and the most important thing to take away from them is the morals.' I thought about this good and long and finally thought well, now, here's a way I can make the *Bible* work for me."

My world is crazy. I came here to learn about witchcraft and am now getting a lecture on Christianity.

"Anyway, kid, I done come around full circle again, but that ain't the point. The point is that this ol' mean nun actually talked sense and *made* believin' in the *Bible* work for me. So, if you can't even believe in your poor mother and what she believed in, then you best just leave here right now." For the first time,

Mickey appeared on the verge of tears. I could tell she missed my mother almost as much as I did. "But leave the rest of the chicken," she added as an afterthought.

Mickey was right. You have to believe in something, and the least I could do is believe in Mom and what she stood for. Sure, I still felt a little betrayed about the deceit—or at least, lack of forthcoming information—going on in my family, but my mother always did try to live the best life she could. For her family, friends, neighbors—through witchcraft, Christianity, good Samaritanism, whatever—Mom shone as an outstanding example of the selfless kind of behavior everyone should strive for. So if she believed in something, I should at least *try* and understand it.

"You're absolutely right, Mickey," I said. "My mom earned my trust. I'm here to learn and soak up your knowledge, oh great mentor." I mock-bowed.

"Damn straight, kid-o!" She whooped and hollered, and I do believe she enjoyed being bowed to.

Chapter Seven

I cut short my meeting with Mickey, as it was time to pick up Dad. I had so much more I wanted to ask her, to learn, but it had to wait. If there's anything I'd learned about Mickey, she's more forthcoming with information when she does things in her own time.

Dad and I prepared chicken cordon bleu, and it worked out moderately successful. Not really into cooking, I accidentally allowed the chicken to cook too long. Dad gave the chicken a workout with his mouth, attempting to tenderize the meat with his teeth. Truthfully, after my snack with Mickey, chicken kinda sickened me. Dad looked puzzled but said nothing when I bagged the chicken bones.

After dinner, I excused myself and told Dad I still had homework to complete before going to bed. A half-truth, at best. I finished my school homework in study hall, but I did have a lot of work of another sort to complete. I had a long night ahead of me.

Earlier, Mickey walked me through some "basic protection spells" and said I wasn't ready for anything else. So I sighed complacently and listened.

"But you're going to have to do it at midnight," she warned.

"Mickey, it's a school night. I can't be up that late doing witchcraft spells."

The inevitable hand-smack of reason caught the

backside of my head. I needed to learn how to predict her attacks and know when to duck. "Wahhhh," she whined. "*Cry me a river*, boo-hoo. Honestly, do you want to protect yourself and your friends or not?"

"Of *course* I do."

"Well, then, schoolboy, I don't wanna' hear no more crying about how you're not going to get your beauty sleep. The very idea! A witch who's complaining about a 'school night.' I swear! For this spell to work, you either need to do it between twelve and one p.m. or between twelve and one a.m."

"I'll be in school tomorrow at twelve p.m." I sighed. "So I guess I have to do it tonight."

"Kid, I don't make up the rules. Just do as you're told and quit your whining."

So, going on eleven p.m., Dad had gone to bed, while I prepared a protection spell for our home. I didn't really think Bellman would come after my dad, but just in case he thought it'd be fun to burn our house down or something, I wanted to be prepared.

Even though Mom left some candles in her office, there weren't enough. Before I picked up Dad, I made a stop at the mall and bought twenty-eight twelve-inch white candles. The clerk looked questioningly at me and asked if I had a romantic evening planned. I grinned, nodded, and carried my bewitching booty the hell out of there.

I cut each candle painstakingly into twenty-four sections, leaving the wick to connect the pieces. Dividing the candles into sets of four, I wrote the days of the week backward on them until I had seven sets of four representing each day. The candle industry was going to owe me big-time.

Out in the garage, I gathered the shovel and spade. I banged my head on a low-lying shelf, muffled a curse, and hoped Dad would sleep through the ruckus. Now came the hard part.

I carried the tools, a flashlight, and my box of candles out through the backdoor as quietly as I possibly could so as not to wake Dad. Even though he knew I was learning about witchcraft, Mickey warned me the fewer loved ones knew about my witching ways would be best. She said it'd keep them out of trouble—whatever kind of trouble that may be—and the spells would be more potent for it.

Flicking on the small flashlight, I clenched it between my teeth and scurried to the far north corner of the yard. Here, I dug a seven-inch hole in the shape of a dove. After surveying my creative gardening, I didn't think it resembled a dove too much. But surely a lack of artistic talent shouldn't be held against me by…whoever or whatever. I placed the candle imprinted with "*yadirF*" inside and lit it, slowly watching it burn through one of the notches. I kneeled and cupped my hands over it several times while a slow but steadily increasing wind gust picked up around me.

Reading Mickey's scribbling from a paper napkin, I chanted a slew of Latin words. Mickey fit the definition of "frugal" to a tee, and I made a mental note to buy her some paper or note cards. Next, I placed a gold foil-wrapped chocolate coin into the hole. Mickey told me I needed to use gold coins. I asked her where I could possibly find or afford those. She smiled, left the room, and came back with a plastic serving bowl full of the chocolate coins.

"Mickey," I said, "this is Halloween candy."

"Well, of course it is, dummy! But it'll work. The only thing that matters is that it appears gold." Apparently, the spirits didn't look too carefully at details.

As I watched the first candle burn down, the slow lonely blast of a nearby train's horn gave me a jolt. It grew louder and more pressing, as if saying it was coming for me—*chug, chug, chug*—*I'm almost there*. I used to think the train sounded comforting in the dead of night, knowing that somewhere life still carried on as life crawled to a temporary halt while I slept. But now, it struck me as a wild, unleashed banshee, howling in the night, a portent of doom.

Even though the night wind brought a cooling chill with it, sweat rolled off me as I moved to the east corner and repeated my candle ritual.

I stepped around to the front of the house. While digging another dirt-engraved dove, headlights turned onto the end of my street. The vehicle crept closer, and I suddenly had a bad feeling. I dropped the tools and backed up slowly toward the large oak tree in the center of the yard. The auto slowed to a near crawl before stopping in front of my house, engine still running. I snuck a peek around the huge oak trunk—more than enough width to cover my thin frame—and saw the dirty white van that had been patrolling the neighborhood pedaling cold, out-of-season treats. The tarnished bell no longer sat on its roof, but most definitely the same van.

A strong ray of light splashed from the driver's side and scanned my yard back and forth, carefully avoiding the house windows. It crossed over the tree I hid behind twice and settled on the tools I left by my hole in progress. Sweat dripped from my brow as I held my breath. I strained for a glimpse into the driver's compartment, but could only make out a shadowy figure behind the blinding light.

"Richard?" A voice called. "Richard, is that you?"

The van's driver snapped off his flashlight and quietly sped away. I breathed a sigh of relief as the taillights vanished over the small incline of the street.

Suddenly, Mr. Cavanaugh stood ten feet in front of me, fully dressed and looking quite puzzled. Why he was up and about at this time of night boggled my mind; the man's a human cat.

"Oh, hi, Mr. Cavanaugh," I said as calmly as possible. "How are you?" I reacted as if I ran into him at the corner drugstore.

"I'm fine, Richard." His hands tucked comfortably into his khaki pockets. "What are you doing out here this time of night?" I could've asked him the same thing. This guy knew more about my comings and goings than my father.

"I'm...uh...digging a mole trap." It constantly astounded me for my recent capacity for lying on the spot. "They're sure bad this time of year."

"At this hour?" He pulled his hands out of his pockets and folded his arms across his chest, the international sign of an adult suspecting teen mischief.

"Well, it's a full day of school tomorrow, so I thought I'd get it over with tonight."

"Does your dad know you're out here?" His beady eyes narrowed into slits.

"He's asleep right now." I held my finger up to my lips and whispered "Shhh" to persuade Mr. Cavanaugh to lower his voice. "But he knew I was going to do this, so I don't think he'd mind so much."

"Who was in that van? Was that a...little friend of yours?" The way he said "little friend" sounded creepy, to say the least. And just how old did he think I was?

"Nope, never seen him before." I assumed it was a *him*. "I think he was lost and was reading address numbers."

"Hmmm," he said emotionlessly. "It's probably not safe for you to be out alone this time of night, Richard. Remember what happened to that boy at your school."

"Oh, yeah, I remember. I'm being careful. I'm almost finished."

"Well. Okay..." He finally walked back to his yard.

"Good night, Mr. Cavanaugh," I said quietly. He walked up onto his porch, leaned over, hands down on the railing, and continued to watch me. Okay, how much longer can he keep this up? I gave another little wave, hoping he'd take the hint he could relinquish his one-man neighborhood watch patrol for the night. Determined to outlast me, I finally gave the battle up to the nosy neighbor. I sighed, went around to the back of the house, and crept inside. I'd have to finish later.

****

Okay, with the house protection spell on hold for now and the clock registering at twelve twenty-eight, time had pretty much run out. I needed to finish the spell by one a.m., or it wouldn't work, according to Mickey. I could start fresh tomorrow with the "Saturday" candles, but I risked a day of non-protection. Not liking the sound of that, I had to work fast.

Now I needed to make protection spells for my

friends. Earlier, Mickey prepared one, patiently showing me the steps, so I could duplicate it later. She called it the 'Bottle Spell' and claimed it was one of the easiest and surest ways to protect my friends.

She'd dragged me back into her kitchen and instructed me to sit down at the table again. On her tiptoes, she strained to reach inside a tall cabinet. She pulled out a large rotating plastic rack full of spices and cooking condiments and plopped it down in front of me. Like an elderly game show model, she gave it a grand spin and stopped it with her finger.

"Okay, Tex, I'm gonna need frankincense, black powdered iron, sea salt, and some oakmoss. You grab those, and I'll be right back." She sped out of the kitchen, leaving me to gape at her amazing variety of kitchen and witch condiments. Tucked in next to the cinnamon and parsley sat the frankincense and other items she requested. I saw a little bottle marked with a piece of masking tape, entitled "Eye of Newt." I wondered what might happen if she baked a cake and mistook the "Eye of Newt" for cinnamon. Note to self: *Never eat Mickey's baked goods.*

She bustled back in with a cardboard box marked "tools" and dropped it in front of me. She pulled out a black bowl, possibly made of clay, and what looked to be a pharmacist's tool. "My mortar and pestle," she explained. I accepted this matter-of-factly and marveled at how my life had changed so much within the last two days when I took this for granted. "Pour those ingredients in there and stir," she ordered. *Hell's Kitchen?*

She rummaged through her magical bag of tricks and pulled out some old parchment paper, black thread, and a white candle. She grabbed a black ballpoint pen from a small stand and whirled on her heels, snagging an empty root beer bottle out of her recycling bin. "You know how hard it is to get soda in a real bottle anymore, kid?" She moved fast, a whirling dervish of blue hair and floral patterns.

"Now, cut that parchment into four equal strips." Ninja-style, she threw a pair of scissors at me and they landed with a dangerous sounding *whack* on the table. I had no idea where she pulled the scissors from.

"What next, Mickey?" I spread the four strips in front of me evenly.

"What's the name of that goddamn bully at your school?" On fire and in command, she moved like how Red must've in his glory days on the basketball court. But we now played on her field, and she *owned* it.

"Write the following on one of the pieces of paper with that pen," she demanded. "'I neutralize the power of Bob Bellman to do Tex McKenna any harm. I ask that this be correct and for the good of all. So mote it be!'"

I did so unquestioningly.

"Now, roll it up, tie it with that black thread, and stick it in the bottle." Feverishly, she paced back and forth, hands folded behind her back, staring at the ceiling as if dictating a letter to me, her secretary. "Put the dry ingredients in there with it."

"Um…do you have a funnel?"

"For cryin' out loud!" She grabbed one out of a kitchen drawer. No matter how cluttered her house may be, Mickey knew where every little utensil hid. She tossed the funnel at me. I fumbled my way through getting the ingredients into the bottle.

Mickey walked up behind me and yanked a long hair out of the back of my head. "Ouch! *Seriously*! What *is* it with you and injuries to my head?"

"Oh, shut up, cry baby." She handed me the single hair. "You've got plenty to spare. This is the final ingredient. Won't work without hair from you and your friends. Now put it in the bottle."

She then instructed me to seal it with wax from a burning candle while rotating it counterclockwise. "Now, here's the most important part. You need to get a hair from each of your friends and do just as I did…and of course, I don't *need* to tell you to put *their* names on the other three parchment pieces instead of yours, right?" She looked at me, disapprovingly. "You kids today need everything spelled out for you."

"Um, I can remember to do that."

"Next, you're gonna have to get it to them somehow." She closed her eyes, lost in thought. "It's best not to tell them yet…for their own safety. But mostly, if they don't believe in witchcraft, the spells may not be potent at all. So, what they don't know, won't hurt 'em."

"Well, how am I going to do that? 'Hey, guys, here's a bottle of weird crap. Don't ask questions, and never leave home without it.' They'll think I'm a drug dealer or something."

"It's best if you can put it under their pillows, so they always sleep on it," she said, ignoring me. "But I've found that folks usually find a lump in their bed. How about if you sneak it into their backpacks? Or their lockers? If you do the lockers, it'll probably only offer school protection, though…"

"I think I can manage that."

"But remember, if they open the bottle…the spell will be broken." She wagged her finger at me. "Okay, kid, that's enough for today. Remember to call first next time. Were you born in a barn?"

"No, Mickey."

"And, kid, this time…don't forget to bring the mashed 'taters, too. Whoever heard of having chicken without the 'taters?"

****

Once I saw Mr. Cavanaugh had finally gone to bed, I went outside and finished the first night of the house protection spell. Witchcraft is hard, monotonous work. I needed to do this ritual once every night of the week and then repeat it one week each month. When's a witch supposed to sleep?

Inside, I made a beeline to my mom's office and searched through her closet. I found Mom's mortar and pestle, which I guess belonged to me now. Part of my legacy passed down from generation to generation. More interesting than a gold watch.

I took the three beer bottles Mickey had begrudgingly given me—she could've gotten five cents each on their return—and prepared the spells for my friends. I opened the little plastic baggies full of the ingredients Mickey had "loaned" me and stirred them in the mortar, now only missing a hair from each of my friends.

I needed to be (witch) crafty tomorrow in obtaining those hairs. But it had to be done, no matter what. If this truly would be successful in rendering Bellman powerless against us, I'm all in for the long haul.

I only wished I'd been one day earlier.

Chapter Eight

As I dashed into class, Ian sat in his seat fidgeting as usual. Okay, no time like the present. I reached over and snatched a black hair out of the back of his head.

"*Ow*! What the hell, man?" He looked dumbfounded as we gained an audience of onlookers.

"Oh, suck it up. Just wanted to make sure you were awake."

"Whatever! I *am* awake now." He punched me in the shoulder. I winced, more than it merited, putting an end to our game of macho one-upmanship. Discreetly, I put the hair in an open lunch bag in my backpack, next to the three beer bottles rattling about. I had to be very careful for more than one reason, as beer bottles filled with questionable content would give Hastings cause to suspend me. Somehow I had to find the time and place today to finish the enchantments. Maybe I'd skip the boiler room lunch ritual and go out to my car and seal the deal.

Once the bell rang, I raced toward Olivia's class and caught her as she left the room.

"Hey, O'," I said. "Everything cool? Still avoiding Bellman?"

"Yeah, trying to. As much as it's killing me." She grinned. I knew asking Olivia to do something against her proud code of conduct was hard for her. But I loved her for trying.

"Wait!" I leaned toward her. "You have something in your hair." I yanked at a hair and pulled it out. She let loose a surprised yelp.

"*What*? Did you get it?" She fluffed her hair to wipe away the imaginary debris. "Next time give a girl a little warning, would ya'?"

"Yeah, must've been make-up or something." Okay, two down. I tucked the hair in another plastic baggy with her name on it. "Gotta go. Hey, maybe you should have lunch down in the 'Dungeon of Dorks' again."

Olivia rolled her eyes and made a gagging sound. "Gross."

Since I invited Olivia to lunch in the boiler room, I thought it best I not blow it off. I'd have to stealthily hit the bathroom to fulfill my protection spells. Quick, quiet, and careful, the only way to go. Melting the candle wax to seal the bottles could be problematic, though.

Josh shared my second hour class, algebra, and I snagged a runaway hair from the back of his turtleneck. Plenty to go around. I carefully placed the hair in the third baggie, mentally celebrating the conclusion of step number one in Operation Witchcraft.

Before lunch, I ran upstairs to the least-used smaller bathroom, nestled between the cooking and home economics classes. I thought it'd be an unlikely place for Bellman to conduct his business. As I approached the farthest stall next to the frosted window, I passed two students. I shut the stall, flipped the latch, and dropped my backpack onto the dirty floor. Carefully, I grabbed Olivia's bottle and baggy. I pulled the hair out, twisted it into the bottle, and crammed it down with a pencil. I waited until I heard the other two students leave and pulled out a book of matches. My hand shook as I lit a match and held it to the candle, watching the wax drip ever so slowly onto the open bottle lip. I verified the cork was securely sealed and repeated the procedure with Josh's bottle. I must've burnt through six matches for the two bottles. Fingers trembling, I grabbed Ian's hair, when the bathroom door cracked open. Startled, I dropped the hair. I checked the floor around my feet, found nothing but dirt. Dammit. I'd have to get another hair from him at lunch.

Carefully wrapping up my tools and bottles, I flushed the toilet and scurried out of there, too scared to look at whoever had come in. I rushed down the stairs, ran down the hall, took a left past the gym, and bounded into the safety of the shop class and the boiler room below.

My friends were already there, Olivia in my usual chair. Her arms crossed angrily, she slouched with her feet slung out across the cement floor, while the boys laughed and carried on. Business as usual. Red enthralled his fans by bragging about his car.

"Hey, guys." I sat on the floor behind Ian. "Sorry I'm late."

"We were getting worried you ran into Bellman," said Josh.

"No...ran into bad sushi or something."

Olivia's nose wrinkled as if she couldn't believe the crap she had to endure. "*Gross.*"

I noticed she hadn't touched her lunch. I couldn't blame her. Red's cavernous environment with his hanging pin-up collection didn't exactly render it the most appealing place to eat.

I eyed Ian's back, looking for a fallen hair. No such luck. Why, of all days, did Ian have to be well-groomed today? I spotted a lone spiky hair standing out and gave it a quick tug.

"*Goddammit*, Tex," he yelled. "What *is* it with you and pulling hair today?" Angry, he whirled around, seconds away from snapping.

"Hey, he pulled the same crap deal on me earlier today," said Olivia. "Tex, is there something you want to talk about?" Josh and Red just stared, baffled. "Have you been reading 'Hair Fetish Monthly' again?" Red snapped to attention, as if he'd discovered a new unheard of porn magazine.

Olivia's joke worked to calm Ian down. "Sorry…" I said lamely, "I thought it was funny."

"What*ever*," said Ian. He threw his hands up resignedly, signifying he didn't accept my behavior, but would at least tolerate it.

Humiliated, I casually pocketed Ian's hair and tried to change the subject. "Hey, so, whose house are we hanging at tonight? It's Halloween, in case you geeks forgot."

"Zombie-Fest!" Ian pumped a fist in the air. A living dead movie marathon had been born last year, our new tradition. Too old to trick-or-treat and not cool enough to be invited to Halloween parties, we had to make our own fun. Then again, we knew too well what kind of real-life ghouls frequent the popular parties.

"I'll ask my parents," said Josh. "Shouldn't be a major issue since my brothers are at school, and we can hang out in their room." This suited me just fine. I could stash the bottles on my friends there, maybe even putting Josh's under his bed. Since it was supposed to be a cold night, I could hide the others in their coats.

"Cool," I said. "Olivia? Ian? You guys need a ride?"

"Yeah, sure," said Ian. Olivia enthusiastically nodded. Oddly enough, Olivia enjoyed the gore-fests more than the guys. She reveled in the bloodletting and found it endlessly amusing when one of us turned away in disgust.

"All right," I said. "Let's just get through the rest of this day. It's Friday, and then we won't have to worry about Bellman all weekend." Although I'd probably have another encounter with him in gym. "Red, will you be around again at seventh hour? Just in case?"

"Sure. No problemo." Red grinned, heavy on the charm, and stole a glance at Olivia, who wanted no part of this "boys club."

"Cool. Okay, let's meet at O's locker after seventh hour. Um...cut me some slack if I smell a little 'gymmy' after gym, though." Another nose wrinkle from Olivia. I could do no right by her today.

Once I found out what we were doing in gym, my heart pounded and rocketed up into my throat. Time, once again, for that most honored tradition of gym coach selective sadism, dodge ball. And this meant, we the underclassmen, would be put up as a sacrifice to the opposing team of upperclassmen, led by Bellman.

While the freshmen and sophomores counted off for attendance and showed proof of wearing jock-straps (by pulling the strap out with the thumb), I surveyed the upperclassmen at the opposite side of the gym. I didn't see Bellman—and he's hard to miss. Taller than most students, his ape-like form stood out like King Kong among a bunch of chimpanzees. At first, I felt relief, but then a crawling feeling of impending fear crept up on me. And I didn't understand *why*. Then it hit me, like a pummeling dodge ball blow to the face. If Bellman didn't attend gym, where *was* he? And since Jensen doubled as the upperclassmen gym teacher, he'd surely know if Bellman cut class. Bellman wouldn't risk anything to miss football practice. Would he?

****

After I opted to use the early exit strategy for dodge ball, I contemplated sneaking into the locker room, but Sowers sat in a folding chair guarding the door. With a warning to make sure we showered, he dismissed us. I pushed ahead of the other students and threw on my clothes with record speed. I felt an urgent need to get to Olivia's locker as quickly as possible.

As I rushed past the shop class garage, I contemplated gathering Red for a safety escort. But since nothing really'd happened yet, I didn't want to waste up his goodwill for what may be nothing more than unreasonable paranoia.

My friends had gathered around Olivia's locker, giddily planning the night's events.

"Dude, you're right," said Ian. "You *do* smell." The others laughed, but once they saw how panicked I looked, they stopped. "What's wrong?"

"Have any of you seen Bellman today?" I asked, my voice a pitch higher than usual.

"Yeah, I saw him this morning," said Olivia. "What's going on?"

"Let's get out of here." My unwarranted dread rose like a tsunami.

We left by the front door. "Bellman wasn't in gym class. And since he was here earlier, that scares me." We walked along the sidewalk running parallel to the gym toward the parking lot.

"Well, he's probably at football practice," said Olivia. "I mean, he loves football more than anything, right? Except, of course, spreading terror and pain to puppy-dogs and kittens." No one laughed.

Josh darted his head about nervously and popped his skateboard out of his backpack. Probably for a fast getaway, if needed.

Silence fell over us like a death shroud as we sped up, eyeing the Bucket far off in the distance. Since I'd been coming to school later, I had to park in the very last lot, which felt like miles away. Around us, students made their way toward their cars, full of Friday energy. We reached the first grassy island between the lots and continued our slight descent. The Bucket gleamed under the sun like a golden steed, waiting to whisk us away to safety.

We set foot on the second grass-covered island, flanked with large oak trees, all of us determined to reach our target as fast as possible. As we entered the last section, the parking lot had thinned out. Keys in hand, I pointed them toward the Bucket like a beacon.

A sudden squeal of tires shrieked. The revving of a motor blared out like a hideous mechanized dinosaur. A car sped toward us, the huge shiny grill smiling hungrily. I saw Bellman's awful, green grimace behind the windshield, mimicking the grill.

"Look out!" Josh grabbed my arm and wrenched me toward the safety of the tree-surrounded island. I grasped Olivia's hand, and the three of us tumbled upward next to a tree. Ian stood in the lot, frozen before the oncoming car. He raised a hand in useless defense, and the right side of Bellman's car connected with a sickening, wet *thud*. Ian rolled off the backside of the car and fell to the pavement. Bellman's car ripped through the parking lot, never slowing, and ratcheted out into the street.

I sat stunned beneath an oak tree's shadow. Students screamed, cacophonous gibberish. Both of Olivia's wide eyes were exposed, her hair swept back by our fall. Josh stood up, ambling unsteadily as if going to be sick. Ian sat in the parking lot, rocking back and forth, cradling something in his hand. I ran over to him. The skin from his pinky and next two fingers had been flayed off, hanging limply like a grotesque pink and red banana peel. The damaged flesh scooped up, he cradled it in his now-mangled appendage. Staring blankly at his hand, he appeared to be in a weird mixed state of calm and shock.

Josh buzzed over on his skateboard. He found an abandoned soft drink cup, poured out the remaining soda, and gave it to Ian. "There's still some ice in there," he blurted out. "Put your hand in it. *Hurry.*"

I gripped Ian around the chest and pulled him to his feet as carefully as I could. He stumbled around like a drunk, his legs unsteady. Students gathered in a circle around us, most of them trying to figure out what happened. I unlocked the back door of the Bucket and dragged Ian in. His blood drained onto the cup's ice at an alarming rate. Olivia crawled in, wrapped her arms around Ian and held him tight.

I pushed Josh into the passenger side and hopped in after him. With shaking hands, I jabbed the key into the ignition and froze in a panic, trying to remember how to get to Clearwell County Hospital. The only other time I'd been there, I had been in a daze, and the Fates were playing a cruel repeat loop on me.

"*Go!*" yelled Olivia, snapping me out of my shock. I floored the pedal, hit the streets, and ran through every light, lucky not to have been t-boned.

"Ian, are you all right?" I heard Olivia asking, as if from a hundred miles away.

"Hell, no, I'm not all right," said Ian, the calm tone of his voice belying the seriousness of his situation. "My fingers are in a drink cup." Amazingly, he chuckled.

"That sonofabitch crazy-ass *psycho*," Olivia shouted. "He tried to kill us!"

"Yeah, he did." The most cool-headed of us now, Josh displayed a surprising knack for calm under pressure. "He'll get his," he added quietly.

While I certainly hoped Josh's statement to be a self-fulfilling prophecy, I didn't know what to make of his implied vow of retribution. Always the most innocent and kind amongst the four of us, I hated to see crazies like Bellman change Josh for the worst. I didn't want his world corrupted, and it made me hate Bellman more than I thought possible.

"Let's just get to the hospital," said Josh. I turned and looked at him, noticing he had torn his turtleneck, and his arm bled. "Just drive..." he said, trailing off into an unsettling stillness.

****

Miraculously, we reached the hospital ticket-free and alive. I left Ian and the others in the car, burst through the emergency room doors, and shouted at the top of my lungs, "He's hurt *bad!* You *gotta* come get him! His *fingers* are cut off!" Or something like that…I didn't really remember, still in shock and running on freaked-out fumes.

They pulled Ian out of the car, lifted him onto a stretcher, and wheeled him through the doors as he still held his hand—and parts of it—in the soda cup. Helpless, I stared as if caught in a bad dream. They ushered us into a waiting area where we sat and tried to make sense of what had just happened.

"That son-of-a-bitch was going after me," I said. "And he got Ian…who has never done anything to him." Pissed off, my anger helped to cover up what I really felt. Guilt. If not for me, Ian wouldn't be lying in there right now.

"Tex…" said Olivia, "you've never done anything to Bellman either. He's just…crazy. You can't blame yourself." She leaned up against me and laid her head on my shoulder. "It's not your fault."

While I knew this to be true, I couldn't be totally blasé about it. Or, I could blame the damned Fates, who just seem to have it in for me and my loved ones. I mean, what possible life lesson is there to take away from this? Life sucks, try to get through it, some don't make it very long, look out for monsters, and then you die?

Josh paced the floor like a nervous, expectant father, when Ian's parents arrived, pale and breathless. Mrs. Stapleton had been crying, her eyes red-rimmed and swollen.

"How is he? What do we know?" Mr. Stapleton's jowls quivered slightly like those of a basset hound.

"He's in surgery," I said. "He's been there for

forty-five minutes. We really don't know anything yet." It had been Josh's idea to call Ian's parents. Those in charge at the hospital probably put a call in anyway, but Olivia and I couldn't even think straight enough to realize it needed to be done.

"What *happened*, Tex?" asked Mrs. Stapleton, on the verge of tears again. I wanted to remain calm, to keep her likewise. Sometimes tears are as contagious as vomiting…once you see someone do it, the floodgates open.

"This crazy kid at school…" I halted, wondering what I should tell and what I shouldn't. *Bullshit*. Bellman tried to kill us. No way would I hold back from ratting because of some misplaced code of school ethics. That bastard exhausted the statute of limitations long ago, and I should've gone forward after he tried to choke me half to death. Right now, a suspension seems minor while my friend remains in terrible condition.

"His name's Bob Bellman," I continued. "And he tried to run us down in the parking lot. He actually tried to kill us. He's a…bully. And he's crazy. Ian didn't do anything to him, and this Bellman kid was after me. I'm sorry…Ian just was in the wrong place at the wrong time." This sounded a lot worse—and cold—once I said it.

Mrs. Stapleton unleashed the tears again. And I joined her, needing that release after caging it for the last hour and a half. I hugged Mrs. Stapleton awkwardly, sloppily sobbing, and saying, "I'm sorry…I'm so sorry," over and over again. I let go and sank back down beside Olivia, hiding my head in shame between my hands. I couldn't tell if Mr. and Mrs. Stapleton blamed me or not, but it didn't stop my guilt.

****

Thirty minutes later, a doctor came out, tugging at her mask. "Mr. and Mrs. Stapleton?" she called out. Sweating profusely, dark stains covered her blue scrubs. Mr. Stapleton bounced out of his seat, pulling his wife behind him. The doctor led them away into another room. Through the glass windows we watched, hoping to catch a sighting of good news.

"Too bad we can't read lips," said Josh.

"I hate waiting," I said. It seemed like that's all we'd been doing. "Waiting Room" should be changed to "Waiting Really Long Room."

The doctor left the room after shaking hands with Mr. Stapleton. Ian's dad hugged his wife, shook his head tiredly, and approached us.

"Well, Ian will be all right," he said, staring down. "But they're not sure about the extent of damage to his left hand. They sewed what skin they could salvage back on him as best they could, but there'll be more skin grafts." He looked me in the eye with sadness and relief. "They're not sure if he'll ever recover the full usage of his fingers…or the amount of muscle damage yet. Time will tell the full story. He's also bruised badly and broke a couple of ribs, but that's the least of our worries. He's going to be in rehab for some time and looks like he'll be missing quite a bit of school." Well, there's the silver lining, I thought.

His glassy-eyed gaze took us all in turn. "The doctor did say that whoever had the good sense to put his fingers on ice may have helped him out immensely." We all looked at Josh. "So…thank you, son," he said, offering his hand.

Josh stood up and accepted it uncertainly. He stammered a bit. So often overlooked, this little bit of human kindness and gratitude felt alien to him. "Well," he said shyly, "I only did what I expect any of us would do." Absolutely not true, as Olivia and I had been in such shock, we couldn't even speak, let alone act. "I guess all those hours watching *E.R.* paid off."

Mr. Stapleton drew him in and hugged him tightly. "Thanks again, Josh."

"Can we see him?" I asked.

"No," Mr. Stapleton replied sternly. "He's going to be in recovery for a couple of hours, and then it's family only." Okay, I thought, he's mad at me. He shut his eyes for a moment and sighed. "Try tomorrow…I'm sure he'll want to see his friends."

"Okay, thanks, Mr. Stapleton. And I'm sorry, for what it's worth."

He stared at me. "Fine, Tex…but I want *all* the details. I'm going to prosecute this kid." I'd never seen Mr. Stapleton angry before. I wondered if Ian inherited his manic-depressive state from his father. His face burned bright red, his clenched teeth bared like a challenged dog. If I didn't know him to be a civilized man, it wouldn't surprise me if he went over to Bellman's house with a shotgun. *Scary*-angry.

For once, I welcomed the sudden appearance of a teacher. "Tex," Mr. Jensen said from across the waiting room. He waved and quickly propelled his huge mass toward us. "How is Ian doing?" Mr. Stapleton introduced himself to Mr. Jensen and filled him in on Ian's questionable condition.

"I'm so sorry for this…" said Mr. Jensen. Slowly, he wagged his head back and forth. "I'll make sure

Bellman gets expelled. And this time, Hastings won't be able to prevent it. There were too many witnesses, and Bellman's gone too far." I couldn't believe Mr. Jensen jumped out on that limb—especially in front of Mr. Stapleton—and blatantly dissed Hastings.

"Expulsion's too easy for this...this *kid*," said Mr. Stapleton. "I want this guy to go to prison for what he did. And I'm going to see that he does."

Mr. Jensen grimaced. "Mr. Stapleton, I don't know how to tell you this. Bob Bellman is...in the eyes of the courts...still a kid. He's seventeen years old. Chances are he'll get off with a slap of the wrist and put on probation." Mr. Jensen placed a large hand on Mr. Stapleton's shoulder, half for comfort, I thought, and half for protection, in case things got out of hand.

Mr. Stapleton's nostrils flared. "Well, Mr. Jensen, we'll see...we'll *just* see." He stormed off, leaving behind a trail of curious observers behind him.

Mr. Jensen turned back to me. "They already pulled in Bellman, and he's sitting in a jail cell now."

"Where'd you hear that?" It sounded too good to be true.

"From the horse's mouth. He actually had the balls to call me and wanted me to bail him out." He smiled in a painful way and shook his head. "Can you believe that? I asked him what he did, and he told me they 'accused' him of running over 'some kid.' I told him I hoped they kept him in there and he should call his father." Bellman didn't care enough about what he did to even learn Ian's name, apparently. "I'm sorry, Tex. The good news is that I'm *not* backing down on this one. Bellman will be out of your life soon enough."

How I wish that were true.

****

"Oh, *crap*." I spun on my heels and looked at the clock on the waiting room wall. Five fifteen. I completely forgot about picking Dad up. I ran outside, dug out my cell phone and called his work number.

"Dad?"

"Son, is everything okay?" The nerves in his voice came through loud and clear. Both of us had been programmed to hate getting phone calls from one another because it usually signified something bad. "You're late…"

"Dad, Ian's been in an accident. He's going to be all right, but there're some complications with his hand." I told him the story.

"My God." I could picture Dad, his eyes closed, concentrating, while thinking how he could "fix this." "Do you want me to come to the hospital? I could get a ride."

"No, Dad, it's all right. Ian's not allowed visitors tonight anyway, so we might be coming home soon. Is there any way you can get a ride home tonight, though? I don't know how steady I feel to be doing a lot of driving." I hoped his co-workers hadn't already started piling out to begin their weekends.

"That shouldn't be a problem. But be careful…as always."

"As always," I said. "Thanks, Dad."

****

As my shock finally waned, my mental processing grew more clear-headed. I saw Olivia and Josh talking to Mr. Jensen and ran down to my car.

I buried Olivia and Josh's protection spell bottles deep within their backpacks. As an afterthought, I

133

grabbed Ian's bottle—fat lot of good it did him—and tucked it into my jacket pocket.

I went back inside and asked if Ian was still in recovery.

"We just got word he's being moved to room 411," said Mr. Jensen. He noticed my look of uncertainty. "That's a good thing, Tex…it means he's on the road to recovery."

"Okay," I said. "Looks like there's not much more for us to do here tonight, so why don't I get you guys home?"

Both Olivia and Josh looked somewhat relieved to hear this and sprang to their feet. "So, I guess Bellman canceled Halloween this year," said Olivia.

"Yeah, I guess we can add that to his list of crimes." I figured none of us felt much like celebrating, and it almost felt like a betrayal to hold Zombie-Fest without Ian. "We'll hold a 'Post-Halloween Zombie-thon' once Ian gets out."

I drove Josh home first and then dropped off Olivia. For the most part, a quiet drive as we all tried to sort through and make sense of the terrible events of the afternoon. At seven o'clock, I turned around and headed back toward the hospital.

****

I saw a sign stating visiting hours ended at nine p.m. I walked past the night nurse, nodded at her as if I had every right to be there, and took the stairwell up to the fourth floor.

I opened the door to the hallway. Room 411 was situated at the far end. I wandered down the sterile hallway, gazing at the floor, adopting a concerned relative's demeanor, when Ian's door opened. Mrs.

Stapleton came out, wiping tears from her face with a well-used tissue. Quickly, I ducked into the closest bathroom. Once again, I staked out the farthest stall and quietly perched on the toilet, latching the swinging door back into place. It seemed like I'd spent a lot of time performing covert operations in public toilets lately.

My legs wavered with weakness once nine p.m. finally arrived. I stood up, stretched, and waited another ten minutes. Peeking into the hallway, I saw the overhead lights snap off one by one like falling fluorescent dominoes. I crept out the door and walked past the nurse stand in the center of the wing. A young, pretty nurse narrowed her eyes at me curiously. I smiled weakly and said, "I left my phone in my brother's room. I'll just be a minute." I didn't pause for her rebuttal, self-consciously humming a nonsense tune to display my innocence.

Opening Ian's door, I shuttled past someone sleeping, snoring loudly. Too loud to be my friend. In the bed closest to the window lay Ian, a broken toy soldier, his arm in a cast and attached to a series of wires and props. An I.V. hooked up to his good arm.

I took out the bottle and placed it stealthily underneath his pillow. He stirred, moaned. His eyes opened slightly.

"Tex?" he whispered, so far removed from the Ian I knew, all his fight and fury gone. Memories rushed back of Mom at her weakest in the hospital. How I hated this place.

"What's up, Ian? Just doin' a quick drive-by…see how you're doing. That one nurse is hot, you lucky bastard."

He laughed once and then coughed. "Not so

lucky…I'm going to have an ass-hand…"

"You're not going to have an ass-hand." I had to laugh. "They're not going to take skin from your ass…at least, I don't *think* so. Just make sure you keep it clean."

He laughed again and then winced in pain. "How is everybody?

Anybody else hurt?" Undoubtedly on some sort of strong pain reliever, he didn't have good recall at the moment.

"Josh cut his arm, but we're okay." Ian's roommate's horrible snoring stopped and turned into a droning wheeze, very similar to what I thought of as a death rattle.

"Hey, I've put something under your pillow, and it's very important you keep it with you at all times. Don't ask questions, just do it, okay? I know you'll probably not remember everything I'm telling you, but you've got to try. Ian? Do you understand?"

"Keep under pillow…" he sighed, sleepiness overtaking him. "Goddamn tooth fairy, Tex…" With that, he conked out. I brushed the hair lightly off his forehead.

"Sorry, Ian," I whispered.

I sped past the night nurse, patted the phone in my pocket, hollered, "Got it, thank you, good night," and ran the hell out of there and into the night.

Chapter Nine

On Saturday morning, I gathered Olivia and Josh to return to the hospital. The once colorful orange and yellow barrage of fall leaves had fled prematurely, the gloomy start of winter settling in early. Skeletal tree fingers reached up from the graves of yards and scratched at the coffin cover of sky. The dull, overcast atmosphere matched our moods perfectly.

"How'd you guys sleep?" I felt them out, hoping they hadn't found their protection bottles.

Josh said, "Okay, I guess." But it looked as if he didn't get much sleep at all. Olivia just stared blankly through the dirty windshield, looking like an adult after New Year's Eve.

We drove by the emergency room, having a slow day compared to last night, and parked. As we walked through the lot, I hung my arm around Olivia's shoulders. She'd been uncharacteristically quiet.

"What's going on, O'?"

She sighed. "I'm just sick of these assholes at school. We didn't do anything to them. We didn't start anything. And now one of us is badly jacked up." The return of the ire in her voice encouraged me. "And, now, you should see the crap they're posting online."

Frankly, I'd fully expected this, surprised it took this long. I warned my friends it would happen and to just ignore it. I also knew Olivia would blow off my plea to let it lie.

"What have they done now?"

"Some of the usual suspects are saying some bad shit about us." She waved her hands exaggeratedly. "They're calling you guys a bunch of 'fags' and me your 'fag-hag.'" At this, she almost cracked a smile. "I don't care *what* they call me, but they better leave my boys alone."

"Just don't let it get to you. Don't even look. They're so damn obvious."

"Oh, no, O', don't back down from nothin'. They've also put up some crappy-ass photo-shopped pictures of us."

Morbid curiosity got the better of me. "What photos?"

"They must've taken your freshmen yearbook photos and put your faces on this photo…of three naked dudes hugging each other. I mean, it doesn't even look real. These morons can't do anything right."

Surely, Bellman's Neanderthal tendencies kept him off-line, so he must've put his football pals up to it. Or maybe Johnny Malinowski. "Olivia, you *aren't* getting on there, are you? You're not fighting back, right?"

"*Hellz,* yeah, I am!"

I knew Josh had enough common sense to not look at their web pages. Or at least, enough good sense to not respond to their senseless viral taunts. But I could tell his interest had been stoked. Olivia, on the other hand, insisted on carrying on in battle, even against overwhelming odds.

"Olivia, you know, you're just going to make matters worse. Way worse than they already are." A sudden cold wind whipped up around our legs, blowing parking lot trash around us. I couldn't help but notice the irony: us being "trash magnets."

"Don't worry about it, Tex. These dumb-asses can't hold a candle to me when it comes to a battle of the wits." Olivia did have a nasty talent for turning things back on people and insulting them with her sharp tongue.

"Look, just because you feel safe behind a computer screen, doesn't mean that'll carry over once you leave your house." Exasperation claimed me, near ready to throw in the towel. "We've seen how dangerous they can be. I don't want to be visiting you guys in the hospital, too."

"What're you saying to them, O'?" Josh appeared nervous, his natural state most of the time.

"Oh, I brought out the big guns, and said if they're so threatened by, and interested in, homosexuality, then they're obviously closeted gays themselves." Olivia guffawed, the wind carrying it far. "Then I told them that football was the gayest thing in the world. A bunch of dudes patting each others' butts, hanging out and showering together, and playing with balls!"

Even I had to laugh at Olivia's defense. "God…you're really gonna rattle the monkey cage." Josh managed to muster a small smile as well.

The wind died down along with our amusement. "But…" said Olivia, suddenly solemn. "There's more…" She hesitated.

"What?"

"Someone anonymously posted that…you killed your mother." She turned around to look at me while walking backward. "I couldn't let that go…"

I hung my head. "Bastards…"

"And…that led into another tangent. All these other jackasses jumped on the bandwagon, the shit hit the fan, and they started saying how they thought that one of us—probably you, Tex—killed Matt Rimmer." Olivia's visible eye glistened, a hint of a tear forming. "I'm sorry…"

I took in a deep breath and let it out slowly. For them to bring my mother into this felt unspeakable. And now murder accusations? Much too surreal to comprehend. I know how things start online, quickly ballooning out of control, which is why I rarely go onto the usual social media hang-outs. Every idiot with access to the Internet feels braver by hiding behind the comfort of a computer screen, saying any harmful thing that pops into his head, and the devil take the hindmost. Most of these bullies are what you'd expect—the so-called popular elite at school. But some of these people are among the downtrodden—just like us, unpopular faces in the crowd, trying to survive. Yet given an opportunity to elevate their self-worth, they'll pile on and try their hand at viral bullying. I suppose some of them think it's their in to being accepted as popular. Whatever their reason, it's not right…and I think they're even worse than the popular kids.

"Okay…" I said. "Radio silence." I had to regroup, shut my eyes, and concentrate, a move I picked up from Dad. "Now that our names are being tossed around as murder suspects, it's more important than ever to keep *quiet*. We do *not* want the cops talking to us anymore, especially at school. That'll just give the gossips more crap to talk about."

Olivia grasped the sense in that. "It's hard, Tex…to see them talking about us like that. I'll *try* and stay off…but you'd better talk to Ian, too."

****

"Hey, guys," said Ian. Hoisted up in bed, his wrapped arm pointed skyward like a waving mummy. "'Bout damn time you got here." His voice sounded like he'd suddenly developed a three-pack-a-day smoking habit.

"Hey, you." Olivia placed her arms carefully around his neck and kissed his forehead. "We were worried about you."

"Takes more than a speeding psycho to take me down." He grinned then cringed as if stubbing a toe. "Ow! Everything hurts."

"Hey, you're going to be missing some school." I smiled, trying to keep emotion at bay. "Lucky guy…"

"That's what you called me last night," croaked Ian. Uh-oh. As far as Olivia and Josh knew, I hadn't come back here last night. Redirection time needed.

"Ah, that's the drugs talking," I countered. "Hey, I hear you've been chatting online to the bad guys… What's up with *that*?"

He grinned. "What the hell else am I supposed to do in here?"

"You can't have a computer in here, can you?" Josh's eyes widened as if considering maybe the hospital didn't seem like such a bad place to stay, after all.

"No, but I've got this." He grabbed his cell phone from underneath the sheets with his good hand. "Don't tell them I've got it. Wait! Maybe you should. Then they'll send in 'Nurse Goodbody' to do a full body search."

Olivia groaned. "God, *always* such a pig." She

smiled, though, and backed down quickly from staging a searing women's rights lecture.

"Dammit, Ian, we've been through this," I said. "Leave these baboons alone, or you're just asking for more trouble."

"You're kidding me, right? After what that asshole did to me, I ain't backing down from him or his idiot entourage. Besides...have you seen what they've been saying about us?" Ian struggled to sit up, then collapsed back into the pillow.

"Yeah. Olivia told me. What've you been saying back to them?" I knew it would be bad. Whereas Olivia reveled in the art of making these buffoons trip up in their own stupidity, pure rage fueled Ian's Internet counterpoints.

"They were calling us 'killers'. You believe that crap? Us? So, I wrote that Bellman was the murderer. I mean, he tried to kill me!" Drops of sweat formed on Ian's forehead, a physical manifestation of his rising ire.

"You need to stop it right *now*. Please?" I thought maybe the softer approach might work better. It couldn't hurt.

"Oh, *whatever*, Tex. It's hard as hell to text one-handed anyway." He looked at his wired-up hand. A momentary flash of inspiration gob-smacked me. Maybe I *would* let Nurse Goodbody know about his cell phone.

"I heard Bellman's sitting in jail," said Josh. "And he's going to most definitely, probably, maybe, be expelled."

"Way to commit, Josh," said Ian, laughing. Sometimes it scared me how Ian could suddenly switch mood-swings. Like father, like son, I guess. "You should see what my dad's planning on doing."

"Yeah, we kinda' got a taste of that last night," said Olivia. "He's going all Five-O on Bellman's ass!"

"But, Mr. Jensen said he probably wouldn't do any time since he's a minor," I added.

"Hey, buzz-kill," said Olivia, "let us have our golden moment." I couldn't deny what she said. But as the resident buzz-kill of the group, I'd learned false hope ended up *much* worse than no hope in certain situations.

"Don't worry," said Josh, nearly under his breath. "He'll get his." I'd forgotten Josh said this in our mad race to the hospital yesterday, a creepy, reoccurring mantra that worried me.

"Well, I hope so." But the realist in me didn't believe it. "Ian, I'm really, *really* sorry about all this…this crap. If it weren't for me, you wouldn't be all wired up like a cyborg…"

"I don't blame you. *You* didn't run me down. This psycho was just looking for somebody to run down, I guess, and I happened to be the one." Ian's heartfelt reasoning hit home, making me glad I remained his friend throughout our golden school days. "Guys, *seriously*. Thanks for getting me to the hospital. And, Josh…thanks for the ice. I heard it may've saved me some nerves or something."

"No prob, bro." Josh pretended he was going to fist-bump Ian's bad hand and then pulled back.

"No fist bumps," yelled Olivia as we all shared a much-needed chuckle.

****

Sooner than later, I knew I had to talk to Ian about

the protection spell. And I had to do it alone because the rules of witchcraft have thus spoketh! The best method would be just to level with him. If anybody'd believe anything so outlandish, it would be him, since he knew me the longest.

Ready to send Olivia and Josh down to the cafeteria ahead of me, a voice suddenly called out "Richard? Richard McKenna?" I whipped around, fists half-raised in defense, until I saw the fluorescent light beaming off Detective Ryan Cowlings' bald head. At least I thought it might be Detective Cowlings of the Clearwell Police Department, but all bald middle-aged men tend to look alike to me. And these days, I wanted positive proof about everyone.

"Um...yeah?"

"I'm Detective Cowlings." Okay, check. "I believe we spoke last week at your high school? About Matt Rimmer?" Apparently, all shaggy-haired teenage boys looked alike to Detective Cowlings as well, since he split his gaze between Josh and me.

"That's right," I said. Josh shrunk back against the wall, his fear of authority figures in full force.

Detective Cowlings rubbed his bald pate as if polishing a bowling trophy. "I was hoping I could talk to you for a few minutes? Alone?"

"Okay, sure." I turned to my friends. "I'll meet you down in the cafeteria...stick with the chips. I remember them as safe." Olivia squinted at Cowlings suspiciously, grabbed Josh's arm, and led him down the hallway.

"It shouldn't take too long," called Cowlings after my friends, holding his hand to his mouth for unnecessary amplification. A nurse, who I assumed to be Nurse Goodbody, shot Cowlings a disapproving scowl.

"Let's go to the chapel." Cowlings sped by me, headed for the elevator. "That girl. She your girlfriend?" Impatiently, he punched the down button twice.

"No. Yes…I don't know," I stammered.

He shot a quick, intense glance at me. "I see." I didn't really think he did see, but obviously, I didn't either. A Muzak version of Neil Diamond's "Cracklin' Rosie" played in the elevator. Cowlings hummed along. "What's her name?" he asked while fidgeting with a button on his suit jacket.

"Olivia. Olivia Furman." Another whip-snap of his head as he glared at me as if he'd just solved the Matt Rimmer murder case. Surely, those incriminatory head-snap stares would end in whiplash. Good thing we were in a hospital.

Silence reigned during the rest of our long, uncomfortable elevator journey. More nervous than a squirrel with a nut allergy, I started whistling "Going To The Chapel" when he fired off round three of his potent stares.

We sat in a back pew of the small, empty chapel. He stared at me and sighed. I didn't know what to say, surely the onus started with him.

Finally, he said, "Richard, I wanted to talk to you away from your Vice Principal Hastings." He smiled a large toothy grin. "He thought it was his investigation last time we spoke."

"Yeah, he can be like that." Okay, maybe Cowlings didn't seem so bad after all.

"Tell me what happened to you and your friends

yesterday." His demeanor suddenly became one of a kindly priest at confession. He leaned toward me with a concerned look. Reaching into his jacket, he withdrew a pocket notebook and began jotting down words.

I wondered if I should tell him about the fire extinguisher incident or leave it out. I didn't want to see Olivia get dragged into this. But I realized my story didn't make a whole lot of sense without it. So before I spilled all, I asked, "Detective Cowlings, would it be possible for you to keep one person's name out of this? I mean, from school, Hastings, and the rest of the powers that be?"

"I can't make any promises until I hear your whole story, but unless it has a direct bearing on my murder investigation…if it's high school hijinks…well, that's not really what I'm after. Relax, Richard, I'm just looking for some facts. I just want to talk a little bit."

I told Cowlings the entire story, beginning with Josh's shower incident late last year. He nodded— sometimes in empathy, sometimes as if trying to piece together a puzzle—and kept scratching away and flipping pages madly in his notebook.

"So…do you *like* Bellman?" I asked. "I mean for the murder of Rimmer?"

He snapped his head at me, then tempered it with amusement. "Richard, have you been watching *CSI* lately?" Well, yes, yes, actually I had. Dad's favorite show, after all.

"Sorry. I'll keep my TV cop lingo out of it and leave it to you."

"Since you asked…I don't 'like' anyone at this point for the boy's death. Even if I did, I couldn't tell you, you know that."

"Right."

"You'll be glad to know the Bellman boy is still cooling his heels in our jail cell. His dad wanted him to stay in overnight to learn his lesson." He stretched his thin legs out in front of him underneath the pew. "That's the good news...the bad news is his father is already looking to lawyer him up as we speak."

"That figures," I muttered.

"You're aware he'll probably just get probation on this, aren't you? I know it's not fair, but his age is helping him here."

"Yeah, I was already warned about it. What's his story on the incident anyway?" I probably could've guessed, but I wanted to know what we were dealing with.

"At first, he denied having done it," said Cowlings. "But after we told them there were numerous witnesses, he changed his story to say it was an accident, and he lost control of the car. He claims he panicked and left because he was afraid."

"That's total bullshit!" I remembered where we were and whispered "Sorry" to the empty chapel.

"Richard, do you think Bob Bellman would have any reason to have killed Matt Rimmer? As far as you could guess? Or know?"

"It's like I told you and Hastings. I didn't really know Rimmer, and my only encounters with Bellman have been acts of terror. As far as I know, they were teammates and friends...although the thought of Bellman even having any friends blows my mind. If you're asking me if Bellman is capable of murder...the answer lies in the hospital bed in room 411."

"His father gave him an alibi of being home the

night Rimmer was murdered. I have to assume it's the truth…for now."

"You don't say." Unable to hide my disappointment, I rolled my eyes.

"Richard, there's something I did want to let you know." He leaned in conspiratorially. "Around the police station, people are assuming that whoever killed Rimmer must've been a large, athletic man to have been able to overpower this young football kid." He whipped off his glasses for dramatic effect. "I'm not so sure this is the case…"

And here we go, I thought. I nervously swallowed, which I'm sure looked suspicious to Cowlings.

"Rimmer was smashed on the back of his skull with an iron bar several times…and then the killer continued to beat Rimmer while he would have been unconscious. The perpetrator finished the job by choking the life out of him with plastic or rubber gloves." Cowlings held me captive in his crossfire stare, no expression whatsoever. "So…I believe that it could have been anyone…of any size…maybe even a female."

"Oh." I already knew where this would head.

"You say…this…" he quickly flipped back a few pages in his notebook, "Olivia Furman…she's the one who was upstairs with you?"

"That's right."

"She's the same one who took out Bob Bellman earlier this week with a fire extinguisher?" Cowlings nonchalantly flipped through the pages of his notebook, while looking for connecting incidents.

"Yeah…but Olivia would *never* do something like kill Matt Rimmer, if that's what you're thinking." I couldn't believe he suspected Olivia, even though the news would bring great personal joy to her.

"Well, it certainly doesn't look like it," he said, chuckling. The many mood swings of Detective Cowlings proved unpredictable. "My point is...it could be anybody. Where were you the night Matt Rimmer was murdered, Richard?"

Boom. He finally got around to asking me what I'd been dreading. "I don't even *know* when he was murdered! If it was a school night, I'm sure I was at home eating dinner with my dad."

"Settle down, Richard. I've got to ask these questions of everyone connected to Matt Rimmer."

"But I'm not *connected*!" Hello, world, would you please quit spinning out of control for a couple of minutes? Two weeks ago, I considered myself just a typical bullied high school student, looking to survive algebra and Bullying 101. Now, I've narrowly escaped a murder attempt and find myself under suspicion as a murder suspect. All because Matt Rimmer had called me "fag" a handful of times.

A long pause settled over Cowlings as he stared at me, almost. "Okay," he finally said, "I'll look into it. What about your friends? Did they hate the Rimmer boy as well?"

Once again, my inner censor malfunctioned. "First of all, Detective, I didn't *hate* Matt Rimmer. I didn't like him...but I didn't *hate* him. He was just a...I don't know...casual bully in my life at the worst. Really, I never even gave him much thought. So do you mind stopping with all of the 'hate' talk?" I didn't know if I helped or hurt my case.

"When we talked earlier...you said he called you

'fag' several times. How did that make you feel toward him?"

"Look, it's just something we learn to live with. I'm sure you never had to deal with such things when you went to school, so you couldn't possibly understand…but as unfair as it is, my friends and I pretty much accept it as a fact of life."

Cowlings glared at me and sighed. "Richard, you'd be surprised. I *do* understand. I was taunted and teased at my school for being gay. And sadly, it doesn't stop there. I'm the only gay law enforcement officer in Clearwell, Kansas."

Whoa, true confession time. I did not see this coming. Maybe the heavenly atmosphere of the chapel had worked wonders on him.

"But, I persevered, and I knew I was going to graduate at the top of my class and police academy, no matter what obstacles were placed in my way," he said. "And I never once even thought about killing the bullies…the assholes…the people who wanted to beat me down for being different."

"*Exactly*," I yelled. The echoes in the chapel prompted me to bring my voice down. "That's what I've been telling you. I wouldn't—neither would my friends—ever resort to their level, especially not murder, for God's sake. We're just trying to get through, hoping the next level of life is better."

Another long awkward silence followed as Cowlings peered into my soul. "Okay, Richard…I believe you. Do *not* let me down," he said, smiling warmly now. "I'm going to want to talk to your friends. They're in the cafeteria, right? And I'll want to speak to Ian as well."

"Go easy on them, copper." I managed a quiet laugh.

"I will." He stood up to leave then turned around. "Richard…is there anything else you want to tell me? Anything you've noticed that's not…quite ordinary?"

"Actually, yes…there's this weird ice cream truck." And I told him *most* everything I could remember about it (excluding the house protection spells, of course). His head buried in his notebook, his bald scalp nodded frequently during my tale.

"We're familiar with this ice cream driver. I've already spoken with him, and he seems harmless enough. He has an alibi. I wouldn't worry about it."

Huh, really? The truck seems pretty damn creepy to me.

"Okay, policing awaits. I gave you a card last time we talked, right?"

"Um, yeah, but I think I threw it away." At the time, I didn't think I'd need it. "Could I get another one?"

"All right. But *keep* this one. I have to pay for them out of my own pocket." He held his hand out to me. "Thanks. I'll be in touch."

"Okay." I squeezed his hand hard as Dad always taught me to do. "Detective Cowlings?"

"Yes?"

"Call me Tex, okay?" As one of us, I felt he earned the right to do so. He gave me hope. Not only because he seemed like a savvy cop who had our best interests at heart, but he'd also been one of the downtrodden. He withstood the hells of high school and made something out of his life. I wanted him on our team.

"You got it, Tex. Be careful."

A lot of adults had been telling me that lately. Maybe it's time to heed their advice.

****

I poked my head into Ian's room. Still sawing wood, I bypassed the mystery-sleeper roommate. "Hey," I said.

"Hey." One-handed, he fiddled with his cell phone before quickly stashing it under his sheet.

"Busted! Tell me you're not back on the social media hangouts." Dumb thing to say as I'm sure I fueled his fire instead of tamping him down.

He laughed and waved me off. "Tex, what the hell is *this* all about?" He pulled out the spell bottle from underneath his pillow.

"Okay, are you sitting down?"

He giggled and then coughed. "Don't make me laugh, you dumbass."

"Do you remember what I said last night?" I braced for the upcoming encounter. Even though we'd been lifelong friends, the truth would admittedly be hard to accept.

"Barely. I thought it was a dream, until Nurse Goodbody found it and asked me what the hell it was. I remembered then what you said and told her it was a good luck charm."

"Good."

"What are you doing, Tex?" he asked seriously. "You're not dealing or something stupid, right?" He rolled the bottle around nimbly in his good hand.

"No, of course not. *Now*, who's being the dumbass?" I sat at the end of his bed. "Hey, by the way, a cop's gonna want to talk to you soon. About what Bellman did to you."

"About damn time. It's payback time, bitches."

"But, before he gets in here, I've got to talk to you myself. What I'm about to tell you, stays here, right?"

"Sure, buddy...like in Vegas!"

"All right. This is hard, so I'm going to jump right in." I took in a deep breath for show, to let Ian gauge my seriousness. "You remember my mom, right?"

"Yeah...uh, sure." Never one for displays of emotion, Ian generally tried to steer clear of any topic that called for it.

"I recently found out she...was a practitioner...of witchcraft." I waited for Ian to laugh, but to his credit, he just stared calmly and waited for me to continue. "She was born into it and apparently had...I dunno...special powers."

"Okay," said Ian slowly.

"And she passed those powers onto me."

"What the *hell* are you talking about, Tex?" His words expressed doubt, but the way his eyes lit up showed excitement to learn more.

"It's true, according to my dad. And I've been learning some minor spells and things. This bottle's supposed to protect you from harm."

"Why couldn't you've gotten it to me a day earlier?" Amazingly, he smiled. "Wow, Tex...I don't know what to say..."

"Well, please don't say anything right now. Just keep quiet, but more importantly, keep the protection spell with you as much as possible, okay?"

He stared at the bottle in his hand. "So...you're a...*witch*? Why not a warlock?" I suppose our many years of watching horror movies together had prepared Ian better for this revelation than most people.

"I really don't know." Constantly, I've wondered the same thing. "It's just the word that's been used by my dad and my…mentor."

"You have a *mentor*? How friggin' cool is *that*?" His roommate rolled over with a loud *snurk*.

"Ian, shhhh. It's important we keep this between the two of us." It actually felt good to have someone know my secret, particularly a close friend. Both Ian and I grinned ear to ear.

"I want to meet your mentor," he said, quieting down. "Is she an old witch with a black pointy hat and all that crap?"

"Something like that." The image of Mickey in a black witch's hat seemed kinda scary.

"So…does this stuff work? Can you put a hex on Bellman or something?"

"It's complicated. I'm not supposed to do anything potentially harmful to people—or do good things for myself—because it may turn bad."

Ian nodded as if this made total sense to him. "Do Olivia and Josh know? *Omigod*, you've gotta tell 'em!"

"No, they don't. And no, they can't know. Not right now, at least. It's for their own good because the spells won't work if they end up not believing. So, please, don't tell them."

"Well…why'd you tell me?"

"Because…because, first of all, I knew you'd believe. Because we totally believe in one another. Also, because I didn't think there was any way around it, since your so-called Nurse Goodbody—or somebody—was sure to find the bottle eventually. I had to make sure you'd keep it with you."

"Cool. I won't tell them. But you've got to promise

me something in return." Ian stared at me with wild-eyed anticipation.

"What's that?"

"Tell me everything...I mean, *everything*...about what you've learned about witchcraft."

I obliged Ian gladly because I hadn't seen him this giddy about anything for some time. So I settled in and told him about my witchy induction week.

****

Feeling fairly good for the first time in days, I bypassed the elevator and ran down the stairs to the hospital lobby. I found the cafeteria, where I remember Dad and I'd shared many somber, bad meals, and saw Olivia and Josh cutting up at a corner table. Coffee cups and chip bags littered their holding area.

"Hey, guys," I said.

"*Omigod*," said Olivia. "Guess who's a murder suspect and has two thumbs?" She hitched her thumbs toward herself.

"O', that's not quite true," said Josh, attempting to calm her down. Her outburst of murder talk attracted quite a bevy of interested onlookers. "He just was asking us some questions..."

"*Yeah*, but he wanted me to give him a freakin' *alibi!* How cool is *that?* He wanted my alibi!" She stood up and squealed with delight.

"Olivia, shhh, be quiet. Everyone here's going to think you're a crazed ax murderer." Even though her glee felt glorious, I fought the urge to not join in. "Come on, let's get out of here."

I grabbed Olivia by the arm. With Josh tugging her other arm, we practically dragged her out of there. We'd almost made it to the cafeteria exit, when Olivia turned and yelled, "That's right. Alibi! Alibi! I ain't got no alibi! Uh-huh!" She hooted, twirled, and kicked up a leg like a demented cheerleader.

No way recovering from that, we lifted her between us and ran like hell to the parking lot, laughing the entire way.

Chapter Ten

Olivia indeed had no plausible alibi to give Detective Cowlings and basked in the afterglow for several days. On the night in question, she told him she was home alone while her mother worked, so she had nothing concrete. The excitement anyone—let alone an investigating detective—would seriously consider her a murder suspect filled her with crazy glee. Three days later, Josh and I finally told her to cool it because it grew old, and she didn't lend the situation the necessary seriousness. But she saw it as a total win for Women's Rights.

"Olivia," I said, "what happens if Detective Cowlings actually considers you a likely suspect and arrests you?"

Josh nodded in agreement.

"Oh, he's not going to arrest me. I've got right on my side." She squealed delightedly.

"Okay, whatever. Just don't go around and broadcast you're a suspect, okay? We *don't* need any other accusations lobbed our way. Things are bad enough already."

Josh did have an alibi. He'd been home that evening with his parents who worked during the day. I'm glad he wouldn't have to endure any more terrifying visits from Clearwell's finest.

I didn't know what Ian told Cowlings, but I'm

pretty sure he'd been home that evening as well. None of us had much of a social life, and if we weren't with one another, then we could usually be found at home. Such is the life of being a social pariah…but at least it is usually made for watertight alibis.

****

For once, I experienced a quiet week at school, and I couldn't have been happier. Buzz in the hallways said that Bellman had been expelled for the rest of the school year. Even though Ian had paid for it in full, I couldn't help but feel great relief.

Josh told me he spotted Bellman a couple of days after school, hanging out at the abandoned gas station across the street where the stoners and smokers go for a fix. Probably waiting for his football pals to finish practice. I would've worried, but even Bellman wouldn't be stupid enough to try something again while he awaited his sentencing. I also suspected Josh knew this. Josh said he'd skateboarded past the gas station several times, taunting Bellman from a safe distance. I warned him to be careful, but when it came to his skateboard, Josh had no fear.

Because he finished his homework in study hall, Josh started leaving his backpack in his locker. In trying to come up with a plausible way to tell Josh he should carry his backpack everywhere he went, I realized nothing would fly. But I reasoned it'd be okay since Bellman had been temporarily neutralized.

Taking advantage of my newfound downtime, I read up on witchcraft at the local library. It's amazing what you can accomplish when you're not focused on escaping death at the hands of a bully. I wanted to prepare myself for my next visit with Mickey. To do this, I had to either acquire knowledge or invest in some protective headgear for my head. There was so much conflicting information regarding beliefs, spells, and the whole nine yards, it ended up confusing me, trying to sift through it all. Practitioners seemed to have their own styles and ways, but at least I had some useful background information that might keep the slapping hand of Mickey Goldfarb at bay. And for several glorious, bully-free days, I realized what it was like to live a normal high-school kid's life. Except for my being a witch, of course.

****

Wednesday morning, Mr. Jensen huffed into sociology class, something clearly on his mind. He opened the floor—as he did every Wednesday—to talk about current events.

"Okay, class, what's on everyone's mind today?"

Susie, the cheerleader, shot her hand up in the air. "Mr. Jensen, I'd like to talk about Bob Bellman. I think it's totally unfair that he was expelled." A few groans arose from the class, while a couple clueless individuals nodded their heads in agreement. "Don't you think a suspension should've been enough?"

I looked over at Ian's empty chair. Talk about unfair. Where were Ian's cheerleaders?

Mr. Jensen sat down, sighed, and rubbed his hands over his face. "Class? Does anyone have an answer for Susie?" He surveyed the room until his eyes locked onto mine. "Tex? What do you say?"

I sat still for a minute, debating whether to speak my mind. Compassion overrode my sense of sitting on the sidelines. "Yes, I'd like to say something about…Bob Bellman." When I said his name, I enunciated through gritted teeth, barely keeping my anger in check. "Bob Bellman is an animal. Yeah, he's on the football team, and I'm sure at least *some* of you will miss him. But I've seen Bob Bellman do unimaginable things. This new…incident…is the straw that broke the camel's back. Bob Bellman's mind doesn't operate like everyone else's. He has no moral compass, no consideration for other students. He's like a rabid animal, and we all know what we do to rabid animals, right?" By this time, I couldn't stop even if I wanted to.

Susie sunk down at her desk and sobbed quietly. If her argument weren't so damned stupid, I would've felt pity for her.

"Thanks to…Bob Bellman," I continued, "my friend, Ian Stapleton, may never fully regain use of his hand." I looked again at Ian's sad, empty chair. "So, Susie, if you want to talk about fair, let's consider Ian who did absolutely *nothing* to Bellman. Frankly, if I had my say, I believe Bob Bellman should be locked up for good along with the other animals in prison. So, no, I don't believe it *is* fair he's been expelled. I think it'd be fair if he was locked away…but I doubt that will happen." Ready to continue with my angry rant, I put the brakes on because it felt too cruel with Susie sobbing.

"Okay, thanks, Tex," said Mr. Jensen, his mouth upturned in a barely perceptible grin. "I'd like to add that as your teacher, it would be unprofessional of me to comment on what I think. But as a fellow human being on this world we share—that we *must* share—I couldn't agree with Tex more." He acknowledged me with a quick nod and let it just as quickly vanish. He stood, cleared his throat, and paced the length of the chalkboard. "Okay, unless anyone has anything else they'd like to discuss, let's open our textbooks."

After that, no one dared discuss anything.

****

That October day felt a little on the cold side, but the sun still managed to peek out. In a display of our freedom from tyranny, we left the claustrophobic confines of the boiler room and ate our packed lunches at one of the picnic tables by the parking lot.

"Have any of you seen Ian this week?" I peeled back the tin foil from my chicken cordon bleu and ate it like a cold burrito. I quickly decided to never again eat chicken cordon bleu cold.

"I saw him yesterday after school," said Josh. "I think he's doing all right. He's cool with no school…and he's trying to keep up with his homework." Josh nibbled at the corner of his peanut butter and jelly sandwich.

"Damn, Tex, what the hell are you eating today?" Olivia looked repelled. "Don't you ever eat any regular food?" She wrinkled up her nose.

"Ah, this is just something Dad and I cooked up. Is Ian staying off social media?"

"Hell, no," said Josh. "I think that's what's keeping him going. If anything, he's enjoying the hell out of it, I think."

A football landed with a loud crack in the middle of the table, spilling my iced tea.

"Hey, pussies," sneered Johnny Malinowski. Two other football thugs flanked him. "Give me my ball back, faggots."

Great…and so it starts again. Different day,

different bully. "Get it yourself," I said defiantly. Josh almost tried to retract his head inside his turtleneck.

"We know how you *love* to play with balls, Malinowski," said Olivia.

Malinowski's eye-slits were usually so narrow, you couldn't see his pupils. But after Olivia's insult, he strained to open them in a wide-eyed, crazy gaze. He grabbed the ball from the table, threw it hard into my back, and caught it on rebound.

"Shut up, bitch," he screamed at Olivia. *Thump* went the ball again into my back. It hurt, but I wouldn't let Malinowski know that. Ridiculously, I kept eating my lunch, while he repeatedly tossed the ball at my back.

"You're the only bitch I see here," yelled Olivia. She stood and positioned herself between me and Malinowski, erecting a human roadblock to end his football fun. The other two football Cro-Magnons snickered.

"You faggots got Bob expelled and off the football team." Malinowski's sudden quiet calm proved unsettling, to say the least.

"You're crazy," I said. "We didn't do a damn thing. Last time I checked, your buddy tried to run us over! Like that's our fault." A few curious student onlookers had gathered at a safe distance, unwilling to intervene.

"Don't you ever get tired of having your fag-hag do the fighting for you, McKenna?" I guess he changed the topic because he couldn't counteract the logic I'd proposed.

"And look at you," I said, "picking on a girl with two of your friends in tow." Looks like I'd completely given up my golden rule of staying off the radar. These bullies would never go away. They were like a hydra— you cut one head off, and there's another eager one to replace it. And trying to ignore it only seemed to make matters worse. I stood up.

"I should drop you freaks right here," said Malinowski. He let go of the football, opening and shutting his wiry fists.

"Come on, Johnny," said one of the gorilla sidekicks. "Leave the faggots alone. The bell's about to ring." With their buzz-cuts and round girths, they were Tweedledee and Tweedledum in football letter jackets.

Malinowski ignored his cronies. Tweedledee grabbed his arm, and Malinowski swung on him yelling, "*Arrr*" like a drug-fueled pirate.

"Cool your shit, hotshot," said Tweedledee. "We don't need to lose you from the team, too." I never would've thought Tweedledee would be the voice of reason. Malinowski grudgingly stalked off with them.

"This isn't over, McKenna," he growled.

As an afterthought, Tweedledee came back and shoved me hard. "Just stay out of our way, fag," he said. I guess he didn't want me thinking he had a soft side. The three raced off, laughing merrily as a good time had been shared by all.

"Well…" I said, "*that* was a fun lunch. Back to the boiler room tomorrow."

"*Nooooo*," Olivia yelled in mock terror. Oddly enough, the three of us doubled up in laughter. Either we'd learned to cope with bullying better, or it just didn't seem as bad. After you've been nearly strangled and run over by a speeding car, what's a little name-calling and football toss to the back? Maybe, hope sprung eternal, after all.

****

After the disaster with Ian, I'd totally forgotten to continue my home protection spell ritual, the furthest thing on my mind. I also needed to call Mickey as I hadn't talked to her since last week. I wanted to ask her something.

I flipped through the Clearwell white pages and found her number.

"Hello," she answered after six rings.

"Hi, Mickey," I said, again too loudly.

"Who *is this*?"

I guess we had to go through our greeting ritual even while on the phone.

"It's Tex McKenna." Long, really long pause. "Elizabeth's son?" I added, hoping to jog her memory.

"Where've you been, kid? I'm absolutely starving!"

****

That night, Dad and I made chili. Easy and quick. We could usually eat it for days afterward. I ate light, as I knew I'd be sharing chicken again with Mickey and thought it only polite to join her. We went through the motions of our small-talk dinner ritual, and I told Dad of my plan to see Mickey. I hated to do it, but I had to borrow ten bucks from him as my allowance had already been long-blown on chicken and candles.

After a quick run-through at Chicken Heaven, the guard of Castle Goldfarb proved a little easier to bypass this time. She still spent a good length of time scrabbling with her door chain, but at least she didn't put me through the usual ordeal of back and forth at her front door.

It surprised me to see Mickey had shed the usual bathrobe and fuzzy pink slippers in exchange for a floral-patterned (of course) sundress. Maybe calling her ahead of time from now on would be worth it.

"Kid, what the *hell* is going on at that school of yours, anyway? Murders, hit-and-runs, bullies... Is it built over the pit of Hell or something?"

After she saw how seriously I pondered this, she let out a loud, phlegmy cough. "That's a joke, kid. Dammit, you sure are gullible!"

We sat down at the kitchen table. "I brought you mashed potatoes and gravy this time." I offered her the red and white bag for inspection.

"Well, what do ya' know about *that*?" She stared at me as if this required an answer.

"Uh...I don't know anything, really."

"Too much, kid...too much. Have some chicken." She pushed the bag across the table toward me. "Well, I was actually getting worried about you when you didn't ring for five days. That Billson boy is your bully, isn't he?"

"Bellman...yes, he is."

"Doesn't look like our protection spells worked so well for your one friend."

"I...didn't get it to him soon enough." I glanced down at my chicken breast, feeling guilty over failing Ian. "One day earlier, maybe he wouldn't be in the hospital..."

"Well, anyway, you do know these spells aren't absolutely fool-proof, right?" Great, yet another rule she hadn't told me until after the fact.

"Mickey, I'm sorry I didn't call earlier. I didn't mean to worry you. I was just concerned about my friend and everything else."

"Oh, sure," she said, laughing. A few pieces of chicken crust flew across the table from her mouth. "Forget all about the old lady. You kids today." She swiped at the crumbs with a small red and white paper napkin. "That's okay…it gave me a chance to catch up with some of my stories. I'll tell you what, that Sonny….mmmm."

Uh-oh, I thought, as I watched her eyes fill with dreamy longing. Before we got back to the lustful leanings of Mickey Goldfarb, I thought it best to change the subject.

Mickey's cat patrol grazed by my legs, purring like well-oiled machines. "Mickey, could you put your cats up again? Please?" A black cat snapped its head up, staring at me with green eyes, disbelieving this brazen kitchen intruder.

"Okay, Sampson," she sighed. "Skeedaddle on upstairs. The rest of you, too." Like furry, ambulatory bullets, they shot upstairs, their offended meows ricocheting off the walls.

"Is your friend going to be all right?" Mickey placed one of her hands on top of mine.

"Well, he's probably never going to have the full use of his hand again. But it could have been worse, I guess."

"It could *always* be worse, kid. Remember that, and you'll be a happier boy. Come on, let's go outside for a bit." She pushed aside the mess on the table. "Clean-up can wait for a few minutes." She shot up from the table and turned around to stare at me. "Well? Are you coming or not?"

I sat next to Mickey on the porch swing as she lit a

cigarette. She expelled a huge smoke-ring, puncturing it with her finger. "Ahhhh, nectar of the gods."

"Mickey, can I ask you something?" I knew I probably shouldn't, but I'd been curious since our first encounter.

"Sure, kid, ask away."

"On our first meeting, you said the doctor told you to quit smoking, so now you only smoke outdoors. What's that all about?"

She swatted me on the back of my head with a *thwack*. I'd have to learn to anticipate her Punishing Hand of Infinite Pain. "Doesn't that school teach you anything? So I don't get second-hand smoke." She cackled hysterically. "Did you sleep through science class? Honestly…"

"Huh…okay." Her laughter slowed like a toy operating on a dead battery.

"What can I do for you tonight, Tex?"

"My dad told me that it might be possible…well, to talk to my mother."

She glared at me and finally said, "Yes, kid, it's possible." She stared off into the night sky. "But I don't know if it's the wisest thing you could do…"

"Why?"

She drew up her tiny shoulders and dropped them with a sigh. "First of all, you need to make sure you're ready for something like this. It can be very painful and emotional sometimes."

"I understand. I think I'm ready for it." I couldn't be sure, not really, but I knew I had to at least try.

"Secondly," she continued, "it's not a solid science. You can't even be sure who you're talking to. There're a lot of spirits out there in the netherworld, some good, some bad. Sometimes, bad spirits pretend to be good spirits." This thought chilled me. I had a hard enough time making sense of the world of high school, let alone the complications of the spirit world.

"Okay," I said, giving it a second thought.

"Thirdly, it can also be hard on the spirit you're trying to communicate with. If the spirit of your mother, say, is in her final resting space, you might be disturbing her and bringing her somewhere where she doesn't want to be. It can be a real struggle for a spirit to return there. It can also be hard on her emotions." On a tangent, Mickey counted off details on her fingers. "Having said that, your mom should be okay, since she was such a powerful witch."

"I…didn't know any of that. But I kind of got the impression Mom *wanted* me to contact her. I think that's why she told Dad I could talk to her after she was gone…and why he told me that."

"Well, I'm game if you are, kid." She jabbed out her cigarette in the ashtray. "Don't say I didn't warn you." Thrusting her finger at me, she closed one eye and squinted with the other.

"Will I be able to see her?" I felt suddenly afraid.

"No, kid, you're definitely not ready for *that*. There are ways to do that, but I'm not going to put you through that. Not on my watch." She poked me in the chest. "I don't even try to conjure up spirits in the physical realm!" While disappointment loomed that I wouldn't see my mother, part of me felt relief, as Mickey may've been right. I didn't know if I could handle it. I appreciated Mickey's looking out for me, though. It felt comforting knowing some adults, like my dad, did that.

"Okay, are we going to use scrying?" I asked.

She looked at me warily as she bounced off the swing. "Has somebody been reading library books on witchcraft?"

"Yeah...some."

"Don't *do* that!" Her lightning-fast snake of an arm reached out and bit me on the back of the head. *Swack!*

"Ouch!"

"Nothing in those books but a bunch of know-nothing scholarly mumbo-jumbo written by a bunch of eggheads who get their information from a buncha' other books! That could be dangerous to you, Tex, if you start trying their spells." Hands on her hips, she glowered down at me.

"Okay, got it...books bad." My school teachers probably wouldn't agree, but I didn't want to argue the point.

"Now...let's go call your mother," she said, rushing off into the house.

Mickey led me back into the kitchen, cleaned off the table, and carefully placed the used chicken bones in plastic baggies again.

"For the cats," I offered, hoping to say something that wouldn't merit a head-slap.

"For the cats," Mickey agreed primly with a nod. She pulled open an orange-painted drawer beside the sink and grabbed a handful of paper napkins, probably accumulated from visitors bearing chicken.

She tossed the napkins in front of me. "Here. Make yourself useful and tear these napkins up into small square pieces, then write 'yes,' 'no,' the letters of the alphabet and the numbers zero through nine on them." She handed me a black magic marker.

From another drawer, she snatched a small silver bell, a piece of green ribbon curling off the top. She flipped open the kitchen window and tied the bell to the handle, letting it dangle in the still, night air.

I finished my assignment and awaited further direction. Mickey hummed off-key, having entered her witch zone again. She stretched up to the cabinet above the sink, straining to open it. Failing this—incredibly—she got a chair and climbed onto the kitchen counter. Teetering, she reached for a wine glass.

"Mickey, let me get that." But before I stood up, she'd already hopped down, wineglass in hand, as lithe and quiet as one of her cats.

"I still got it," she exclaimed proudly. Damn, she sure did. I wondered if she'd like to come to school and kick some bully ass.

"Okay, Tex, put the 'Yes' at the top, the 'No' at the bottom, and put the 'A' next to the 'Yes' and keep going clockwise," she ordered. "The numbers should all go down at the bottom by the 'No.'." She lit two candles and placed them on the opposite sides of the table, so as not to disrupt the circle of paper I had created. She sat down facing me, setting the wine glass upside down inside the circle.

"Mickey, is this an Ouija Board? Don't you have a proper one?"

I think she felt this deserved a head-slap, but she couldn't reach far enough across the table to do the deed. Note to self…don't sit next to her. "Kid, this ain't the Parker Brothers for cryin' out loud." I wanted to ask her about her Etch-A-Sketch but realized I'd be courting future head-slaps. "Poor folks got poor ways," she added.

"All right, I'm sure you know the object of this and how to do it," she said. "It works best if you ask questions, keep them simple…and remember, it could get a little emotional for you." She stood up, crossed the kitchen quickly, and flipped the lights out. She sat down. The candles' flames reflected off the tip of her gravity-defying glasses, her eye-sockets dark caverns.

"Put your fingers on the tips of the base of the glass," she directed. "And don't go doin' no funny business by trying to push it. Just keep your fingers light. I'll start." She placed her lean fingers on her side of the glass.

I assume she'd closed her eyes—I couldn't really see her face as the table and our hands were the only things lit by the candlelight—and she began to hum softly. At first, I considered it some sort of opening chant, but I think she just felt the mood. Repeatedly, she cleared her throat of phlegm…definitely not part of a ritual.

And still we waited, a seeming eternity. Suddenly, a cool breeze gently brushed my cheek. The hanging bell emitted a timid ring, making me nearly jump out of my skin.

"Okay," Mickey whispered so as not to wake the dead…even though that seemed kinda the point. "Is there a spirit present with us?" Uncharacteristically soothing, her tone lulled me into a zone of my own.

My fingers trembled lightly on the edge of the wine glass, either from fear…or a sign from the spirit world. The glass slid smoothly across the table to the paper marked "*Yes*."

"We're looking for Elizabeth McKenna," intoned Mickey. "A loved one comes calling."

The bell rang more consistently now, swinging in the unexpected night breeze. The cold air blew back my hair before growing warmer. It felt as if I were a kid nodding to sleep, my mother kissing me good night.

"Are you Elizabeth?" asked Mickey.

The glass scooted to *Yes*.

"Okay, Tex, we've established contact…ask your mom what you want to know."

I guess I should've been better prepared for this. After longer than a year of trying to adapt to the loss of my mother—and trying to make sense of why she had to die—I didn't know *what* to say or ask.

"I…love you, Mom," I said. Mickey let out an exasperated sigh. I'm sure she wanted to avoid any Hallmark Moments, but she didn't say anything.

Me too, the letters spelled out one by one. The little bell tinkered away at the window, swaying gently back and forth.

"Are you happy, Mom? I mean…wherever you are? Are you good?"

The wine glass shot directly to *Yes*. It continued rolling around the table until it pointed out the letters *miss you*.

"Mom, I miss you too." Even though tears dampened my cheeks, I hadn't realized it until now. "I miss you so much…it's not fair…I miss you…"

Our fingers followed the wineglass around another journey across the table. *Be okay*, it said.

"What does that mean?" I asked, forcing the words through my choked voice. "Are you telling me to 'be okay,' or are you saying everything *will* 'be okay?'"

The bell jangled furiously. The warm air turned cold, as cold as an icy swimming pool on a hot summer day. The wine goblet furiously whipped across the table.

Danger, read the homemade Ouija Board.

"Who's in danger, Elizabeth?" asked Mickey. "Are you in danger? Or is it Tex?" The bell pulled taut at the ribbon, ringing out in shrill terror, as if afraid of being snatched into Hell. The cold breeze transformed into more than just a breeze, a frigid wind whipping by me, seemingly—impossibly—out of nowhere.

Tex, responded Mom via the Ouija Board. *Trust none.*

"What danger, Mom? *Who* can't I trust? *Why?* What do you *mean*?"

The wine glass whipped back and forth frenetically. Our arms strained in every direction, attempting to keep our fingertips attached to it. *Can't stay*, it read. *Luv...* The wine glass flew off the table, smashing on the floor as if the spirit world hung up on me angrily. The cold wind blew across the table, spreading the napkin pieces in the air as if shot out of a confetti cannon. The bell rocked ferociously back and forth, finally snapping against the windowpane, tearing the ribbon and falling to the floor with a hollow clunk.

Mickey ran to the kitchen light and flipped it on. I pounded my hands on the kitchen table, crying and ranting hysterically. "Don't go! Don't *leave* me again!"

"Well…" said Mickey. "*That* went well."

****

Mickey somehow managed to get me on my feet and led me into the living room. "Come on, kid, before you break my table." She pushed me down onto her sofa with a grunt and sat next to me. "Shhh, Tex. It'll be all right."

I was wound down, experiencing the dry, hiccupping sighing that signifies the end to a long bout of crying. Mickey patted my shoulder several times, dared once to slip an arm around my back before snagging it back abruptly.

"I should've listened to my gut," she said finally. "I thought it might be too much for you right now."

"It's like I've lost her twice. She says she loves me, and then she leaves…again…" More tears. "It's not fair. It's just not…fair." In a state of shock again, it seemed like my new norm.

"Oh, hush, Tex. Snap outta it! Do you really think you're the only one who's ever lost a loved one? I lost my Herbert twenty years ago…to a heart attack…but I didn't mope around about it." I half expected a wake-up slap to the back of my head. "At least you got to tell your mom you loved her again…to get some sort of closure—"

"She was too young to die, Mickey—"

"Yes, you were dealt a bad hand," she continued. "But everyone gets one now and again. It's part of life, and you need to start living it again. You overly-dramatic emo kids today, I swear. It's all self-pity and woe is me and hand-wringing and—"

I surprised myself with a chuckle. "You know what…*emo* is?"

"Well, of course I do," she crowed triumphantly. "I wasn't born yesterday." Well, yes, I thought, sometimes clichés *are* true. "And now more than ever, you better shape up. Your loved ones, your friends, your father, are all counting on you…especially now with the message your mother gave you."

With newborn panic, I recalled what Mom said.

"What'd it mean, Mickey?"

She focused on her hands. "I'm not sure. It could be taken as any number of things. With the cold air and wild bell ringing, I suspect that something else…something dark…was making its way toward us. I think your mom got out early because she didn't want this possibly bad spirit finding its path to us. I 'spect she was protecting you." Mickey must've noticed my wide-eyed fear and quickly added, "But I wouldn't worry about your mother, kid. She was one tough, smart cookie. She knew her craft well. I'm sure she's okay. But she was definitely warning you about something. Either you're in danger, or someone around you is."

And this ended my short half-week of feeling safe, happy endings all around. One more strike against Bellman would surely land him in prison, regardless of his age, so I didn't think I had anything to fear from him, at least for now. So what could I be in danger from?

"I don't *understand*, Mickey. Why couldn't she've given more complete answers? More information? What exactly am I in danger from? A car crash?" I'd feared those since Mom's accident.

"You gotta know something, kid. It's hard for a spirit to communicate with us. And as I said, I think she was keeping a bad spirit at bay, as well. *Trust* me. You don't want to mess around with bad spirits." She wagged her finger at me like an irate judge's gavel. "Either way, I think she was telling you to be careful."

"And to trust none…or no one."

"That's right, so you be careful out there, kid. Word of advice from ol' Mickey…don't go anywhere alone if you can help it." She placed her hands on her knees and sprung up out of the sofa. "Well, I'd say this has been more of a lesson than you needed right now. Next time, we'll cover something less...stressful...say, like the beauty of nature and your place in the world." She chuckled at her joke.

"That sounds about my speed," I said, nodding.

"Heh, kid, you're something else. Now, if you learned nothing else from tonight, you damn well don't go messing with *any* of this by yourself, you got that?"

"Yeah, pretty sure I do."

"And don't go trying to contact your mom again. Ouija Boards don't work with less than two people, anyhow. And you 'specially better not try and contact her using an even stronger spell. You could even end up dead—or worse!"

I wondered what could possibly be worse than death, but after tonight's supernatural events, I didn't want to know. "Believe me, Mickey, I won't contact my mother again." Just too painful to handle and I didn't want to cause Mom any pain or unrest.

I stood and walked toward the door, with Mickey hot on my heels. "Remember to be careful. And call me if you need me."

"Thanks, Mickey." I surprised myself by throwing my arms around her and hugged her tight. "I mean thanks for teaching me about witchcraft and stuff...but really, thanks for everything."

Hesitantly, Mickey hugged me back. She patted me once, and then the moment ended. Sorta' like a guy hug, but even more awkward. "Kid, you're going to get me all emotional...I don't *do* emotional."

She shut the door, but I saw her smile.

****

I drove home, thinking about what I learned tonight. First of all, Mickey was, as usual, right. I needed to quit playing the helpless victim in a hopeless world. Time to be proactive and take back the night. My friends counted on me. Last week, Olivia mentioned they more or less look to me as their leader. What kind of leader would I be if I moped around about the unfairness of the Fates and then you die? In retrospect, I suppose there's not much I could've done about Ian's situation. But what if there had been? What if I'd told someone about what Bellman had done in the past? Or what if I had stood up to him? Sure, I would have taken a pummeling, but Hastings wouldn't have been able to overlook it. I would've made sure of it. Okay, Mom, *this* one goes out to you. Today, I choose to live and crawl out of my former shadow-world.

In spite of my newfound bravery, the troublesome issue of Mom's warning pecked at my mind like a hungry chicken. I had no idea what she meant, but I wouldn't sit back and wait for it to happen, either. Eyes open, brain alert, utilize all the help I could get. My new Golden Rule.

Midnight set in as I reached home. I didn't recognize the car in the drive. Immediately panicked about Dad, I shoved a couple of cats off the front porch and reached for the doorknob.

Mr. Cavanaugh leaned over his porch railing. "Tex, is everything okay at home?"

"I really don't know, Mr. Cavanaugh," I blurted out. "That's what I'm about to find out, I guess."

"Kind of late for visitors."

"*Whatever.*"

I pushed open the front door. In his wheelchair, Dad sat next to the sofa. Way past his bedtime.

"Tex…" Concern marked his face. "Where have you been? I've been trying to call you…"

"Sorry, Dad. Mickey makes me turn off my cell phone when I'm at her place. What's wrong?"

Suddenly, someone stood from the chair next to the sofa.

"Hello, Tex," said Detective Cowlings. "We just found Bob Bellman's body down by the Missouri River."

"What?"

Chapter Eleven

"What?" I repeated, dumbfounded. Even though I'd heard the words, they made no sense. I stumbled into the living room and collapsed onto the sofa next to Dad. Hands in pockets, Cowlings appeared ready for a casual stroll.

"A couple of hours ago, Bob Bellman's body was found down by the Missouri River," said Cowlings as he sat next to me. "The KCMO police received a tip—from Bellman's own cell phone—there was a body underneath one of the bridges by the river."

"I can't believe this is happening." Unsure how to react or feel, all I managed to muster was a dull incredulity. "How did he die?" But I knew the answer already.

"Beaten and then strangled…just like the Rimmer boy." Cowlings peered at me inquisitively, hoping for a "tell" in my reaction. I'd never been one with a great poker face.

"Good Lord," Dad whispered. Clearly, the realization that murder had touched him and his family had taken hold. "Did you catch the killer, Detective Cowlings?"

"No…but apparently we didn't miss the perpetrator by much." As he manically scribbled in his ever-present book of clues, I snuck a peek. My underlined name sat atop one of the pages.

"The Kansas City, Missouri Police Department gave me a call after they sent a squad car down to the river and found his body," he continued. "They saw he was a Clearwell student, and this was the second murdered victim from there." He glared at me while flapping the notebook against his thigh. I really hated Detective Cowling's dramatic pauses.

"So…is it the same killer?" I asked. "The same one who killed Matt Rimmer?"

Dad sat in stunned silence.

"It sure looks that way, Tex." Cowlings picked a piece of lint from his suit pants and studied his finding. "Unless…there are *two* killers." I half-expected a dramatic musical *zing* to take us to a commercial. Alas, no commercial break for me.

"Anyway, I drove down to the crime scene." Now speaking like a jovial uncle who's had too much to drink at Christmastime, Cowlings grinned. A scary grin. "A homeless man had phoned in the tip. Apparently, that wasn't the only thing he did…" Another dramatic pause. I wondered whether he picked up this technique from police training to make suspects nervous, or if social awkwardness caused it. I decided my first guess to be more likely. It certainly made *me* nervous.

"The homeless man was sitting under the bridge, trying to stay warm by covering himself in old blankets and boxes. He saw a car pull up and a male got out, who then proceeded to open the trunk and drag a large bundle out, dumping it quickly, and then taking off like a bat out of hell."

"Well…you have a witness, now," said Dad. "Isn't this a big break in the case?" Dad looked hopeful, also applying what he and I learned from watching crime shows.

"You would think so," said Cowlings. "However, the witness was no help at all. He was smashed out of his mind, and the only useful piece of information we got out of him was that the perpetrator was male…and I'm not even sure that was reliable."

"Wait, you said you had a tip?" I said. "From Bellman's phone? Does this mean someone *else* called in the tip? Using his phone? Could it have been the murderer?"

"Sounds like a pretty good episode of *CSI* you've got there, Tex," Cowlings said. "I wish we had more to go on. No, the homeless man snagged Bellman's phone and his shoes for himself. He also tried to wrestle his jacket off him, but gave up halfway through. Bellman was a big guy, and at dead weight, a drunken homeless man wouldn't get too far. Instead of cutting his losses, he called the police, hoping for a reward. He didn't much care for my reward of a burger and fries…" Cowlings smiled, reflecting on the memory. "Anyway, he's lucky he got that because he tainted the hell out of the crime scene." He turned toward me like a cat prepared to pounce on an unsuspecting mouse. "So far, we have no clues…and one more body."

"Why are you *here*, Detective?" Dad asked. "*What* can we do for you?" Obviously getting pissed now, Dad fired up his Protective Mode, set to stun.

"Would you mind if I talk to your son in private, Mr. McKenna?"

"Absolutely I would mind. He's a minor still, and I believe it's the law that I be present if this is a police matter. Anything you talk to Tex about, I have a right to hear as well!" Dad's hidden reserves of strength never cease to surprise me. While he takes a beating, he rises to the occasion immediately after. *Go, Dad*!

Cowlings' smile flipped over into a sneer as he undoubtedly silently cursed the crime shows we watched. "Well, technically, this isn't *truly* a police matter in which you need to be present, Mr. McKenna..." Cowlings paused, thinking better of it. "Okay, you win." No moss on Cowlings, he realized he wouldn't win against an irate father, and he'd probably gain more cooperation if he kept matters friendly. "I just have a few quick questions for Tex." Dad rolled around in front of us, a referee in a boxing match. "Where were you tonight, Tex? Kind of late for a school night..." The book flipped open again, as Cowlings alternated scribbling and glancing furtively at me.

"I was at Mickey Goldfarb's house."

"I've already *told* you that, Detective," said Dad. We now formed a wary circle (okay, triangle) of predators, each one with a different goal and enemy in mind, close enough to feel each other's heated breath—and emotions.

"I understand that, Mr. McKenna," said Cowlings. "I just needed to hear it from Tex. To make sure he's not in trouble. Now, Tex, who is Mickey Goldfarb, and why were you there so late?"

"She was a friend of my mom's," I said. "I recently found out about her and wanted to hear more about my mom."

"Yes, I was sorry to hear about your mother. My belated condolences to you and your father." Although the sentiment seemed genuine, I wished it weren't during an interrogation. "But you were there until almost midnight?"

"That's right. I guess time really flies when I talk about my mother." I looked to Dad for backup, and he nodded reassuringly.

"I see. Would this...Mickey Goldfarb be able to back up your story, Tex?"

"Yes. But I wouldn't contact her until morning. She's an old woman...and kind of cranky."

Cowlings smiled. "Good. I hope it checks out."

I fished into my wallet for Mickey's address Dad had given me several weeks back. "It will. Here's her name and address."

"Thanks." Cowlings eyed the paper skeptically and then placed it into his jacket pocket.

"Surely, Detective, you don't think Tex had anything to do with the...murders of these boys." I hated that I'd added one more thing for Dad to worry about.

Cowlings shut his little black book and weighed his words carefully before speaking. "If it's any consolation, Mr. McKenna...Tex...I really don't *want* to think Tex had anything to do with this." He craned his head, looking at us both in turn. "But, *please* understand something. Tex's name keeps coming up when connected to these two boys. And with Bellman's running over his friend..." He flipped open his book to check a fact. "...Ian Stapleton...well, some people are already talking about Tex as having motive."

"No...oh, no." Dad shook his head slowly, looking as if he'd just aged several years.

Always quick to turn a bad situation around, Cowlings added, "But, I'm not 'some people.' I don't put much weight on gossip and personal vendettas. If you ask me, no, I don't believe Tex is who I'm looking for. But I have to follow up on everything." He turned his attention to me. "I'm glad you have a solid sounding alibi for tonight, Tex."

"Um…thanks?"

"Too bad I can't say the same thing for your friend, Olivia, for the night Matt Rimmer was murdered." The master of hope deflation, Cowlings took home the gold medal. "Her alibi is pretty much non-existent. Her mother tried to verify Olivia's whereabouts, but I know she was working the night in question. However," he chuckled and rolled his eyes, "I've never seen anyone so enthused to not have an alibi and be considered a murder suspect. I don't think it was her, either."

I smiled. "That's good…but don't tell her that."

"Yeah, I get that." Cowlings and I laughed as Dad looked on, puzzled.

"Now, the best thing that came out of Ian's mishap," continued Cowlings, "is he definitely has a rock-solid alibi for tonight. I haven't talked to Olivia or Josh about tonight yet, but I'll get to them. I have a few other…well, leads, I guess…to follow that I think are more urgent."

I didn't understand why Cowlings shared so much about his case with me. Maybe he thought I might be a good source of inside information. Or he just wanted to put our minds at ease. Good luck with that.

He got up to leave but not without one last dramatic sting. "Something's not quite right here, Tex, and I think *you* understand that."

I did feel something wrong, something off, and not just because my mother warned me earlier about imminent danger. Somehow, someway, these murders involved me. And the only possible link I could think of…both victims had bullied me.

Turnabout being fair play, I delivered a dramatic pause before speaking. "Detective, I can see why you're suddenly seeing my name everywhere. If you're talking to other kids at school, and I'm thinking the football team, in particular, of course they're going to throw my name around. I found out today they blame me for Bellman being expelled from school."

He raised an eyebrow. "Yes, I've been talking to some football players."

"Again, I can tell you neither my friends nor I had any real connection to Matt Rimmer…and if he could, he'd probably tell you the same thing. The Bellman story is different, as you know. But we would never, *ever* murder anyone. The *only* possible thing that connects us to both murders is we had the unfortunate luck to be victims of those bullies."

Satisfied, Dad sat back and entwined his hands across his chest. "Well, Detective, are we done here?"

"Yes. For now. I'll see myself out." He walked toward the door, swung it open, and said, "Be careful, Tex. For whatever reason, it seems the killer has now entered your orbit." Quietly, he pulled the door shut behind him.

Still facing one another, Dad and I stared about the room, not knowing what to say. Nearly one a.m., I felt too wired to sleep.

"Son…Tex? Is there anything else you want to tell me? Anything at all? Are you holding back anything from that detective?"

"Dad…no. You don't really think I have anything to do with this mess, do you?"

"No, of course not. I just wanted to make sure you weren't...forgetting something important...or protecting one of your friends." *Ah, that's what he thinks.*

"Dad, you know *everything* I know." Not completely true—he didn't know about the fire extinguisher encounter, but I felt that tidbit rather irrelevant at this point. "And you know my friends. They wouldn't *do* this."

"I know, I know...you're right." But Dad didn't look too reassured. "What was all that about Olivia's not having an alibi...and being excited about it?"

"Dad...come on, Olivia's no murderer!" He narrowed his eyes intently, so I realized I needed to elaborate. "Look, everything Olivia does is usually weighed in terms of what political or social concerns she's championing at the moment. Lately, she's been rallying against authority figures for being sexist."

"I don't understand..." He probably thought how girls had changed quite a bit since his high school days. I guess I understood that. Olivia still puzzled me at times.

"Well, when some authority figure—say, Cowlings—considers her worthy enough to be a murder suspect of a guy, literally twice her size...I think she sees this as a positive victory for womankind."

"I still don't understand it..." he said, a tiny smile hovering over his lips, "but she doesn't sound like the murderer of the century, either."

"No...she's not." I couldn't wait to tell Olivia about this. She'd appreciate Dad's questioning her notoriety.

"Son, do you think you should maybe stay home

from school tomorrow?" The creases on his forehead rippled, each wrinkle representing a different worry.

"No. I can't run away from the boogeyman. It's giving in to terrorism." I needed to maintain my new vow to face life and live it. Of course, my constant terror stayed glued to me like a shadow. "School goes on, and so does life."

"Fine… But I want you to call me at lunch and when you get home. Deal?"

"All right, deal."

"And, son? Be careful…I mean it."

"Always, Dad." I gave him a reassuring pat on the back and he returned the favor, although I don't think either of us felt very reassured.

****

Before I slept, I needed to text my friends. With the wee hours upon us, I'd probably wake them up, but if they didn't know about Bellman already, they sure needed to.

My phone had been off since about eight. The message indicator lit up with ten messages…all from Olivia.

—Omigod call me! Did u hear? Where r u? I need 2 talk 2 u!—

No sense in finishing them. Obviously, Olivia'd heard the unsettling news. No word from Ian or Josh.

I sent out a text to Ian and Josh first:—*Hey, did u hear about Bellman?—*

Then I called Olivia as I knew she'd be awake.

"*Omigod*," she screamed. "Where have you *been?* Did you *hear* about Bellman? It was on the news and—"

"Olivia," I said in a hushed voice, "calm down.

187

You're going to wake your mom." Out-of-breath, she panted as if she'd just run a marathon. "Yeah, I just had a visit from Detective Cowlings. He told me they found Bellman's body down by the river."

"What happened to him? Did he kill himself? Did he kill Matt Rimmer and then kill himself in a love pact or something?" I couldn't tell if Olivia was being serious or just had way too many nervous hours to concoct this crazy scenario. I thought *wouldn't her explanation solve a lot of problems to everyone's satisfaction?* Then I quickly erased it from my mind, as it seemed a little too unnecessarily vindictive.

"No. It looks like whoever killed Rimmer also killed Bellman. He was beaten and then strangled." I could feel Olivia's disappointment through the phone. I believe she thought all along Bellman had done in Matt Rimmer. "Some homeless guy found him, and he messed up all the evidence and was too hammered to provide any real information."

Silently, Olivia processed this. "Do Ian and Josh know?"

"No, I don't think so. I texted them, but they're probably asleep. Ian's probably conked out on some wonder drug."

"I've got to call them," she said excitedly. "Ian'll be happy!" Sadly, I agreed. I guess I couldn't really blame him.

"O', don't call them. They're probably asleep. They'll find out soon enough in the morning."

"Whatever. You know, this means there's a serial killer in Clearwell! And he's going after football players. *Omigod,* I wonder if it's someone we know?" Amped up on adrenaline—and probably caffeine—

Olivia managed to put into words something I wanted to desperately avoid. "Does Cowlings think you did it, Tex?"

"I don't know. Maybe. I do think he's one of the good guys and just wants to find out who did it. He commented on your lack of alibi, though…" An uncontrollable grin spread across my face.

"Get *out*," she yelled. "I was home alone again tonight."

"Well, he's going to talk to you, probably soon."

A small silence weighed very large. "Tex, *what* does it mean? I mean…really? Do you think *we're* in danger? Or just the football pigs?"

"I think we need to be careful." Mom's unearthly warning echoed in my mind. "As long as there's a killer, taking out students…I'd say we need to watch each other's backs more than ever."

"We always do. Wow! I really don't know *how* to feel about this…" She sounded as dazed and confused as I felt.

"I know what you mean. Part of me thinks this is some scary, sick crap. But the devil on my shoulder is telling me Bellman won't rise to terrorize anyone ever again, so it's a good thing…and I feel a little guilty about that."

"Yeah, as crazy as it sounds, I feel the same way. But, you know Bellman would be laughing if it was one of us, right?" I wish I could share her method of justifying her guilt.

"Oh, I'm sure you're right," I said. "But it doesn't matter, 'cause we're better than Bellman."

"Damn skippy!"

"O', it's late, and I need to get to bed. But do me a

favor, will you?"

"Sure, anything."

"Carry your backpack with you, wherever you go from now on, okay? And try and help me convince Josh to do the same thing—"

"What's *that* all about?"

"I'll explain it all to you tomorrow, all right?"

"Okay…whatever. Later." She hung up.

To protect my friends, it's about damn time I explain my witch status to them and what I wanted to do. I could trust them. It felt like a betrayal by not doing so. Let the Witchcraft Rules be damned, my friends had a right to know. More importantly, they had a right to survive. And if I faced ridicule and mockery from them…well, it's worth it if it meant keeping them alive.

Chapter Twelve

Before I climbed out of bed, I checked my phone.

—*Dude!*—the one message read from Ian. Still not a word from Josh.

I directly rang Ian's cell phone, hoping he wouldn't face the wrath of Nurse GoodBody. "Hey."

"I can't believe it." Voice back to ear-banging decibels, Ian didn't rein it in a bit, pretty much elated. "My dad called me first thing this morning and told me the news! Do they have any idea what happened?"

"Looks like whoever killed Matt Rimmer got Bellman, too." With one eye on the clock, I didn't want to be late for first class. And I needed to free up my cell phone in case Josh or Olivia tried to get a hold of me. "Cowlings hit me up at home last night and filled me in with the gory details…he was beaten and strangled."

"Wow…just…wow. I really thought Bellman killed Rimmer."

"Yeah, I think all of us kinda thought that." Phone glued to my ear, I rushed downstairs, popped some bread in the toaster, and multi-tasked the crap out of breakfast. At the table, Dad slowly ate his way through a bowl of cereal.

"My dad seemed kind of…pissed, in a way," said Ian. "He wasn't going to get his day in court. I think he was looking forward to that." I imagined Ian's dad, ranting at the heavens because a serial kill stole his sweet revenge.

"Yeah. Look, Ian, I gotta get my dad to work. Just remember, the threat of Bellman is gone." I pulled open the refrigerator to grab some butter, stuck my head in, and lowered my voice, "But this means there's still a psycho out there. You still have the bottle I gave you, right?"

"Right."

"Well, keep it with you wherever you go, okay?" I shut the refrigerator door, feeling Dad's eyes knifing into me.

"Whatever, I already said I would, Tex. Hey, let me know what happens at school today. I can't wait to hear." For the first time, maybe *ever*, Ian sounded as if he wished he could be there.

"No worries."

"Hey, I get out tomorrow and get to go home. They said I could probably go back to school next week, too."

"Great, ass-hand." I couldn't help but smile, even though Dad grimaced at the language. Whatever. I'd heard him yell a few choice words himself when he broke a dish or got a splinter.

I hung up and wolfed down the toast, while Dad impatiently tapped his watch to let me know we were running late.

"Ian's going home tomorrow," I managed between bites.

"Good news. I still wish you'd stay home today."

"No can do, Popperoo. Besides, I have an algebra test today." I didn't, but I knew he wouldn't argue against the dictates of scholarly pursuits.

I swallowed the last bit of toast, tossed the napkin

into the pedal bin, and checked my text messages one last time. I still hadn't heard anything from Josh.

****

After I pulled into the school parking lot—nearly twenty minutes before class, as I didn't need to avoid Bellman any longer—I leisurely strolled up the sidewalk. I brushed past *Principal Who-Are-You-Again, good morning, nice day, whatever, gotta go,* standing on the steps. I suppose the principal thought it'd be reassuring after the tragedies the school had faced. Sorta we would be comforted by his authoritative presence. Whatever. Half the students didn't even know the man from a sock.

At her locker, Olivia stood isolated, edgy, at unease. Anxiously, she looked around like the proverbial lost sheep, her usual larger-than-life persona on break.

"Tex, thank God! Josh hasn't made it yet, and he's not answering my texts."

"Yeah, same here. Maybe he overslept and missed his ride or something." Josh had four different methods of getting to school—the school bus; his parents, if they weren't running late for work; me, on occasion; and his preferred mode of transportation, his skateboard. Since the weather held up decently today, I'm sure he would've opted for his board, so my argument about missing a ride didn't hold much water.

"I'm scared." Olivia's visible eye captured a glazed-over sheen to it as if she hadn't slept the night before. "I mean, he's gotta have heard about Bellman by now, and he would've been all over the phone with us."

"Let's not worry yet." But I didn't feel my words,

couldn't believe them. "Hey, we got time; let's go see if he called in sick at the office." I didn't know if they'd divulge that information, but we had to try. I grabbed Olivia's arm, bracelets clanking around her wrist, and dragged her through the crowd of students. A multitude of faces bestowed upon us even more attention than we'd ever had before at Clearwell High. Groups of students huddled around their lockers, stopped their conversations to stare at us as we passed. Hushed whispers followed in our path, chasing us like the vengeful ghosts of Matt Rimmer and Bob Bellman. I finally understood why Olivia had looked so...*scared*. It hit me we were apparently the student body's number one murder suspects. *J'Accuse!*

I quit dragging Olivia and instead placed my arm protectively around her shoulders. Seeing Olivia truly scared for the first time since I'd met her frightened me even more. Nobody put Olivia in a corner.

After we pushed open the doors to the office, the pelican glare of Mrs. Carbody blasted us with visual bullets. Busy sorting papers (or pretending to), she hovered over the greeting desk (from Hell!), and finally stopped to glower at us.

"Yes?" As always, Mrs. Carbody looked archaic in her outdated paisley-patterned dress, ready to explode at the seams.

"Um, hi, Mrs. Carbody." Man, I hated coming here. "We're, like, worried about our friend Josh Berillo. He's not here, and kinda wondered if you might, maybe, tell us if he called in sick today?"

Her face broadened into a sickly, condescending smile. I halfway expected a fish tail to flop out of her pelican-like jaw. "Well, now, it's against school policy—as you may or may not know—for students to be privy to this information." She emphasized the word "privy" by raising her inflection to a bird-like shrill.

To our left, the large, foreboding door of doom swung open. Arville Hastings, in his monstrous yippee-kay-holeness, loomed in the doorway, leaning against the jamb, arms folded. A half-grin cocked up the side of his square head.

"Look, Carbody," said Olivia, regaining her fire, "Josh is our friend, and we're worried, so I think that gives us an in to your '*privy*'!" She screeched the last word in imitation of Mrs. Carbody, whose smirky grin swallowed into pursed lips.

"Mrs. Carbody," I said calmly, trying to do my best good cop routine since Olivia already owned the bad cop gig. "Surely you understand with these unfortunate… tragedies that have happened lately, we're just concerned about our friend's well-being?"

Mrs. Carbody stared at me and then looked to Hastings, who took it all in with amusement. Good times. He nodded to Carbody and mumbled, "Fine."

Olivia blurted out a victorious, "Hah!"

Obviously angry at being overruled in her domain, Mrs Carbody returned to her endless paper shuffling, slapping the piles on her desk.

"Well, let's see. Berillo…Berillo…Berillo…" Eyes on Olivia, she blindly turned the papers over. "Here we are." She smacked the stack of papers, a physical embodiment of an exclamation point.

"Why, yes, indeed. Mrs. Berillo called in for Josh this morning. He's *sick*. If it's fine with you, may I get back to work?"

Olivia snorted at Mrs. Carbody's Victorian

melodrama, but relief sung clearly in her outburst.

Hastings barked, "Get to class…it's about to start."

Arms linked, we bolted out of there, trying to beat the bell. We parted ways, and I made it to sociology with only three minutes to spare.

Time enough for one last text to Josh.—*Sorry yur sick. Let me know how u r.*—

****

Usually so locomotive, Mr. Jensen ambled into the classroom, holding a large cup of coffee. He looked tired as he squeezed into his chair. Leaning back, the chair groaned. Thumb and finger supporting his face, he gazed at us wearily.

Great, here comes another tear-jerking session where we hear about the greatness of Bob Bellman from classmates and have to express our innermost feelings on sudden and unexplainable death. Susie, resplendent in her cheerleader uniform, sobbed silently, head buried on her desk. A particularly hard week on Susie. Oddly enough, no one rushed forward to comfort her this time.

I looked at Ian's empty chair. My friend would be back soon, edgily scrunching back and forth behind his desk. Sure, he'd have his casted hand permanently wired up into the air, like the kid the teacher never called on, but I couldn't wait. I missed him.

Finally, Mr. Jensen, baggy-eyed, set down his coffee cup and said, "Okay, open your Soc books to page 199. Start reading Chapter Five…" He grabbed a stress ball off his desk, squeezed it repeatedly, the whiffing release of air the only sound in the room.

Wow, a complete turnaround from the parade thrown for Matt Rimmer's death. Maybe the powers that be told Mr. Jensen to keep it on the down-low because they didn't want to panic the school. Or since Bellman had been expelled, it would've broken some sort of school rule to rave about the great loss of the king bully. Or maybe—just maybe—some wise teacher thought it'd be in poor taste to honor Bellman after what he'd done to Ian. Either way, I was hellishly glad we didn't have to sit through a day of praising the wonderful legend that was Bob Bellman.

Experiencing a hard time concentrating, I endlessly reread sentences that didn't register, total jibber-jabber. Distracted by Susie's crying and the air deflating from Jensen's tennis ball, I looked around the classroom, not the only one. A few students stole glimpses at me, some rife with distrust, others filled with dread. I knew they thought I'd killed Bellman. A sudden crazy-ass insight smacked me as to what it must've been like to be Bob Bellman—feared and hated by other students. The outrageous irony dug deep I hid my face in my book and didn't look up again until the bell rang.

****

I suffered a long and strange morning until lunch break mercifully arrived. Now or never, I told Olivia to meet me at my car at lunch. I had no idea how she'd respond to the news that I'm a witch. Total dread.

Josh's no-show at school raised my dread levels to off the chart. Yes, his mother had called in sick for him, but why didn't he respond to my texts? I stepped up the frequency in sending my messages.

—*Are u ok? Where r u? Call me!*—

Maybe he didn't want to text me at school for fear I'd get my phone taken away from me. But, now, I didn't really care.

197

A boulder of fear slammed through my stomach, I met up with Olivia at her locker.

"Hey," Olivia greeted me. "God, has everyone been weirder than crap with you all day? Like you're a huge freak show or something?"

"Yeah. Creepy. I never thought people would think of me as a killer, but...I can clear a room like *that*!" I snapped my fingers. People stepped out of our way, Moses at the Red Sea. "Have you heard from Josh yet?"

"No..."

"Okay, I'm calling him." Phone held to my ear, we walked into the parking lot. After six rings, I got dumped into voice mail. "Josh, give me a call. I'm getting kinda worried."

At the Battle Bucket, I opened the passenger door for Olivia. Before I could say anything, she plunged into a plastic bag full of carrot sticks and started gnawing. "What's up, Doc?"

"Okay," I said. "This is going to sound messed up, but there's something I need to tell you..."

Olivia continued to chew on her carrot, watching me expectantly. "Tex, you're not dying or something, are you?" Her eye glistened in the cold day sunshine.

"No, nothing like that. Well, I hope not, at least." I reached for a deep breath and braved myself. "I'm a witch."

She stared at me blankly as if what I said hadn't been a big deal. The crunching of her carrot reached epic proportions of cacophony in the enclosed car. Suddenly, she raised her fist, pumping it in the air. Ah, here we go...took a while to fire up her synapses.

"Shut *up*," she screamed. "What do you *mean* you're a *witch*?" Torn between extreme giddiness and disbelief, her ear-piercing threatened to blow out the Bucket's windows. Her fists shuddered above her, holding onto invisible, anti-crazy handlebars, grounding her from this flight of lunacy.

"I just found out recently. I found out my mom was a witch, and apparently, I inherited her…talents. Or whatever."

"Omigod, shut *up!*" Lunching students passed us, looking in at the commotion. They probably thought we were planning our next murder. "Do *something!* Make Malinowski a toad or *something!*" Her smile broke wide while she contemplated the new possibilities for us.

"O', it doesn't work like that. I can't just turn Malinowski into a frog. Even if that were possible, I couldn't do it because I guess it's getting into black magic, which is a big no-no. I'm not really sure what I can do, at this point. Mickey's been teaching me some stuff, but she's taking her time."

"Mickey? Who's Mickey? Your talking mouse?"

"Mickey's my mentor. She knew my mom and taught her stuff. She knows witch stuff." I gestured toward Olivia's backpack on the floor. "Hey, didn't you wonder what that bottle was doing in your backpack?"

"What bottle?" She began to rummage through her backpack, finally snagging the spell at the very bottom. "Aha! Shows you how much I ever get into my backpack. What is it?"

"It's a protection spell." Olivia started to open it. "*Stop!* It won't work if you open it." She halted and gave it a quick shake.

"*Omigod.*" Her hysterics went into round two. "Does *Ian* know? Does *Josh* know? They better not have found out *before* me!"

"Well...I sorta' had to tell Ian...just to protect him. It was the only way to get him to keep the bottle with him in the hospital. It had nothing to do with trust or anything like that, O'."

"Why didn't you *tell* me, Tex? You *know* you can trust me!" She jabbed me on the shoulder.

"I know. Believe me, there's no one I want on my team more than you—you've always got my back. But Mickey told me sometimes if you tell a person about a spell, it'll lessen its impact and may not work."

"Whatever." She shrugged. "But, you better not keep any more secrets from me."

"I promise."

"Okay, when are we going to start your witch education? I want in on this. I can be like your apprentice or something!" Damned determined to headline "Project Witchcraft," I couldn't stop her. Actually, the thought of sharing my witchcraft education with her comforted me.

"Well, I don't know how Mickey will like it if you come over." I knew well she would definitely *not* appreciate it. "But, maybe you can help me with research and practice and stuff."

"*Omigod,* this is so gonna kick *ass*," she screeched.

My cell phone buzzed.

A message from Josh that chilled me:—*I'm scared*!—

—*Josh*!— I wrote back. —*Where u been? What's wrong?*—

I let out a huge sigh of relief as I held the phone up to show Olivia. As an afterthought, I texted, —*Nothin to be scared about. Bellman's gone.*—

I sent the message and felt instant relief.

"Come on, O'," I said. "It's time to go back to the hallowed halls of Clearwell High for some fine learning experiences."

****

During the rest of the afternoon, I constantly peeked at my phone to see if Josh had written back. By the time gym class rolled around, full-on panic set in again. Maybe he's just really sick. My paranoid alter ego kept nudging me in the other direction, though. Since when would being sick keep a dedicated texter like Josh down?

And just *what* was he afraid of, anyway? Surely, he'd heard the news about Bellman by now. While getting ready for gym, I quickly shot out another text to him: —*Have u heard Bellman's dead?*—

Probably not the most sensitive text in the world, but, hey, it got the message across efficiently. Stomach-churning silence responded.

I bucked the no-call during class school policy and rang Josh. Dumped to the robotic message woman again, I hung up and flung my phone into the locker. That did it. After school, I'd drive over to his house before I dropped Olivia off.

That particular gym class proved horrifically long. As we did nothing but run laps around "The World's Smallest Indoor Track" the entire hour, my mind worked itself up into a lather of overblown hysteria. I honestly didn't even remember running as I watched the clock on the gym wall tick by slowly. Surely I'm just letting my imagination run out of control. But a deep, gnawing feeling in my gut—not unlike hunger— told me something different.

****

I practically dragged Olivia down the hall by her arm. "Wait a minute, dammit," she said. "I've got to grab my backpack. And quit pulling me around like I'm your damn suitcase!"

"Oh, crap, sorry." Totally driven, I didn't realize my brutish behavior. We pulled a u-turn toward her locker. "I'm just really, *really* concerned about Josh. We need to get over to his house asap."

The corners of her mouth curled down, her eyes flashed with alarm. "Okay." She grabbed her backpack and slung it over one shoulder. I don't know how she carried it, as it looked heavier than her.

We swam through the ocean of students, shoals of apprehensive minnows parting before the killer sharks. I tossed her bag in the Bucket's back seat and sped out of there, carefully trying to avoid a repeat performance of mowing down a student.

Even though a cold November day, sweat beaded my brow. "Seems like we've made a lot of getaways in the Battle Bucket lately," I said. "Good thing she's trustworthy." I knew Olivia hated when I referred to the Bucket as female, but I thought to lighten the mood. I failed miserably.

"Your car's not a her," she said emotionlessly under her breath. "What do you think's wrong with Josh?"

"I'm not sure. He's not acting right, and he's scared." I raced around a corner, bounding over a curb. I cursed, hoping it wouldn't flatten the tire. "Try and call him again, would you?"

"Sure." She tapped the speed dial option. "No answer."

"Yeah, that's what I've been getting all day." A trail of leaves swirled up behind us as I rocketed along.

Finally, we pulled in front of Josh's house. The driveway sat empty, not unusual. Both his parents worked during the day, and his brothers were away at college. But the sight of the front door open wide on such a cold day froze me with fear.

"Oh, crap…" I jumped out of the car and dashed through the yard toward the front door. In my haste, I'd forgotten to let Olivia out and heard her cursing from the Bucket. In seconds, she scrambled out of the driver's side.

"Josh?" I yelled through the open door. "Hey, Josh, man, where are you?" The door looked as if it had been kicked in. The flimsy deadbolt had given away along with a piece of trim. My heart pounded in my chest, wanting to burst out and run back to the safety of the car.

"Oh my God," whispered Olivia when she saw the damage to the door. Her hand flew to her mouth as if wary of hurling. Carefully, we stepped inside and surveyed the interior.

"Hello!" I yelled through the hallway to the left. We peered into the living room, where the TV and gaming console lived. No sign of Josh in there, his usual habitat. My breathing skyrocketed into realms of irregularity, like an out-of-shape man on a treadmill. Olivia took my hand, ignoring my sweat-drenched palm.

Other than the front door, the house appeared normal enough. We approached the long, narrow staircase leading up to Josh's bedroom. I strained, peering up into the shadows at the head of the stairwell.

Slowly, we climbed the steps, each one creaking softly, complaining of our offending weight. At the top of the stairs, I saw Josh's closed bedroom door. "KEEP OUT" read his homemade sign. If only this prophecy claimed truth.

I pushed open the door. Unmade covers twisted and strangled across the bed. For a teenage boy, Josh always kept his room shockingly immaculate. The full-length mirror at the foot of his bed had fallen over and smashed on the floor. A drawer jutted out of his dresser, clothes strewn across the room. The top of the dresser sat barren as if someone had swept an arm across it, the debris lying in a sad heap on the floor. Josh's favorite skateboard lay on its back next to the bed, the wheels up toward the ceiling like a dog waiting for its belly to be scratched. That seemed the eeriest sight. I couldn't help but think this one stubborn dog waiting for its master to come home would be disappointed. A struggle had taken place here, with Josh nowhere to be found.

"Tex, what if there's someone still in the house?" Olivia whispered.

I thought about searching the house, but what next if I found the culprit? What would we do? Yell "Aha! Caught you!" and wait for sudden death and strangulation?

Too frightened to speak, I squeezed Olivia's trembling hand with my own. I gestured for her to follow me. On the way out of the war-torn remains of Josh's bedroom, I grabbed a brown turtleneck off the floor as an afterthought. Olivia shook her head and raised her free hand in a questioning fashion. I held a finger to my lips and led her slowly down the staircase.

My legs quivered as if I'd just endured a monster workout.

I really didn't want to do it, but I thought a photo of Josh might come in handy, the one on the refrigerator door. We stepped across the landing, bypassing the damaged open door.

"Go wait for me in the car," I whispered.

She shook her head. It's nearly impossible to argue with Olivia in full voice, and trying to do so in mute silence proved hugely futile. I gave up, and we entered the kitchen.

The kitchen floor linoleum squeaked with every footfall, a mouse-like warning about our intrusion. Amidst a blur of photographed smiling faces of various family members covering the refrigerator, I plucked a head and shoulder shot of Josh. Not a particularly spectacular photograph by any means, but it showed Josh smiling sheepishly. I knew why his parents cherished the photo. It captured Josh brilliantly. His large eyes stared off into the horizon—seeing all and doing absolutely nothing—conveying his warmth, quiet inner strength, and deadpan sense of humor perfectly. I tried to rearrange the photos slightly to make up for the missing space and made a silent vow to return the photo when I could.

A low rhythmic banging from the basement door shattered the silence. On instinct, I whipped around. Still connected at the hand, Olivia tumbled after me, almost falling into the refrigerator. She tugged on my arm and whispered, "Let's go!" Teetering side-to-side, she resembled a child performing a "potty dance."

The banging stopped. My heart raced again, paralleling the earlier thumping sounds. I considered checking out the basement and then thought better of it. Probably just the plumbing. We needed to get out of there. Before we messed anything up. Or before something worse happened.

Clamping my two acquisitions to my chest, we tiptoed out of the kitchen. The thrumming from the basement blared out again, kick-starting us into a panicked gait. I bashed into hanging pots and pans, knocked over a lamp in the living room, and leaped through the front door.

Once we tumbled into the car, we were breathless. Olivia locked her car door and I followed her lead.

Pale as a Kabuki actor, I reached over to hold Olivia's hand. We sat in terrible silence, our rapid breathing the only sound on that quiet, cold day from hell.

I whipped out Cowlings' card from my wallet and dialed the number.

On the second ring, he answered. "Detective Cowlings."

"Detective…it's Tex…Tex McKenna…" I waited for his response.

"Yes, I remember you." He chuckled. "You're the only Tex I know." His tone shifted suddenly from amusement to suspicion. "What can I do for you?"

"We're at Josh Berillo's house… He's missing, and it looks like there was a fight…or something in his room." My words jumbled together. "I think someone kicked in the door!"

"Where *exactly* are you now, Tex?"

"We're in my car in front of his house." Olivia fidgeted with a long strand of hair, twirling it around her finger repeatedly.

"Wait…did you go *in* the house?"

"Yes, then we got out as fast as we could!" Cowlings had a way about him that made me feel everything I did always proved the wrong move.

"Okay," he sighed. "Is there anyone else in the house? Or parked nearby you?"

I looked around even though I'd previously scanned the neighborhood. "No…no, I don't think so. But we didn't look everywhere in the house." A chill ran down my spine as I conjured an image of a killer lurking in the basement.

"Stay where you are. I'll be there in ten minutes," he said and hung up.

After five minutes, a patrol car pulled up behind us. Via the rear-view mirror, I watched a young, lone police officer talking on his radio. Ever so slowly, he got out of his car and walked toward my side, one hand on his right hip.

Anticipating him, I rolled down my window. With her head craned back, Olivia blatantly watched his every move.

"Tex McKenna?" he asked, although it seemed like more of a declaration.

"Yes, hi, that's right." I squirmed on the car seat, not comfortable being this close to the long arm of the law. "I'm the one who called Detective Cowlings a little bit ago."

He stared at both of us long and hard, then leaned into the car slightly, his hands now resting on the windowsill. "Okay. I'm Officer Bensen. Wait right here until I come back."

"Sure, okay, you got it," I said, trying not to sound like a crack addict or whatever. Of course, the harder I tried, the worse I sounded. "Um, be sure and look upstairs first, and then we heard something in the basement and…um…"

Officer Bensen locked his stone-cold eyes on mine.

"Ah…okay. We'll be waiting in the car." I splayed my hand about the car for unnecessary clarity.

Bensen pulled out his radio, sputtered some indecipherable words, and cautiously approached the open door.

"Tex, you sure have a way with the cops," said Olivia.

Soon, a brown Cadillac parked on the opposite side of Josh's driveway. Cowlings stepped out, skillfully pulling his overcoat on with one arm while reaching in his suit jacket pocket for his notebook with the other hand.

He nodded at me in a half-hearted salutation, pulled open the back door, and scooted in. "Tex. Olivia," he said. "You'll be glad to know I contacted Mrs. Berillo, and she should be here shortly."

Suddenly, Cowlings dropped the pleasantries. "I'd rather not continue to find you kids involved in what could possibly be bad situations." I thought about this impossible-to-decipher sentence and had no idea how to respond.

"Detective, our friend is missing," I said into the rear-view mirror at Cowlings. "We *don't* want to be involved in bad situations either!"

Olivia turned around, facing Cowlings, one jean-jacketed arm draped across the seat back. "You *really* don't think we had something to do with this, right?" I guess her enjoyment of her fifteen minutes of fame as a murder suspect had ended.

I finally realized how stupid I felt to have a conversation with a rear-view mirror and twisted around in my seat. "Detective, we're wasting time here! I mean, it's obvious something's happened—something *bad*—and we just want to find our friend."

"So do I. Tell me—from the start, whenever you determine that to be—what happened." He snapped open a new notebook. I wondered if he now had a library devoted solely to me.

I told him everything, except for my grabbing Josh's shirt and photograph. He didn't say much, nodding here and there, scribbling haphazardly. By the time I finished, Officer Bensen stood at the front door, wearing gloves and waving to get Cowlings' attention.

Cowlings slid out of the car. He, like Bensen before him, leaned into my front window, both hands firmly placed on the windowsill like an angry carhop stiffed on a tip.

"I'll tell you what, guys," he said not unkindly. "I'm going to let you go home now. I know it's been an upsetting and a long day for both of you. Keep your cell phones on, but stay *home*. Be careful. Do *not* do anything to impede my investigation." He straightened and placed his hands on his back as if it pained him. One final time, he poked his head down inside again, his confidence seemingly lacking this time. "I'll find Josh," he said, then hesitated. "I just want you both to be realistic." He looked as if he debated finishing his thoughts. "Okay?" Apparently, his discretion won out over blunt truthfulness.

"Okay." But we weren't going home.

I drove a block before either one of us spoke. "Sorry, O'. We have to make a stop first. Time's important because Josh could be counting on us."

"Where are we going?" she asked.

"To Mickey's."

She stared at me, first with fear, and then confusion set in. Finally, she grinned and yelled "*All right*!"

Hang on, Josh. The cavalry's coming.

Chapter Thirteen

On the way to Mickey's house, Olivia tried her best to pump us up with her unflagging optimism. "Yeah! With your witchy mentor's help, we'll find Josh in no time." Although I appreciated her valiant effort at keeping the faith, I couldn't help but recall Cowlings' rather ominous final words about "being realistic." Because I ain't nothin', if not realistic. But maybe a faint glimmer of hope lay in my witch status…and how's *that* for "being realistic?"

"I hope so, Olivia." Pretty much by-the-numbers, I drove in a half-lucid dream state. I couldn't think straight or even concentrate on the traffic surrounding me. My reflexes dulled, my senses numbed, and nothing seemed as it is or should be. The world as I knew it stopped making sense. Olivia said something else, and I couldn't hear her through the overwhelming sense of dread and fog clouding my head, my only certainty that terrible danger claimed my friend.

I snapped out of my reverie when we reached Mickey's house. Her white picket fence acted as my guiding light, welcoming me up the path to Josh's salvation. Despite the freezing turn of the weather, her flower garden still thrived in life-affirming full bloom.

I suddenly realized I hadn't called Mickey, and even worse, I brought a stranger to her home. I fervently hoped they'd hit it off, and Mickey wouldn't mind. Boy, talk about naïve.

I knocked on the door. "Mickey, hi. It's Tex." I hoped to forego our usual game of "knock knock, who's there?" The endless clatter of the chain signaled her arrival as Olivia and I shuffled, trying to stay warm in the chilly wind.

She yanked open the door and immediately frowned. "Dammit, Tex, you're supposed to call."

"Sorry, but it's an emergency. We need your help." Olivia stood behind me on the small porch, sneaking furtive glances at the neighborhood witch. "This is my friend, Olivia."

Olivia nodded politely and said, "Hi. Tex has told me a lot about you."

Mickey peered at Olivia through her glasses. "Oh, he *has*, has he?" She burned Olivia with a slow, judgmental take as if she were a rotten side of beef. She lingered on Olivia's spider-webbed leggings. "It's a little late for Halloween, isn't it, girl?"

Olivia let out an irritated huff. "Yes, it is, so maybe you should take your mask off!" *Oh boy.*

Stunned by the personal attack, Mickey glowered at Olivia. She chuckled once, built momentum into a loud bray, and polished it off with the inevitable coughing fit. "Heh! Good for you, girly. Come in then. You're letting out the heat!" She pinched my arm and shooed Olivia in with a flourish. When she slammed the door with a bang, her cats shot upstairs to safety.

"Tex, you didn't tell…this girl everything, did you? You know it harms the potency of your…work."

"Yes! *This* girl has been told everything," said Olivia sarcastically. "And *this girl's* name is Olivia!" Her visible eyebrow arched down toward her nose.

Time for Fireman Tex to put out some fires. "Mickey…it's *fine*. I had to tell Olivia about my being a witch because we're in trouble." Mickey exaggeratedly whipped her head between the two of us. "It's okay…she believes," I added meekly.

"Well…I suppose the damage is done," she said with a loud sigh. "What trouble are you in this time? It's always an emergency with you, kid."

"Our friend, Josh…he's missing. And I think he's been taken…or worse." Hearing my words brought back the terror we'd been operating under for the last ninety minutes. "We need to find him…*fast*."

"Oh. I see." Lost in thought, Mickey scratched her chin, one eye cocked toward the ceiling. "Okay. Sit down."

Out of the corner of my eye, I saw Olivia fishing for my attention but thought it'd be rude to return her astounded smirk. I put my hand on her back and ushered her to the sofa. She sat with a wind-rushed *flumph.* Quietly, she said "Whoa" while sinking deep into the depths of Mickey's devouring sofa. I returned a knowing glance. Mickey disappeared into one of the back rooms while chattering to herself.

"Tex, what's going on?" whispered Olivia. She grabbed my arm, forcing my full attention. "What are we doing?"

"I really don't know yet."

Mickey reappeared, her pink slippers flapping, holding a large map and what looked like a green pendant.

"Tex, move that coffee table out of the way," ordered Mickey.

I flipped up out of the bowels of the hungry

cushions—a trick I learned from Mickey. I did as told, careful not to knock over the various knick-knacks on the table.

"Now, I saw you brought in a sweater or something," she said. "Was that the boy's clothing?"

"Yes." I unfolded Josh's turtleneck. "I also brought a photo." I waved the photo in front of Mickey as solid proof. At the time, I had no clue why I had thought to bring these two items from Josh's house. Maybe I had read about it in one of my undercover studies, or chalk it up to witch's intuition.

"Well, we don't *really* need a picture. But sometimes it helps. Good boy, Tex." She smiled approvingly at me, her obedient puppy. "Spread out the map."

Olivia jumped up and helped me straighten out the map over the floor. A large, very detailed map of the Greater Kansas City metropolitan area unfurled before us. I spotted Clearwell and noticed that even tiny alleyways were shown.

"All right, now…you, Olivia," —She extended a gaunt finger in her direction.— "Give me that chain you're wearing."

Olivia unfastened the plain, thin silver necklace and handed it to Mickey. "Um, will I get it back?"

Mickey grabbed it and exhaled noisily, ignoring Olivia. She quickly tied the green pendant on the end of Olivia's chain. "It helps that the chain's from a friend. Tex, grab my fire poker."

I snagged a rusty fire poker from a small copper scuttle, the only tool there. I passed it to her, handle first.

She squeezed the turtleneck tightly to her chest.

214

She mumbled a litany of words in a barely audible tone, head tilted toward the ceiling, her eyes shut. "Okay, what's your friend's name again?"

"Josh. Josh Berillo." Olivia hovered behind me, slack-jawed in awe.

"Lemme have that picture." Mickey placed the sweater on the floor beside the map. With cat-like speed, she grasped the photo from me and repeated the turtleneck ritual. She then took the pendulum and chain in one hand, letting it dangle about an inch above the floor while wielding the poker in the other.

"Is today Thursday?" she asked in a low, even monotone. The pendulum awoke from its neutral position and bobbed up and down.

"Is it Halloween?" She popped open one eye, peeking directly at Olivia. Olivia rolled her eyes. The pendulum began to swing back and forth, to signify no.

"Okay, good," said Mickey. She stepped onto the map carefully, her slippers crinkling the paper. "I should probably get this laminated," she said to no one in particular. "Is Josh Berillo now in the vicinity of this map?" The pendant responded with a wide-swinging *Yes*. She walked toward the Clearwell area. "Is Josh Berillo now in Clearwell?"

No, answered the pendant, flinging back and forth. Olivia pressed her fingers to her mouth to stifle a gasp.

Mickey walked in circles around the map, stopping at large areas, repeating the question over different vicinities. She had worked her way toward the center of the map. The pendant continued to respond with *No*.

"Is Josh Berillo now within the North Kansas City area?" The pendant answered with a definitive *Yes*. I sat up on the edge of the voracious sofa, Olivia joining me.

Mickey suddenly stopped dead and said, "Wait a minute." She tossed the pendant to me as she ran out of the room, the back ends of her slippers slapping loudly.

We both studied the pendant. I wondered if I should ask the pendant if Josh was still alive. But I chickened out. I really didn't want to see the pendant deliver a very final *No*. Besides, maybe the pendant was aligned—or whatever—to Mickey and only Mickey.

"Tex, this is *creepy*," whispered Olivia.

Not knowing what to say, I nodded in agreement.

Mickey rushed back into the room, another couple of maps tucked under her arm. She deftly kicked the larger map aside and instructed me to spread out one of the new maps. It was a detailed map of the North Kansas City, Missouri area. Mickey once again went through her routine until the pendant settled on an industrial area by the railroad. She asked about specific streets, but the pendant began to swing in small circles.

"Hmmm," she said, finally addressing us. "My spirit helper is either tired...or unsure. That's what it means when the circles begin. But I have it narrowed down to between Ninth and Twelfth Streets, on the East Side by the railroad tracks." She grimaced at us painfully. "That's probably all I can do for you kids with this. Unless...you want to ask something..."

I knew what I wanted to ask but didn't dare. Olivia swallowed hard and blurted out, "Ask if Josh is all right!" I grabbed her hand, and we held on tight.

"Are you sure you want to do this?" Mickey asked. I've learned when Mickey issues one of her half-warnings, it's best to heed it. Instead, we both nodded, unable to find our voices.

Mickey hesitated. Her shoulders sagged briefly as

she cleared her throat. "Is Josh Berillo all right?" The pendant stood absolutely still for one long, agonizing moment. It began to slowly wobble, unsure of which way it wanted to go. Its movements became more pronounced, more confident in its resolve. Back and forth, a dog's rhythmic wagging tail, the answer definitively stated *No*. The pendant came to an abrupt stop the way I thought my heart might. Olivia crumpled, her shoulders shuddering as she buried her face into my arm. Too stunned and defeated to cry, stone-cold shock negated any emotion.

"I'm sorry, kids," said Mickey. "Maybe my spirit guide isn't always one hundred percent right." But she didn't sound very sincere at all.

A sick, cold gut instinct told me to believe in the spirits.

After a few minutes, my shock trickled away as a profound sense of loss tidal waved its way in. A salve to my crushed soul, tears of loss and rage unleashed. Olivia and I huddled together, hugging, sobbing. Mickey, no longer the Iron Queen of Witchcraft, appeared befuddled, uncomfortably out of her element. She didn't have a spell to handle two crying teenagers in her home. Her efforts at consoling us felt awkward, sadly comical at best. She tentatively patted our shoulders, issuing hollow condolences, such as "He's in a better place," or "Josh's life isn't over yet, you know," which of course, just made matters worse.

When the tears ran their course, I realized whatever the outcome should be—and maybe, just maybe, hope still persisted—we needed to quit wasting time blubbering and call Cowlings. I gathered Josh's photo and shirt and helped Olivia off the sofa.

"Mickey," I said, my voice still shaking, "I have to call the police about this." Through my swollen eyes, Mickey looked like a blue-topped blur.

"Well, I agree. But you know…you should make the call anonymously. You don't want the cops nosing about your business of witchcraft. That's what your mom did those years back when she helped to find that kid who went missing." She wiggled her lecture finger, although with my impaired vision, I saw two digits. "What're you gonna tell the cops how you knew where to look for your friend?"

She made sense, but I couldn't make any logically based decisions now. "Okay, we'll call anonymously."

"And be careful of what phone you make the call from," she warned. "According to my stories, they can trace *any* phone now. I'd use a payphone." Mickey rubbed her chin again, shrewdly concocting a plan to outsmart the police. "I think there's one down at the Shop-Kwik, still."

"All right."

"And be sure and disguise your voice," added Mickey. The criminal underworld really lost one shrewd crime lord to witchcraft.

"Okay. Thanks." The awkward and inevitable moment of not knowing how to end our visit set in. I didn't know if Mickey still found hugs taboo because "Mickey don't *do* emotion." I gambled. She responded with her uncomfortable half-hug.

"Go make your call and then go home and sleep," she said. "That's an order." She looked at both of us.

Unbelievably, Olivia threw her arms around Mickey's neck. Holding on for dear life, Mickey acted as her emotional life preserver. As light as a feather,

Mickey caressed Olivia's back. Olivia started crying again and buried her face in Mickey's shoulder.

"I…um…I didn't think your spider-web stockings were really all *that* bad." Over Olivia's trembling shoulder, Mickey gave me a helpless look. I bet she'd received more hugs this week than since birth. I let them hug it out for another minute before I interjected.

"Come on, Olivia. We've got to go make a phone call."

On the way to Shop-Kwik, Olivia's focus clawed its way back. "You think Josh is dead, don't you?" The directness and coldness of her question took me aback, although it shouldn't have, considering the source.

"Truthfully? Even though I don't want to say it? Yes." I glanced over at her, and she looked as if I had just struck her. "Maybe I'm wrong, O', but…you know me, I hate giving out false hope." I reached blindly for her hand and latched onto it. "I've become a big believer in Mickey's world of spirits." I told her about contacting my mother. She stared out the window silently.

"Besides…if Josh is down by the railroad tracks," I added, "that doesn't give me much hope at all. Why would he be alive and not contacting someone?"

"Maybe…maybe he's being held by someone," she said.

"Maybe." This scenario opened a whole new world of terrors as I imagined the worst implications possible. I hastily changed the subject. "Hey, do you think you're up to making the phone call?"

"Sure. But why me?" A little bit of life sprung back into her.

"Well, I think Cowlings may recognize my voice."

I almost added "and because he no longer suspects you," —but Olivia didn't need another blow.— "And I can't disguise my voice very well." She nodded in agreement.

Mickey proved right about the payphone at Shop-Kwik. When you grow accustomed to living with your cell phone, it's funny how you actually forget about things like payphones.

We parked in front of the shop and I gathered some change from out of the Bucket's ashtray. While I deposited fifty cents into the phone, Olivia glanced about conspiratorially. "Don't forget to disguise your voice," I said, as I dialed Cowlings' number.

Our faces pressed together closely, we hovered over the phone receiver. "Cowlings," answered the detective on the third ring.

"Yes, I say, is this Inspector Cowlings?" She spoke in an outrageously stereotypical Cockney accent. I rolled my eyes.

"Yes it is," he said hesitantly. "Who am I speaking with?"

"Never you mind that, guv'nor! Oi've got a clue for you to follow up on, then." She scrambled for the paper with the street numbers on it. "Look for that missing lad, Josh Berillo, down in the ol' North Kansas City industrial area. Say, somethin' loik between Ninth and Twelfth Street, then. By the railroad tracks." Olivia owned her performance art. Her head swayed back and forth as she unrolled her hand in the air with a royal flourish.

"Why don't you tell me how you've come by this information and my name and number, please?"

"Afraid Oi can't do that, guv. But please…hurry,

inspector!" With that, she slammed down the phone, and we high-tailed it to the Bucket.

I shook my head in disbelief.

"What?" She threw her hands into the air.

"*Honestly*, Olivia. Bleedin' Mary Bleedin' Poppins, ain't we now, guv?"

"*You* said to disguise my voice!" Despite everything, we both managed a slight grin.

I pulled into Olivia's driveway and turned off the ignition. We let the encroaching darkness outside devour us in silence. The trees in Olivia's yard stood as naked reminders of their past lives, their shed skin of leaves blanketing the once green lawn.

"Looks like you've got some yard work ahead of you," I finally said. Best not to leave Olivia on a down note.

"Yeah, you better get on it for me," she shot back. We contemplated the mass of leaves and thought it could wait, the last thing on our minds. "Tex...what are we going to do?" A tear touched her eye, a glistening jewel, sad, yet beautiful. "I mean, if Josh is really...*gone*? What are we going to do?"

"I...don't know." I gulped, trying to be strong and failing miserably. As the truth that Josh may be out of our lives forever settled over me, my voice cracked. "I know...I'm going to miss him..." My words faded away. The endless parade of tears marched onward again. We sat in the car sobbing, uttering sad remembrances of Josh.

Olivia scooted across the seat closer to me. She cradled my face in her hands, leaned in, and kissed me. I kissed her back, taking warm solace in her soft, wet lips and her fresh vanilla fragrance. Our arms wrapped around each other. The inside of the windshield fogged as our breathing became more pronounced, more unified.

I pulled back, gently placing my hands on her shoulders.

"What's the matter?" she asked. Her hand jolted up to her mouth. "*Omigod*, is it true, Tex? Are you *gay*?" Like an old horror movie damsel in distress, she held the back of her hand to her mouth in shock.

"*What*? No. What are you *talking* about? Look, several weeks ago, I had a normal life, I guess. Now I'm a witch…a murder suspect… I've lost a friend…" I released a brief anguished sob. "And I'm afraid for our lives."

"I know. I understand…I just thought…you and I…" she trailed off, appearing ashamed in her assumption.

"*No*! It's not you, Olivia. I *do* like you. I may…even feel more than that for you…" I swept her hair aside so I could see both her eyes. "Let's just get through this…all this *shit*…before we decide whether we… I don't want to be like that couple in a horror film that ends up making out because all their friends are dying around them." I managed a meager smile and wiped away what I hoped was the last of my tears.

She returned my weak smile, a hint of hope playing around her lips. I leaned in and hugged her. She placed a light, lingering kiss on my cheek. "You're right." She released her arms from around me and lowered them to her lap, staring at them like a chastised schoolgirl.

"I think about you. I want to think about *us*. But right now, there's just too much confusion…too much fear…and a whole lot of unknown stuff I hate to even think about."

"Okay." We stared out the window. She reached in front of her and drew a small heart in the rapidly dwindling condensation on the windshield. She looked at me and smiled shyly. *Since when had she ever been shy about anything?*

I grinned back. It took me all this time to realize I loved her. Soooo dumb. *But I've gotta stay focused.* "We'll circle back to this, Olivia, I promise."

"We'd better."

"Hey, listen. Your mom's at work, right?" She nodded. Suddenly, it felt like business as usual. "Maybe you'd better come with me to pick my dad up and have dinner with us until she gets home." The thought someone had abducted Josh while he was home alone made me fearful for her.

"Okay, now you're just being crazy. Obviously, you forget I can take care of myself." She dug into her giant purse and plucked out a can of pepper spray. She splayed her massive array of keys between her fingers, reminding me of mammoth bear claws. "*Snikt*," she said.

"I know you can take care of yourself, but we really don't know what we're facing here. I mean, Josh was...*is*...pretty resourceful as well."

"I'll be okay. I've already got Cowlings' number—and the local cops—put onto speed dial, and I never leave home without my trusty phone."

"All right," I sighed. "Just call me if anything—*anything*—goes weird or something. And put the bottle spell under your pillow and keep it there. It's supposed to be most effective there for whatever reason."

"Dealio," she said. I got out of the car and quickly

raced to her side, letting her out. I gave her another hug, this time full-bodied. And maybe I lingered a little too long.

"*Omigod*! I just remembered! Josh's backpack—with his bottle spell—is in his locker at school. Do you think that's why…" She didn't finish, but it wasn't necessary.

"I don't know. Could be. Please…put yours under your pillow, okay?"

"I will." She ran to her front door. With a glance over one shoulder, she shot me a quick, dazzling smile before she went in.

I barely made it in time to rescue Dad from work. As always, he acted genuinely happy to see me. I wondered if I should tell him about Josh, but didn't want to worry him needlessly. Then I remembered my parents using that same excuse for not telling me about Mom's cancer. Quite a hypocritical little witch boy. Also, I've learned Dad can be a good ally in certain situations, and really, couldn't he be in danger himself, maybe? After what happened to Josh, anyone could be a target.

"Dad, something happened today," I said very deliberately. "It's Josh. He's gone missing…and I think someone snatched him."

Dad's hands rested on top of his legs before falling to the Bucket's seat as if he lost control of his muscles. "Oh, no…not Josh…no." Dad liked Josh and found him to be respectful and not nearly as "wild a card" as Ian.

I debated telling him how witchcraft played a part. I had the feeling the topic made him uncomfortable. But, I'd been wrong about people before, so I forged ahead and told him everything. I definitely spared him my earlier spiritual encounter with Mom, though.

Anguished-looking throughout my recounting, he just nodded thoughtfully at appropriate times. When I finished, a protracted calm filled the car. For a while.

"You think Josh…has been killed?" Dad shook his head. "How did this happen? Josh was a good boy…." He appeared ready to cry. I hoped he wouldn't, as I'd had more than my fair share of tears today.

"I don't know, but we alerted Cowlings, anonymously. He's looking into it." He gave me a despairing look. I felt he didn't share the faith I had in Cowlings' capabilities.

"Tex, this is serious. You've *got* to be careful. I don't know if it's safe for you to come home after school by yourself. Maybe you and your friends should all stay together until all the parents get home."

"I thought the same thing, but Olivia already punted the idea." I now regretted telling him everything. "Don't worry, Dad, I *will* be careful. Any sign of a problem, I'll have the cops all over it."

I could tell this didn't allay his fears. "Son, I want you to be careful with this witchcraft stuff, too. Don't get in over your head." He looked at me, cautiously sizing up the situation to see if he'd overstepped any boundaries. "Just be careful. That's all I'm saying, and I'll leave it at that."

Upon arriving home, I noticed the "cat pack" out in full force. I brushed a handful of cats off the porch with the back of my coat arm, carefully avoiding skin contact. "Sorry, Dad. Apparently, I'm neighborhood catnip now."

To my surprise, Dad nodded casually and said, "Yes, your mother used to have the same problem."

We ate in silence as I stared at the phone positioned beside my plate, mentally urging it to ring. I wanted news, but I also dreaded the inevitable finality of what I expected to hear. Neither of us felt like watching TV, so I excused myself early and went to bed. I texted Olivia and Ian—home now and ready to return to school on Monday—to touch base.

—*Right as rain*— Olivia returned immediately.

—*Can't believe I'm ready to go back to school!*— texted Ian.

I decided Ian should hear the news about Josh via a human voice so I called him.

"What's up?" he answered, more jovial than usual.

"Ian, I have to tell you something…it's about Josh." I told him the heart-rending tale.

"Bastards." Ian's righteous anger stoked his defense mechanism against falling prey to vulnerable emotion. "Josh…" he said before falling quiet.

"I know… I'll let you know when I hear something. But I don't expect it to be good." I hung up and nervously paced the floor. I held my phone at arms-length, anxiously checking it every few seconds to see if I missed a call.

About eleven fifteen, the phone rang, startling me even though I expected it. I answered on the first ring.

"Tex…it's Detective Cowlings. I'm sorry to call so late, but I knew you were waiting for my call." He hesitated, coughed once. "There's no other way to tell you this, Tex, but we found Josh's body down by the railroad tracks in North Kansas City. I'm sorry."

Oddly, I reacted with cool calm, probably because I'd been prematurely wrapping my head around this news for the last eight hours. "No. Josh…" I tried to feign surprise and shock. But I just felt dead.

"If it's any consolation," Cowlings continued, "it doesn't look like Josh was beaten like the other two boys. He was strangled. And it looks like he went fast and didn't suffer." Some words of consolation. The idea of poor, innocent Josh being strangled to death didn't exactly bring me peace of mind. "That's what's odd," said Cowlings, brainstorming aloud, "I'm not so sure we have the same killer here."

Great, I thought, now we're dealing with *two* killers? "How…how'd you find him?" But I knew the answer.

"That's another strange thing, Tex." His voice tightened considerably. "We received an anonymous tip from a girl pretending to be British." A long pause stopped our conversation, as I visualized Cowlings whipping out his overused notebook. "*You* wouldn't happen to know anything about that, would you?"

"*No,*" I blurted. When I'm caught off guard, my love of the English language fails me miserably. "I'm not a girl…or British!" *Way to go, Tex, that'll get him out of your hair.*

"I hate to do this to you…" He released a long sigh. "But I'm going to need to talk to you and your friends tomorrow. Will you be at school? I know it'll be hard on you…but I'd recommend your going. It actually might be the safest place for you and your friends."

I nearly let rip a lunatic's laugh at the irony of school as a safe haven. Last week I had feared for my life at Clearwell high, and now, Cowlings presented it to me like a shiny gift-wrapped present full of comforting safety.

"Yeah, okay, I guess so," I said.

"Needless to say, I hope you and Olivia can account for your whereabouts after you left Josh's house, right? I assume you *did* go home when I told you to." Cowlings delivered this assumption like a military officer to a subordinate who'd blatantly ignored direct orders.

"Well, I did make a quick stop at my friend Mickey's house."

Silence again. I imagined him counting to ten, trying not to lose his cool. "Ah yes, Mickey…Goldfarb." I heard the flippity-flip of his fact-checking through the phone. "She's certainly quite the charmer, isn't she? You have some strange friends for a teenage boy."

I'll just bet *that* had been a fun encounter for Cowlings. "Well, strange is more interesting, sometimes." I suspected my goodwill with Cowlings had about run dry.

Cowlings said he'd talk to me tomorrow and hung up.

I called both Olivia and Ian with the conference call option.

We talked through the night, sharing many stories, laughs, and tears. God, yes, there were tears. And anger. Anger was expressed frequently as we wondered why such a terrible thing could happen to someone like Josh. Out of the four of us, he was by far the sweetest, and thus, the most vulnerable to any situation. We wondered why he didn't call the cops and guessed his fear of anybody in an authoritative position won out.

I didn't share this with the others, but a very unsettling notion threatened to swallow me alive. What if Josh *did* call the cops? And what if a cop was the killer? It seemed a stretch, but the message my mother sent me—*Trust none*—kept clanging in the back of my mind like Quasimodo leaping onto his large bell.

But mostly, we shared great stories about Josh. I guess you could say we held our own personal mini-wake for him. When the conversation would turn hateful——or morbid—I'd steer my friends back to what made Josh so great. Yet, all the while, my mind kept churning over a horrific image of Josh, staring upward with his round, innocent eyes and the last image he would have seen. Someone strangling him. Maybe someone he knew. His last thought, *Why*?

Olivia wanted to bail out on school tomorrow, but I told her of Cowlings' warning. She hesitantly agreed to go. I made sure Ian's mother would be at home with him throughout the day. We got off the phone at nearly three-thirty in the morning, and I still couldn't sleep. Finally, I drifted off and dreamt about Josh during last summer, the best of times, when he taught us how to skateboard. The dream played out like one of those gloriously hot, comforting summer days we shared as we took turns falling and bruising and laughing until the sun went down. Then Josh quietly and effortlessly stepped onto his skateboard, the wheels rolling of their own accord, and slowly drifted up the street and over the hill, waving sadly until he was out of our sight.

When my alarm went off, I realized I'd been crying in my sleep.

Chapter Fourteen

Still numb, I stumbled down the stairs and met Dad for a quick, silent breakfast. He still fought for me to stay home today, but I gave him Cowlings' explanation about it being safer at school. Begrudgingly, he agreed.

Dreary-eyed and foggy-minded, I made my way to school. I'd downed three cups of coffee, but all the caffeine in the world couldn't wake me up enough to fully face the next seven grueling hours. Parked in the lot, I checked in with Olivia and Ian.

—*I'm here, at least physically*— texted Olivia.

—*I'm ok*— responded Ian.

All right, everyone should be safe for another seven hours at least.

As I sleep-walked into sociology, Mr. Jensen watched me. Once I sat down, he came over to talk quietly to me.

"I'm surprised you're here today, Tex. I'm truly sorry to hear about your friend, Josh. I didn't know him, but I understand he was a good kid."

I just nodded vacantly, rather than run the risk of crying at school. It all seemed like a bad dream, the discomfiture compounded by my lack of sleep. And even though Jensen tried his best to make me feel better, it only made things suck more. I felt light-headed and a little nauseous.

Jensen briefly placed his bear-claw hand on my

shoulder before returning to his desk.

"Quiet down, class," he said, glancing furtively around the room. "As you all know by now…we've lost another student…Josh Berillo." He paused, looking in my direction. "Does anyone want to express their feelings?"

How the hell do you think I *feel*? I realized Mr. Jensen didn't intend to make a horrible situation awkward, but that's what it turned into. No one raised their hand or said anything.

"Tex, would you like to say a few words?" I knew it. And dreaded the hell out of it. A lump birthed in my throat.

"Josh was a great guy…" All I could muster before I lost control. Everyone watched me, expecting more, but I couldn't continue. I looked down at my open textbook and shook my head slowly.

"Okay, then, let's get started," said Mr. Jensen.

Now I was pissed. I knew Josh as a quiet guy and didn't know many—if any—of the students in this classroom, but surely one of them had something to say about him. And no fanfare and hullabaloo for Josh? When Matt Rimmer died, they damn near threw him a memorial parade. I could understand their skipping the glory for Bellman, but not Josh. Would it have hurt them to announce over the intercom? Did they really think Josh didn't matter as much as Rimmer, simply because he lagged in popularity and didn't play football?

I almost threw up. Ready to ask Mr. Jensen to be excused, the intercom buzzed and beat me to the punch. I hoped I'd get summoned to Hastings' office again; at least I'd get out of this claustrophobic nightmare. As if confronted with a gorilla in the zoo, my fellow students heeded the zookeeper's warning to avoid eye contact with me for their own safety.

Sure enough, Jensen hung up the intercom and once again approached me.

"Tex, you're wanted in Mr. Hasting's office," he said softly. "Would you like me to go with you?"

"No." The last thing I wanted. I just needed to get the hell out of there. I snatched up my book, threw it in my backpack, and stumbled toward the hallway, feeling the gazes of the curiosity-seekers burning a hole in my back.

As I walked down the long hallway, the searing neon lights guided the way. Rings pulsated around the lights like they did when I'd gotten too much chlorine in my eyes from swimming. I cursed Hastings and company for ignoring Josh's murder and built up quite a bit of rage, Ian style.

When I opened the office door, Mrs. Carbody slapped a handful of papers down on her desk. She tilted her head and looked at me expectantly.

"Yes?" she asked, smiling ever so slightly and ever so sourly.

Without saying a word, I ignored her, walked to Hastings' door, and pushed it open.

Hastings sat at his desk, shooting eye daggers at me. Detective Cowlings straddled the edge of the desk with one leg dangling down. Spread on the desk in front of them lay Josh's natty, blue canvas backpack. The beer bottle protection spell stood straight up on Hastings' desk like an out-of-place buoy in the desert.

Hastings leaned back in his chair and entwined his fingers behind his square head. "Richard...are you and your friends practicing Satanism?"

Oh, crap.

"*No!*" I said, a little too emphatically. "Why would you even ask me something like that?" Nothing had prepared me for this. Thinking fast on my feet came hard enough, but due to emotional trauma, this felt nearly impossible.

"Would you care to explain this?" Hastings picked the bottle up and rolled it around between his thick fingers.

Cowlings looked on disapprovingly. "Ah, Mr. Hastings, please don't touch the bottle anymore." Hastings cocked an eyebrow up, glared at Cowlings, and set the bottle down on his desk.

"What is that?" I asked. Then I thought I didn't want to leave Josh open for accusations of Satanism, so I quickly—maybe stupidly—changed my story. "Ohhhh…*that* must be one of the good luck charms I made at my friend's house." I rubbed the back of my head as if it aided my sudden recall.

"And which friend is this, Tex?" asked Cowlings. Already prepared for me, his notebook sat open in his lap and his pen poised. "Please explain…"

"'Tex?'" asked Hastings while staring at Cowlings. "Why 'Tex'?"

Cowlings gave Hastings an annoyed look and went back to writing. "Go on, Tex."

"Let's see…" I squinted and looked upward. "Some time ago, my friend Mickey told me about an old family tradition of hers—good luck charms—and how to make them. I thought it was funny and asked her to make a couple of them for me. I gave one to Josh." I attempted to smile to show good times. "But, really…*Satanism*? We would never get into anything stupid like that." Sweat formed on my forehead, augmented by the amount of coffee I'd had.

"Uh-huh. And when did you make these good luck charms?" asked Cowlings.

"I really can't remember…" I said. "Quite some time ago, though."

"You really can't remember?" Cowlings repeated. He looked at me suspiciously and with obvious disappointment. "Tell me when."

"I guess it wasn't too long ago, but I really can't recall. It was just something to do, really…we don't actually believe in good luck charms." I needed to sit down, so I wouldn't fall. Then again, I didn't want to get too comfortable. If I remained standing, I could get out of there quicker.

"When Mr. Hastings unlocked Josh Berillo's locker this morning, he opened up the bottle before I arrived," said Cowlings. He tightened his lips into a thin, hard grimace and pulled out a small folded piece of paper from his pocket. "He found this. It looks like a…spell of some sort. Let me read it to you, Tex, and see if it helps jog your memory." He yanked his glasses out of his front pocket and put them on in one quick motion. "'I neutralize the power of Bob Bellman to do Josh Berillo any harm. I ask that this be correct and for the good of all. So mote it be.'" Carefully, he put the paper back in his pocket, took his glasses off, and waited for explanations.

"Oh, yeah, now I remember. I think we made them last summer. It was after Bellman attacked Josh in the shower room in the spring." I thought if I allowed for more time to pass, this would lessen the impact of their findings. "You remember that incident, don't you, Mr. Hastings?" My upper lip curled up involuntarily in anger.

"I seem to recall you and the Berillo boy were involved in some sort of skirmish with Bellman," said Hastings, smiling, yet…not.

Ignoring Hastings, I turned my attention back to Cowlings. "To tell you the truth, I hardly remember this 'good luck charm.' It was just something interesting for us to do. We were bored last summer."

"I see." Cowlings twirled his glasses around by the ear-piece. He turned to Hastings and asked, "Mr. Hastings, would you mind terribly if I borrow your office for a few minutes? I have some official police business to talk with Tex about." Hastings stared at Cowlings as if he couldn't believe the cop's gall. "Alone," added Cowlings firmly.

Hastings grunted and slapped his hands on his desk. He stood and faced Cowlings. "I'll be in the hallway if you need me." The door slammed on his way out.

I couldn't help but smile at Cowlings after this showdown. He didn't smile back.

"Tex, just what in the *hell* is going on here?"

"Pretty much what I told you, detective."

"'Pretty much,'" he bounced back.

"Pretty much."

"That's not good enough. I know you're not telling me everything. You're not lying, but you're not telling the truth, either." I thought I saw the bald patch on top of his head turn red with anger.

"It's just a 'good luck charm.' We never even took it seriously. We're really *not* into Satanism or—"

"It's not just this goddamn good luck charm, Tex, and you know it," he said, cutting me off. "Every time I turn around, there you are! You and your friends. I've got three—*three!*—murders on my hands, and you seem to be embroiled in all of them!" He crossed the room and stopped in front of me, his face a couple of inches from mine. "Then last night, I get a tip from an obviously teenage girl—*obviously* doing a terrible British impersonation—about where Josh Berillo's body can be found. How many teenage girls do you know that are involved in this, Tex? I can think of one. Your friend, Olivia."

"Actually, Bellman and Rimmer knew a lot of cheerleaders. Have you talked to them?" A worthless reply, but beggars can't be choosy. And frankly, I didn't much care, anyway.

"Shut the hell up!" I'd never seen Cowlings angry before. He always seemed like a warrior when it came to keeping his cool. "And now, our friend Mr. Hastings stupidly contaminates any evidence we may've found in Josh's locker by digging his fingers into everything. And he's already determined it's Satanic foul play and tells me that's why you kids are the killers!"

My knees gave way, and I collapsed into the chair, unfeeling from head to toe. "Detective Cowlings…we're *not* Satanists…and we're *not* killers…we're just fairly ordinary kids…"

Cowlings violently swatted his hand in the air as if warding off a mosquito attack, I suppose his method of cooling down. Whatever works, just please let it end. He turned his back toward me, hung his head, and stood akimbo.

"Tex, you're making my job *very* difficult. You do

understand I'm trying to catch what some people are now calling a serial killer, don't you?"

I nodded silently, fully understanding this as my best course of action.

"Do you know how many murders I've had to deal with, Tex? Do you? In the quiet, little town of Clearwell, Kansas?"

"Not many…I guess."

"That's right, Tex, and usually—if they happen at all—they're robbery related. But not this case…" He looked up at the ceiling as if appealing to the great gods of justice. "And now, I fully expect our amateur police friend Hastings to start spreading his theory about Satanism. Sure, there're random cases of Satanism in Kansas…but they don't end in serial killings! Soon enough, they're going to send in the FBI, and that's just going to make my headaches even worse!"

"Sorry?"

"And during this *cluster*," he continued, "I have Tex and his friends withholding more knowledge than they're letting on. I don't know if you're playing detective yourself, or something much worse, but it has to stop! *Now*." He walked around to Hastings' desk and sat down. "I don't feel you're the killer, Tex…I don't want you to be and thankfully, your alibis pan out. I've already checked with Mickey Goldfarb about yesterday—another lovely meeting with her, by the way—and now I get the grand pleasure of calling her again to ask her about this…good luck charm. So, not only am I tasked with finding a thus-far impossible to locate 'serial killer'…I also find myself in the unenviable position of being protector to Tex and his crew. I'm not a goddamned *babysitter*!"

"Thank you." I gulped, my throat dry.

"But…it's becoming harder and harder to do. Not only am I trying to keep you alive, but I'm also struggling to keep gung-ho idiots like Hastings from accusing you and your friends. You've got to admit …some of this evidence looks pretty bad."

"I swear to God, Detective, we had nothing to do with the killings."

"I want to believe you, Tex." He stood in front of me, grasped my arm, and yanked me to my feet. "But you've got to start telling me the *truth*." Even though I stood close enough to smell the mint on his breath, his voice lowered to the point I had to strain to hear him. "Everything."

I wondered if I could trust Cowlings with the information about my newfound witchhood. It would certainly help matters…if he believed it. On the other hand, if he *didn't* believe it, I'd pretty much sign my own declaration of guilt as being a card-carrying Satanist and thus, by default, a serial killer. When it came to things otherworldly, I suspected Cowlings put no such stock in the notion. I didn't want to become someone's bitch in prison—so I opted to lie. So much for my newfound belief of "honesty is the best policy."

"I'm telling you everything I know, Detective."

"I wish I could believe you." He sighed and sat down again. "You can go."

"Goodbye," I said quietly.

"Oh, Tex, you know Josh's name may get dragged through the shit-heap once news of this…good luck charm…gets out, don't you?" This ploy smelled like Cowlings' last stab at getting me to tell him what he wanted to hear. It felt sadistic, almost.

It also struck a nerve. I stood in front of the door, dumbstruck. Bad enough that Josh had been murdered and his memory ignored at school. And now, the possibility the muckrakers would haul his name through this murder business, claiming he's a Satanist, and quite possibly involved in the killings, didn't sit right by me. Josh did not—his *memory* did not—deserve this.

Oddly enough, the outer office sat empty. Hastings probably puffed away angrily to some faculty lounge. No doubt, Mrs. Carbody kept busy by—I don't know—pulling hairs out of a cat somewhere or whatever. And the two nameless women who normally lurked in the back were nowhere to be seen, either.

An urge overwhelmed me. I vaulted the front desk and slid to the other side. Dashing over to the intercom system, I quickly figured out how it operated. Practically archaic compared to hooking up some of the electronics we had at home. I flipped on the standing microphone and pressed the button labeled ALL CLASSROOMS.

I cleared my throat as a screeching sound emanated above me over a loudspeaker. I turned the volume down and spoke calmly into the microphone.

"Attention, students of Clearwell High." I had no real idea of what might come out of my mouth. I just knew it had to be done. "I'm sure you're all aware of the sad passing of fellow student Josh Berillo by now. If you're not, well now you are. He was murdered sometime yesterday, and his body was found last night."

Several students—out of class for some reason—stopped to stare at me through the window of the office. Paul Jacobson, the constant stoner, actually pumped his fist in the air as a sign of support.

"For whatever reason," I continued, "the school's powers-that-be have decided that Josh's not worthy enough of a day devoted to him, as Matt Rimmer had been accorded. If anything, Josh Berillo is *more* worthy! Let me tell you something. Josh, unlike Matt Rimmer or Bob Bellman, never insulted anyone, never hurt anyone… never intruded on anyone's private lives…he never judged anyone for who they were, or who they weren't. He was a great guy. And I know some of you know this…and knew Josh…"

More people gathered in front of the windowed wall. A few began to clap. One disembodied voice yelled, "Go, Tex!" From behind the growing throng of students, I could see Arville Hastings' square head bobbing back and forth, as he tried to push his way through the crowd. Not much time left.

"You know what? You know what made Josh so great? He was always there; he always had your back. He was the nicest guy I'd ever met. And he was a skate god!" More cheers erupted from the crowd as Hastings parted the sea of students. "And—like most of us here at wonderful Clearwell High—he was one of the downtrodden…one of the underdogs…one of the guys you people won't go out of your way to be nice to because he wasn't popular. Well…you *suck*!" Hoots, hollers, and whistles ripped through the hallway. "If you learn only one thing from the senselessness of Josh's death, make it this: don't write *anyone* off. Don't do it. Make friends with someone who you've decided is not worth your time. Don't belittle someone for being different, and for God's sake, don't bully them! Do it today. Because I feel sorry for anyone who wasn't friends with Josh Berillo...you don't know what you missed..." I paused, fighting back tears.

The door flew open. Hastings bounded through the swinging wooden door set into the front desk. He came toward me, a furious, charging bull. He snaked an arm around my neck while reaching for the microphone with his other hand. I held the mike out of arm's reach.

"Our fine staff of school counselors is standing by to talk to you about..." Hastings cut me off as he dragged me backward on the rolling chair. Even though I now sat far from the intercom system, he tightened his grasp around my throat. Helplessly, I looked out at the students massed in front of the windows. They stared at the pandemonium, flabbergasted.

"Oh, you're in *big* trouble now, Richard." I looked into Hastings' flaring nostrils, his breath hot on my face.

"That's enough, Hastings," said a voice from behind us. "I think Tex's been through enough today. Besides," Cowlings continued, "you wouldn't want to be accused of student brutality. Particularly, when there're many students watching you right now."

Hastings let me go. He straightened up and noticed the angry and frightened students watching the fracas. Several of the braver students booed.

"Ah, okay, Richard..." Attempting to gain control, Hastings cracked his thick neck. "Ordinarily, I would recommend suspension for such a blatant disregard of school property and authority, but given the circumstances, you'll be given a detention next Monday." He mustered a fake smile, waved to the gathered students to dismiss them, and stormed into his office.

Cowlings bent over and said quietly, "Nice job, Tex. Stupid but nicely done." He tapped my shoulder with his notebook and rejoined Hastings in his office to continue his police business.

I sat there stunned for a moment before I made my way out into the hallway. A few kids cheered their approval as I stepped through the crowd. Kids I didn't even know congratulated me, patting me on the back and ruffling my hair. Several letter-jacketed football players stood, backs against the lockers, scowling at me.

At first, I couldn't help but grin. So, this is what it felt like to be popular. Then I immediately suppressed my smile because I remembered what it all meant. It wasn't about gaining popularity, or even notoriety. It's about the loss of Josh. And about others like him. I hoped to maybe awaken some students' minds about not letting kids slip through the cracks. About not letting them float through school like drifting ghosts, barely visible to most people, making only faint impressions, if any. The elite considered these students annoying flies, buzzing past the immaculately coiffed social status climbers, to be swatted away on their never-ending search for recognition among the popular. The sad thing is that students like Josh have so much more to offer than the thugs and the bullies, but no one gives them a chance, because being popular is the goal that is brainwashed into everyone since toddlerhood. And here at Clearwell High, popular usually equated with sports, cheerleading, money, appearance, or other such criteria that the vast majority of the student body never stood a chance of achieving.

I wondered if I had practiced some of the same

behavior. After all, here were students congratulating me on my impromptu act of defiance. Yet I didn't know them, nor can I say they'd ever made much of an impact on me before this moment. I didn't even recognize some of them. But I could see in their faces the same sense of desperation with which I constantly lived. Sadness, fear, and most of all, a yearning sense of *dammit, world, look at me! I'm here, too!* I felt sick…hypocritical. I, too, ignored some of these other ciphers.

I made my way through the crowd, mumbling my thanks. As I stood in front of Olivia's locker, I pretended to fiddle with the lock, trying to blend in with the walls. I'd never had a problem doing this before, and now, people wouldn't leave me alone. School pariah and murder suspect one day, hero for the downtrodden the next. Back to being bullied tomorrow. I wanted no part of it.

The bell rang, more students piled out of classes, and more well-wishers congratulated me in passing. I guess I shouldn't be so hard on myself and hoped maybe what I said might have gotten through to some of them. Right now, there seemed to be a sense of giddiness in the hallways that the underdogs had won one. And here I spun at the center of this maddening vortex.

But, really, would anything change in the long run? The bullies will be out in full force, probably going after me now more than ever. Fine. I'm just not going to take it anymore. Sure, I may get some bruised ribs, or a black eye out of the deal, but I'm now prepared to pay that price. No one should have to live a life based on fear. And the adult bullies—the vice-principals, the gym teachers, whatever—would they stop their behavior? I doubted it. But what does one do to combat those in charge? What options are open? I did what I could this morning. I knew it wouldn't change their behavior—but maybe, just maybe—it might open the eyes to some of the cool adults and teachers around.

Still…my friend Josh had died. Nothing could bring him back. And at that moment, I hated this school with a passion because, in the long run, I blamed it—its protocol, bullies, *everything*—instead of some faceless psychopath, for letting Josh vanish off the face of the earth.

My head throbbed. Exhausted, the urge to puke hit hard.

A loud shriek shot through the hallway. Olivia rocketed down the hallway, pushing kids out of the way, barreling toward me. She threw her arms around my neck, buried her head in my chest, and nearly knocked me over.

"*Omigod,* Tex! That was *too* goddamned *cool!* Josh would be *so* proud of what you did." She bounced up and down, her flats slapping the floor.

"Shhhh. People are going to think you're trying to kill me." Thank God she came around when she did because what she said made it all worthwhile. I did think Josh would've liked it.

"Tex, everyone's talking about how *awesome* that was. You did Josh *justice*." I found myself the main attraction of every passing student's interest, and Olivia just turned it into a three-ring circus.

"Olivia, cool it."

"Can't help it, can't help it, can't *goddamn help it*!"

"Olivia...you wanna get out of here?" I pulled her arms from around my neck and held them to halt her gymnastics.

"What do you mean?"

"I'm kind of sick over this whole thing. I don't like the hero worship...and I haven't slept for ages...and there's Josh...and I can't even think straight. I want to get the hell out of here."

"*Cool!* Let's bounce."

"Would your mom mind? I mean, if you cut school?"

"*Hellz* no. She didn't even want me coming in today."

"Okay, tell you what...I don't think my dad would care either, as long as we stay together."

"Cool."

"But let's do it by the rules this time. I'm already in enough trouble." The bell rang, threatening the beginning of the second hour. The students lost interest in me and rushed off to their classes. I grabbed Olivia by the hand and led her to the nurse's office.

Surprisingly cool about the whole thing, Nurse Cranky grinned at me. Chuckling on occasion, she seemed somewhat amused by my hijacking of the intercom system. Perhaps she'd been a survivor of the downtrodden back in the day for whom I had become an unofficial poster boy. She made us jump through some hoops and what-not, but I realized that's what her job entailed.

I told her we were upset over our friend's death, and we really needed to go home. Probably providing TMI, I explained to her my mother had passed away, and my dad couldn't drive, so I asked her about the possibility of my driving us home.

"Absolutely not," she said, lips pursed. "You know that would be against school policy." Her small mustache twitched. "Let's see what we can do…"

Luckily for us, Olivia's mom jumped at the chance to pick us up under the stipulation we go to Ian's house since his mother would be there. Through some quick phone-jockeying, Ian's mom gave the thumbs up, and I called Dad to get his permission to do the same. He, of course, acted more than happy to oblige, as there would be four of us together. Safety in numbers and all that. Once again, he would have to have a co-worker give him a ride home, but he didn't seem to mind. I had to leave my car at school, but the Bucket could take a bullet for a day if it meant getting out of there.

"All right, kids," said Nurse Not-So-Cranky-Now. "Lie down on the cots until Mrs. Furman gets here." She hummed some old-time country song and went about her business.

****

Super-amped to see us, Ian greeted us at the door with an ear-to-ear grin, a different look on him. Although black half-moons circled his eyes, nothing dampened his enthusiasm.

"What *up*?" With his arm still extended up in a cast, he resembled the poor guy who no one would high-five.

"Ian… Goddamn, it's good to see you!" Olivia carefully embraced him. With his good arm, he gave me a secret fist-bump behind her back.

"It's great to see you up and around," I said.

Behind Ian stood Mrs. Stapleton, smiling. "Hi, kids, come in, come in." We obeyed, and her smile vanished. "I'm sure sorry to hear about Josh. He was such a nice boy. Are you kids doing okay?" She wrung her hands as if prepping for surgery.

Olivia answered, "We're trying."

Upstairs, Olivia hopped onto Ian's bed while we sat on the floor. Olivia told Ian what'd happened today.

"Ohhhh, shit." Ian kicked his feet in the air, laughing. "Why is it I miss the only good things that happen there?"

"You didn't miss *that* much," I said. "Really…it wasn't much at all…"

"Oh, Josh would've *loved* it," he screamed. Suddenly he stopped laughing. A hush fell over us as we realized Josh would never be able to enjoy even the telling of it.

Chapter Fifteen

A cold, windy Saturday provided the backdrop for Josh's funeral, much too early to be this frigid. I sensed a winter storm looming. Call it witchcraft or just an accurate weather sense, but the way the sky melded several tints of gray with dark clouds speedily rolling in felt like an omen of even worse things to come.

Ian's parents offered to pick up Dad and me, as they knew my car was still at school. The five of us piled into their van and attended the church services. Josh's parents sat in the front pew along with his brothers, back from college. They looked typically anesthetized after their tragic loss. I know the feeling well, having already attended too many funerals for someone my age.

The preacher blathered on about how Josh had departed to a better place and yadda, yadda, yadda. Occasionally, an attendee would rip out an agonized sob, jarring me from my stupor. One poor kid, in particular, wailed throughout the entire service, his anguished howls echoing throughout the large church. I didn't recognize him but assumed him to be an old friend from Josh's previous school, or maybe a cousin. Another kid comforted him by wrapping his arm around his shoulders, tormented shudders bouncing both of them in unison.

We sat next to Olivia and her mother. Impossibly,

Ian, Olivia, and I had cried all of our tears out the day before, given our head start. Only half paying attention to the surrounding proceedings, we sat immobile in stony silence.

After the church services, Mr. and Mrs. Stapleton took Dad home, as he wouldn't be able to get out to the gravesite part of the ceremony. "Tex, you be sure and get a ride home from someone, okay?" he said as I assisted him into the Stapletons' van.

"Yeah, Dad, but I want to go to the Berillo house, and I might try and get my car later."

He looked doubtful and reiterated, "Just be careful." I watched the van pull away as a low rumble of thunder sounded above; the Fates getting restless and demanding to play.

At the gravesite, Red stood not too far behind the Berillos. As the cold wind blew his curly red locks about his face, for the first time since I'd met him, he appeared less than cock-sure about everything. Obviously on the losing end of a macho battle with his feelings, gritting his teeth and looking skyward, he fought against the tears, but they fell like rain, anyway. Over to the far left of Red—to my great surprise—loomed Vice-Principal Hastings and directly behind him, Principal *Who's This Guy Again*. Hastings wore sunglasses (totally unnecessary with the overcast skies) and chomped gum like a cow chewing cud. His hands rested idly within the pockets of his too-tight suit pants, and he apparently couldn't have been bothered to wear the accompanying suit jacket. Principal *Mystery Man* stared down toward the ground, his hands folded in front of him in a well-rehearsed display of respect.

The turnout made me happy. With at least seventy

people in attendance, I recognized half of them as Clearwell students, a lot of whom I vaguely knew by passing them like ships in our high school ocean. I'm ashamed to think I'd underestimated the number of kids Josh called friends, as they all looked appropriately devastated.

Not one to miss a party, Detective Cowlings lurked in the background. Respectfully, he kept his distance and didn't join the gathered mourners, but he remained painfully obvious, particularly while scratching away in his omnipresent notebook. On occasion, I'd sneak a peek his way and catch him staring back at me. The wind whipped what little hair he had up and over, thus negating the effect of the cue ball cover-up. Didn't fool anyone anyway.

The thunder continued to bubble up throughout the ceremony, but it didn't rain. Nature having a good yuk, warning us that at any minute, we would be at her mercy.

When the ceremony concluded, I approached the Berillo family, the hardest thing in the world. Instead of comforting words, I gave both Mr. and Mrs. Berillo long, hard hugs, the kind of condolences I wish I'd received at Mom's funeral.

"Tex, who would take my boy from me?" Mrs. Berillo gargled her words with wrenching sobs. "Who would do this? *Why*?" She pulled back from our embrace, peering into me as if I had the answer.

"I don't know, Mrs. Berillo." For her benefit, I sought strength. Didn't work. I only found anger. "But I'll find out...I'm going to find out." All I could muster. My vow of vengeance probably didn't supply much comfort to the Berillo family, but I needed to try and do something about it. *Way* past time.

Ian and I hitched a ride from Olivia's mom to the Berillo house. I didn't look forward to the gathering, but I had to go. I remembered when Mom died, and people came over to the house after the funeral. An endless wave of well-wishers spouted the same useless clichés over and over. At the time, I remembered thinking *how are casseroles supposed to help?* But I soon realized I misplaced my anger onto these visitors, who were obviously just as uncomfortable with loss and sorrow as me. When you're forced into it, everyone finds a different way of coping.

Packed to the rafters with friends and family, the Berillos' small house was eerily reserved and quiet, a far cry from the rollicking family meals I'd enjoyed there in the past. Josh's twin brothers grabbed me by the arm and dragged me into the hallway for some privacy.

"Tex, do you have any idea who's responsible for this?" asked one of the brothers. I wanted to respond with his name, but I never could tell them apart. Muscle always looked the same to me.

"No. I don't." I shook my head. "It's just…weird." One of the brothers grimaced as if I belittled the impact of Josh's death.

"Could it've been one of the bullies who picked on Josh?" asked the other one. Well into their third stage of grief—anger—they were primed and pumped for some ass-whooping. As much as I would've enjoyed sending them after someone like Johnny Malinowski, I figured it best not to fan any sort of mob mentality, deserved though it may be.

"I've no idea. It may or may not have been one of

Clearwell's bullies. It just doesn't make *any* sense."

"If you find out anything…I mean *anything*," said brother number one, "you call us." He slipped me a small piece of paper with their cell phone numbers on it. "We're going to be in town for a while, helping Mom and Dad…and stuff."

I verbally agreed although I wouldn't call them. The thought of more violence flipped my stomach like an omelet. There'd already been too much bloodshed.

Clearly out of their element, Olivia and Ian stood in the kitchen as I rejoined them. Ian appeared ready to bolt. "Dude," he whispered, "this *sucks*."

"I know, but we need to be here for Josh."

I had to replace Josh's photo on the refrigerator. At the moment, we were alone in the kitchen, so I discretely tacked his photo back on the refrigerator. His visage stared back at me serenely. I dragged my thumb across it and whispered, "Goodbye, Josh."

The atmosphere of morbid sadness and despair permeating the house grew tangible. Poor Mrs. Berillo couldn't stop crying. Her husband joined her on occasion, his entire body racked with violent spasms. The twins circled the house, their rage building, fire stoking their eyes. Guests delivered their condolences to the Berillos and whispered their suspicions to others. Gossip quietly and quickly spread, heads shook condescendingly, and lips tightly pursed in disgust.

I felt stifled. I needed to get out of there. Very all too reminiscent of Mom's funeral and after-gathering.

"Hey, guys, I gotta go. O', could your mom make sure Ian gets home?"

"Yeah, but where are you going?" asked Olivia. "What are you going to do?" Visibly agitated by my early rabbiting, she got in my face.

"I need fresh air. This is just too much for me…" I could tell they didn't understand and added, "It reminds me of when my mom died." They nodded. "I think I'll go get the Bucket from school."

"How're you going to get there?" For a second, excitement gripped Ian, hoping to escape the uncomfortable proceedings with me.

"I'm just gonna walk. School's not far, and it's still light outside." But just barely. As dusk dropped, the intimidating clouds turned even darker, some nearly navy blue, one small step away from black.

"You *can't* walk, and you *can't* go alone," spat Olivia in an uncustomary quiet tone. "You're being a dumb-ass!"

"Maybe I am. But I really, *really* have to get out of here." I looked over at Olivia's mother, deep in a heavy but hushed conversation with Mrs. Berillo. "And it looks like your mom's gonna be here a while." No argument from Olivia.

"Okay, but, text me as soon as you're in your car and headed home," she said. "I mean it, Tex." She swatted me on the shoulder, leaned closer, and whispered "*Dumb*-ass!"

While I didn't disagree with Olivia's assessment of me as a dumb-ass, I thought I'd start screaming if I stayed there any longer.

With one last round of hugs and condolences, I left Josh's family. Pretty much an expert at this behavior now, I knew exactly what *not* to say. Leaving the twins with handshakes and light guy-hugs (but not *too* huggy!), they reinforced their offer of retaliatory payback.

****

After the oppressive atmosphere of the Berillo house, the cold night air felt like an unexpected slap.

The skies growled, rumbled, teased, and threatened a deluge but stayed stubbornly dry. Eerie, purple-skied nights foreshadowed worse weather. But for now, the heavens remained constipated, and all the angrier for it.

As I walked over the hill, I saw good ol' Clearwell High. It looked so different on a weekend night. Heavy robes of night cloaked the long building. The usually bright streetlights lining the entry drive napped in darkness. A shadow of its daily, bustling self, the school looked dead—a skeleton deprived of its inner organs and muscles.

I hurried down the long winding drive toward the parking lot. Across the street sat the abandoned gas station, hiding in the gloom. By day, a den of iniquity for the pot-smokers, but at night, even they had deserted it. I thought of Josh's last week of life when he'd taunted Bellman there. The ghosts all marched out in full force tonight. At least in my mind.

Fallen leaves crunched beneath my feet as I crossed over the descending islands between the lots. A low, long rumble roared above me, the accompanying lightning bolt firing up the sky for several long seconds. There sat the Battle Bucket, waiting for me like a loyal steed.

I unlocked the door and slid onto the cold seat. My car key slipped into the ignition, but the Bucket wouldn't catch. "Come on, come *on*," I whispered, afraid to stir the ghosts. The engine kept trying to rev up but gave up and slowed to a down-winding death groan. "Bucket, don't fail me now." But I knew it was no use. "Not so loyal now, are you, Bucket?"

A light snap cracked outside the car. *The wind blowing the leaves*? Something scratched across the passenger side window. A dark figure in a ski jacket stood outside. With a sudden flash of movement, the window shattered inward, showering me with glass shards. My scream sounded ridiculously feminine, a helluva time for such a thought. A black-gloved hand reached inside and grabbed the door handle. I snatched my skateboard from the floor, swung with all my might at the intruding arm. I made contact, and with a satisfying thud, the person fell backward, grunting. A male sound, caveman style.

The keys still in the ignition, I wrenched open my door and jumped out of the car. Flipping the skateboard onto the ground, I pushed off with one foot, keeping the other firmly on the board. As I sped by my attacker, he scrambled on the ground trying to get to his feet. But I didn't look closely, too scared to.

With momentum building, I propelled myself across the pavement. The board ratcheted and echoed throughout the empty lot. My target lay ahead, the football field. If I could cross it on foot and exit through the far fence, I'd be able to shake my attacker off in the streets beyond.

I dared a glance back. The person ran in the opposite direction. A car roared. Tires shrieked like banshees. Bright headlights pinpointed my back as I reached the field. Kicking the board up into my hands, I ran onto the turf. The car raced parallel with me on the street opposite the fence, trying to beat me to the exit. I couldn't outrun a car. The car came to a screeching halt in front of the fence exit. Waiting for me.

Fists flailing in the air, I turned and ran back toward the school. The car spun out in a loud, ferocious u-turn. I slammed up against the gym exit, immediately pulling at the doors. Locked. With nowhere else to run, I raced to the back of the school.

Across the football field, the intruder's tires squealed. Echoes of death bounced off the empty school buildings.

Break into the school and hide? No. Sitting target. Better to take my chances outside.

Carefully, I crept along the back wall of the school. With shaking hands, I fished my phone out. The Fates had indeed settled on playtime. No charge.

My desperate panting sounded magnified, way too loud. I tried holding my breath but was too winded. At the far edge of the brick building, I peeked around the corner. I couldn't see or hear the car. After gently placing the board down, I hit the pavement and began to ride. At slower speeds, the oiled wheels made little noise.

At a sluggish pace, the board carried me along the short edge of the building toward Red's garage. All lights off—my last hope shattered.

I passed the garage door, prepared to bolt into the circular drive along the front of the building for a last, wild, Hail Mary getaway. I stopped and peered around the building's edge. In the center of the drive sat a silver car, lights off, engine quietly idling.

Two choices. One, speed by the car and get out to the main street, hoping to take the driver by surprise. Not a good plan. Two, back up, scramble over the privacy fence flanking the apartment complex next door and wind my way through the residential neighborhood.

Much better option.

Quietly, I clutched my skateboard and hunkered down, running as best I could through the grass. At the fence, I climbed, the skateboard pinched between two trembling fingers. Even though the fence stood at nearly six feet tall, I managed to scramble to the top. The skateboard slipped from my grasp. Head over tail, it flipped as if in slow motion. It struck cement with a loud, hollow *clump*, sharp as a gunshot.

From around the corner, bright lights flashed with far-reaching knives of illumination. Tires shrieked. The headlights rounded the corner as I jumped from the top of the fence into the apartment parking lot.

I darted between two apartment buildings. Never slowing, I took a quick look behind me. The car sped backward into the street, whipped around, and wrenched into the apartment parking lot. As I ran through the grassy strip between the two buildings, I pounded on tenants' doors. But I didn't take time to stop. Or wait. Just *knock knock, who's there, no one,* and onto the next. As long as I kept to the grass, between buildings, the murderer couldn't get me. At least by car. But I didn't feel great about my chances.

I tossed the dice of life and exited the apartment complex lot onto another residential street. The car sped through the parking lot, hurtling over speed bumps at a breakneck pace, to get around the buildings. To get to me.

As soon as I crossed the street, the silver car bounced out of the parking lot, headlights bearing down on me. I jumped into a residential yard, eyes locked on the backyard fence beside the house.

Foomph. Zzzzzzz…

At the fence, I turned around. The maniac had bumped the curb into the yard, the tires sizzling in the grass. The front door lights of the house flashed on as I hopped the fence with one bound. The car backed up, sped away, scurrying to meet me on the next street.

Over the next fence, my jeans snagged and tore on the chain-link edges. I tumbled down the other side. My leg buckled underneath me, a sharp jag of pain electrifying my body. The car roared down the street in front of me.

Change of course, sideways-ho. I hurtled through multiple yards, most mercifully free of fences. A row of houses stood between me and the killer, nothing else. I stopped, closed my eyes, and listened. The car slowly ambled past my position, now a good several house-lengths away, the engine quieting with distance.

Suddenly, a little rat of a dog yapped loudly, nipping at my heels. *Crap!* Unsuccessfully, I tried to shush the dog by whispering to it.

Yip, yip, yip…

Shit, shit, shit…

On the street, the car stopped, grew louder, and reversed toward the barking dog. Quickly, I jumped over the fence, braved myself, and ran like hell through the front yard toward the street. Before I reached pavement, the oncoming taillights grew larger at an alarming rate. I dashed across the street. Fishtailing in reverse, the car swam toward me. The tail end of the auto barely missed me, the ensuing rush flapping the back of my shirt up. I tore into the yard. Car brakes slammed on. Gears shifted as the car lurched forward slowly and then stopped. I felt eyes peering into my back as I continued my survival run. The driver once again raced down the block and turned onto the next street, attempting to cut me off.

This time I went up the street through the backyards. I couldn't keep this up much longer, not with my aching leg.

About four houses from the top of the street, I peeked around the corner of a large bush. The silver car slowly rumbled by. It crawled another two hundred feet or so before the headlights shut off, the motor idling, the car at a standstill. If I could make it another two houses up the street, it would put about four or five houses between us. And he'd again be facing the wrong direction. That left only two more blocks to clear and reach the safety of Josh's house.

One more fence to climb before I'd sneak across the street behind my attacker. My one-move vaults were history. It now took me several slow and clumsy moves. Once at the top, I tumbled down over the fence. I crawled toward the front of the house, my leg on fire, my gaze locked down on the car down the street. At the large oak tree in the front yard, I hugged it for dear life. The driver still hadn't made a move. Waiting...*hunting*... Every bush and mailbox my camouflage, I slowly duck-walked my way to the street. By the end of the driveway, flanked by two bushes, I'd resorted to all fours.

Another automobile pulled into the top of the street, headlights on high. An additional beam snapped on from within the driver's compartment. Fantastic time for the skiff ice cream man in the white van to show up. Caught between a serial killer...and a serial killer.

Glimpsed in the van's sliver of light, I watched the silver car slowly pull out. Quiet as a ninja on wheels, it motored down the street, headlights still off. Once it topped the hill, the speed picked up, followed by more squealing tires. One killer down, one to go. Maybe they're the two killers Cowlings suspects. Lucky me.

Do I make another mad dash for it? Or do I lurk in the backyards until dawn? Probably the latter. The van driver might not even know about me, not tonight at least.

I stood halfway up, ducking the flashlight from the van while it swept back and forth through the yards. When I turned around to make my way to the backyard again, the front porch lights popped on, flooding the yard with brightness. Startled, I bolted up. The van's flashlight targeted me. I yelped and stumbled backward. The van pulled up in front of the driveway. The driver jumped out, his engine still running. I scrambled toward the backyard, footsteps quickly catching up behind me. My leg numbed, slowing me down.

A voice called out behind me, "Hey! Stop!" A hand snagged my arm as the ice cream killer took me down to the ground. My chin cracked on the driveway. A man in T-shirt and jeans stared at us from his porch.

"Call the cops! Now!" I pleaded.

"Goddamn it, kid," said the man who'd tackled me. "I *am* the cops!"

****

After Detective Brittaglia flashed his credentials to the man whose home we'd invaded, I climbed into the van next to him. I looked around, not a single Bomb Pop or ice cream cone to be found. Instead, a detached police radio sat in the front, a fenced holding area behind me. I massaged life back into my leg and let out a long, obvious sigh; I'd had my fair share of fences for a while.

"Well, you don't *look* like a serial killer," I said. "You don't even look like an ice cream man."

Smiling, he turned toward me. He wore enough hair product to qualify as a fire hazard. "You've kind of been a pain in the ass, you know that? What in hell were you up to?" With no malice in his voice, something unusual, I felt somewhat at ease. *Somewhat.*

I told him everything that happened after I left Josh's house. He nodded sympathetically. "Tell me everything you can about the car that was pursuing you."

"I didn't really see much. Didn't you see anything?"

"Kid, I didn't even see the car. Just took it as a neighbor's parked vehicle since the lights were off."

"Well, I didn't see anything, either. Maybe, kinda, I think it was silver."

"You *think* it was silver? What about the year and the make?"

"As I said, I think it was silver. It was dark. It could've been white or light blue. I don't really know much about the makes of cars or anything like that." I felt lame, but cars were not what you'd call a passion for me.

Brittaglia shook his head—his turn to sigh belligerently—while he picked up his radio receiver. He phoned in an APB for a silver car, make and year unknown.

"Your girlfriend called Cowlings when you didn't call or text her back," said Brittaglia. "So we sent a cop down to your car and saw there'd been a scuffle. And with all the neighborhood complaints of a prowler…well, you weren't too hard to find."

Thank God for Olivia. Proven right once again…I am a dumb-ass.

"So, you work with Cowlings? All this time? And Cowlings didn't think to mention this to me when I told him about you?" This knowledge could've saved me nearly two heart attacks.

"Well, you're not exactly on a need-to-know basis, Richard. Once Cowlings told me you had suspicions about me, at least we dropped the pretense of being an ice cream man." He pointed at the bell, lying discarded on the floor.

"Next time, you guys should spend a little bit more money if you want to look like a non-serial-killing ice cream man."

Brittaglia chuckled. "Department's not exactly loaded with cash. I'm actually on loan from the Olathe police department."

"Could you please take me home?" I didn't want to worry Dad sick, although I knew that boat had probably already sailed. Let's just hope it's not the Titanic.

"That's where we're headed. I know where you live, cruised by there quite a few times. I suspect Detective Cowlings is waiting there for you already."

We pulled in the driveway, and sure enough, Cowlings' car loomed large and lawly in front of the house. *Great.* I looked around for Mr. Cavanaugh, but it must have been too chilly for one of his nosy nighttime vigils. Nowhere to be seen, all his lights turned off, about the only scary adult who hadn't come out to play tonight.

Dad and Cowlings had assumed the same positions they'd been in last time I arrived home for an interrogation.

"Tex, are you all right?" A map of crevasses and fault lines etched into Dad's face.

"I'm a little bruised and scraped, but I'll live."

"Tex, tell me everything that happened, and don't leave anything out." Cowlings' notebook perched on his lap, his pen hovering over his lip.

As I recounted the story, Dad fidgeted, his hands twisting the entire time. "What did I tell you about being careful? You should *never* have gone off alone." He was pissed and rightfully so.

"Sorry, Dad. I really thought it'd be okay."

"What can you tell me about your assailant?" Cowlings asked.

"I know he was male. When I whacked him with my skateboard, I heard a definitely male...groan, I guess you'd call it."

"Did you recognize the voice?" Cowlings' eyes lit up behind his glasses.

"No. It was just *Ugh*! I wasn't paying attention to voice recognition at that point." Realizing my snark might be a bit much, I added, "His voice was muffled, and I was in the car when he fell backward. I think he was wearing a ski mask. Maybe not."

"What about the color of the car?"

"I think it was silver. It might've been white or light blue. Look, I was running for my life! My powers of observation weren't at their peak."

Silence swept the room, broken only by the slap of Cowlings' notebook against his thigh. "Tex, think hard about what I'm about to ask you before you reply. Why do you think the killer went after you?"

I honestly had no idea, unless I knew something I

shouldn't. But I couldn't fathom what. Then realization gobsmacked me. The killer perceived me as a threat. Even more unsettling, the killer apparently knew about my car at school and had waited for me. Unless, of course, the killer might just be balls-out crazy and simply targeting random Clearwell students. I miss the good ol' days of Bob Bellman and his wacky, sadistic, bullying hijinx.

"I don't know, Detective." I tossed my hands up.

"Did you say anything at Josh's funeral?" asked Cowlings. "Or at the Berillo household afterward? Anything at all? Did you *hear* anything?"

I recalled my conversation with Mrs. Berillo. Stupidly, I'd told her I planned to find out the killer's identity. But this seemed an unlikely reason for the killer to target me. And I also thought it best not to tell Cowlings. He didn't like my playing Tex McKenna, Boy Detective.

"Sorry, Detective, I got nothing. Wait…" I considered mentioning Josh's brothers and their readiness to form a vigilante party of two but decided against it. The Berillo family didn't need to borrow any more trouble.

"Yes?"

"Ah, nothing. It was just a bunch of old ladies at Josh's house whispering rumors about the killer. I didn't really hear anything, and I don't think they fit the bill of who you're looking for."

Dad remained reverently quiet. I believe he now saw Cowlings as an ally instead of a harassing policeman.

Teeth clenched, Cowlings stood up and walked toward me. "Explain something to me…" I could tell he worked hard at keeping his anger in check. "At first, it looked like our killer was targeting Clearwell High School football players. Okay, that gave me a little something to work with. Not much, mind you, but it was something—at least a discernible pattern."

He stared at me for confirmation I understood this. I nodded in agreement, wary of where this might lead.

"Now, the killer has seemingly switched his choice of victims to you and your group of friends," he continued. "Why is this, Tex? What's the connection?" He wouldn't be satisfied until I gave him an answer. I sat on the sofa he'd just vacated. What *is* the connection? It made no sense. And it scared me.

"Detective, the only possible thing that links everything together in this…mess, is the victims were either bullies…or the bullied."

"Yes, I've figured that out." A faint glimmer of a smile crossed Cowlings' lips. "*Why?*"

"I don't know, I don't know, I don't know…" I felt two years old again and getting a stern talking to for misbehaving. "God, I don't know!" I buried my face in my hands, trying to concentrate. A sudden, horrific thought hacked away at my brain. I looked up at Cowlings, tears beginning to form around my eyes.

"What is it?" Cowlings placed a reassuring hand on my shoulder.

"Tell the Detective everything you can, son," said Dad.

"What if…what if…" I began and halted. The thought nearly pummeled me, too painful to complete. But I had to put it out there. "What if Josh *saw* something? Something terrible. Something he shouldn't have seen?" The idea gushed out, thinking out loud, trying to make sense of my newly incoherent world.

"Go on, Tex." Cowlings released my shoulder and grabbed his "comfort" notebook. "Why do you think this?"

"Well, the day Josh…went missing," I said, choking up, "he'd sent me a text saying '*I'm scared.*' At first, I thought it was just about the usual round of bullies, but…later on, that didn't make sense because Bellman was gone." Breathing loudly through my nose, I beat back the inevitable torrent of tears through sheer force. "I also knew after Bellman was expelled, he was hanging around the old gas station across from the school. Josh'd been taunting Bellman by skateboarding in front of him…staying out of reach. I *think* he did that the night Bellman was killed."

"Uh-huh."

"What if Josh was still around when the killer grabbed Bellman?"

The room filled once again with a heavy, ominous silence, interrupted on occasion only by my pathetic whimpers. Dad rolled over, handed me a tissue, and wrapped his arm around me.

"Shhhh, Tex, it's okay," he said. "You're doing great."

Through blurry eyes, I glimpsed up at Cowlings. He'd crossed the room to the fireplace, resting an elbow on the hearth above it. As if in deep concentration, he shut his eyes.

"Thanks, Tex," said Cowlings finally. "I know you've just lost your friend. And I know this is hard for you. But I wish you would've told me this earlier."

"I didn't think any of it was that important. And I'm really just…guessing right now." I gained control of myself and let out a cleansing sigh.

"This all makes a little more sense. Now we just need to figure out why the killer went after you. Did Josh text anything else to you?" He looked suspicious again, probably getting used to my withholding information.

"No…on that day, I only got the one text from Josh. And he wouldn't answer his phone. I don't even think I talked to him the night before." The memories came hard. So much had happened in such a short time.

"All right." Cowlings snapped his notebook shut. "I won't give you the usual spiel to call me if you think of something because I think now you know *anything* might be vital. *Right*?" He stared at me coldly.

"Yeah…"

"Oh, and you might want to call your pseudo-girlfriend Olivia. She's been pretty worried about you." Cowlings made his way to the front door.

Oh, crap, Olivia! She's going to kill me! "Okay, I will, thanks." I pulled out my phone but remembered the battery had gone AWOL on me.

"By the way, Tex, here're your car keys. You really shouldn't have left them in the car. You never know, there might be a criminal around." Cowlings took out the ring of keys from his pocket and tossed them in my direction. I held up a hand to catch them. They smacked hard against my fingertips before falling to the floor with a clank. An athlete I'm not.

"Oh, thanks," I said, embarrassed at my lack of physical dexterity. As for leaving my keys behind, I kinda' had other things on my mind at the time.

"Good night, Tex…Mr. McKenna," he said, shutting the door behind him.

Obviously anxious to talk to me, Dad said something, but I'd already dialed Olivia's number on the land line. "Sorry, Dad. I've got to let Olivia know I'm okay."

She answered on the first ring. "Tex?"

"Yeah, it's me." I prepared myself for an onslaught of verbal abuse. "I'm okay."

"You *dumbass*!" She screamed and cursed at me non-stop for a few minutes. I accepted my punishment accordingly.

"You're right, Olivia, I'm a dumbass." Dad winced at my language. "I'm really sorry…you were right."

"Tell me what the hell happened, *dammit*! And don't leave anything out!"

Once again, I relayed the story of my close call with the killer. Cold silence on her end met me.

"Oh my God," she whispered. "This is…scary…"

"I know. And I think we're all definitely in danger." Dad strained to listen in, hanging on to every word. I lowered my voice to get a little bit of privacy. "Don't go anywhere alone. Always be with someone. If your mom's not home, or if I'm not available, go to Ian's, but don't stay alone. Is your mom home now?"

"Yeah, she's downstairs baking or something."

"And she's not working all weekend, right?"

"Right…well, she'll go to church tomorrow."

"I hate to tell you this, O', but I think you better go get some religion yourself with your mom tomorrow."

"*Gah*! Don't make me do it!" Even after what I'd been through, I could always count on Olivia to make me smile.

"It's just for one hour. The killer is *not* going to go after you there."

"*Fine*. Will you go with me?"

"Ah, no. I've got a lot to do tomorrow with my dad and other stuff." A partial truth at best. I *did* have a lot to do, but it didn't involve Dad. And, honestly, I didn't feel ready to go back to church. Not yet. Not Mom's thing. Again, I realized my hypocrisy, but I thought saving a person's life kinda compensated for my sin.

"Whatever," she sighed. "What's next? We can't run and hide forever."

"I'm going to find out who did this, Olivia," I said quietly. I glanced at Dad to make sure he couldn't hear me. "I'm going to use my witchcraft to find out who took Josh away from us." I pressed my lips together in anger. "And then I'm going to get the bastard."

"Don't you *dare* be a dumbass again, Tex! You let me know what you're doing, and don't you do it alone! You're not the only one who gets to give orders around here. You stay in constant contact with me."

"Okay, okay…I'll call you tomorrow. I've gotta go." Ending with my Dad's constant mantra to be careful, I hung up.

I hated to already prove Olivia right again, but what I needed to do tomorrow night would definitely be considered text-book *dumb-assery.*

Chapter Sixteen

Dad wanted to stay up a while longer, I assume more for his peace of mind than mine. I get it. He desired comprehension and through that, a little bit of comfort. That's the way Dad rolls. Anything he understands, he thinks he can fix. But if it soars beyond his comfort zone, it unsettles him deeply. My eyelids felt like leaden window shades. Exhaustion had set in, but after one look at Dad, I knew I had to do what I could.

We stayed up for another hour, revisiting the events. He'd ask me a question, or tell me to repeat something for clarification, particularly when I resorted to deliberate ambiguity. I tried my best not to increase his worry-load, but he saw right through me.

I assured him the name of the game now would be the "buddy system." I wouldn't go anywhere alone, and I would try and make sure at least one adult hovered over us at all times. He leaned back and nodded with a large, semi-satisfied sigh.

We talked about getting the car fixed tomorrow, but I put that off. I told him Red could surely fix it for parts cost at school Monday and if not, give us a diagnosis. Right now, though, my priorities leaned toward preparations for tomorrow night. But I didn't tell Dad that.

Before I went to bed, I plugged my phone into the

charger and saw a ton of missed texts from Ian and Olivia. Too tired to text, I gave Ian a call, something teens don't usually do.

"What's up?" Ian answered. "Olivia texted me earlier and said you were missing. Damn, man. After what happened to Josh, don't pull a stunt like that. Everything cool?"

"Well, define *cool*." For the umpteenth time that night, I told the story.

"Dude, that's messed up."

"I know, right? Hey, isn't your Mom always home?"

"Yeah, never leaves the place, drives me crazy."

"Okay, cool. Hey, do you think she could run us somewhere tomorrow afternoon since my car's dead?"

"Yeah, probably. Where we going?"

"We're going to the mall…"

"Dude, I don't know, that sounds kind of…chickish. But what the hell, I'm dying to get out of here. Why are we going to the mall?"

"I've got to buy some witchcraft supplies," I said.

****

The abnormally cold weather hung around like a vulture looking for carrion. That morning, the skies floated in a dull, solemn gray, but at least the thunder, lightning, and brain-freezing wind had blown outta town. Even though we were only in November, it felt like the despairing negative degrees of February. I checked the weather on my phone. Sure enough, the forecast for tomorrow called for snow. I couldn't believe it, but that's Kansas for you.

Backtracking a bit, Dad hesitated to let me go out. I told him I needed to get out and clear my head, but that didn't fly. After I explained to him Ian would be my shadow, and his mom had promised to drop us and pick us up at the mall doors, he finally relented.

"You do *not* leave the mall for any reason," he said. I knew he didn't want to let me go. Dad struggled with giving me more freedom and letting me find my wings, possibly because of what happened to Mom. Eventually, though, he thought it best not to fight me on this. And I loved him all the more for it.

"I won't, Dad, I promise." I bent down and gave him a quick one-armed hug. "See ya." When the car horn blared in the driveway, I grabbed my winter coat. Like a roller derby superstar, Dad speedily shot to the front door and looked out to make sure Mrs. Stapleton sat behind the wheel. He gave a curt wave, which she returned.

As an afterthought, I turned around and said, "Hey, Dad, please double-lock the door after me, and don't let anyone in, okay?"

He stared at me quizzically and then grinned. Embarrassed, I realized I had just "fathered" him. "I'll be all right. Believe it or not, I can take care of myself," he said, still grinning. I really didn't think my dad would become a target for the killer, but after yesterday's events, I couldn't be too sure.

I piled in the back seat of the car. "Thanks a lot, Mrs. Stapleton."

"Of course, Tex," she said. "If it's for school work, it has to be done, right?"

I shot Ian a puzzled look. He furrowed his eyebrows, slightly inclining his head as if to say, "Just go with it."

"Um, yes, school work waits on no one," I said.

When Mrs. Stapleton pulled in front of the mall's large front doors, she placed the car in park and stared out the front windshield. Finally, she said, "Ian, are you sure I shouldn't go with you?"

"*Mom*! No!" Ian scrunched down a bit, embarrassed, hoping no one had overheard this exchange.

"Okay, okay." Mrs. Stapleton tossed her hands in the air and spread her fingers. "I just worry."

"I know, Mom. We'll be okay, and we'll see you in about three hours." He jumped out of the car, and I followed suit. Mrs. Stapleton craned her neck to see that we safely entered the mall. Ian dismissed her with a quick, impatient wave.

To me, the Maple Leaf Shopping Center resembled a huge, ghastly eyesore of prefab concrete buildings connected like interlocking toys designed by an off-his-meds architect. Full of department stores, clothing boutiques, health food outlets…yet you couldn't find a single bookstore. For some reason, teenagers had made this the in place to go, where they spent endless hours cruising the two long levels, seeking out what amusement they could. Most of these kids didn't have any money to shop—excluding the spoiled, rich kids, natch—just looking for some excitement to be found under the garish lights. I guess I couldn't blame them, as there wasn't much for kids to do in Kansas, especially if you didn't drive. I'd only been there a handful of times before. On those occasions, Mom had carted me along with her on shopping sprees. Seems like such a long time ago.

Many of the shoppers and mall-walkers gaped at Ian, with his splinted upraised hand. After a while, he got sick of it. Turning angrily proactive, he'd say, "Hello," or "Good day to you too," or to one unfortunate woman, "Be careful, what I have is contagious." He asked me if he should switch to *Heil, Hitler* due to the unfortunate positioning of his arm. I pleaded with him to not do so.

"I had to tell my mom we're doing a sociology paper on the cult of shopping," Ian explained. "She wasn't going to let me out of her sight until I came up with that."

I nodded. We all had our parental battles.

Not too long after our shopping binge started, Ian whipped out his phone and began to text one-handed. Quite efficient at it, his thumb flew across the screen.

"Uh-oh," he said. "We got trouble."

"What's up?" I didn't want any more trouble.

"We'd better go to the food court," he said with a resigned sigh.

We rounded the corner. Standing in the center of hundreds of cheap plastic tables and chairs, waited Olivia. Her button-adorned purse slouched sassily off her shoulder while she impatiently tapped a black-sneakered foot. One hand perched on her hip, and the other held her cell phone open as she glared at it.

Oh, crap! I'd considered it mistake-worthy not to tell Olivia about our trip to the mall, but I honestly just wanted to keep her safe at home. In the here and now, looking at a pissed-off Olivia, my reasoning seemed kind of askew. But I figured the killer wouldn't target two teen boys in a mall, whereas Olivia would be dangerously alone if she made a trip to the bathroom. Sexist? Maybe. Caring? Sure. In trouble? *Absolutely*. I primed myself for a severe tongue-lashing.

Olivia met me with a blood-chilling glare. "Oh, *here* they come," she yelled. People sitting at the nearby tables stopped eating their artificial tacos and corn-dogs to watch the commotion. "Hi, *girls!* I can't *believe* you'd even think to go to the mall on your own! How many times have I *tried* to get you to go? You little girls would probably get *lost* without me!"

While I felt ashamed and embarrassed, Ian giggled. I nudged him to shut up before things got worse.

"Olivia, I'm sorry," I said. "I was just trying to protect you." She whipped the hair over her eye behind her ear, the better to glower at me with. Her hand doubled up into a fist and pounded her hip.

"You *don't* get to protect me! I think I've proven I can take care of myself. What's going to happen to me at a mall that wouldn't happen to you girlies?" Some of the food-court patrons gathered their trays to move farther away from the eye of Hurricane O'.

"Sorry, sorry, sorry," I said. "I also didn't think you'd approve of what I'm going to do, to be honest." *Uh-oh, I actually said that out loud.*

"And *what* is it you're planning on *doing*? Didn't you learn your lesson last night?" She visibly shook with rage.

"I'm going to perform a simple…witchcraft spell," I said, lowering my voice. "There's nothing to it, really. I'm just going to see if a spirit will tell me who the killer is." I shifted my eyes left to right, making sure no one still sat within earshot. My hand cupped to my mouth probably made me look more suspicious.

"*Gah!* So *stupid!* I can't *believe* you were sending me to church while you two girls were going *shopping*."

275

Ian laughed again. If looks could kill, Ian would've been a goner.

She grabbed a Styrofoam cup off a table and took a long drink out of the straw. "Okay, I've got my shot of caffeine. Let's get shopping." She pulled her giant purse tighter around her shoulder and brushed by us. She turned around and asked "Well? Are you coming or what?"

We hurried to catch up with her. "How did you know where to find us?" asked Ian.

"Because you dumb-asses only answer your phones half the time, I called Tex's dad, who told me," she spat. "Mom dropped me off here on her way to church. By the way, Ian, your mom's giving me a ride home."

"Okay," said Ian, humbled. I wish I possessed Olivia's magical effect on Ian. Some witch I am.

"You've *got to* quit doing this *crap* to me." She walked in front of us, backward, making sure she held our attention. Along with everyone else's attention in the mall. "I mean *really!*"

"Okay," we both said.

"Now, gimme the witchy shopping list…"

****

Before we'd set out on our shopping spree that morning, I'd told Dad I had to go upstairs and finish my homework since I didn't get a chance to do so on Saturday. I went into Mom's study and did an inventory of what I needed to purchase.

Pushed up against the back wall loomed a curious piece of furniture. An antique, wooden, rectangular box stood at about five feet tall and approximately three feet wide. It reminded me of a monster-sized drawer resting on its end. Or an unfinished coffin, because these days that's the way my mind rolled. Ornate hand-carved leaves ran around the trim edges. A small, cream-colored curtain, drawn across on a metal rod, hid an empty shelf behind it. Melted wax blemished the top of the cupboard.

As a kid, I remember asking Mom about the piece. She called it her "special armoire." I never knew what she meant. But when you're young and naive, you accept parents' answers as truth and absolutely knew things would clear up with the wisdom of age.

It had to have been her altar. I doubted I could find one at the mall, so I checked this off my list. In her closet, I found some incense, on the crumbling end of its life. I took a whiff, thought it smelled decent, and decided even crumbling things would burn and give off the proper aroma. Another item off the list.

In her desk, I found some parchment paper. Check. I couldn't find the last important item in her office, however.

Having struck out upstairs, I rummaged through the junk silverware drawer—not to be confused with our utensils drawer—and searched in vain for a dagger. A lot of dull steak knives jam-packed the drawer, which didn't come close to defining a dagger to the best of my understanding. So I planned a trip to the knife store at the mall.

****

Hesitant as three rabbits crossing a highway at rush hour, we entered Greydon's Knives. An overweight clerk looked up from his hunting magazine, eyeing us suspiciously. Olivia shook her head and sneered with obvious disdain at the knife-ware on display. Ian, on the other hand, found his new candy shop. Delighted at the sheer number of potentially damage-causing weapons, beckoning like shiny, metallic sirens, he touched everything not locked up under the glass case the clerk leaned on.

"Can I help you, kids?" He finally stood up and flipped his magazine onto the counter.

"Uh, yes," I said. "Do you have anything by way of daggers?" I'd never foreseen myself asking this question to anyone.

"*Daggers*? What kind of 'dagger' are you looking for?"

"We're putting on a small Renaissance Festival at school." Olivia enunciated perfectly, attempting to sound older. At least she didn't pull out her cockney accent again. "We would like something rustic, old-fashioned, and quite beautiful." And here we go, next stop the East end of London.

The clerk grinned. "I think I know what's going on here. You kids wouldn't happen to be practitioners of the black arts, now, would you?" The way he said practitioners took forever as he dragged it out with at least four extra syllables. He leered creepily at Olivia while ignoring Ian and me.

"Well, not exactly," continued Olivia, "but I do believe that's the exact sort of item we're looking to purchase."

"Uh-hmmm." He turned around, opened a cabinet behind him, and brought out a brown box, setting it down gently on a piece of cloth in front of us. With great reverence and more than a little show, he opened it. Within lay an arrangement of jewel-handled knives with twisting blades. Daggers, I suppose. Ian's eyes positively sparkled.

"Yes, this will do splendidly. What is the going price for the cheapest knife here?" Olivia gave a haughty sniff.

"The 'going price'?" he guffawed. "Well, the going price for the cheapest knife here would be…I'd say…about two hundred fifty dollars." We stared at each other, stunned. I'd been prepared to go up to thirty dollars tops, but no way could I swing this. Based on his supercilious look, I suspect he hiked the price up on us young rubes.

"I see," said Olivia. "You wouldn't happen to have anything second-hand, would you?"

A slow, rumbling chuckle built, then exploded from the clerk's large quivering belly. Clearly the most fun he'd had in a while. "Now, the going price for these here Black Magic artifacts is expensive, because, believe it or not, this is where I make the real cash. You wouldn't *believe* how much black magic business I do here in Kansas. Why in the world do you think I opened up a store in the mall? Do ya' really think all the other teeny-boppers out there want to buy knives?" He swept his chubby hand toward the mall's hall.

"No, I suppose not." I saw Olivia's internal struggle not to rip him a new one, while Ian and I just stood by helplessly.

"Now, far be it from me to judge you for your personal…ah…beliefs, little lady." *Uh-oh.* "But if you want the goods, you got to pay the price." He stood there, mouth open, strands of saliva forming bridges between his upper and lower teeth.

Olivia clamped her lips tightly. "Could you rent us one for the night?"

"Hmmm, I've never had a request for something like that before. But for you, I suppose I could make an exception." Ever so delicately, he pulled out the smallest knife in the box. "How does fifty bucks sound, little lady?" *Uh-oh, again.*

"It *sounds* like…" To my amazement, Olivia stomped on her brakes. "It sounds like I need to confer with my associates." She turned around to face us. "Tex, how important is this to you?"

"Forget it, O'," I whispered. "I only have thirty bucks."

"How *important* is it?"

"I just want to put an end to this nightmare. I thought this might be the fastest, best way to do it. I mean, what's the point of my…powers…if I don't use them for good?"

"Fine," she said. "But, promise me right now you're *not* going to use it as a weapon of any sort. *Okay?*"

The thought had never crossed my mind. "No way. You know me better than that."

She twirled around to face the clerk and whipped out a twenty-dollar bill from her pocket. "*Sold!*" The money slammed down onto the counter, prompting me to jump a bit. "Tex, let's have your thirty dollars."

Before I could object, the clerk said, "Okay, I just need to see picture ID that you're twenty-one, or a signed approval from a parent." He chuckled again. "You kids didn't really think I was going to sell you a dagger to go perform black magic acts with live chickens, did you? I mean, I've got to abide by the law. No minors."

Olivia snatched up the twenty-dollar bill and

stashed it back into her pocket. "Okay, listen to me. I'm so glad we supplied some entertainment value to your sad, empty life, and you got some laughs." The second she crossed her arms, I actually pitied the clerk. When he started putting away the knives, I felt relief.

"But I'll *tell* you something," she continued. "The *next* time you string somebody along like that, just remember they have a life. And you'll go home, read your hunting magazines—doing only *God* knows what while you're looking at the pictures—then you'll come back to your stupid, sad little store of *stupid* toys and *weapons.*" The clerk's ever-present grin vanished. She turned on her heels and said, "Let's go, boys." We left the store, Ian and I laughing.

Olivia said, "Wait a minute," and ran back to the open door. "And don't you *ever* call me 'little lady,' again, you…*you gross man*!"

Okay, I thought, we *do* need Olivia. How in the world we ever got anything accomplished without her is one of life's great mysteries.

****

We finished our shopping spree with four white candles and a robe. I didn't think it mattered what kind of robe I used—a robe is a robe, right?—so I bought the cheapest bathrobe I could find.

Olivia stood in the checkout line, just shaking her head. "Jesus, Tex, do you want some lovely bubble-bath to go along with that?"

"Are you planning on a nice romantic dinner for one?" chimed in Ian. The checkout girl stared blankly at us.

"Funny, guys." I realized my purchases did make it look like I planned to pamper myself.

"You should've gone for the robe I pointed out to you." Olivia sneered with disgust at the brown robe I picked out. "Honestly…so sucky."

We waited by the front doors until Ian's mom showed up. "I still need a dagger," I said, wondering if a steak knife would do the trick.

"I've got an idea," said Ian. "My dad goes hunting with a special knife he uses to gut deer with." Olivia feigned a throwing up motion. "Would that work?" I thought it couldn't hurt to try; probably better than a rusty steak knife.

On the way home, Ian asked his mom if we could stop by their house first because he had to give me something for our school assignment.

"Well, you know me, kids," sang Mrs. Stapleton, delighted to be able to help further our academic pursuits. "Education is everything!"

Ian raced into the house, leaving us to make small talk with Mrs. Stapleton. Five minutes later, Ian returned holding a bogus stack of papers. He opened the back door, handed me the papers, and quietly dropped a large knife into my lap. Quickly, I scrambled to hide it in my coat pocket.

Mrs. Stapleton dropped me off first. "Say hello to your dad for me, Tex," she said.

"Okay. Thanks for the ride, Mrs. Stapleton. Bye, guys. Text me tonight." I got out of the car, shooing cats all the way up the sidewalk. Before I reached the front door, Olivia had already texted me.

—*Yur sure this spell isn't dangerous, right?*—

I stood on the stoop, typing, and freezing. —*Yes. Just going to contact Mom or friendly spirit. Nothing dangerous.*—

Sadly, I found myself withholding the entire truth to her again. I didn't intend to speed-dial Mom or a friendly spirit on my conjuring network.

"Dad, I'm home," I yelled through the chained and bolted door, glad to see Dad took my suggestion to heart.

"Just a minute." His voice sounded muted, far away, probably from the kitchen.

"Did your dad lock you out of the house, Richard?" called out the all-too-familiar, nasal voice from next door. Out on his porch-vigil and bundled up to beat the cold, Mr. Cavanaugh indulged in his favorite past-time: getting all up in my business.

"Yeah, something like that, Mr. Cavanaugh." Under my breath, I cursed. Cold jags of air spat plumed from my mouth.

"You must've been especially naughty," he purred.

Hurry up, Dad.

Once unlocked, I flew inside, hoping Dad wouldn't notice the plastic bag I carried.

"How was the shopping adventure?" He eyeballed the bag. "What'd you buy?"

"Ah, I bought…a bathrobe. It gets cold upstairs going to the bathroom in the mornings."

"Oh… You should've told me, son, I would've been happy to buy you one."

"Dad, you and I both know it came from you anyway since my allowance is my only income."

"Glad you see it that way," he said, laughing. "Come on, dinner's about ready."

****

We finished dinner—chili again, welcome on a cold night—and jumped directly into putting the dishes away.

"Did you and your friends have fun at the mall today?" Although Dad concentrated on drying a bowl, he couldn't help but sneak glances at me.

Honestly—unbelievably—we *had* had fun. Something I just realized. I found this astonishing, in the light of everything going on, particularly the death of Josh. It gave me a little bit of hope.

"Yeah, actually, we did."

Dad made arrangements for a work friend to pick both of us up tomorrow morning and drop me at school. I said goodnight and bounded up the stairs. Almost ten-thirty, it was a little too early to perform my spell, but not too early to start on the preparations. Soooo many preparations in witchcraft. Maybe I could find an apprentice on Craig's List.

With my plastic mall sack of goods in hand, I entered Mom's study. Carefully, I rolled up the large multi-colored rug covering most of the floor and scooted it underneath the window. I always thought it odd Mom had such a large barren space in her study, with nothing on top of the rug. But now I easily put two and two together. While I drew a large chalk circle on the hardwood floor, I envisioned Mom doing the same thing in the past.

I laid the library book—an old musty tome called *The Book of Ancient Witchcraft and Spells*—next to the circle and opened it to one of the bookmarked pages. With painstaking detail, I copied symbols, ancient lettering of some sort, pentagrams, and hexagrams lining the inside of the circle. I drew another circle within the circle, enclosing the drawings, leaving plenty of blank space in between them.

Dragging the altar across the floor, I positioned it in front of the circle. Next, I set four candles in small holders on the corners of the altar. Incense rested in a small oval bowl at the center of the candles.

At eleven-thirty, I had about twenty minutes before I could perform the ritual. With time to kill, I pondered how Mickey wouldn't approve of my doing this potentially dangerous spell. But I wanted to keep her out of this entire serial killer business. Bad enough my friends and loved ones were drowning in the consuming whirlpool of madness. Whether by accident or design, too many people had been either hurt or killed lately, and it fell on me to stop it.

I put on my ill-fitting robe—Olivia would've hated how it looked—and fastened it tight. I lit the candles, careful to avoid dripping wax on the altar or my floor drawing. Before I lit the incense, I opened the window wide to let in a breeze, hoping it would diffuse the scent so as not to awaken Dad. The cold air blew lightly in, flapping the cream-colored curtains ever so gently. For ten minutes, I stood silently, nervously, gauging the wind, and determined the candles wouldn't blow out. Step one complete.

I lit the incense and waited for the sickly, sweet odor of exotic perfume to permeate the room. The smell grew so intense my eyes watered, but it didn't take much for this allergy-ridden witch boy to show symptoms. Cat hair and everything else witchy seemed to bother the hell outta me. Surely, there's a special witch allergy pill for us outliers or something.

The next step—one I picked up from an Internet video (probably not the best source, but hey, desperate times and all that)—involved carefully pouring a ring of salt around the drawn circle. Not wanting to take any chances, I sorta kitchen-sinked my way through this entire deal, combining several different methods and spells of conjuring—like a chef creating a hodge-podge recipe in the kitchen—with the salt providing cautionary comfort, nothing essential.

Finally, I placed the hunting knife within reach next to the circle. Okay, just a few more minutes until showtime.

Two different methods had been presented to me during my research. The first involved conjuring up a spirit on the so-called astral plane. Even though this sounded safer and possibly less scary, I didn't have the necessary crystal ball it called for. And I certainly didn't want to take another day to find a crystal ball store. The second method, the one I chose, clearly came with some risk. I planned on dialing up a spirit on the physical plane. Mickey'd kill me if she knew—even books and Internet articles warned against it—but to me, it felt like my only option left.

I didn't want to conjure—or contact—Mom again. The thought of disturbing her, or placing her in some kind of danger in the spiritual world, weighed too heavily on me. Of course, the same went for Josh. No way could I tolerate seeing his tortured spirit, especially if I yanked him out of a nice, peaceful afterlife of some sort. As of now, I really don't know where my thoughts fit in regarding the spiritual world—especially the afterlife—but from what I've seen lately, it gives me pause there might be something out there.

But I sure didn't mind dredging up the soul—if he ever had one—of Bob Bellman from the bowels of hell.

I wrote his name on a piece of parchment paper

and placed it next to the bowl of incense on the altar. Grabbing the knife, I pantomimed the sign of the pentagram in the air in several different directions. Leaning over, keeping my feet perfectly still so as not to come anywhere near the circle and salt, I grabbed the parchment paper. I stared at it intently, chanting Bellman's name over and over again.

My breath held, I stared into the center of the circle. I pulled out my cheat sheet and slowly read aloud, "I command and conjure you, Bob Bellman, to appear before me within my magical circle in a safe and friendly manner." A slew of Latin words, which I attempted to read without slaying the ancient language, followed.

The air thickened, what I imagined London fog to be like, only denser. Time stopped, not a sound to be heard. A musty, rancid odor tortured my nostrils. My eyes flooded with irritation, worse than before from the incense. The earlier breeze vanished, the curtains hanging on the window still as death. Behind the altar, the windowpanes blurred. From a non-existent light source, a greenish tint eerily lit the room. An unearthly green blob—indistinct shapes mashed together— appeared, rotating, stopping within the center of the circle. Smoke circled and danced around the green mass. A pair of eyes, white as snow, formed at the center of this miniature tornado, staring back at me, unblinking. The all-too-familiar face began to form around the eyes, smoke swirling in and out as if teasing the spectral figure.

Soon, Bellman's unibrow knit together above glaring eyes, followed by the nose, mouth, and green teeth, at home within the rest of his green face. The neck followed, the chest dropping down, birthing itself. Legs sprouted through the smoke, oddly detached and stepping out of line like an errant chorus girl. The full figure danced awkwardly about, shimmering, breaking apart, and reforming every few seconds. No arms, though. *Good, harder for him to throttle me from beyond the grave.*

Okay, with the curtain drawn back, the bad guy on stage, it felt like my cue to jump into witchy action. I cleared my throat, then did it again.

"What is your name, O spirit?" Well, duh. But proper protocol and all.

A loud ear-ripping shriek emanated from nowhere before Bellman's mouth opened, exposing Bellman's eternally rotting teeth. *"Ro...bo...ert...Bel...uh...man,"* replied the thing. Unbelievably, the spiritual Bellman spoke even more inarticulately than the late, not-so-great living version.

"In peace I welcome you, Bob Bellman, and in the name of the Mother Earth, the fire, the wind, and the water, I command you to stay where you are until dismissed and to answer all questions I put before you truthfully." Upon seeing Bellman again—an even scarier than living Bellman—my junk tried to crawl up into my stomach. Suddenly on fire, sweat soaked me from my hair, my pits. My throat dried up, more arid than a desert. I thought this ugly chapter in my life had closed forever. Too late for regrets, all in.

A loud screech reverberated around the room. Green mists churned and merged, formed and reformed his body, a petulant puzzle in progress.

"Who killed you, Bellman?"

Abruptly, wind blasted through the window,

stronger than before, and snapped the curtains back and forth. Then radio silence. Within the circle, green smoke obscured the figure. Kinda a major worry.

"Who killed you, Bellman?" I asked again, louder.

Bellman's death visage poked out from the green wisps again, the blank eyes unseeing, the mouth gaping even wider. An awful banshee-like wail filled the room, ricocheting off the walls and ceiling. Suddenly, an arm appeared out of the clouds of Hell, a fat sausage-like finger extended, pointing at me. The crazed howling continued.

A huge, unnatural gust of wind barreled through the open window, knocking the curtains and rod to the floor. Startled, I lost my footing and stumbled backward. Attempting to counter-balance, I flung myself forward, arms stretched out. I fell to my knees with a loud *thwack!* My right hand landed on the salt and chalk circle line. I quickly pulled my hand out as if burnt. But the two concentric circles had been broken.

The altar slid across the floor backward and slammed against the window. The candles blew out, then tipped out of the candlesticks to the floor. I looked up into Bellman's face leaning out of the circle directly above me. Grinning. Still sitting, I scrambled back, a panicked crab. Slowly, the thing lurched toward me, a cloud of green enveloping its lower body. I scrabbled to get up on shaking legs. With the knife, I frantically drew the sign of the pentagram several times. But the creature's movement hastened. Next to the broken circle, I saw the book lying on the floor. My last chance.

I jumped to the right. The creature flailed about but couldn't turn very quickly. Staying out of arms' reach, I snagged the book. Intense heat rolled off of Bellman, growing more intense with each step closer. Quickly, I flipped the tome's pages until I reached another bookmarked spell.

"I banish *you*, Bob Bellman, to return to your sphere of origin. By the authority of the true Mother of Earth, I *command* you to depart and harm *no* one on your travels," I stuttered, words tumbling together like a verbal avalanche.

Bellman's spirit stopped. Its arm still extended, the accusatory finger still pointing at me. Suddenly another death-wail bounced off the walls, ringing in my ears so badly, I dropped the knife. The knife *thunked* into the wooden floor, the handle wobbling to and fro, an inch from my big toe.

The thing quivered and shook. Its eyes moved apart, rolling across its dead face like scattershot pinballs. An ear rotated around to the front of the head. As the green mists encircled it, tighter and tighter, the spirit eroded and strangled until it became just a thin, roiling wisp of smoke. It disappeared with an anti-climactic *plip*.

Abominations from hell vanish with a plip*?*

The room temperature dropped, frigidly so. As fast as possible, I dashed to the circle and rubbed it out with my foot. No sense leaving the door to Hell open, thank you very much. I shut the window quietly, but it probably didn't make a difference now since much louder things had occurred in the room.

For a few moments, I sat on the floor, hyperventilating. Recovering. After feeling like I could walk again, I picked up everything witch-related, stuffed it into my plastic shopping bag, and hastily tossed it into the closet. With one last look around the room, I ensured I hadn't forgotten anything. Once I pulled the door shut behind me, the furnace's welcome warmth embraced me. In the hallway, I peeked down the stairwell to see if Dad had awakened. Miraculously, all lights stayed off.

I tiptoed to my room and collapsed into the bed. As an afterthought, I got up again and locked my bedroom door before getting back under the covers. It probably wouldn't keep ghosts out, but it couldn't hurt.

Bellman stayed true to form in death, a vindictive, crazy bitch from hell. Or had he really meant to implicate me in his murder somehow by pointing at me? I pulled the covers over my head, still terrified of my boogeyman.

And no doubt about it, I screwed this one up royally.

The two women in my life—Olivia and Mickey—kept proving they were right, while I still hadn't graduated from dumbass class. I shouldn't have attempted this hare-brained spell, and tomorrow, I'd ask for Mickey's help, something I should've done in the first place.

One way or another, this ends tomorrow.

Chapter Seventeen

Dad's friend dropped me off at school a little bit earlier than usual. Snow had already started falling in large, lethargic puffs of thick wetness. As we pulled in front of the school, the streets remained free of accumulation, but a light dusting covered the grassy areas.

First things first, I hurried toward Red's Den of Iniquity and clanged down the metal stairs to the boiler room.

"Hey, Red." Cemented in his usual chair, he pored over an issue of *Penthouse*. Startled, he closed the magazine and scrambled to hide it under his chair.

Once he saw a friendly face, it didn't take him long to regain his composure of cool. "Texas-Style, where you been? Haven't seen you in a while. Everything all right?" He withdrew the magazine and waved it in greeting.

"I dunno. Just…there's been a lot of crap going on lately. Got a scare Saturday night." Once again I retold the long saga of my ordeal with my mysterious pursuer.

"Man, that sucks. Wow, I can't believe it." He wagged his head, red curls bouncing in agreement. "They catch the guy?"

"No. Hey, I was wondering if I could ask you a favor?"

"Sure. Anything for you, buddy."

"Could you take a look at my car?" I hated pulling the favor card, didn't like taking Red away from his regular duties, but I also knew he liked playing hero. Shameless, I know, but I'd gladly return the favor to him. If I could ever offer anything of value to him, of course.

"No problem." He stood up and stretched his lanky body. "Let's go." Dressed in his usual coveralls, he was one of those super-humans who never needed a winter coat. "Hang on...is your window still busted out?"

"Yeah, I guess it is."

Red bolted up the stairs while I trailed behind him. At a metal shelving unit jam-packed full of tools, he grabbed a large piece of cardboard stashed behind it. On the way out, he snatched his toolbox.

While students arrived in droves, we made our way through the school, out into the cold, and down the long curving sidewalk. We must've made quite the sight together. Both of us taller than a lot of the students, I imagined they wondered what the Tall and Gangly duo were up to, headed in the opposite direction. The snow fell heavier now; the wind whipping up, distributing it mainly along the curbs and sides of the building.

"Hey, I didn't get a chance to talk to you at the funeral, but I'm sure sorry about little Joshie," he said. "He was a good kid."

"Yeah." I sighed. "He was a really good friend." I pulled my coat tighter around me as a sudden blast of north wind bit into my face and blew back my hair.

"You did him proud, though, with your speech on Friday. I heard Hastings was all pissy over it." He smiled, nodding lazily at me, the snowfall not bothering him in the least.

"Crap! I forgot I got a detention for it. I'm supposed to serve it today. But I don't know if I'll be able to make it. I've got something important to do."

"Well, you'll probably earn more if you skip it, Tex. Maybe your dad can call in for you or something." A great idea and I wished I'd thought of it earlier. I'd better phone him later.

"Whoa." Red let out a long whistle, a practiced one on dogging girls, no doubt. "They really did a number on your window." There the Bucket sat, lonely and abandoned, the snow already blowing in through the broken window. I half expected to see it roped off as a crime scene.

"Yay, I've finally got air conditioning."

"Pull the hood open," Red ordered.

I opened the door and pulled the latch. While Red's head vanished underneath the hood, I sat in the Bucket shivering, trying to stave off the cold. Snow blew in and settled on me, melting immediately from my body heat.

It didn't take long before he waved a hand, his head still under the hood, and yelled, "Turn it over, Tex." I turned the key in the ignition, and to my amazement, it fired right up.

Red came around to the open window, bent down, and said, "Your distributor cap was off. It either fell off…or someone took it off."

"Huh." Shocker.

"You really should lock your car," he said. Regarding neglect toward automobiles, Red took it as a personal insult.

"Actually, I'm pretty sure I *did*." Or at least I thought I had.

"Well, old cars like these…they're not too hard to

get into with a clothes-hanger or a Slim-Jim. You might think about a car alarm."

"Just thought nobody'd ever want to mess with my junker. No offense intended, Bucket." I gave the car's dashboard a reassuring pat, not wanting to piss her off again or whatever. "Anyway, thanks tons, Red. I owe you."

"No prob." He wiped his hands on a red, filthy rag. "Let's get the cardboard in, so you don't freeze to death."

****

"Dude," said Ian, "I'm back and ready to kick some scholastic ass!" His hand still hiked up in the air as if on an eternal quest for acknowledgement, he grinned like he'd just inherited millions. Out of morbid curiosity, some students snuck glances, but just as quickly turned away when either one of us challenged their stares.

"All right! Fist-bump, while O's not here!"

Ian formed a fist with his good hand and met mine enthusiastically.

"So, how'd your dream date with yourself go last night?" He lowered his voice, enjoying the cloak and daggerness of it all.

I shook my head. "Total wash-out. I'm bringing in the big guns after school, though…this has gotta end."

"What're you talking about?"

Mr. Jensen walked into the room and torpedoed directly toward Ian. He smiled, an alien look for him, particularly over the last month or so. "Welcome back, Ian." He smacked him good-naturedly on the shoulder. "Hope you kept up your sociology homework."

"Yeah, thanks, Mr. Jensen." Ian squirmed, trying to

hide his pleasure. And, by God, I think he blushed. "There wasn't a whole lot to do, so, yeah, here's a big stinkin' pile of sociology for you." He reached into his backpack, fiddled about, and pulled out a batch of papers.

"Good deal," said Mr. Jensen.

****

"How'd it go last night?" shouted Olivia from down the hallway.

"Olivia, shhhh. Don't let the whole school know about it, okay?"

"Whatever. If you would've texted me last night like you were supposed to, then I wouldn't be sharing with the world."

"Sorry, but it was about one when I was done. I thought you'd be asleep."

"The *hell* I was." She stamped a foot down.

"Anyway, it didn't work. It was pretty messed-up actually."

"What did you do?" She eyed me suspiciously. "Were you being stupid again?"

"Yeah, I guess you could say that." The stark terror vividly new again, I recalled what I'd conjured up from the netherworld. "I'll explain later."

Olivia glowered, waiting for me to divulge more information.

"But it's all cool now," I added quickly. "I think I've a follow-up plan that'll work, though, and I'm doing it after school. I'm going to ask Mickey for help."

"So glad you're coming to your senses. You should've done that in the first place." I couldn't have agreed with her more.

"Listen, Red fixed my car, but I was wondering if

you'd be able to hook a ride with Ian after school and maybe hang out at his house until I give you the all-clear?"

"Gah! Stop making plans for me, *Dad*. I'm a big girl, dammit!"

"I know, but the end is in sight. Just do it for me this one last time, okay?" I placed my hands on her shoulders. "It's going to be over soon...*trust* me."

"Yeah, seems to me I've heard those words before...with pretty shitty results."

I said goodbye to Olivia and raced to the bathroom to secretly call Dad. School policy frowns upon phones, blah, blah, blah, but extenuating circumstances trumps policy.

"Hey, son, everything okay?" Fatigue and worry formed his voice.

"Yeah. Dad, I need a favor from you. It's important."

"Okay..." He knew when I asked for favors, he usually didn't like the outcome.

"Can you call the school and let them know I can't make my detention today? Tell them because of the snow or...whatever..."

"Why? I mean, frankly, I'd rather you didn't tarry after school anyway, but...what are you up to?"

"I have to go see Mickey. I need her help with something. Dad, it's *important*."

"And you'll be with Mickey? And then you'll come home?"

"Yeah. I'm not sure how long it'll take me, so for one last time...can you get a ride home?"

"Fine," he said with a long, obvious sigh, "but be careful."

"Always, Dad, always."

"I recall hearing that from you before…and it didn't really mean much, now, did it?"

Man. When it rains, it pours.

****

One hour before school let out, the snow decided to dump down heavily, a total freak storm for this time of year, but not unheard of in Kansas. In gym class, ants invaded my pants as I continuously glanced out the window. Outside, a blanket of snow covered the entire football field, possibly six inches deep. It looked like it wouldn't let up any time soon, either. Already nervous and fidgety, the snow just made me more anxious about the job I had ahead of me.

As soon as the bell clanged, I ran into the locker room and threw my clothes on fast. I sped through the hallways, past the students who seemed excited about the first big snowfall of the year. One of the first students out the front door, my foot sank into the snow on the step. My tennis shoe came up wet but gave me good traction. I high-tailed it down through the parking lot, jumped into the Bucket, turned the ignition, and prayed it'd turn over. It did, and I carefully, but quickly, backed out and pulled into the street.

Visibility barely existed, no more than a foot's worth. The rusty, bent wipers scraped across the windshield with a series of grunts, spreading the dirty slush, making matters worse. Just yesterday, the skies hovered in gray, the grass had turned yellow, and the remaining leaves wore a dark, vibrant orange skin. Today, everything dressed in their finest whites. The Fates decided to perform a purifying ritual on Clearwell, Kansas and wanted to flush the evil away.

If only.

Buoyed by the gray tape Red had affixed on both sides, the cardboard held steady on the passenger side. I wanted to speed up but knew I'd better keep it slow and steady, Dad's boring motto. At the first stop sign, the Bucket decided it didn't want to stop and slid to the side, nearly depositing me in the ditch. Revenge, no doubt, for having abandoned it for several days. Halfway through the intersection, just several inches from the ditch, the Bucket finally gave me a break and wobbled to a stop. Several cars blasted their horns, one driver's middle finger raised in a fine salute, as I gave them a shaky wave in return. I took a deep breath and continued my perilous journey.

I topped out at about ten miles an hour. What should've taken fifteen minutes nearly tripled in time. Finally, I pulled in front of Mickey's house and unclenched my alabaster white knuckles from the steering wheel. Panting heavily, the inside of the windshield fogged up in seconds. While the trip wracked every last nerve, I dreaded what lay ahead of me even more.

Carefully, I trudged up the snow-hidden sidewalk. Not taken by surprise this time, Mickey's flowerbed still held strong, even in the storm. A last act of defiance by the flowers. They wouldn't give up their lives without a battle, stubborn as Mickey, their caretaker.

I pounded on the door, wishing I had the foresight to bring gloves. The requisite scrambling of the chains and locks ensued. Finally, Mickey belted out, "Who is it?"

"It's Tex, Mickey." Large snowflakes melted upon

my face while I shivered through the storm. "I really need your help this time!"

She opened the door and quickly ushered me in. "How many times I gotta tell you, kid? Call first."

"Sorry, but it's an emergency." I stomped my soaking wet shoes onto her, yes, floral patterned, greeting rug. "I didn't have time to call. I was in school all day."

Unnatural light emitted from her TV, the only illumination in the house. A frozen image of some bland soap-stud, shaking and stuttering on freeze frame, flickered spasmodically. The resulting lights flashing strobes resembled a cheap rock concert.

"Let me turn off the VCR, then." She grabbed a huge remote and pointed it at the television. And I had to wonder what a VCR was, but the answer had to wait.

"There. Now, what's all the hullaballoo? My stories are waiting for me." She rested one hand on her waist impatiently, while the other swung the large remote like a weapon.

"The killer's after me. Everyone I know's in danger."

"Oh! Sit down, then." Her attitude shifted from impatience to concern.

As I sank into her quicksand sofa trap, I explained everything as fast and succinctly as I could. Mickey gasped audibly when I told her about the killer chasing me. She shut her eyes, leaned back, and nodded on occasion, the only sign she hadn't fallen asleep.

"And…there's one final thing I gotta tell you," I said. "Last night I conjured up the spirit of Bob Bellman, trying to find out who the killer is." I grimaced and actually bent forward, proffering my head in a dope-slap sacrificial position.

She gasped again. "*You* actually conjured up a spirit? On the physical plane?" She appeared in awe, her mouth open, lower lip quivering. "Only third-level witches and coven leaders can achieve that. You must be more powerful than I thought." She patted me on the back. I pulled up in surprise. *Crack*! Her hand caught me sharply on the back of the head. An even bigger, more painful, surprise.

"You idiot! Do you know how dangerous that is? And you did it by yourself? Stupid!" She smacked the back of my head again for emphasis. "Haven't you been listening to a thing I've taught you?"

"Sorry, sorry, I'm sorry. I didn't want to involve you anymore. I didn't want you to be in danger, too." I lifted my head and dared to look into her eyes.

"You don't need to worry about my safety, kid. I can take care of myself." I thought she surely meant protection spells. But from out of nowhere she suddenly brandished a large, shiny knife. "This pig-sticker will get any killer comes after me!" She continued to wave it in the dark room, admiring the sharp edges that glinted from the TV's light show. Just as quickly, the knife vanished again. I wondered—but not too much—where she kept it. And if she had many of them placed strategically throughout the house.

"Anyway, it *is* impressive you conjured a spirit, you being a newbie and all. But it's a dangerous game you're playing at, kid." She plucked her lip, lost in thought. "The spirit still may be lurking around somewhere…."

I doubted it as I remembered the twisting, imploding green miasma that had vanished with a tortured wail. Seemed pretty final to me. But I didn't want to disagree with Mickey on anything, not now. "I know, I'm sorry, and I won't do it again. I was stupid."

Silence overcame us as the tick-tock of the grandfather clock against the wall reminded me of my urgency.

"Mickey? I really gotta hurry."

"Okay," she finally said, "what do you want to do?"

"I know I've got a lot to learn yet and I'm not ready for, well, tons of stuff, but I need to find out who the killer is. It needs to happen *now*. Before any more of my friends are attacked or killed."

Mickey tapped her bony finger against her lips. "All right, then, I'll be right back." Like a jet at take-off, she flew upstairs, shooing her cats along the way. I heard thumps and bumps and nearly ran upstairs to see if she'd fallen when she came back carrying a box and a large silk bag on top of it.

"Scoot that crap off the coffee table," she ordered. I obeyed, carefully grabbing the magazines and knickknacks off the table, and setting them gently onto the hardwood floor. "Oh for God's sake, kid," she said, rolling her eyes. "Don't be such a namby-pamby! Just sweep them onto the floor." I looked at her questioningly but did as told.

She placed the silk bag onto the now empty table.

"What are we doing?"

Deep into her witchy zone, she pulled out a large, oval dark mirror from the bag and set it at the edge of the table. I leaned forward to get a better look.

"Don't look into it," she screamed. I fell back into the enveloping sofa with a *whoomph*. "*We're* not going to do anything, kid. *You're* going to do some mirror scrying." She stood over me, glaring, until I understood the implications of what she said.

"I think you're a more powerful witch already than I am, so you're probably gonna have better luck at this." She pulled two orange votive candles out of the box and placed them, one on each end of the table. She tossed a book of matches at me, which I, of course, didn't catch. "C'mon, fumble-fingers, light those candles up." I lit the candles as she scrambled away again.

She brought back a small bowl with several pieces of brown incense lying within and slammed it down in front of me. "Okay, now light the incense." It took several attempts, but I finally succeeded in igniting the incense, and the acrid, perfume smell filled my nostrils and burned my eyes.

"Don't tell me you're allergic to incense, too?" she asked as she noticed my squirming.

"I don't know. Yeah…maybe, probably I am."

She giggled hysterically. "Oh, Tex…you just slay me." She shook her blue-haired head. "Okay, I'm going to walk you through this. But do *not* look directly into the mirror."

Of course, once Mickey said this, I wanted nothing more than to sneak a glance at the forbidden mirror. Its surface appeared to be painted black with a smooth, acrylic finish. Grapevines or some such foliage adorned the golden-colored oval frame. Tin foil appeared to be stretched across the backside.

"Mickey, why didn't we try this before? I mean, why didn't we try a spell to find out who the killer was earlier?"

She stopped what she was doing and sat next to me with a sigh. "Because, first of all, I told you it only works *sometimes*." Her fingers extended with each point. "Secondly, you *have* to be emotionally connected—in a strong way—to what you're trying to find out. I didn't think you were before, not with them bullies dying, but you are now. Thirdly, now that I see how powerful you are, I think you can pull this off." She'd counted down to her pinkie finger. "Finally, with witchcraft like this, there's always a chance of great danger. You never know what you're going to get." She stared at me, her lecture completed.

I nodded. "Okay…let's do it."

"Go grab a wooden chair from the kitchen. And carry it! Don't drag it across my floor." I hurried into the kitchen. Before I returned, Mickey had quickly scrawled a chalk circle, not unlike the one I had drawn the night before, on the floor.

"Carefully put the chair in the circle…and *don't* break the circle." Again operating in unbridled drill sergeant witch-mode, any semblance of an addle-brained blue-haired woman had flown the witch-coop.

I put the chair in the scraggily drawn circle with about an eight-inch clear circumference between the chair and the chalk line.

"Now, sit down, Tex." I sat. "Shut your eyes and do some relaxing breathing exercises."

"I don't really know how to do that." With my eyes shut, it unnerved me I wouldn't see the inevitable coming head-slap.

"Oh, for God's sake, kid, just relax. Breathe in, breathe out…keep doing it." For nearly five minutes I breathed deeply, amazed at how loosened up I felt.

From a seemingly far distance, Mickey quietly intoned, "You're looking for your inner eye, Tex. This is the eye that's in your mind. Look for it and ask it to help fill you with white light. You'll understand once you see it."

Mickey's voice changed into a whisper, a guidepost from across an expansive ocean. Alone now, I swam in a sea of comforting darkness. My body tingled pleasantly, the warmth embracing me, far removed from the blizzard happening outside. The darkness diminished, replaced by a glowing, warm light, growing and expanding constantly. Thrumming in a pleasant rhythm. Now I saw myself as if in a dream. I walked through the blinding white light, no boundaries, walls, or ground underneath me. Simply *there*.

"Tex. Hi, my love," said my mother. Bit by bit, she materialized in front of me, a light mist comprised of more shades of blue than I ever thought existed. I tried to speak, but as happens in dreams sometimes, I couldn't.

"I'm so proud of you, Tex," she said, smiling. Her entire body came into a light, shimmering focus. She wore the same outfit she wore on the day she'd told me the news her cancer had gone into remission. "What you're doing is the right thing. It's a dangerous, dark path you've chosen to go down, but you may be the only one that can end the cycle."

She reached out and caressed my face, her fingers light as whispers. "I wish I could tell you everything will be all right…but I can't see the future." Her smile slid away. "Don't go in alone, Tex. Bring someone you trust."

I couldn't see myself now, only her. But I felt love,

as strong as faith. My entire being filled with calm resolve and love and protection from my mom. "Now, go do what you need—what you *have*—to do, Tex. My hero." She vanished gently into a luminous swirl.

This time, unlike the last time I'd contacted Mom, hope and happiness filled me, something in short supply lately. I wanted to stay and bask in the inner eye if this indeed truly existed, but I knew I needed to move on and complete my task.

"Tex? Tex, have you found your inner eye?" asked Mickey from miles away. Her voice echoed in my head like a firecracker's report in an empty field. "Tex, can you hear me?"

"Yes." I found my voice on the physical plane. Semi-awareness fluttered back to me, but I managed to hold onto the dream-like stage as well.

"Good, now stay in touch with your inner eye and ask for assistance from the Great Mother of Earth."

Eyes still closed, my head nodded slightly as if someone else drove the vehicle of my body. "Oh, Great Mother of Earth, I call upon you for help in answering my questions." I didn't know if the syntax, or intonation, were correct, but it felt right and flowed smoothly from my mouth.

An even-brighter light and warmth filled my mind and body, head to toe.

"Can you feel her, Tex?" Mickey's voice sounded louder and closer now. "Is she there?"

"I think so." I nodded again.

"Slowly open your eyes and gaze upon the mirror and be careful not to see your own reflection in it."

I opened my eyes and looked down upon the mirror resting on the table, holding my head rigid so as not to see my reflection. The shiny black surface had been replaced by a whirling miasma of black clouds and an occasional beam of radiance, like the sunny aftermath of a spring thunderstorm.

"Visualize something, Tex. Think of a pink circle."

I did so, and a pink circle materialized out of the wisps of black smoke. "Now, think of a fruit," she said.

I thought of a red apple. The pink circle shrank, transforming into a strange, photo-negative appearance of a shiny red apple.

"Did you see these things, Tex?"

"Yes."

"Good, now ask your question."

I hesitated at first but realized I needed to. Half-awake, half-asleep, I stared at the red apple and realized I couldn't turn back.

"Great Mother, who is the killer of my friend, Josh Berillo?" I gulped, suddenly more aware of my immediate surroundings.

The entire surface of the mirror lit up brightly before filling up with the black smoke again, spinning endlessly and recklessly as if fighting to escape the boundaries of the mirror's frame. The apple rolled and tumbled then dissolved into a purée. The smoke pulled back, and the features of a face formed, one element at a time. Finally, the smoke rolled away, leaving a black and white, but extremely clear, photo-negative image of a face.

I let out a yelp of shock. My eyes snapped open. I jumped up, full awareness shooting back into my body like a syringe full of adrenalin. Helpless, I chanted, "No, no, please *no*," over and over again as I held my head, trying to keep my brain from exploding. The image on the mirror expanded, shattered into jagged smoky shards, before reverting back into its original state of dull blackness.

I stumbled back, still crying out "*No!*" Bile rose in my throat. I couldn't believe it. I just couldn't believe it.

Mickey jumped from the sofa and snapped on the lamp in the room. I stood, traumatized. Any sense of my inner eye had long vanished, to be replaced by cold, stark terror, disappointment, and nausea.

"Sit down, Tex," Mickey ordered. She reached high and placed her arm around my shoulders. "Before you break something."

I obeyed and fell back onto the sofa.

"Did you see him?" she asked. "Did you see who the killer is?"

"Yes…" I whispered. "Didn't you?"

"I didn't see a damn thing. Do you know who it is?"

"Yeah, I know him." I told her his identity, and she looked just as shocked as me. After several deep breaths, I stood up and said, "I've gotta go."

"Now, hold on, Tex!" She scrambled to her feet, trying to keep up with me. "What do you think you're going to do?" She rushed after me, her pink slippers slapping rudely at the floor.

"I'm going to go confront him…and end this." Driven by a fierce sense of determination and anger, nothing could stop me.

"You can't go off and do this by yourself!" I suddenly remembered what Mom had warned me to do. "Besides, there's a goddamn blizzard outside!"

I looked out Mickey's window and couldn't even

see the street through the flowing, whirling snowflakes.

"Mickey, I can't tell anyone about this without telling them I'm a witch. Can't you see that? And I'm not going to involve my friends." She blinked at me, lower lip trembling. "And I've *got* to make sure first. I can't call the cops until I'm *absolutely* sure."

For once, Mickey lacked a snappy comeback, a head-slap, anything. Finally, she said, "Well, if you're going to do a damn fool thing like this, wait here a minute." She began to paddle off, then turned around. "I *mean* it, Tex. Just wait a damn minute, okay?" I nodded as she hustled off into the kitchen.

She reappeared brandishing a black Sharpie and what looked like an old-fashioned burlap potato sack. "Here." She pointed the Sharpie at me like the sharpest knife in her arsenal. "Draw a big pentagram on this."

I thought it crazy, but probably no less crazy than the things I'd witnessed in the past month. Struggling with it, I managed a primitive pentagram on the rough material. I went over the lines several times, thickening them to about a quarter-inch wide.

"Now, attach this to the front of your car," she said. "And I have a spell here somewhere…" She grabbed what looked like a plastic recipe box from the side table by the sofa and flipped through it frantically. "Here." She yanked out a note card. "Put that burlap in front of your car and before you leave, read this spell."

I took the card and noticed it was mostly in Latin.

"That should at least keep you safe on your drive," she said. "But, Tex, I'll tell you what I'm going to do. I'm going to give you thirty minutes, and then I'm going to call the cops. You ain't gonna' tell me no different either." Her finger wagged like an ecstatic dog's tail in my face.

I knew her mind wouldn't change, but thought I could haggle a bit. "Fine, but at least wait forty-five minutes. It took me thirty to get here in the snow."

She looked at me, suspicion touching her eyes. "We'll see."

"Thanks again, Mickey," I said, already one foot out the front door.

"You be careful," she called from her door. "You just be careful!" Through the unrelenting snow, I turned and gave her a thumbs-up. And I swear I heard her say, "I don't want to lose you, too," in a quiet as snow voice.

I trudged down Mickey's sidewalk—possibly eight inches of coverage now—and made it to the car. The wind tossed my hair, mad as hell. My ears numbed from the frigid temperature.

I punctured a hole in the burlap with my hood ornament and managed to tuck the other end into the grille. Even given the sharp winds, the bag seemed to be holding firm. I read the spell Mickey'd given me. A barely visible red glow bled out from the pentagram on the burlap bag. The snow in front began to melt away as if exposed to a heat source.

I yanked open the car door, and a sudden, violent gust of wind nearly took the door off its hinges. The wind played tug of war with me, but as the winner, I pulled the door shut. The engine turned over on the first try. *Good girl, Bucket. I promise I won't abandon you again.*

Slowly, I inched into the street. Even though visibility was nearly nonexistent, the headlights proved the spell successful. In front of the car, snow tossed back up into the sky, the world's greatest snowplow. Snow flew to the left and right, the spell clearing a path for me, even melting some as I chugged along. I peered in my rear-view mirror and saw the cleared path behind me quickly filling up again. Briefly, I wondered if I could get a job snow plowing this winter? That's a big no to witchcraft for personal gain.

Obviously, the snow crews had been wholly unprepared for a November snowstorm. I didn't spot a single plow and the side roads hadn't been touched. Either that or the snow fell at such a wicked pace the city employees couldn't keep up with it. But I carefully traveled on, the snow blowing out of my way, a quicker journey this time.

Not too late, four-forty, I hoped against hope I could still find him at school.

Foregoing the parking lot, I pulled into the circular school drive. I slid to a halt in front of the main side doors, locked my car, and kicked the snow aside as I walked through the entrance. Good, still open, and all lights burning brightly on the dark confrontation ahead of me.

Wet footprints trailed behind me as I walked up the stairs to the second floor. I approached the door. Light leaked out from beneath it. I braved myself, took a deep breath, shut my eyes, and opened them.

I knew what I had to do—what I must do—as I slowly pushed the door open to Mr. Jensen's classroom.

Chapter Eighteen

"Why'd you do it?" Anger barrelled through my fear, shooting from the pit of my stomach to my gritted teeth. "Why'd you kill them? Why'd you take my friend from me, Red?"

Red popped his head up from behind the open hood of the car in the garage. Momentarily dumbfounded, he recovered quickly and flashed his award-winning smile. Adorned in his dirty coveralls, he brandished a large oil-covered wrench in his hand. "What're you talking about, Tex?" His wavering grin spoke volumes.

"I *know* you killed them, Red. I just want to know *why*."

Red's face transformed into one of a stranger. His brow furrowed, his eyes cold. An ugly sneer replaced the genial smile, a long way from the fair-haired, good-time, golden boy I'd become friends with and even admired.

"You gotta understand something, Tex." He crossed the garage in lengthy strides. "Do you have any idea what it's like to work at a school—a school where you once were the most promising athlete, one who would go places—and you end up as a *janitor*?" When he said the word "janitor," his voice pitched high. "I was set to go to any school of my choice on a free-ride scholarship, but I blew my knee out. Then my choices became…limited."

Slowly, he approached me, his wrench swinging by his side. I backed up to the opposite side of the garage, positioning the car between us.

"And those punks Rimmer and Bellman were shit! They taunted me. They *teased* me! They'd say things like 'Hey, I saw your trophy in the case…too bad you're a janitor now!' and 'Wow, I hope I make it big like you someday…the world's oldest high school student!'"

The outrageous irony of the situation floored me. "You mean to tell me…you killed them…because you were *bullied*?" A giggle seeped out, then the dam broke releasing hysterical laughter.

"Shut your *mouth*. You don't understand!"

"You don't think I understand what it's like to be *bullied? Bullshit*! What kind of life do you think I've lived since I started here?" Like a panther and its prey, he stalked me around the car as I kept moving.

"But your whole goddamn *life*?" He stopped, the wrench pointing at me like a hanging judge's gavel. "I'd had enough. You gotta understand, something. I *was* those punks! I used to get all the chicks, the awards, the favored treatment. Everyone loved me…and then it was taken away." His upper lip curled, his face a twisted visage of evil. "And that one night, after football practice, Rimmer actually came in here and said to me—just as sweetly as he could—'Are you ever going to graduate, Red?'" He grinned and repeated, 'Are you ever going to graduate, Red?' I just…I kept hitting him with a crowbar. He was unconscious, and I tossed him into the trunk of my car. Then I dumped him."

I looked toward the hallway door waiting for Mr.

Jensen to come in.

"The funny thing is, Tex…" His smile came back, but this time not a good-natured smile, but one swimming in malice and insanity. "The funny thing is I liked it." He licked his lips. "So, when I saw Bellman hanging out by himself at the old gas station…well, I grabbed my crowbar and went over there and did the same thing to him. The last straw was when I heard what he did to Ian. I did it for *you guys*, Tex!" For a moment, I saw the sincere side of Red shine through, protector of the underdog. He was insane, no doubt about it, possibly even more so than Bellman, but I felt he truly believed that he did it for us.

"That's just…*crazy*, Red," I said. "Yeah, those guys sucked, but we didn't want you to kill them for us. And…and…what about Josh?"

"I didn't want to hurt little Joshie." Sadness weighed his gaze down. "But when he was riding around on his damn skateboard, he saw me do it. I stuffed Bellman in the trunk of my car and saw Josh staring at me from across the street. I yelled at him to stop, but he took off faster than shit. I knew he was afraid of the cops, so that gave me a bit of time. The next day, when his parents were gone, I went to his house, trying to talk sense into him. But…I knew it'd never work. I kicked in the door, went upstairs, and…" His prominent Adam's apple bobbed up and down as he swallowed. "I didn't want to! I *had* to!"

"He was your *friend*!" A mixture of emotions threatened to overwhelm, to confuse me. I almost pitied Red.

Like a dime, though, he turned again. "Do you really think I would've picked *you* guys as friends?

You're the kind of geeks I crushed in high school. Now...I was one of you..." He slammed the wrench down onto the car, denting the body of his dream project he'd slaved over all semester.

"You're nothing but a sad, failed bully, aren't you, Red?" His eyelids flew up, exposing dilated pupils. "Why'd you go after me, then?"

"I couldn't be sure what Josh might've told you. Nothing personal." He shrugged. "And at Joshie's funeral, I heard you say you were going to catch me. But...I'm going to get you first."

Red released a guttural scream and ran after me. I darted to the left, and he countered by lunging after me.

Blown knee or not, Red still packed amazing speed. He tackled me from behind, arms around my legs. I went down onto the cement with a sickening thud. My chin felt like it split open. I wriggled around and saw Red raise the wrench above me, his mouth gaping open, roaring in incoherent rage.

The hallway door slammed open with a *thwack*. Mr. Jensen launched himself into the room, all three hundred pounds of him in a miraculously fast display of locomotion. He grabbed Red by the shoulders, practically carrying him across the room, as they slammed down onto the cement. They rolled and grappled as I scrambled to my feet. Red forced his way on top and grasped Jensen by the throat, his other fist raised high to deliver a blow. I grabbed the wrench Red dropped. With shaking hands, I swung it into Red's back. He yelped and twisted around, snarling.

He bounded off Jensen and leaped at me. I waved the wrench wildly in front of me, trying to ward him off. A few lucky blows landed on his outstretched arms, but it didn't stop him. He came at me fast, an unrelenting force from Hell.

"Hold it," yelled a voice behind us. Detective Cowlings stood in the doorway, legs straddled and gun pointed at Red. Two uniformed cops backed him up, guns aimed as well.

Red looked like he'd just awakened from a bad dream. Shock filled his eyes, then fear, then a heavier than sandbags sadness. He crumpled to the floor, his head cowering between his knees, sobbing. He rocked back and forth as the two cops approached him warily.

I went over to Jensen to check on him. "Are you all right, Mr. Jensen?" I extended a hand to help him up, even though I knew I didn't have the strength to do so.

"Yeah, Tex, thanks." He coughed several times, cleared his throat. His hand engulfed mine. I pulled, but as I suspected, he pretty much had to get himself up on his knees. "Didn't do you much good, though, did I?"

"Did you hear everything?"

"I sure did." Another weird cough, a cat spitting up a hairball.

"Well, then, you did great, Mr. Jensen."

The two policemen escorted Red away, his hands cuffed behind him. Still sobbing, he looked over his shoulder at me and stopped. "Sorry...I'm sorry, Tex...so sorry."

"Yeah, I'm sorry, too." My voice choked, full of loss and sadness.

Of course, Cowlings watched the entire transaction with great interest. "Well, Tex, here we go again," he said, for once smiling. "Your friend Mickey called me, told me where I could find you, and what you were up to." His smile vanished. "Is that cut on your chin okay?

Let me have a look at it." He tilted my head back and carefully probed at it with his gloved fingers. "Yeah, I don't think you'll need stitches. Now…why don't you tell me *how* you discovered who the biggest killer in Clearwell, Kansas, history was?"

Uh-oh.

"It's like he told me, Detective," interjected Mr. Jensen. "I didn't believe him at first either, but when he told me his suspicions…well, I thought it merited further investigation."

"You two are *not* policemen," said Cowlings. "You don't do my job. And where did these suspicions come from, Tex?"

"I can't really remember right now, Detective." Even though I never felt more clear-headed than I did now, I played up the woozy act. "But when Red fixed my car window earlier this morning, there were a few things he said that sounded…weird."

"Like what?"

"I don't know. *Oh*! I think he asked me if I needed help fixing my car window before I told him it was broken."

"Uh-huh," said Cowlings. "You didn't think he could've seen your car in the parking lot?"

"Hmmm, doubt it. He always parked on the opposite side of the school, by his garage."

Cowlings shook his head. "I don't believe you, Tex…but whatever…for now." He stared at both Jensen and me. "The important thing is you can both give me a detailed report, right?"

Mr. Jensen said, "Oh, I'll be glad to."

I nodded.

"And you both absolutely, positively, heard him

admit guilt of the murders?" Excited at the potential outcome, Cowlings damn near glowed as he probably envisioned a ginormous gold star in his detective work.

"Absolutely, positively," echoed back Mr. Jensen, with a Cheshire Cat smile. Great, surrounded by two adults who were way too giddy about a serial-murder case. Once again, I nodded dumbly in agreement.

"Okay, I'm going to look over...Red's...place of work here with a fine-toothed comb and check out his car. If all goes well, we'll have some corroborating evidence that will seal the deal. I'll look forward to getting your statements in the morning, all right, fellas?"

"Sounds good, Detective," said Jensen. And I, of course, nodded like a dutiful little schoolboy.

"Tex, once again, I have to say, nice job. *Stupid* and dangerous...but nicely done." Cowlings patted me on the back. Mr. Jensen joined him and clapped me on the back as well as he escorted me out to my car.

Then I went home.

****

The next day, I awoke to a pounding at the front door. I looked at the alarm clock and saw that it read three-thirty p.m. Unbelievably, I'd slept completely through school. Dad obviously knew about it, and let me sleep the sleep of the sleepy.

When I'd arrived home the night before, as soon as I walked inside, I pretty much collapsed right in front of him. Like a babbling brook of an idiot, I explained everything to him as fast as I could, not letting him get a word in edgewise. I didn't have the time or mood for a lecture. His anger soon dissipated into relief, as he rolled his chair over and hugged me. I didn't let go.

Mutual relief rolled off us like steam in a sauna. A long hug worked better than words at that moment. Maybe now a semblance of normality would re-enter our lives. We may as well've cheered, *Bring on the mundane and humdrum.*

Exhausted, I went to bed. As soon as I hit the blankets, they hit back and knocked me out.

So, now, not only had I slept through school, but the door hammering possibly meant the cops wanted to hose and phonebook me since I missed giving my statement. Or maybe Hastings finally nailed the goods on me for missing detention, two days running.

I groaned and rolled over, wishing the noise away, and attempted to sink back into sleep. Suddenly, stealthy footsteps rushed up the stairwell. I looked around for a weapon and ridiculously settled on a candle from my nightstand. I held it toward the closed bedroom door, shaking in my hand like a very successful divining rod.

Slowly, the door opened on squeaking hinges, followed by a loud high-pitched shriek.

"Where the *hell* were you today, Tex? And *why* in the goddamned hell didn't you text me?" shrieked Olivia. "And are you going to attack me with a *candle* or *what*?"

"Sorry." I dropped the candle. "Force of habit. Paranoia dies hard."

She burst in, a human hurricane. The door slammed behind her. Arms akimbo, she stood over me, her anger rising like a hot air balloon. "*Well*?"

"Sorry, O'." I've had to apologize a lot to her lately. "Honestly, after last night, I was so drained and exhausted, I fell asleep. I guess I've been asleep for nineteen hours or so." She paced my room back and forth, shooting me an occasional icy glare.

"I was worried," she said, calming down. "There's been so much talk at school I didn't know what to think!" She spotted my phone next to my bed, grabbed it, and held it face forward toward me. "*Twenty-six* messages and *sixty-two* texts! Don't you *ever* check this *damn* thing?"

All I could muster was, "I'm so tired." While I hoped it might buy me the sympathy vote, nothing could have been more accurate.

"You're not the only one who's been through hell lately, you know!" She slipped off her black flats and pulled the blanket down. "Scoot over. You *don't* get to have a monopoly on being tired either." She crawled in next to me. "I've heard the stories, but I wanna hear it from you."

With a deliberate sigh, I explained the entire tale to her from the moment I left school until the time I hit the sack last night. I asked her what happened today.

"Well, apparently, they found a bloodied crowbar in Red's trunk and remnants of bloodied coveralls down in the boiler...or something," she sneered. "I can't *believe* we were sitting in that...*gross* place, right next to where that creep was burning his murder clothes! What *did* I tell you about him, Tex? *Gross!*"

"Yeah." Although the thought of everything— especially that it happened and *why* it happened— seemed so pointless and ultimately sad. I nearly teared up again in my vulnerability. More sleep felt like the antidote I needed.

"And Cowlings was looking for you," she added.

"Great. I'm going back to sleep... You can join me

if you'd like to."

"Okay. No *snoring*!"

I smiled, and we both slept for another couple of hours, comfortable at long last in the realization we would awaken once again—relatively speaking—to a safe place to exist.

****

One month later, not much had changed. We were still mourning the loss of Josh while the rest of the student body moved on from the shock of the killer janitor who cleaned up vomit in between murdering people, to preparing for Christmas vacation.

Cowlings finally tracked me down and took my statement. Obviously, he remained skeptical of many things I told him. But he appeared pleased with how things turned out for him, so he took it all in stride. Happy ending and all that. He did leave me with a simple warning.

"Tex, it's not that I don't like you," he told me upon shaking hands goodbye. "I do. But I hope I don't see you within my professional capacity again."

"You and me both, Detective." I grinned and shook his hand. Hooray, no more need for Cowlings in my life. Or so I thought. But that's a story for another time.

For the first couple of weeks after the ordeal, people treated me differently. Very discomfiting. Some wanted to lionize me as a sort of hero, which I just shrugged off. But most of the students just sort of stared and whispered. Let them. In another month, it'd be forgotten anyway. Then they could get back to the important things in life such as joining the popular kids and wondering who would win the all-important title of Prom Queen.

Johnny Malinowski pretty much ignored me for those first two weeks as well. But soon enough—the Christmas Spirit had overtaken him, I suppose—he reverted to calling me fag and other such enlightened names. I paid him no attention until the third week when he shoved me. I stopped, turned around, and shoved him back, hard. He slammed into the lockers, a stunned look on his face. He didn't say another word, and I kept on walking as if nothing had happened.

Other students stared at this display, a few smiling, wishing they'd been the ones to do it, I guess. He left me alone for the remaining few days of school, but I'm sure he'd roar back with a vengeance come the start of school in January. Types like him always do attack again, like rabid dogs, acting on gut instinct. Let him come. But he wouldn't find me sitting back and taking it any longer. Sure, I might receive a few punches, but after everything that'd happened recently, a threat like Johnny Malinowski felt downright laughable. Besides, I had a new Golden Rule to live by—if he, or any of the other Neanderthals crossed the line into violence, I'd directly take it up with a sympathetic ear like Jensen until I got satisfactory results. I'd lived most of my high school life in the shadow of fear and dread. No longer acceptable. If they branded me a rat, so be it; I've been called much worse.

Ian still brandished his arm in the ever-heavenward pointing splint, but it was due soon to come off. His Christmas present, he told everyone laughing. We'd join him in his obvious delight, but we also understood that underneath that jolly exterior lurked the highly likely fear he'd never again regain full use of that hand.

Through it all, the three of us adopted *Josh*

would've loved this as a mantra, as if he were lurking somewhere within earshot. I say it's true, as I had definitely become a firm believer that a hereafter existed. Whether heaven, some big ball of energy, a parallel earth, we start over as worker ants, whatever, I had no clue. I didn't want to dwell on it either. Teenagers shouldn't be thinking of such things. But we kept Josh alive the best way we knew how.

I remembered what I'd said on the intercom that day, which now seemed so long ago, and accepted my own words as a challenge. I sought out the shadow people, kids I'd never noticed before, and if I didn't downright befriend them, I made a note to learn their names and say hi.

"Son, one of the most important things you should do with people," Dad told me once, "is learn their names and always address them by it. People like to hear their names." As a general rule, Dad nailed it, although there were exceptions. I, for one, still hated to be called "Richard."

With varying success, I even tried to invite some of the shadow kids into our little tight-knit group. Generally, Olivia or Ian might smirk—not fans of change, I guess—and I'd nudge them and chastise them later. Sometimes, though, the new kids proved obviously too freaky to hang with. But I kept trying.

For some reason, nothing ever came of my missing my detention. Nobody ever said anything; I didn't get any calls to go to the office for a meeting with Hastings; the hall patrol didn't shoot me down on sight. Nothing. I didn't ask because missing out on that fun suited me just fine and dandy. I don't know if a higher power such as Jensen intervened—or even Cowlings—

but I didn't look a gift horse in the mouth. Cool. But Hastings still lurked around the hallways like a stone gargoyle, glaring at me every chance he could. One time, he even gave me the silly two fingers pointing from his eyes thing, like he couldn't get enough of me. Maybe he had an inappropriate crush on me or whatever.

****

Just a few days before Christmas, on the wonderful last day of classes, I gave Olivia and Ian a ride home. Unnaturally mild for a late December day (and even though we suffered through a whiter than white November), it looked like we'd get to enjoy a damn-near balmy Christmas.

They both wanted to hang out, but to their disappointment, I told them I had something important to do. Olivia shot me a look of suspicion, instantly remembered danger didn't currently lurk around the corner, and let me go with a hug.

Package under arm, I walked down Mickey's sidewalk. I hadn't seen Mickey since that night in November and felt guilty for it. Not that I blew her off. Rather, I think she just reminded me of everything that'd happened and all the resultant danger that connected, at least in my mind, with the practice of witchcraft. Utter nonsense, I know—witchcraft had nothing to do with Red's psycho turn—but it still scared me to think of things like Bellman, his demonic form (of which I still have nightmares), my mother, and especially, the cruel, unjust murder of Josh.

Around the sidewalk, the sunflowers and weeds had finally given up the good fight and gone into hibernation. Sadly, the joyously full of life flowerbed had departed this mortal coil as well.

I knocked on the door, holding the heavy package unsteadily with one hand.

"Who's there?" she cried out after a seeming eternity.

"Merry Christmas, Mickey," I yelled. "It's Tex."

Rattle, rattle, shake, shake, and the door swung open. Surprised, she smiled, wider than I'd ever seen her do so. She didn't even seem to mind I didn't call first.

"Tex, kiddo, where've you been?" she cried. "Come in, come in!" She opened the door and waved the cats upstairs.

"Hi, Mickey. Sorry I haven't been by. I've just been sort of freaked out by the stuff that happened last month. I'm sure you heard all about it."

"Oh, yes, indeed! It was almost as good a tale as my daytime stories." And this was probably the highest compliment Mickey Goldfarb would ever dole out. "I heard everything about it, kid. Are you some kind of big-time hero now? Too good to come see ol' Mickey?" She actually looked hurt.

"Well, that's one thing I came to talk to you about. If it's okay with you, I know I need to learn more about witchcraft. I need..." I paused, searching for the right word.

"Refinement," she said. "Yes, you sure do need that, kid." She smiled again, a very toothy smile.

"I've got some time off school. Could we start the day after Christmas? If I'm going to be a responsible witch, I can't think of a better mentor than you, Mickey."

"Okay, kid, twist my arm. Just don't forget the

chicken." She playfully wagged her finger in my face and burst out cackling. "You know I never really expected you to bring me chicken that first time. I was just sort of testing you." Her throaty laugh turned quickly into a coughing spasm.

"Oh, *now* you tell me." I rolled my eyes exaggeratedly. "Hey, here's the other reason I came by…" I held the package out to her. "Merry Christmas, Mickey."

She grabbed the package and began to rattle it. I winced, hoping she wouldn't break it, but I didn't want to interrupt her obvious joy at receiving the gift. "You didn't wrap up chicken, did you?"

"No." I sighed. "Open it."

"Kid, I didn't get you anything." Her lips pushed toward her nose, while the corners of her mouth drooped.

"That's okay." I laughed. "The spirit of Christmas and all that jazz, don't you know? Besides, you've given me plenty."

She ripped open the present with savage ferocity. "'Digital…Video… Recorder,'" she read slowly off the box as if in a foreign language. She stared at it for a long time before she asked, "What the hell is it, kid?"

"It's a DVR. It'll make recording your stories a lot easier, and the quality will be better, too. I noticed you were still using a VCR, and I thought—"

She thrust the package back into my chest. "Now, you just take that back right now, Tex. I don't need to be messin' with no new electronic gadgets or anything like that."

"I'll be glad to hook it up for you and show you how to operate it—"

"Kid, that ol' VCR has seen a lot of years on it, and I'm betting it'll see a lot more, too." She gave me a conspiratorial wink, nudging me in the side. I had no idea what she meant, but I knew you couldn't argue with her.

"Okay, Mickey, fine." I didn't do a very good job hiding my disappointment. I'd taken out a small loan with my dad at his bank to purchase it.

"Oh, kid, don't get your panties up in a bunch." She laughed. When I heard this, I had to laugh as well. "I appreciate the thought, but *really*…save your money for something else, all right?"

"If you say so. Well, I better get home. So…I'll see you the day after Christmas?" I looked around her house and noticed she hadn't set up a Christmas tree, nor had she any decorations around. I turned to leave, and as an afterthought, I said, "Hey, Mickey, can I ask you something?"

"Sure, kid."

"Do you have any Christmas plans?"

She turned her head sideways, so I wouldn't be able to look into her eyes.

I let her off the hook and said, "I ask because every Christmas day, it's a tradition at our house to invite friends and family to come and go as they please. It's nothing fancy, but we keep a big vat of clam chowder heated up the entire day. I'd really like it if you could come."

Her eyes lit up behind her gravity-defying glasses. "Are you actually asking me to come to your party, kid?"

"Yes, I am."

"To get out in the cold and travel across town on

Christmas?" A smile cracked across her face.

"Mickey, it's going to be about sixty degrees, and I'm only—what—ten minutes away?"

"Okay, kid." She sighed, unsuccessfully keeping her gruff persona upfront. "You drive a hard bargain. I'll come if it's that big a deal to you." She smiled as giddily as one of Clearwell High's always cheerful cheerleaders.

"Great! No presents, no fancy dress, just bring yourself. Anytime between ten a.m. to ten p.m. Let me write down my address." I reached into my coat for a pen.

"I know where you live, kid." She swatted my arm out of my jacket. "I'll be there, already"

"Cool. Bye, Mickey." Before she shut the door, I stole a glimpse at her grinning as wide as a jack-o-lantern.

****

The second I walked in the door, Dad said, "Son, we need to talk about something." My heart bang, bang, banged at the door of my ribcage. Every time he'd start a conversation like this, it usually was the harbinger of something awful. Surely, his health hadn't taken a turn for the worse?

"What's wrong, Dad?" I sat down at the kitchen table next to him. I remember some very hard conversations happening here.

"I don't know how to say this, Tex, so I'm just going to come out with it." He cleared his throat. "Son…what would you think if I started to date?"

Flabbergasted didn't even capture how I felt. At first, relief rolled off me that I wouldn't lose another parent. Then, a sharp tinge of pain shot through me as if

Dad betrayed Mom's memory by even considering such a thing. Then I realized how ridiculous that sounded. I couldn't expect him to live the life of a monk. Like everyone, he deserved happiness. His only job shouldn't be to ensure his kid's happiness. And I'm sure Mom understood and blessed his decision. Finally, I thought…oh, boy, am I going to have fun with this. Payback time!

"Woooo, Dad, who's your little friend? Is she someone special? Is she your little girlfriend? Is she a nice girl? You know what I mean, right? She hasn't been around the block now, has she?" Like an idiot, I grinned.

"So. I take it, you're okay with this, son?" My God, Dad blushed. Something I thought I'd never see in my life.

"Whatever, Dad." I cut my silly line of faux-parental inquiry with a laugh. Time to cut him some slack. "I think it's great. Is she coming to our Christmas open house?"

"Yes, she is." He looked greatly relieved. "Her name is Ruth Crandall, and she's a librarian new to the area. I met her at the bank when she took out a loan when she moved here."

"Now, Dad, isn't that a conflict of interest?" I assumed my father-knows-best creased eyebrows.

"I'm not a doctor, lawyer, or such. I'm but a mere banker." He splayed his hands. "I haven't been on a date with her yet, but I invited her over, and she seemed very pleased with the offer."

"Father, do I need to…have the talk with you?" I hefted one eyebrow, apparently not done with putting him on the spot just yet.

"Okay, Tex, I think we're done with this conversation."

"I'm talking about responsibility here, Dad. One mistake could ruin your future."

"Shut up, Tex. Go to bed."

****

The next morning, Dad could barely function, and I assumed all responsibilities for cooking the first vat of clam chowder.

"Tex, which tie do you think looks better?" He held up two gaudy, horrible green and red ties.

"Neither. They're both terrible."

"But…your mother always loved when I wore these ties."

"Oh, no, she didn't!" I burst out laughing. "She hated both of them. It was one of our little inside secret Christmas jokes." I wondered how he could've been so oblivious to this. "Did you honestly never see her making the throw-up sign when you'd parade those ties around every Christmas?"

He thought about it for a minute. "Is that what she was doing?"

I sighed. "Dad, let me pick out your tie."

The first guest arrived at ten a.m. sharp, and it was the very aforementioned Ruth Crandall, bearing some sort of casserole. Pleasant and pretty in sort of a bland Midwestern way, she couldn't hold a candle to Mom's beauty. I realized that wasn't fair, as I might be more than a little biased. But I loved the way she doted on Dad and even laughed at his stupid, corny jokes.

Olivia and Ian arrived next. Olivia stared slack-jawed at Ms. Crandall, while Ian batted his eyes behind their backs. Clearly, we had an unexpected burgeoning romance on our hands.

People came and left throughout the day, with our core five staying the entire time. It did my heart good to see Mr. and Mrs. Berillo show up, even though they didn't stay very long. Mrs. Berillo hugged me and thanked me for being such a good friend to Josh, while Mr. Berillo seemed sort of despondent, just kind of wandering around with his hands in his pockets. Both of them had that hollow-eyed look you get when you've lost someone close, and you're unsuccessfully trying to put your life back together again. I told Mrs. Berillo I should be thanking her for Josh, one of the greatest people I'd ever known. Before the tears began, she said they couldn't stay and had to go. I hugged her again and shook Mr. Berillo's hand on the way out, telling them to please stay in touch. I doubted they would, though, as I undoubtedly reminded them of their painful loss.

Mickey showed up around four p.m., looking like the Queen of Bloody England. She wore a jazzy, sequin-enhanced blue dress and even sported a matching hat, complete with a veil. She'd applied make-up either hastily—or by poor eyesight—as it looked rather hit or miss. Either way, she didn't look like the bathrobe-wearing Mickey I'd grown accustomed to. Regardless, she looked great in her old-fashioned way.

Playing it to the hilt, she extended her hand royally to everyone and clearly enjoyed the attention lavished upon her. To my amusement—and to the obvious discomfort of Ruth Crandall—once the eggnog rolled out, she entertained the troops with some rather bawdy stories from her past. I loved Mickey, and I loved seeing her letting her blue hair down.

As the night drew to a close, I grabbed Olivia and dragged her out onto the front porch. Still in the fifties and unbelievably nice, a perfect full moon lit the sky brightly.

"Remember a month ago, when I said we would have a talk?" I grabbed her hands.

"About damn time, Tex." Momentarily emboldened, I leaned in to kiss her.

"Who's your friend, Tex?" an all-too-familiar voice interrupted us. I broke the kiss and saw Mr. Cavanaugh peering at me from his porch.

"Merry Christmas, Mr. Cavanaugh." I withheld the snark, Christmas and all, ho, ho, ho. "This is Olivia."

"Hi," she muttered. Obviously pissed he'd disturbed this crucial moment, she turned to me and whispered, "He's just staring at us."

"That's what he does," I whispered back.

"Does he ever quit?"

I thought about this. "No…no, he never does."

"Hey, Mr. Cavanaugh," she yelled. "Would you like a nine by twelve-inch glossy photo or poster size?" She kicked her leg high in the air as if she were punting a football and screamed "*Hoo-Yah!*" I wasn't really sure what this meant, but it definitely made me laugh.

Mr. Cavanaugh sputtered something like *No manners whatsoever* before retreating to his patio chair.

"Come on, O'," I said, pulling her with me. "Let's go to the other side of the deck."

I kissed her again. The memory of how she felt, smelled, and tasted came flooding back to me. A wonderful memory.

This time she stopped. "Okay, this is fun and everything, but you're not doing much talking. That's what we're supposed to do. What exactly does this all mean?"

"Well, I guess this makes you my Witch Bitch." I smiled. "That is, if you'll have me," I added hastily, a little less cock-sure of myself.

"Hold on, hold on! I may be a bitch at times, but the only one who gets to refer to me as a bitch is myself, got that?" She stabbed a finger into my chest.

"Okay."

"Secondly," she continued, "what's with this *my* crap? I'm no one's property!"

"It was a joke, Olivia."

"Finally, I prefer the title Witch Handler because you're *not* leaving me out of stuff anymore!" Obviously angry, a sunshiny smile managed to break through her stormy demeanor. "Now, kiss me again, and I'll make up my mind."

She stretched up, grabbed the back of my head, and we kissed. After we caught our breath, she said, "Okay, Tex, looks like there're two romances going on here tonight."

And we kissed Christmas away.

Afterword

Although this is a work of fiction, every incident of bullying did actually happen to either a friend or me while we were in high school. To this day, a close friend of mine still doesn't have the full use of his left hand due to the same automobile attack you've read about in the book. Times have changed since I was in school, but unfortunately, bullying remains. This book is dedicated to the downtrodden "ghost people" in high school who believe there is no recourse or hope from the constant bullying they endure.

Have courage; stand up for yourself, and don't worry about the fall-out if you need to report bullying.

There is hope. Things will get better, count on it.

A word about the author...

Stuart R. West is a lifelong resident of Kansas, which he considers both a curse and a blessing. It's a curse because...well, it's Kansas. But it's great because...well, it's Kansas. Lots of cool, strange and creepy things happen in the Midwest, and Stuart takes advantage of them in his books. Call it "Kansas Noir." Stuart writes thrillers, horror, and mysteries usually tinged with humor, both for adult and young adult audiences. Twenty-something books have been published, all very different in genre, all set in Kansas.

Stuart spent 25 years in the corporate sector and had to bail, splitting his time between writing and real estate. He's married to a professor of pharmacy (who greatly appreciates the fact he cooks dinner for her every night) and has a 29-year-old daughter who's dabbling in the nefarious world of banking.

If you're still reading this, you may as well head on over to Stuart's blog. It's what all the cool kids are doing.

http://stuartrwest.blogspot.com/

Thank you for purchasing
this publication of The Wild Rose Press, Inc.

For questions or more information
contact us at
info@thewildrosepress.com.

The Wild Rose Press, Inc.
www.thewildrosepress.com